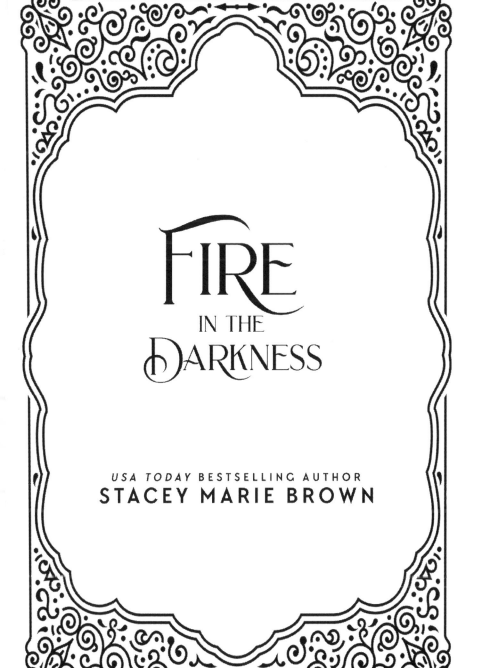

# FIRE
## IN THE
## DARKNESS

*USA TODAY* BESTSELLING AUTHOR
**STACEY MARIE BROWN**

Fire in the Darkness

*Fire in the Darkness Copyright © 2014 Stacey Marie Brown*
Discover other titles by Stacey Marie Brown:
This is a work of fiction. Any references to historical events, real people, or real locales are used fictitiously. Other names, characters, places and incidents are the product of the author's imagination and her crazy friends. Any resemblance to actual events, locales or persons, living or dead, is entirely coincidental.
This book is licensed for your personal enjoyment only. It cannot be re-sold, reproduced, scanned or distributed in any manner whatsoever without written permission from the author.
All rights reserved.
Edited by Hollie Westring hollietheeditor@gmail.com
Cover Design by Jay Aheer https://www.simplydefinedart.com
Design Layout: www.formatting4U.com

# ALSO BY STACEY MARIE BROWN

## Contemporary Romance

**How the Heart Breaks**

**Buried Alive**

**Smug Bastard**

**The Unlucky Ones**

**Blinded Love Series**
Shattered Love (#1)
Broken Love (#2)
Twisted Love (#3)

**Royal Watch Series**
Royal Watch (#1)
Royal Command (#2)

## Paranormal Romance

**Darkness Series**
Darkness of Light (#1)
Fire in the Darkness (#2)
Beast in the Darkness (An Elighan Dragen Novelette)
Dwellers of Darkness (#3)
Blood Beyond Darkness (#4)
West (#5)

## Collector Series
City in Embers (#1)
The Barrier Between (#2)
Across the Divide (#3)
From Burning Ashes (#4)

## Lightness Saga
The Crown of Light (#1)
Lightness Falling (#2)
The Fall of the King (#3)
Rise from the Embers (#4)

## Savage Lands Series
Savage Lands (#1)
Wild Lands (#2)
Dead Lands (#3)
Bad Lands (#4)
Blood Lands (#5)
Shadow Lands (#6)

## A Winterland Tale
Descending into Madness (#1)
Ascending from Madness (#2)
Beauty in Her Madness (#3)
Beast in His Madness (#4)

Stacey Marie Brown

### 10 YEAR ANNIVERSARY!

To Eli and Ember for creating a world that has led me on a 10-year-journey, which I only see growing. You two will always be my first muses.

And most of all to the readers, thank you for loving this world, for allowing me to keep telling you stories within this crazy world. If you have just found me or have been with me since the beginning, you are so deeply appreciated.

Happy 10th Birthday DOL…and here's to many more.

Fire in the Darkness

**For a better understanding of the Fae world, there is a Glossary at the end of the story.**

Fire in the Darkness

CHAPTER ONE

The acrid aroma of cheap, processed coffee and burnt beans seeped down the long food line, assaulting my nose. The strong smells did little to cover up the eye-watering stench of urine and body odor that hovered around me. It had been over four days since I last had access to a shower. No doubt I contributed to this stench.

Although it felt like a lifetime, it had only been a month since I had a roof over my head, a hot shower whenever I wanted, and a warm meal every night. Now I understood what it was to be so hungry the hollow, crushing pain consumed your every thought and action. To be so cold your bones felt like they would shatter.

Another whiff of beans seeped into my nose and my stomach rumbled in response. I inhaled a deep breath and savored the slight tang that grazed my taste buds. Food had been scarce for me, and I had taken what I could when I could. Leaning out, I scanned the dozens of people lined up in front of me. Tired, despondent faces looked ahead hungrily anticipating the food soon to be scooped onto their plates.

Food and water were everyone's biggest concerns. Other necessities, such as medicines and supplies, were used to trade or control the city; a warm shower or hot food was a luxury. What I had taken for granted, I now struggled for every day: clean drinking water, a place to sleep, clothes, food. Some days I lucked out, but most days I didn't. Looted candy bars from convenience stores were my usual dinner.

Red Cross had set up aid and refuge centers around Seattle, but I only used them when absolutely necessary. Four days of not eating or sleeping properly had me seeking out protection tonight.

The line moved glacially slow, my stomach protesting the lack of headway with each tiny step. I had just made the monumental approach to the first stack of trays when two men entered the food tent. Dressed in pedestrian clothes, they looked almost human. But something was slightly off and their attempt to blend in didn't disguise what they really were. Not to me. A few weeks ago, I would have thought they were normal people. Now I knew better. Their stunning, nearly impeccable appearance, complexion, and icy blue eyes told me they were the Queen's soldiers.

Fay. Fairies. Fae. Seelie. They were Otherworlders no matter what description you used. As I was new to the Fae realm, I didn't know much, but I knew enough to know Fae was a general term for all creatures from the Otherworld. Fay was short for Fairy, which was the top of the food chain there. The Seelie Queen was a pure-blooded Fairy.

It didn't matter if a bunch of dancing leprechauns had entered the tent. These men were here for me. I had avoided being caught while on the streets. I wasn't going to break my streak now.

Ducking my head, I flipped up the hood of my "borrowed" sweatshirt. Okay, some people might call it stolen. When I had run from the Queen, I was in nothing but my underwear, Eli's tattered shirt, and a cloak. Everything I had acquired in the last couple of weeks was stolen. The looted stores, with their broken windows, had made it a little easier to swipe clothes and a pair of shoes. With everything in chaos and the Queen of the Otherworld combing every inch for me, my best chance for survival was losing myself deep in the city. Seattle was in complete turmoil and hiding among humans was the only thing that had kept me alive for the last four weeks.

Looked like my luck had run out.

Stooping behind the person in front of me, I watched the two Fays gauge the room. If I bolted, it would only draw attention to me. Hoping they'd look around, not see me, and move to the next tent was probably too much to ask. The two men started at the end of the line, studying each person with impudent regard.

Humans are funny—they ignore their natural instinct because they're afraid of appearing rude to others. I could see their nervous, unsettled glances as the men approached them, knowing something was not right. But they turned away and disregarded their suspicions.

*If only they trusted their intuition.*

As the men moved closer to me, my nose prickled with the smell of magic. Since I had Dark Dweller blood running in my veins, my sense of smell had increased. My sight and hearing had also improved.

Normally Fay couldn't smell magic, but I could now. The sweet, tingling sense that was like snorting a glass of champagne had saved my butt more than once in the last couple of weeks. I had learned to pay attention to the slight indications that told me Fae were near.

Since my escape, the Queen had relentlessly searched for me. In time I'm sure the Unseelie King would throw his hat in the ring for me as well. Evidently being a Dae—half Fay, half Demon—was a hot commodity for both the Light and Dark. They had different agendas, but both wanted to use me as a weapon to destroy the other.

Each step brought my pursuers closer. I needed a plan. Edging closer to the stack of trays, I frantically searched for the best possible escape route.

"Do not even think about running," a voice whispered in my ear. Hands clamped down on my arms as his partner came around my other side, blocking my escape.

The men moved in tighter, pinning my arms to my sides. "Do not fight. You cannot get away from us. All you will do is alarm and upset all these humans by bringing attention to yourself. This will only cause us to do more harm. You do not want that." His voice was smooth, slipping like velvet over my skin. Into my ears.

Like hell I didn't.

I knew what I had to do.

I screamed.

"Help! These guys are trying to kidnap me!" Like I hoped, every head turned our way. People were too weary to jump in and help, but at least it gave me the briefest moment of surprise to break away from my abductors. With all my strength, I yanked my arms out of their grasps. The momentum pitched me forward into a stack of plastic trays. The crash echoed throughout the tent with a deafening clatter. People stood in shock, taking in the scene. Scrambling up, I slid and skidded over the mass of serving trays. One of the Fays leaped, grabbing for me. His foot slipped, and he tumbled. As he fell back, his head smacked on the cement. The other man was right behind him, coming for me.

Seizing a tray, I swung. His face collided with my choice of weapon with an audible *thwack*. This was my only chance. I took off for the exit, trying to maneuver and dodge people as they stood there, dazed. My mistake was looking to see if the men were pursuing me. When I turned back it was too late. A tall bakery cart stood in my path. Plowing into it hurt like a bitch. Sharp, flat metal baking sheets jammed into my ribs, face, and arms as we toppled over together. Gritting my teeth, I waited for it to be over, already feeling blood seeping from the gashes on my hands and arms. The Fay soldiers were on me in a flash.

"Hey." I heard a man call out as people started to respond. "Stop those guys!"

*About fucking time.*

A large hand closed around my neck and pulled me to my feet. "You are not getting away from us again." He tightened his grip, cutting off my air. Panic rumbled deep in my core, and that's when I felt the darkness inside me surge its way up.

I had used my powers minimally since the day I caused Seattle to burn to the ground. Every time I had tried to use them, they caused more damage, more pain. I had hurt so many people. There was this one boy about ten who was searching for food in a liquor store like I was. He startled me, and I sent an entire rack of soda falling onto him. I caused a car to blow up because someone was chasing me for a can of corn. My powers were volatile and unpredictable since the day the Queen forced them to the surface. The energy scared me. Unfortunately, fear brought them out even more.

A large cart shot off the ground crashing blindly into the innocent people in line, knocking over anyone standing in its way, including children.

*Oh, God, no!* It was happening again. Both the anxiety of the situation and the hand tightening around my throat directed the energy towards the standing heaters and lights. A loud buzz whined through the tent. People covered their ears, hunching down in protection. Sparks licked out of heaters, popping and crackling while energy pulsated through them.

"Stop that," the Fay soldier commanded, squeezing my neck harder.

My building panic forced a dozen baking sheets through the air toward him and anyone who stood close. The sharp, metal edges drove into his head and back. Instantly his grip loosened and fell away from my neck as he crumpled to the ground in agony. He wasn't the only one attacked by baking sheets. The other soldier and two men who were trying to help me lay on the ground, blood oozing from gashes on their foreheads and arms. Guilt rooted in my gut. They were only trying to help me, now look what I'd done to them.

Hundreds of eyes stared at me in terror. Kids cried, some with cuts and bloody noses from the cart that fell on them. I choked down my guilt, whirling around and bolting to where I'd be safe from the Fay, and the people would be safe from me.

## TWO

The sun slipped quickly below the horizon. The air clung to the last bit of warmth, hinting at the changing season. It didn't stop the goose bumps from breaking out over my skin, and the hoodie I wore did little to keep in my body heat. The chills soon turned to sweat as I raced through the city, dodging, ducking, scaling over walls, through tunnels, and down alleyways.

I had always hated running and had teased my stepfather, Mark, because he enjoyed running marathons for fun. Lately, it had become easier because I did a great deal of it. I could run farther and longer than I ever imagined possible. Funny the things one is capable of doing when your life is on the line.

My calves still didn't care for all the exercise they were getting now. Lorcan, Eli's brother, had torn them to shreds a month ago. Lorcan was also the one who had turned me over to the Queen. My legs continued to ache, mainly at night when I tried to sleep. I was lucky even to be walking, but the painful leg cramps kept the night of my attack fresh in my mind.

Keeping to the shadows, I slunk down a vandalized back street toward the abandoned warehouses. Dusk enveloped everything in its path. With no electricity, it was harder to see, but it was also harder to be seen.

I had become quite familiar with the shipping harbor. Painful as it was, there was a lot of iron around here that discouraged Fay from coming in after me. The area gave me many places to hide from my pursuers—Fae or human.

Seattle had become a battle ground for gangs and those individuals using the catastrophe as an excuse to act out. Over the last several weeks, I had learned not to underestimate humans. They could be as scary and dangerous as the monsters that hid in the dark, especially when pushed into a corner. A girl alone on the streets was asking for trouble, and it usually found me. But I had no other option. I was stranded in Seattle with no means of getting out. The airport, buses, and trains were down. With no electricity there was little transportation, except on foot.

Even if getting home was easy to do, I wouldn't have gone back. Besides Olympia being over sixty miles away, Mark was gone and my home was likely the first place the Queen would have her minions watching. It would put my friends in danger as well.

Torin, who until recently I thought was a figment of my imagination, was a beautiful Fay who had come to me mostly in my dreams. He had tried to keep me informed as much as he could to what was happening in the Otherworld. But I had seen little of him in the last few weeks. He said it was extremely dangerous to contact me as the Queen was constantly with him. She was obsessed about finding me.

I was on my own now.

Footsteps clicked from the other side of the broken window of the abandoned warehouse where I hid, bringing me back to the present.

"Come out, lass. We know you're there," a man cooed. He couldn't disguise the sinister tone underneath. "We saw you come this way. Running from something? Who else is after you, little Dae?" His voice was raspy and harsh.

Two warning bells rang in my head. First, I had hid here because Fay, like the Queen's soldiers, couldn't be around iron. It made us sick, although in the last couple of weeks, I had become a little more tolerant to it. Barely. Second, the man's voice wasn't Fay. Fay had voices like silk. This meant I had more than one group after me tonight.

"You can't get by us. Might as well come out now," another gravelly voice spoke. There were at least two of them.

Biting my lip, I pressed myself tighter into the corner. My powers would not work well with so much iron around. Not that I wanted them to. I had hurt too many people already, and tonight only confirmed I should stay as far from humans as possible. My powers were not only dangerous but erratic.

I had discovered the best place to hide was in the iron-filled shipping yard. Iron was Fay kryptonite. Being only half Fay didn't make being around iron any easier for me. It was torture, but when your life is at stake, you push through. Either the Queen had gotten wise to my trick and sent Fae who wouldn't be deterred by iron, or there was a whole different group now after me. The chance it might be the Unseelie King's men was pretty good. He probably wanted me as badly as the Queen. Neither option seemed especially good for my well-being.

"You are only hurting yourself being around all this iron. We won't harm you... we simply want to talk."

*Yeah. And I believe that one.*

There was a soft scuffling sound. My eyes darted to the noise. A large rat trotted along the wall, scurrying towards me. I threw myself back into the brick wall, and my hand flew up to my mouth, blocking the scream that clawed at my throat. I had almost gotten used to rats over the past month. I slept with them practically every night. But this was no ordinary rat. The façade of the rat quickly changed in front of me. A small, flesh-colored, gremlin-like creature sniffed at the hem of my jeans.

"Oh crap," I croaked out. *Why did they always disguise themselves as rats?*

The tiny, alien-looking creature, with its bat ears and long claws, looked up at me. A vibrating noise came from its throat as it assessed me. "Did you just purr?" The little creature huffed at me with annoyance, and then tore off up the wall and out the broken window.

It seemed like only a few seconds after the creature's departure when I felt a familiar pull. *"Oh no. Not now, Torin!"* I shouted in my head. He either didn't hear my plea or ignored it because the pull in my head and gut became stronger. *No-no-no-no!* I fought against it, trying to keep myself awake, but it was useless. My mind caved to the pressure, my head falling back against the wall.

"Torin!" I belted out the moment my eyes opened up. We were in our usual place—a forest somewhere in the Otherworld. This seemed to be his preferred spot. Glistening dew sparked the trees in a halo glow. The colors were so vivid and bright my lids blinked a few times to adjust. A deep turquoise stream trickled through the green grass. A fox settled itself into the exact same spot it had in a prior dreamscape with Torin.

"Send me back right now. I have two Fay soldiers and some other unknown Fae after me right now. I'm a sitting duck while I'm asleep."

"That is what I wanted to warn you about. I sent an imp to find you before I tried to contact you." He stepped in front of me.

"Imp?" The tiny, rat-gremlin creature?

"Yes, this one owed me a favor. My sources have to stay off the Queen's radar."

My eyes finally focused on Torin. He could still take my breath away. There was no denying Fay were gorgeous—almost painfully beautiful. His dark hair was tied back neatly, displaying his high cheek bones and crystal blue eyes. His usual outfit of leather pants and tight, black shirt clung to every muscular curve.

"The Queen went on a rampage today. I sent two of my most inane Fay soldiers to come after you, thinking you could probably get away from them. But she knows you are hiding near iron. The fact you seem to handle it when her top soldiers can't, makes her exceedingly unhappy. She's promised a reward to those dark Fae if they bring you back."

"They're already here. That's why I have to go. They could find me at any moment."

A small whine from behind Torin caught my attention. I felt it trying to communicate with me as it paced back and forth.

"Hey, little guy." I took a step towards it. It was a beautiful animal. Red foxes always reminded me of my mother. She had a fondness for them and had spent a lot of time studying them. Now I knew she had come from this realm and had grown up with animals like this.

"No." He grabbed my arm, stopping me from moving closer. "Don't."

I looked back at the little animal. Its gaze locked onto mine, and then Torin's, before turning and disappearing into the brush. Something in my gut tugged, wanting to run after it.

"Ember," his voice dragged my attention away from the empty spot and back to his face. "I need you to be careful. The Queen is determined to capture you. You need to find Lars soon. He will protect you."

"Who is this Lars?"

Torin's hands moved to my arms, pulling me in closer.

"I am not permitted to tell you. The Queen has bound me and has limited what I can say. But I am trying in every way I can to let you know what's going on. Please, trust me." He leaned his forehead against me; his lips mere inches from mine.

*The more time I spent with Torin, the more natural it felt being with him. I couldn't deny he made me feel safe and protected. Even in his limited way, I knew he would do anything for me. He had risked his life helping me escape the Queen a few weeks back. Just seeing me now put him in jeopardy. He was the only one I could turn to.*

*Eli was no longer someone I could trust. Lorcan had confirmed that Eli had been planning the whole time to trade me to the Unseelie King. I had to keep reminding myself Eli was among my enemies. I had to run from him like all the rest.*

"I need to get back," I said quietly but didn't move away from him.

"I know," Torin mumbled. He didn't seem inclined to move either. It was foolish. My body was completely unprotected back at the warehouse, but I couldn't seem to compel myself to go. His head moved slowly toward mine. His lips brushed mine....

My lids opened, and I found myself staring at rafters of the old dingy warehouse. It was solid metal with a few large rollaway doors. The only light came from the windows that were at the very top. At least three stories up.

"Damn it, Torin."

Standing, I quickly evaluated everything around me. There were no dark Fae standing over me, so they hadn't found me yet, which was always a good thing. But how long had I been out? Time was different in the Otherworld. Had hours passed here or merely minutes?

Leaving my hiding spot wasn't the brightest idea, but I needed to know if the men had left or were still outside waiting for me. Moving up to the roof would give me a better idea and advantage. Decision made, I slunk down, stayed close to the wall, and headed for the stairs.

Only a few steps from them, I came to a grinding stop. A gun cocked. "Where do you think you're goin', lass?" A man moved in closer behind me and pressed the barrel to the back of my head. "You're worth a pretty penny." His buddy stepped around to my side. He was tall and lanky; his face long and narrow with a tuft of hair covering his chin. When I peered at him all I could think was he looked like a goat. Not a goat you'd find in a petting zoo, but like one you'd find in the Andes Mountains—tough and bouncing from boulder to boulder. Goat-like or not he had a gun pointed at me.

I tried to swallow my panic. The disadvantage of hiding out in iron buildings was coming to bite me in the ass. There was too much of it for my powers to be strong enough to fight both of them. My magic could destroy an entire city, killing thousands. But here I was defenseless, and officially screwed by a dark Fae with a pistol.

"Move it." The man pressed the gun harder against my head, encouraging me forward. His partner-in-crime pulled out restraints from his pocket. No doubt iron, giving them more assurance they would get their prisoner to the drop-off point for payment.

"I don't think you want to do that," a deep, familiar voice declared from the doorway, his large silhouette leaned apathetically against the door jam.

"And my night only continues to get better and better," I muttered, annoyed at myself for missing my internal warning system that alerted me when my biggest threat was near.

I heard a small scoff. "Now is this how you treat your savior? Your liberator, your rescuer, the redeemer?"

It was my turn to scoff. "Oh, hell. Are you and your ego done preening?"

"Knight-in-shining armor then?"

"Please. Goat-boy here is more likely going to be my knight-in-shining armor than you." I pointed to the guy with handcuffs.

"Ouch," Eli's voice stayed level. He didn't even pretend it hurt his feelings. "Now you're just trying to be mean."

"You haven't seen me even get close to being nasty." I crossed my arms.

"Threat or promise?"

"That's a pro—"

"What the shit is going on?" The man behind me cut me off. I jumped. Eli had a way of making me forget there was anybody else in the room besides us. "Who the hell are you?"

"Someone your mommy told you not to mess with," Eli said calmly. His coolness scared me. I knew this tone, and it meant nothing good. A shadow fell across my vision from above. Looking up I saw Cole and a blonde guy I didn't know come in the top window.

Moonlight, streaming through the windows, was the only light. But when Eli stepped out from the shadows,

I couldn't stop the gasp of air at seeing him again. My traitorous heart slammed against my ribs.

The dark Fae beside me prickled. "This is our take. Get lost." He clearly didn't know who he was dealing with.

"I don't think so. You have something belonging to me, and I'd like it back now."

I bristled at his words. I was a piece of property Eli could sell off to the Unseelie King. It hadn't solely been the Queen's minions who had kept me on the run for the last several weeks. Eli's blood, which ran through my veins, had kept me constantly moving. His blood allowed me to sense when he was near. It had become my warning system but also his beacon—it never let me get too far or him too close. It had turned into a tiring game of hide and seek.

The running had been pointless. There wasn't a place on Earth where he couldn't track me down. So why did I keep doing it? Because the only thing I had left was my tiny slice of false independence. And it now seemed even this was coming to an end.

"Sorry, we found her first. She's worth a big reward, and we're gonna be the ones to cash in."

The man behind me moved, pointing his gun at Eli.

"You really think that's going to stop me?" Eli nodded toward the gun.

"It will hurt like hell and slow you down enough."

Eli's eyes blazed, the pupils shifting into vertical slits. "No more than a pinprick."

Cole and his partner silently walked the rafters, positioning themselves above our heads. This conflict would be over before it started.

I had a limited window of opportunity to get away. Surprisingly, it seemed no matter how many things were stacked against me, my self-preservation wouldn't go down without a fight.

Through the dark shadows, I saw Eli's body start to shift, lowering closer to the ground, his eyes now turning from their bright green to flaming red.

"Holy shit! You're a Dark Dweller," the man yelped. "The Queen led us to believe you were all dead."

"Sorry to disappoint," Eli's voice growled, his words garbled as his form shifted.

The gun went off. The bullet hit the cement at Eli's feet. Sensing movement from above, I felt the whooshing air as Cole and his companion dropped silently down. Like a brilliantly executed plan, the moment their feet hit the ground, I dropped to my knees, getting out of the way of both gun and men.

My feet scrambled underneath me as I scurried towards the exit. The fight behind me was deafening with gun shots, bones crunching, and frightening, deep growls. Taking a quick glance over my shoulder, I could see the outlines of them fighting. Dark Dwellers clashed with shapes of large, spikey-horned goats.

I ran for the door—their reward money was fleeing out the door. I sprinted out the entrance and around the corner, toward freedom.

With a piercing shatter, glass flew out from the window next to my head, raining shards down on me. A body hurled through the window taking me to the ground. I thrashed against the unrelenting force of my assailant.

"Stop fighting me," a deep voice growled. I looked up into his face as fierce, green eyes locked on mine. They were still vertical, in his Dark Dweller state, but his body was all man and pressed up against me. My heart instantly tripped over itself, while my mind tried to look at him as no more than another enemy.

An exceedingly exposed enemy. Eli was naked, his body covering mine, letting me feel everything.

I wrestled against his hold on me. "Let me go."

"Try again."

"Get off of me."

"Nope, not that one either," he replied icily.

"Do you have her, Eli?" The blonde guy stuck his head around the corner. There was something about him I recognized. Had I met him before?

"Yeah." Eli sighed deeply against me, his cock pressing into me.

The blonde guy smirked, shaking his head. "Yep, I would say you definitely do."

"Get. Off. Of. Me. Now!" Embarrassment and anger burned deep. Eli had become the bane of my existence—when I didn't want to kiss him, which was all the time. I wanted to be cured of him since I'd found out he had only been faking an attraction to me. He wanted to get closer to learn more about me and my capabilities before turning me over to the Unseelie King.

Eli's eyes narrowed, his grip only becoming tighter as he pushed off me, pulling me up with him. There was no barrier now between me and all of Eli's glory. And, wow, was there glory. The man was *massive*. I had seen enough porn to know he was beyond anything

I had ever observed. Heat crept between my thighs, blushing my cheeks, my eyes darting to the side, looking away from his unclothed body.

"You're naked."

"And you're observant."

He led me around the corner where a black Cadillac Escalade Hybrid was waiting. "Now get in."

"Are you kidding me?" I tugged against his grip. "You think I'm going to get into the car? I'm not going anywhere with you."

"It is not a choice."

Cole came from behind tugging on some jeans. "We've got to go, Eli, before those Phooka assholes come to."

"Those what?"

"A Phooka. An Irish goblin that turns itself into a goat. Prone to violence, stealing, and vicious pranks. Not nice guys."

I looked around. All the other Dark Dwellers were moving toward the car. By the dim moonlight I could make them out. They were all naked.

*Damn...*

Eli grabbed my arm and hauled me into the backseat of the SUV. "We don't have time for this."

"Watch it," I protested as I fell in. He pushed me over, sliding in next to me.

The magnificent, blonde specimen who, thank God, had pulled some jeans over the lower half of his god-like body, climbed in on my other side, boxing me in. "Cooper." He nodded.

His name confirmed he was the beautiful, surfer-looking guy whom I had overheard talking after being attacked by Lorcan over a month ago. Then I had thought it was a dream. Cooper had said things at the time I didn't understand. Now I did. *"She nearly died. Now how useful would she have been to us dead, huh? Lorcan almost killed our only way out of here."* Cooper's voice still echoed in my ears. As their ticket back to the Otherworld, they would do anything to keep me under their watch.

Cooper's huge, soft brown eyes looked me over. He was definitely sexy although he didn't take my breath away like Eli did. Even so, he did make me whimper with aggravation.

Did every one of these guys have to be sex-on-a-stick? It was ridiculous how extraordinarily hot this group was. If more kept popping up like this, I'm sure I would instantaneously combust from overheating.

A boy of about sixteen opened up the back hatch and jumped in. "Hey, I'm Jared." His excitable voice was at odds with the rest of the guys in the car.

I nodded, craning my neck to get a better look at him. I wanted to laugh, but I shouldn't have been surprised at this point. He was just another hot, young, toned guy. They obviously didn't allow anyone in their group who couldn't also model for some rugged, outdoorsy, men's magazine.

Jared had dark, brownish-red hair, hazel eyes, and freckles sprinkled across his cheeks and nose. He looked sweet and endearing next to Eli's rough and tumbled look. At least Jared was fully clothed. I had little doubt he was related to Cole and Owen. He looked like a younger version of them both.

Cole, leader of the Dark Dwellers, had the same rugged bad-boy look as Eli. There was also little misgiving as to his relation with Owen. They had the same coloring, eyes, and nose. The difference was Owen was the opposite in everything else: neat and tidy with short hair and a freshly shaved face. He was the medic in the group and had operated on me, saving my life after Lorcan attacked me.

Cole jumped into the driver's seat and tore out of the port area, barely allowing Owen time to get into the passenger's side.

"That was awesome," Jared exclaimed from the back.

"Good job with lookout, J-man," Cooper turned back, praising Jared.

"Oh, here you go, E." Jared threw a pair of jeans over the seat.

"Thanks, man."

Eli grabbed them and started to tug the jeans on in the tiny space between the car door and me, his elbows jabbing into me as he moved. I tried to avoid looking at him directly, but couldn't stop from sneaking quick snapshots every so often. I couldn't help it—every inch of him was on display, inviting me to look. Particularly when he pushed his hips up, pulling his jeans over them, putting him way too close to my eye line for comfort. I tried to focus on the digital clock blinking rhythmically on the dashboard in front of me.

The surrealism of my life peaked at that moment, and a giggle burst from me. Everyone in the car turned to stare at me. I cleared my throat, letting the quiet and tension in the car fill the space again. No one talked as we headed to our destination.

Since the Electrical Current Storm, the ECS, I had spent the last four weeks rendered by guilt and disgust. So many lives had been lost. So many dead, murdered by me. Shame and disabling guilt kept me from staying in the shelters most nights. The first time I tried, I had been starving and cold, but when I saw all the frightened homeless children and heard people crying during the night, it was all too much to endure. I left and spent the night in an abandoned gas station instead. Hunger led me back every once in a while, but I tried to avoid people at all costs, especially being a target of the Fae world. I would have preferred to go out into the forest and stay away from people all together, but then I might as well have handed myself over to the Queen. Both the city and humans were my shields, and I needed to be near them.

As we drove through town, I took everything in. Seattle had taken the brunt of the devastation, but the towns within a fifty-mile radius were also affected, including Olympia, my home town.

People were mystified as to what really happened and how it was possible. Not for a moment did they think it could be "Otherworldly." Scientists came out saying it had been a freak lightening super storm. The conspiracy theorists were certain it had been aliens. Funny, they were closer to the truth than the scientists.

Seattle's airport and seaports had been affected, crippling trade. I read in the paper they had moved the trade ports to Vancouver and San Francisco, overworking them. All of this influenced technology and electronics around the world.

The Seattle area had no lights, TVs, refrigerators, or heat. Anything running off satellites, like Internet and cell phones, worked but only if you had electricity or generators to keep batteries charged. None of us realized how much we relied on electricity until it was gone. Gas stations were shut down, too. People siphoned it out of the pumps, quickly drying them up. If you hadn't filled up before... you were up shit creek, no paddle.

Most people who could get out did, knowing it wouldn't be long before everything went to hell. Everyone else either stayed in their homes and locked the doors or went to one of the shelters. Panic led to looting, and gangs had quickly established dominance and took whatever they wanted, whenever they wanted, turning the city into chaos.

The President stepped in, declaring the Seattle area a Natural Disaster. The National Guard set up a perimeter around the city, but they couldn't completely control the hold the gangs already had on the city. You had to learn fast to survive. It was kill or be killed. You stayed away from particular areas and never ventured out at night, not if you could help it. I, on the other hand, couldn't always follow that rule. With a price on my head and a Dark Dweller on my ass, I had to be constantly on the move.

A part of me now was relieved Eli had finally caught me. My pride would never have let me go to him any other way. Although my brain was set on being okay without him, my heart had never fully succumbed to that mindset as much as I wanted it to. I sat next to him again and felt calm and content in a way I couldn't explain. That pissed me off more than anything. Why did logic and reason go out the window when I was near him?

# THREE

The further we drove out of Seattle, the less damage there was. This was the first time in four weeks I had ventured out of the immediate carnage. They were taking me back to Olympia, and I felt sick at this prospect. Getting close to my home suddenly made everything so real. Deep down I wanted to believe Mark was there and life was going on for him and my friends.

Driving down the familiar streets into Olympia caused the truth to collapse heavily on me. Mark was gone. I couldn't go back to my old life or friends. I missed Kennedy and Ryan so badly it left an ache rotting in my bones. And the thought of Mark was like acid being poured into my lungs. He had helped me through each day. I could not surrender to this paralyzing guilt when he needed me. The Queen was keeping him prisoner in the Otherworld the perfect bait to catch me. She knew without a doubt I would come for him. She was right. I would, but I had to be smart about it.

Venturing deep into the unpopulated, rural woodland of Olympia, we turned down a dark, creepy, dirt road. We bounced down the gravel lane for at least fifteen minutes before I saw the twinkling of house lights flickering between the trees. Coming upon an expansive ranch-style house with several cabins off to the side, I immediately recognized it. Not too long ago, I had climbed out the bathroom window of one of those cabins, trying to escape.

"You have electricity?" I leaned forward to get a better view.

"We have always generated our own electricity to keep our compound self-efficient. What the electrical burst did was far reaching but did not affect us too much." Cole's eyes looked back at mine through the rearview mirror.

As we pulled up to one of the side cabins, the car headlights landed on a girl leaning up against a post. Her facial expression, even from where I sat, was streaked with rage.

"Shit," Cooper sighed and looked away from the girl.

"You didn't tell Gabby?" Eli looked over at Cooper with raised eyebrows. "Shit, man."

All the guys, including Cole, looked anxious, which made my blood level rise. The girl was striking, even more so because she wasn't wearing any makeup. Her blue-black hair was cut short in a pixie style. Most girls couldn't pull it off, but she had those high cheekbones, a perfectly proportionate oval face, tiny nose, and rich brown eyes. The only adornment on her face was an eyebrow piercing. Just like the boys, she could have modeled for a magazine.

"Oh man, she is gonna kick your ass." Jared's head popped over the seat next to my head and snickered.

"And then she'll kick your ass when she gets done with mine," Cooper retaliated, wiping the smile off Jared's face.

"Who is she? Another girlfriend or something?" I couldn't cover up the sheer dread bleeding into my voice. *Not again.* I couldn't take anymore of Eli's old or present flames.

"No, worse," Cooper replied. "She's my twin."

"And she doesn't like being left out of things—I mean *really* doesn't like it." Eli breathed out heavily.

My head turned back to the girl. Besides the fact she obviously dyed her hair, everything else about her was similar to Cooper—face structure, eyes, lips. She was shorter than Cooper and about three inches shorter than me. She was a skinny thing, but you could see the muscles cutting her lean frame under her punk rock t-shirt and tight, ripped, black jeans. Tattoos peeked out through the gaps in her clothes.

The moment Cole opened the door and everyone piled out, swear words spewed from her mouth. "I can't believe you bastards. You are such sexist assholes. Leave the helpless, fragile girl at home?"

"Gabbs, there is nothing helpless or fragile about you." Eli laughed as he got out of the car.

"That's right. Remember just 'cause you've grown into the size of a sasquatch doesn't mean I can't kick your ass."

*Sasquatch? Oh God, don't tell me they're real?* I looked worriedly over to Eli, who shook his head.

*At least not in the way you think of a sasquatch,* his eyes relayed to mine. He said nothing personal, but the wordless communication between us slammed my senses. The fact we could do this was something that still baffled me. Almost from the moment we met, we had the ability to interact with our eyes, to know what the other was thinking without speaking a word. After so long without seeing him, it felt very intimate and unnerving.

"Sorry, Gabbs, it all happened so fast I forgot." Cooper shrugged.

Gabby stomped up to Cooper and sucker punched his arm. "That's for forgetting to contact me," she said and then punched him again. "And that's for me missing out on the fun."

Eli grabbed my arm and pulled me out of the car, his grip firm, almost causing me to fall out the door.

Gabby's attention jerked instantly to me. "So this is the infamous *páiste gréine?*" Gabby cocked her head walking closer to me and looked me up and down.

"Gabby," Eli said warningly.

"I'm assuming she didn't say something flattering?" My eyebrows narrowed.

She smiled in response then added, "The *bitseach* is smarter than she looks."

"Eli, we'll put Ember back in the infirmary for now." Cole's powerful voice broke through the tension between Gabby and me. "I'll be there in a minute."

Eli nodded, grabbed my arm, and tugged me towards the cabin I had been in before.

"You know, getting pulled, dragged, and pushed around isn't getting old or anything."

"And having to pull, drag, and push you around is not getting old for me either." He huffed, and his hand clamped down tighter on my bicep as he propelled me into the small room, flicking on the light. The room was tidy and clean as if I had never used it. "And keeping you out of trouble has been like a vacation."

I pulled out of his grip. "What do you mean keeping me out of trouble?"

"You think you made it this long without help?" He cocked his head. "I was always there, Ember, even if you didn't see me or let me get too close. There were more things after you than you ever knew. There was an onslaught of them daily, and I fought most of them back." He tapped at his chest. "Do you know what a huge pain in my ass you have been for the last four weeks?"

"But I didn't feel you there the whole time."

"After a while I learned to stay far enough back so you couldn't sense me and run. I got really tired of you running and putting yourself in more danger. I couldn't keep them all away from you, but it was easier when you stayed put."

My mouth hung slightly ajar. Here I'd patted myself on the back for escaping the Fae who had been hunting me, and I'd only dealt with a small percentage of them. Gratitude, confusion, and anger weaved together in my chest.

"You're my hero, Eli. Is this what you want to hear? Oh yeah, except for the part where you only did it so you could use me as a nice bargaining chip to the

Unseelie King." If he was shocked by my words, he didn't show it. "What do you guys get out of the plan anyway?"

"An ally."

"So, it's true then. You used me. Pretended to care. For what? To get closer to me?" I looked at him steadily, "Why bother going through all that?"

"I had to know for certain who and what you were."

Bile rose from my stomach. "You are disgusting. I would have respected you more if you had kidnapped me like Lorcan had. He may be psychotic, but he was upfront and honest about his intent. He didn't have to fake seducing me so he could learn about me. Was sticking your tongue down my throat the only way you could figure it out? Funny, I don't remember having any powers in my tonsils."

Eli's eyes narrowed into slits and moved in closer to me—a wild cat stalking its prey. "I'm thorough." He was suddenly inches from me, making me stumble back into the wall.

"Yes, you take your job quite seriously. You should get a raise."

"I get plenty of those." He looked me straight in the eye as he backed me farther against the wall.

"Really? It must have been cold then."

His hand struck the wall, next to my head; his other hand following suit on the other side, locking me in. *You really wanna play this game with me again? You didn't fare so well last time,* his gaze transmitted. I held my chin high, making sure I didn't flinch as I looked back at him. "You enjoy playing with fire, don't you? The power is addicting—you crave it."

The truth of his words flooded me. I gritted my teeth together even harder. He leaned in; his lips so close to mine the heat off them tickled my own. I pressed my head back into the wall to hold myself back.

"You think you're so irresistible? You think this shit gets me all wet in my panties like all the other girls? Remember I'm not human. Why don't you go play with something you can handle?"

We stared at each other in a dead-lock before I pushed his arm away, lunging for the door only a few feet away. As I grabbed for the handle, he pushed me up against it. My cheek bit the wood, burning as it slid across the door. His body pressed into my back. A small whimper escaped me. It wasn't from fear. No, it was my damn, stupid hormones disobeying me so ardently again.

"And do you think you were anything more to me than a job? It was my duty. Whatever it took." His breath was heavy on my neck.

Closing my eyes, anger, disgust, and desire battled through me making it hard to breathe. All of my emotions evoked passion, which was the last thing I wanted when I was around him. He moved in tighter. I bit my lip.

"Get off of me."

"See, again I know that's not what you really want. I can feel you, Ember; my blood is in your veins now. You can't lie to me," he bit into my ear.

"Please leave me alone." I tried to keep the pleading from my voice.

"That is no longer an option. Not since the Queen is after you."

"Yeah, and your own brother is the one who turned me over to her."

"Something I should have foreseen. We were so concerned about Lorcan coming to get you we didn't realize he was already here. Waiting. Lorcan is impulsive and has tunnel vision. He has never seen the bigger picture."

Eli flipped me around, pushing my back into the door. It didn't hurt. I could handle a lot more than ordinary people, but the fierceness in which he did it left me gasping for air. "By the time I got to Lorcan's hideout, you were gone."

He had come for me that fateful night, and I could feel the mixture of sadness and betrayal emanating from him. I couldn't stop the words forming, "I'm sorry."

A fiery expression strained his features. "You're sorry?"

"Yes," I replied. "Your brother betrayed you. I know how it feels to be lied to and deceived by family."

"Don't feel sorry for me. I don't need your pity."

Anger rose again, and I seethed out, "Fine. No problem. Get out of my way."

He didn't move. I shot my fist into his gut. Not even flinching, he finally stepped back, letting me go. Yanking the door open, almost ripping it off the hinges, I started to bolt out. My body collided with a wall of flesh. Cole's hazel-green eyes and sexy face looked at me with slight surprise. I immediately jumped back.

"Eli," Cole asserted, seeming to know whom to blame for my retreat. "Play nice."

"I was." Eli turned and walked farther back into the room.

Cole carried clothes as he motioned me back into the room. I obliged, but begrudgingly. "We'll get you other clothing to wear, but until then I took these from Samantha's old room. I figured you'd want to clean up and put on some warmer clothes."

Samantha was another Dark Dweller who had followed Lorcan. Her obsession with Eli had made her hate me beyond the normal disgust of Daes. Even though his interest in me had been a lie, she wanted to follow any course that destroyed me. Lorcan provided it.

"Are those Samantha's? No." I frowned, immediately shaking my head. I resisted the idea of wearing anything belonging to her. I didn't really have room to complain, since all I had was a torn t-shirt, hoodie, and jeans matted with weeks of dirt and grime. But I felt more comfortable in the dirty clothes than something of hers.

"Use them until we can get you some other clothes." Cole tossed them over to me. "I think you remember where the shower is located. We'll be here when you're done." His nose scrunched. Obviously I smelled really bad. I nodded, holding the ball of clothes tighter to me as I headed for the bathroom.

"By the way, the bathroom window is secured from the outside now. Fixed it just for you." Eli's amused tone rubbed at my nerves. Grinding my teeth, I slammed the bathroom door and placed the clothes on the counter: sports bra, white tank, black yoga pants, and a form-fitting hoodie. Sam's style was simple and classic. I couldn't fault her on it, but her smell, mixed with the detergent, made me agitated. *You have bigger issues to worry about,* I reminded myself.

### Fire in the Darkness

Looking at my hideous reflection in the mirror, my mouth fell open with horror. I looked worse than I felt. Turning away from my double, I got into the shower, dirty water swirling down the drain.

# FOUR

Fifteen minutes later I was clean, dressed, and back with Eli and Cole.

"All right, now what?"

"Could you narrow your field of inquiry?" Eli leaned back against the wall, crossing his arms.

Frustration blazed through me. "You have me. Isn't that what you wanted from the beginning? Now you can get back into the Otherworld. Good for you." Neither Cole nor Eli reacted to my statement. Hysteria cracked my voice. "You used me. You've lied to me about everything."

"We did not lie to you, Ember," Cole passed his hand through his reddish-brown hair.

"Kept from me. Same difference."

My entire life had been a complete lie. Learning this had been a harsh reality, and the only person who could really tell me everything I needed to know was dead. Whether it made sense or not, I was angry with my mother for not telling me the truth. Her betrayal ran deep in my bones. But it didn't even come close to the pain of missing her. Her death had torn a hole in my heart. Now that I knew what I was, it made me miss her even more. My fear and loneliness had only been amplified by living on the streets. I would have given anything for her assurance that everything was going to be okay.

"You kept the fact that I'm part Demon from me—that I am a Dae—detested and hunted by the Otherworld. And how about the little tidbit of you wanting to give me to the Unseelie King as a goodwill token? I was only a way for you to get out of here. A pawn." For weeks I had been blocking the hurt I felt—the depths of pain my heart held in. Eli had ripped another hole in my heart.

"I did what I thought was best at the time." Cole folded his arms. "You had just found out the Otherworld existed. I didn't think telling you that you were one of the most feared and most despised species in the Otherworld would help your mental state at that particular time. Telling someone they are part Demon? How do you think you would have reacted?"

I was still trying to comprehend it all. The word Demon had so many definitions and there was so much folklore about them—none of it good. Demons weren't sweet, fluffy creatures, but now I understood they weren't actually spawns of the devil or totally evil either. Nor did they have anything to do with religion or manifesting and possessing people.

I was half Demon but I had yet to possess or torment any souls. Maybe I just needed to give it time. Spending more time with Eli might do it.

"It had nothing to do with my mental state but what was convenient for you. Don't pretend you did any of this for me. Feigning to care about me? That's even more revolting than if you had been brutally honest with me from the start."

"I will not apologize. I did what I had to for my family." Eli timber rumbled.

"Funny, Lorcan said the same thing."

"Yeah, but he obviously wasn't willing to go to the lengths I did."

The need to lunge across the room and smack him was almost too much to endure. Eli and I, jaws set, guns loaded, glared at each other.

"You two being at each other's throats is not going to solve anything." Cole stepped between us, blocking me from Eli. "Eli, if you cannot play nice, I will require you to leave." Eli only looked away. He didn't commit either way, but he wisely stayed quiet.

Cole turned to me, his face looking serious. "I am impressed you lasted on your own as long as you did. Even though we were there helping, you took on a lot of professionally trained hunters. You're smart, but you know you never would have made it without us. You are safest here."

"Am I?" I crossed my arms. "With a bunch of Dark Dwellers who cause even the most dangerous Fae to wet themselves?"

Cole ambled over to a bed and leaned against one of the metal bedframes. "Exactly. No one will even attempt to come after you here. It is in our best interest to keep you alive."

"Oh, I feel so much better," I replied dryly. I knew Cole was right. I was safer with them, but I didn't have to be happy about it.

"Aneira wants to use you to destroy humans and take back Earth, but she will kill you after she is done. The Unseelie King does not want to harm Earth or the humans—humans like your friends and father. The King's fight is only with Aneira."

It was the first time they had called the Queen by her given name. Hearing it suddenly gave her a presence. It made her more than some evil bitch who you'd find in a bedtime story. She had a name, a family, a story. Fairytales always showed the Seelie/Fairy Queen as this good, pure, angelic, beautiful creature. She certainly had an ethereal and untouchable beauty, but she was not good. She was cruel and power hungry. But then no story I'd ever read portrayed the Unseelie King as the better choice. Leave it to me to be dropped into a screwed-up, twisted fairytale.

"Aneira," I repeated her name out loud, needing to say it, to feel the name roll off my tongue.

"Humans and Fae used to share Earth, and legends and stories were close to the truth then. Later it became too dangerous for the Fae to stay because of human discovery and their prosecution of us. The Fae had to disappear to the Otherworld." He rubbed his chin. "Much of the English monarchy is actually based on the structure of the Seelie kingdom. But we don't run around in period costumes like most think. Humans have this idea the Fae are stuck in the King Arthur days and have not progressed with the times. I'm not saying there aren't castles, horses, and moats, but Fae are actually forward thinkers. We do have technology, but we treat our realm with respect, working with it instead of destroying it."

Even if they no longer lived there, it was obvious the guys still considered it home. I could feel the overwhelming desire coming off both men to get back there. Sacrificing me would be simple.

"So does Aneira govern all of the Otherworld?"

"The Unseelie have only a small portion left in the north. The Queen has control over most of the kingdom. Some noble Seelie lords and ladies oversee the various towns and areas in the Queen's domain. Like I said, it's similar to the old English monarchy, but unlike today's sovereign, the Queen isn't purely a figure head. She has ultimate authority, and she's not one for democracy."

"Yeah, kinda got that." Frowning, I pulled my long, damp hair up into a ponytail. "Where do you guys fit into the Fae society?"

Eli ran his hand over his face and through his hair, a habit he had when he got irritated or frustrated. "We don't."

Tilting my head to the side, I stared at him.

He sighed. "We are dark Fae. Though we don't really follow anybody's rule. Unseelie or Seelie. The Queen banished us from the Otherworld a while back." Lorcan had confessed this to me when he held me prisoner. I just didn't know why. "We may not have followed her rule, but she had the ability to banish us. There was a misunderstanding and something occurred that shouldn't have. We were forced from our homes and exiled. We settled here."

"So, you've been looking for some way to get back and 'ta-da' here it is." I motioned to myself.

"I am sorry, Ember," Cole said.

"No, you're not."

"Actually, I am. You are not at all what I imagined a Dae to be. In fact I find myself liking you. You're tough and can hold your own. I wish things could be different."

There was sincerity in his words. It didn't help my outcome though.

"How many others followed Lorcan?"

"There were four others." A flash of anger and pain flashed through Cole's eyes. "Besides Lorcan there was Sam, West, Dax, and Dominic."

I had heard of everyone except Dominic. West's desertion had hurt. I liked him when we had met at Mike's Bar months ago. His going with Lorcan felt wrong to me.

"Did they all feel you weren't 'getting the job done'?"

"Yeah." Eli's gaze leveled, his resentment lurching into me. "For some reason they all thought I got a little distracted—that I had lost focus."

"Did you?" I asked.

Eli stood motionless. An uncomfortable silence hung between us. I could feel Cole's gaze taking in every nuance between Eli and me. The implications of his silence twisted everything inside of me. Emotion flooded through me as we stared at each other; so many feelings I had kept guarded floated to the surface. Light bulbs above our heads began to flicker. Soft pops of energy surged through them, dimming and lighting the room in pulses. Bulbs started to crack and splitter. An endless amount of power hummed through my skin.

"Eli, grab the bracelet," Cole ordered, snapping Eli's attention from me.

Suddenly, sensing a threat, my defenses mounted. Warning bells went off in my head, but I hesitated a second too long. Eli grabbed me. He pulled an object out of his pocket and mumbled something I couldn't hear. A prickle slinked over my skin. I was ready to throw him off, but his hand only went for my wrist, snapping something into place.

The reaction was instantaneous. Energy ripped from my body as if someone cut an artery, my powers pouring from me like blood. I let out a strangled cry and looked down to see a metal bracelet wrapped around my wrist. Eli had slipped it on, yet now looking at it I couldn't see a clip or latch. It hugged my wrist like it was a part of my skin, and there seemed to be no way of getting it off. It took a moment for my body to take in the shock and start to balance out.

"What is this?" I looked up at Eli in confusion, feeling weak and helpless.

"The bracelet is laced with iron," he replied.

"I know that." I shakily gripped onto the bedframe for balance. "I meant what is it?" I pointed at the delicate looking object wrapped around my wrist.

"We have to be able to control you. We can't have you using your abilities on us," Cole stated matter-of-factly.

"So this bracelet is basically my dog collar?" I looked down at the harmless looking band. It was actually beautiful if it wasn't for its evil effect on me. Small Celtic symbols were etched around the band, weaving in beautiful looping designs.

"Basically." Ah, Eli. He never sugarcoated anything for me. "Or, if you'd prefer, I can chain you in the basement. Could be fun."

My eyes constricted into a glare. Air pumped in and out of my lungs, the initial shock of iron began to wear off, slowly becoming more manageable.

"The goblins made it, and you will not be able to break it or slip it off as it is magically bound to your wrist. But I know you will try anyway so have fun with that." A slight knowing smile appeared on Eli's mouth.

"Magically bound? It will never come off? Ever?" Panic filled my chest.

"Only if you know the magic word," Cole replied.

"So say pretty please." Eli smirked. "With sugar on top."

"I'll tell you where you can shove—"

"Shut up the both of you. The two of you are driving me insane." Cole rubbed his forehead. "What I meant was it can only be released from your wrist by a word spoken in Goblin tongue, and only three of us know this word. It's like a combination to a lock."

"Let me guess. He's one of those people?" I nodded my head toward Eli, which only made him grin, confirming I was right. "Oh yeah, this is going to be fun."

"But now with your collar on, I can take you for walks."

I automatically took a step towards Eli. Fury burned through me, but my powers stayed quiet and coiled deep inside me.

Cole grabbed my arm, turning to Eli. "Out." He pointed towards the door.

Eli's eyes narrowed on me like it was my fault he was being cast out. He stomped out of the room. Cole stared after Eli, a contemplative expression on his face. He shook his head and faced me.

"Seriously, the two of you are going to cause me to lose my mind."

"But it's his fau—"

"Ember," he warned, shutting me up. We stood there for a time in silence.

"What's going to happen?" I asked, feeling the weight of the world coming down on me all at once.

"I wish I could tell you something good." Cole clasped his hands together and gave a little shrug. "You are safe here as long as you stay on our property. You are free to walk around within our borders. I don't believe you are rash enough to try and escape. Your freedom and life will never be what it once was. You do understand that?" My shoulders sagged further under the reality of his words. "Ember, tell me you comprehend that? You cannot contact your friends or go back to your old life again?"

I nodded, my throat closing up on itself. My friends were vulnerable simply knowing me, but they couldn't be privy to where I was or have contact with me. I understood early on, when I was being chased by different Fae, that it was better if they thought I was dead or gone. Knowledge would only get them killed.

From the moment I had woken up in the Dark Dweller's makeshift hospital a month earlier, my life had changed. I could never go back to the way life used to be. I lost Mark, my friends, my home, my freedom, my life, and I was responsible for thousands of people's deaths. I didn't grasp how much I had been keeping inside the last couple of weeks. It had been ripping me apart. My legs now gave out, and I collapsed to the ground, sobbing. My elbows settled into my lap, and my hands covered my face as my heart broke.

I didn't know how long I sat there or when Cole left, but eventually the tears subsided, leaving me even more drained and lifeless.

The thought of running away again did cross my mind, but I quickly banished it. It would be stupid. There was nowhere to go—nowhere safe. Plus, Eli could track me down.

As pathetic as it was, he and the Dark Dwellers were my best option for now. At least they would protect me from the Fae who hunted me. My life was secure until they figured out what to do with me. I would use this time to learn everything I could about the Otherworld and myself, while finding out who Lars was.

# FIVE

Sometime later I walked outside, the cool air stinging my face. It was one of those rare, clear nights for the Pacific Northwest and the moon glowed brightly overhead.

I headed into the main house. Cole said as long as I didn't leave their property I had free reign. Well, he didn't quite say that, but that's how I was going to act. I wasn't going to behave like a prisoner, not until they actually chained me in the basement.

The sprawling, one-story, ranch-style house wasn't fancy by any means, but it had a worn, well loved feel about it. It was clean, but definitely had a guy's design sense. Brown, overstuffed leather sofas were spaced around the room, and tree stumps were used for the coffee table and side tables. A giant, flat-screen TV was mounted to the wall.

My feet stopped moving when I saw the television. Images of destroyed houses and people covered in blood played out on the screen. My stomach bottomed out. "Oh God." My hand went to my mouth. I had seen newspaper articles of the devastation, but hadn't seen TV in a month. The vivid images flashed in front of me. A reporter walked in the rubble where people were now picking through it, trying to find any belongings they had left.

"Four weeks have passed since tragedy hit our area. Today people have finally been allowed into their homes. Thousands were left homeless, and everything they had is now gone. Many are just thankful they made it out with their lives since countless did not. So much devastation, so much lost. It is hard to even comprehend. The need is so great here. For those of you wanting to volunteer, please contact this station or the Red Cross." The reporter looked away shaking his head with sadness. Vomit shot up my throat, barely letting me get back outside before it came out.

A hand touched my shoulder. "You okay?" Cooper asked.

The guilt was so oppressive I couldn't talk, or breathe, or even cry. Shaking my head, a tortured sob broke from my lips.

Without a word, Cooper waited for me to calm down before helping me to my feet.

"I don't think I can live with this," I whispered, mostly to myself.

Cooper's arm held me tight against him, keeping me standing. "Yes, you can."

"How?" I looked up at him. He tucked his white-blonde hair behind his ear.

"Because if it hadn't been you, the Queen would have found another way to do it. I know it's hard, but don't let that bitch win. Don't let all those people's deaths be in vain. Honor them by fighting for them. Not with this self-pity."

His words were like a gift to my broken spirit. I unleashed my selfish wallowing and saw it from another view. A river of strength put my legs firmer onto the ground.

Cooper let go, turning to leave, I touched his arm. "Thank you." He looked at me over his shoulder. With a nod he turned around, continuing back to the house.

The clock in the infirmary told me it was midnight. I had tried to sleep, but the images from the news wouldn't let me. Cooper's words helped, but I still felt haunted by the dead. These thoughts would never go away, but I had to learn to live with them and do something to keep this from ever happening again. The fear of the Queen capturing me kept my lids wide open.

Owen had brought me some soup for dinner, afraid my stomach couldn't handle real food yet. My stomach thought differently so I headed to the kitchen, voices stopping my pursuit of food. The door to what looked like an office next to the kitchen was partially open. Peeking through the crack, I could see what was left of the group seated in various places around the room. Cole was at the focal point leaning against his desk. Silently, I pressed myself against the wall next to the doorway.

"Even with the protected wards around our property, we still have to be diligent with our security. They are going to come out of the woodwork for her, Dark and Light. Incessantly. We have our invocations in place, but I don't want us to depend on them and become lax. By now the Phookas have certainly told the Queen who took her. We must be careful and on guard constantly. The Queen will try to find her any way she can. We need to be prepared," Cole voiced his concerns. "We also need to be watchful of her. She is unbelievably powerful for being so young and untrained. Eli was able to put a cuff on her, so at least we have her abilities somewhat contained for now."

"There's even less doubt as to who her parents really are," I heard Cooper's voice pipe up.

"Think we've known for a while," Cole replied.

"Yeah, some of us longer than others." I knew Cooper's jab was meant for Eli.

"I am trying to locate the Unseelie King but so far nothing," Eli's voice spoke next.

My body immediately tightened, and my heart wrenched in my chest. To hear him talk so callously about getting rid of me hurt.

"Wait. I don't understand. Why can't we find this guy? He's the Unseelie King. He shouldn't be hard to find." Jared's teenage tone sounded at odds with the rest of the group.

"The Unseelie King isn't found unless he wants to be," Eli responded. "Plus, the curse makes it harder for us to go through Otherworld channels to find him."

"The curse...." By Jared's voice it was clear he had forgotten what the curse was.

"Seriously, Jared, I am going to start quizzing you. I know you weren't born in the Otherworld, but you really need to know your own history." I could sense Eli shaking his head in exasperation. "Fast re-cap: the Queen banned us to Earth and put a Druid spell blocking us from all entries into the Otherworld, trapping us here."

"Oh yeah, I remember," Jared said, lying through his teeth.

"Sure. One thing you probably didn't know is Druid curses can only be undone by a Druid. Unleashing the enchantment would allow us to go home."

"Too bad the Queen killed off the entire Druid population," Cooper huffed.

There was a long pause then Gabby spoke up, speculation in her tone. "I know you, Eli. I recognize the look. What do you know?"

"What if we didn't have to use Ember? What if I told you I might know of a living Druid?"

"*What?*" Everyone reacted in unison to his claim.

"That is not possible. The Queen made sure every last Druid was killed," Cole said when he got everyone quiet again.

"It's what I thought too, but I think more than we know were smuggled out. At least this one was." Eli stated. "I wasn't sure at first, but now I'm positive she is a Druid of a high bloodline. She, of course, is completely ignorant to this and I think because of that is suppressing it."

Eli's words filtered into my ear and fell heavy into my stomach, twisting and itching with intuition. I seemed to already know who he was talking about. "She was raised by ordinary humans. Her Druid parents must have gotten her out. I've been watching from the moment she crossed my path, and I can feel the magic in her."

Fire in the Darkness

"Why didn't you tell us?" Owen spoke for the first time.

"I wanted to be sure. I didn't want to let you all down if it wasn't true."

"Holy shit! What are the odds we'd find a Dae and a Druid?" Gabby exclaimed.

"I think they were drawn to each other. Sensed each other's magic without realizing it." Eli breathed out. "We only have one chance to get this right, and I want to be sure everything is in our favor. Abducting her will only put more attention on her and us. We don't want the Queen to realize what she is. If that happens—game over. I know this girl needs to be told. She has the blood of a Druid, but she doesn't have the training, and undoing the curse is not an easy process. She needs to learn her magic first."

"But it might take centuries. Druids aren't known for their speed," Gabby exclaimed. "Let's go get her. There has to be *Cliffs Notes* or *Druid Magic for Dummies* she can read really fast. Oh hell, I don't want to wait any longer. Let's use Ember. If that fails, we still have the Druid option."

"*Mac an donais*, Gabby." I could hear Eli jump up from his chair. "This isn't a game."

"I know that, Eli," she bellowed back. "I'm sorry if your little girlfriend gets hurt in this, but we need to stop screwing around and start doing something."

There were a few seconds of silence and, even without seeing Eli, I could feel the anger burning through him. "I have *always* put you guys first. Do not second guess me again. *Ni ceart go cur le cheile*," Eli said, his voice so even it gave me chills.

"Eli." Cole's voice instantly sending calmness through me, the Alpha controlling the room.

"How do you suppose we do that, Eli?" Cooper spoke up. "You think this girl is going to accept she's from an ancient line of Druids who were killed off because the Queen feared them? That she has magical talents and should help us out of the kindness of her heart?"

"That's precisely what I think she will do," he responded. "If her good friend is in peril or threatened—she will do anything to save her."

Charging into the room, my body reacted before my brain. "You will not use me as bait to get Kennedy. You will not bring her into this. Use me! But you stay the hell away from her."

The entire room turned and stared at me. Eli's smug expression halted my fury. Damn him. Of course, he knew I was there the whole time; he had felt me near.

"Who's Kennedy?" Cooper looked between me and Eli.

Eli's stare burned into me. "I never said her name."

He didn't have to. From the moment I met Kennedy I had recognized she was different.

*Like me.*

Maybe like Eli mentioned somewhere inside I had known all along. Why she and I bonded from the moment I moved to Olympia. We had a connection beyond this world.

"Kennedy is the Druid, isn't she?"

"Yes," Eli concurred. "You don't seem very surprised"

"I'm not. I know I should be, but I'm not," I waited for shock and disbelief to find me, but it never did. Kennedy had always been eerily intuitive, seeing more than anybody else. I didn't know much about Druid traits, but if being so insightful that you were almost clairvoyant was one of them, she had it in spades. Kennedy being a Druid made sense, which felt odd to say, but it did. It was another piece of the puzzle fitting into place.

Cole, still leaning against the desk, addressed Eli. "How do you want to handle this?"

"We have to tell her. She needs to know." I stepped further into the room.

"No." Eli shook his head furiously. "That is the last thing we do. Not until we are ready to bring her here."

"Why? What will happen to her?"

"Since I know there's no way you will let this go, you might as well sit down." When I refused, Eli shrugged and continued on. "The basic story you need to know is the Queen grew to fear the Druids. Since they are human and contain their own magic, she has no control over them. Their magic is something the Queen cannot challenge or beat. They used a spell to hide something from her, which she desperately wanted. When torture didn't work, she thought killing off the Druid line would break the curse. So she annihilated the Druid population, but the spell still held. This was around the same time she had put a curse on us. Since a Druid is the only one who can undue this Druid curse, we thought that option was lost to us forever."

"If Aneira knows Kennedy's a Druid, she will torture and kill her and then she can't help you."

He nodded and bile coiled in my stomach, climbing up my throat. This was not much different from what the Queen wanted to do with me, but it felt so different hearing she would do this to Kennedy—sweet, compassionate, loving Kennedy. All I wanted to do was run to her and shield her from anything bad. She couldn't handle this world and the darkness in it like me. Kennedy had been adopted by a loving couple who shielded their daughters from the bad in the world. She had grown less naïve around Ryan and me, but she had such a pure heart. I couldn't let anything happen to her.

"What do we do then?" Panic curled around my vocal chords.

"Until we are ready to bring her in, she has to stay ignorant to everything. Your friends are being watched, the Queen waiting for you to contact them. If anything changes, even in the slightest, they will notice. We can't draw any attention to her."

"Why hasn't Aneira felt her or heard of Kennedy before?" My hands were damp with sweat as they twisted around each other.

"Kennedy has been well protected, and her ignorance to what she is helps. You only sense magic if you are really looking for it and near someone who has it. Magic doesn't have a GPS on it. Plus, hers is so dormant no one from afar would notice. I only noticed because I smelled something different about her. Fay have no real sense of smell; Dark Dwellers do. Also, I sensed something the first time I saw her in the car, when your friends came to pick you up at Silverwood."

I remembered the evening as well. Kennedy had gone into a trance-like state when she first laid eyes on Eli. I had ignored it thinking it was because of how hot he was. Eli had sensed something about her, but she also sensed he was different.

"The moment she is aware of what she is and starts using her magic, she will be recognized as a Druid by the Queen." Cole folded his arms.

My head and stomach ached. All I wanted to do was curl into a ball.

"So what is stopping you from getting her? You have another way out of here now. Since you think Earth is such a hell hole, I'm surprised you're not jumping on that."

Eli's eyes narrowed. "Your friend's life, as she knows it, would be over. She'd have to cut off all ties to her family and friends and leave everything and everyone she's ever known. She'd have to go into hiding here. Is that what you want?"

"Of course not!" Indignation flew out of me, furling me with rage. "I am just surprised you don't. Did you suddenly grow a soul or conscience?"

Eli was in my face before I could even blink. A deep growl vibrated off him. Standing my ground, I held his penetrating scowl.

"Eli." Cole stood, ready to step between us. "Back down."

It took Eli another minute before he stepped back, twitching with aggravation.

"Ember, we'll talk more about this later. I think it's best if you leave. We all could use a break." Cole's hand herded me towards the door.

Obliging his request, I strode out of the room. My hot headedness dissolved with every step I took towards the infirmary cabin now serving as my bedroom.

*Kennedy.* My stomach squeezed into a sick knot. Kennedy's safety was all I could think of. The desire to call or go to her was difficult to ignore. I couldn't, but the notion was still overbearing. Kennedy was a Druid.

*Holy shit.*

From my limited reading on Celtic mythology, I recalled they were human. But each could live thousands of years and cross over into the Otherworld as easily as Fae could. Originally Fae and Druids worked together in harmony. Obviously, the Queen had changed that relationship. Was Kennedy the last surviving Druid? Thoughts tossed around in my head like clothes in a dryer. Growing weary in both mind and body, I curled up on my bed. Some days you were the bitch and some days you were shit that came out of the bitch's toy poodle. Today was one of those days I was the latter.

My lids started to droop when I felt a hand slide softly through my hair. I sensed Eli behind me, but I wasn't ready for him to know I was awake. He stood there a couple of more moments, his fingers gripped the back of my head roughly, yanking my head, his lips next to my ear.

"If you ever eavesdrop on us or challenge me again, I will personally chain you to this bed."

When I flipped over, he was gone.

It took me hours to finally fall back asleep.

*The cool mist of the descending water circled the air, forming clouds clinging desperately to the trees and rocks. The noise from the cascading waterfall was muted and not as forceful as I knew it was in person,*

but it could almost pass for reality. Almost. The place was so familiar, but it was not the place where Torin usually met me. This was not the enchanted Otherworld Forest but the waterfall where Eli and I had spent time together. Where I told him about my mother. Where he had brought me after getting me out of jail. Why would Torin bring me here?

"Ember?" A voice came from behind me. I whipped around. Torin stood before me.

He stepped closer to me, his eyes moving over my body. "I've been so worried. I'm so relieved you got away from the dark Fae. I was too afraid to dreamscape in case you were running from them. I had hoped you would eventually contact me. Are you all right?"

"I'm okay." I nodded, not wanting to tell him who had saved me. I knew Torin's animosity towards the Dark Dwellers, specifically Eli, was strong. "How is my dad? Is he okay?"

"He is fine. The Queen will not hurt him until it suits her."

"That's not reassuring. I need to get him out."

"Em, you do not have the ability or the skill to take on the Queen yet. Lars can train you." He reached for my hand, stopping at the trinket wrapped around my wrist. "What is this?"

"My doggie leash."

Torin's head jerked up, looking around. "Where are you right now? Who has you?"

Biting my lip, I looked down. He was going to freak. "Eli found me. They actually saved me from those dark Fae. I'm back at their compound."

Anger burned up into his face. "Leave. Leave right now."

"I can't." I pulled my arm away from him.

"Ember, it is not a safe place for you. You don't know how dangerous those guys are."

"Where should I go then? I have such great options," I exclaimed. I was sick of everyone having an opinion on whom I should associate with. Everyone had an agenda when it came to me.

"They are killers, Ember, and will only use you for their own benefit."

I crossed my arms, stepping back. "True, but that's no secret. What is your deal, Torin? What do you want with me?"

He stilled. "I do not care what you are or what you can do. I only desire you." He retook the space I had set between us, his hands cupping my face. The sincerity of his tone was hard to deny. "Only you—like it was supposed to be." Torin leaned in.

"I hope I'm not interrupting some romantic moment here?" Eli's voice came out of the dark. I jolted back in shock. "And all these years, T, I figured you for the Shefro type." Eli walked out from the trees, his face and body rigid with anger. As much as he was trying to appear nonplussed, I could feel confusion rolling off him.

"Shefros are miniature, male Fairies," Torin retorted.

"Exactly."

"Whoa—wait, you guys know each other?" Aware they knew of each other, I hadn't realized they were actually acquainted. I looked between the two men.

*They both took my breath away but were so different. Torin was beautiful, almost unreal looking. He was neat, nearly to a fault, dressed in crisp, leather pants and a tight, black shirt. This seemed to be his consistent, off-duty uniform. He was clean shaven, and his dark hair was pulled back with a band. I couldn't deny he was sexy as hell.*

*Eli was physically opposite. His hair was loose, falling to his shoulders in a way that made him look fierce and wild. A permanent thick scruff only emphasized his sharp jaw line. He oozed sexual energy. He was rugged, raw, primal, and pure, uninhibited sex.*

*Both of them were trouble.*

"Yeah, we go way back. Don't we, T?" Eli said but his voice was tight and threatening.

"How are you even here?" Torin demanded. "This should not be possible."

"How am I in the dreamscape with you?" A slow smile spread over his face. "Ask her."

Torin's eyes flicked over to me, and I immediately held up my hands. "I'm not doing anything. I have no idea how he's here."

"Hmmm..." Eli shrugged. "I must have taken a wrong turn then. I thought this was the way to the fairies-gone-wild dream. You know how crazy those water fairies can get." He sighed happily. "Good times." Then with a shake of his head he turned to us.

"From now on, I have a feeling you two little love birds will probably have a chaperone. She needs someone to make sure her suitors have the best of intentions. You understand? Wouldn't want to sully Ember's reputation."

"I have no business with you, Elighan." Torin's face was strained, and I could see it took everything he had to stay calm. "I'm here for Ember. To keep her safe."

"Oh, that is rich coming from you." Under the surface, I could see Eli was fuming. "Why don't you tell Ember what your full title is? How much the Queen controls your harness inside and outside of the bedroom? Think she will be dying to know that little tidbit."

Torin's body stiffened next to mine.

"What?" A memory of the Queen touching Torin in a way that felt possessive and intimate flashed through my head.

"Ember, it is not what you think." Torin faced me. "This doesn't change my feelings for you." His words barely computed in my brain.

"What is he talking about? What are you to her?"

"I am the First Knight of the Queen."

"Oh, come on, T. She knows that much. I think you can do better." Eli raised his eyebrow. "Like, for instance, you are the Queen's consort." Eli's attention turned to me. "He attends to the Queen's needs, and, yes, I mean every one of them."

I took a few more steps back, looking at Torin. He was the Queen's lover? This man who had held me, kissed me, made me feel protected?

"But you helped me escape. Why?"

"Ember, please, let me explain. You were taken from me, but you and I are destined to be together. There was nothing I wouldn't do to find you, even if it meant becoming the First Knight. It's not like that with her. I do not love her."

"*Not like what, Torin? Do you sleep with her?*"

Torin's jaw clenched.

"*That's what I thought. It is exactly like that,*" I spit out. "*You had the audacity to stand there, while under her command, in her bed, telling me who was dangerous and who not to trust?*" I yelled. Anger and hurt filled my words. "*When it was you all along that I needed to protect myself from.*"

"*Ember, please that's not—*" He reached out for me, but I jerked backwards out of his reach.

"*No. I don't want to hear it. I am sick of listening to everyone else telling me who not to trust, where to go, what to do. I've had enough.*" I shook my head. "*Did you and Eli invest in the same handbook—the one telling you how to seduce and twist a girl's mind so much she'd do whatever you wanted?*"

"*There's a handbook? Damn. Now that would have been helpful,*" Eli quipped.

Torin's chest heaved, puffing with offense. "*My feelings for you are real; they are nothing like Elighan's.*"

"*You know nothing of me. You never have,*" Eli uttered through gritted teeth as he lunged forward.

Leaping in front of Eli, I tried to block his attack on Torin. "*Stop!*"

Eli's pupils shifted vertically, his anger consuming him. Instinctively I grabbed his hand. The skin was rough, and I could feel the knife-like claws starting to burrow into my skin. I moved it over my heart. Both my blood and his pumped through it. Taking a couple deep breaths, I felt his body react to mine, his heartbeat slowing.

"*Breathe, Eli.*" *It only took a few seconds before he was back to himself. Dropping his hand, I turned to face Torin, who was watching us intensely with a bewildered, hurt expression.*

"*Torin, I think you should go now.*" *My voice was raw after his duplicity.*

"*Em...*"

"*Do I believe you are going to turn me over to her? No. But how do I know she won't command you to?*" *I demanded.* "*You are sleeping with the Queen. You no longer have a right to judge who I associate with. Eli might not be the best choice, but I'd rather stick with the enemy I know.*"

"*Ember, I...*"

*I turned, rapidly walking away, willing myself to wake up.*

"*Ember!*" *Torin's voice tore through me.*

Wake up, wake up. Now! *I screamed into my head.*

My eyes popped open and only a minute passed before the door banged open, Eli storming inside. In three giant steps he had crossed the room, looming down on me.

I sat up, leaning back against the wall. "Seems a little early for breakfast in bed, but since you're offering, I'll take my eggs scrambled."

"About to scramble your ass." He grumbled, and his hands fisted. "Talk."

I was about to say something smart-ass, but the way red flickered through his eyes, I decided against it. I did have some sense of self-preservation.

"Are you talking about Torin? Were you there, too?" As I said, I only have *some* self-preservation.

"How long has this thing between you two been going on?" Fury dripped over each word as he continued on. "You and him, huh? Never saw that one coming I'll admit. I think it's funny you were getting all bent out of shape over me being a womanizer, when you were coming to both of us at once. Quite an act you got going on there. You probably could give me pointers."

"Fuck you!" I jumped out of bed and got into his face. "You don't know what I've done or haven't done with Torin. You have no right to be pissed. What do you care anyway? Your feelings for me aren't real."

Something dark swept over his face. He stepped back from me. "You're right. I don't care." The pain came fast and swift, reflecting on my face before I could contain my pained reaction. "So how long has Torin been coming into your dreams like that? How did he find you?"

I shook my head. "I don't know how he found me. I never asked because until recently I thought he was another hallucination of mine. He first fully appeared to me right before I came to Silverwood."

"I don't know what his game plan is, but you have to block him from your mind. He is the Queen's Knight."

"Block him? I am not going to block him," I declared. "Plus, I don't have the skill to do that."

"These are your dreams. You have the ability to regulate them."

"Then can I block you out? How did you get in anyway?"

His eyes flickered away for a brief second, and then he shrugged. "Maybe your subconscious was thinking about me."

"Then it would have had me kicking the crap out of you."

Eli laughed, deep and full at the idea of me battling him.

"I can fight."

His eyes grazed over my body, and I suddenly was too aware of my skimpy tank top and underwear. He moved closer to me. "Do you think your little struggle with Sam back at Silverwood was fighting? She wasn't even trying knowing humans were watching her. You could never have defended yourself if she had truly wanted to kill you."

I felt my hackles go up. "I threw her into your windshield."

"Like you, she wasn't expecting your powers. She will never misjudge you again. So don't underestimate her or the rest of us. You are powerful, but we are deadly."

I shivered at his words. Had I only won the fight with Sam a few weeks earlier because I had the element of surprise? The Demon in me was happy to fight, but what if it couldn't defend me from what was out there, or worse, it decided to take the day off?

"Okay, then teach me how to fight."

"Seriously?" Eli scoffed. "You want me to teach you techniques you will use against me?"

"Already scared the student will out-fight and out-wit the master?"

"Oh, good one, little girl. Think baiting me will work?"

I stepped up to him, my hands on my hips. "Yes."

Eli nodded and turned. "Find some pants and meet me in the garage."

Five minutes later, I stood in the garage, which had been turned into a gym with punching bags, a boxing ring, and weights.

"Okay, you want to learn how to fight." Eli walked up to a heavy bag in the workout room. "So, let's teach you." I stood there for a moment, looking from him to the bag. "Come on, Brycin, let's see what you got."

Shaking my head, I moved in closer. I didn't get Eli. Sometimes he treated me like an object to be tossed away after use. Then other times, like this, he was helping me protect myself—from the exact thing I needed to defend myself from—him.

"I don't know how to help you with your powers. But kicking someone's ass the old fashion way? Now that is something I can do. It comes in handy most of the time." He smiled the arrogant, bad-boy smile, which made me melt inside. "Punch it."

I swung my arm back and gave the bag a fisted hit. The bag barely moved.

"Pathetic," he sneered and grabbed my hand in his.

"Lesson one: you need to keep your thumb on the outside of your fist." He curled my fingers, wrapping my thumb over them.

"Lesson two: most movies do it wrong and show people punching with their arm straight. This will only be more painful to your hand than the target; you aim to punch with the first two knuckles."

Eli grabbed my wrist, punching my knuckles against his palm in slow motion to show me the technique. "Keep your arm angled, but your wrist straight as you punch. Try it again." I pointed to the bag. This time when I swung, the bag flew out of Eli's grip. "Good." He looked slightly impressed. "Again." I punched at the bag several more times.

"This is also about protecting yourself, not just learning the skills of fight club. You want to incapacitate your attacker as quickly and efficiently as possible, so you can get the hell out. Again, movies always show people punching each other in the face, which is actually the worst place to aim. Most likely you will miss or hurt your hand. It's also difficult, and extremely lucky, to knock someone out cold in one hit."

His fingers wrapped around my balled-up hand. The touch of his skin on mine made my pulse race. "Aim for their throat or the side of their neck where their carotid artery is." As he spoke, he touched my fist to the spots on his neck he mentioned. "This will cause them to back off immediately. It affects their breathing and will create panic in them. Good time to run. But, if you can't punch there, then go for their sternum or the kidneys. Of course, if you are fighting a male, the knee to the groin is going to put them down every time."

I absorbed every word he said as we moved through different types of punches. He had me using both my right and left hands and practicing defensive moves until sweat poured down my face.

"Okay, let's move to the mat and you can try some shots on me. I'll come at you like an attacker," Eli said.

He pulled his sweatshirt over his head and his tan, ripped chest was beyond distracting. I tried not to respond to that or how low his jeans clung to his hips.

*Nope wasn't paying attention to it at all...nope, not one bit.*

He seemed to know where my mind and eyes were because he responded, "I sleep naked. You're lucky I could find what I did."

Yeah, I didn't really consider him finding clothes "lucky" for me. I turned my eyes away, scolding myself, as I followed him to the mats. I needed to get my hormones in check. Being attracted to a guy who only pretended to like you so he could use you as a trading card to the Unseelie King was not exactly healthy.

"All right, nothing but punches—no actual knee to the groin."

I let my eyes widen with a fake innocence. "Me? Would I do something like that?"

"Yeah, you would. You've probably been dreaming about hitting me there since the day we met."

"*Your* groin is not what I dream about at night." I smirked. Yeah, sometimes I didn't play nice either, now knowing my dreams with Torin bothered him.

It worked like a charm. His eyes narrowed, and he came at me in a blink of an eye with speed no human possessed. I reacted before I could think. Ducking and turning to the side, I slipped out of his reach. Whirling around his body, I took the opportunity to strike, targeting his kidneys. My fist plunged into his side. *Bulls-eye.* We turned to face each other. His eyebrows were hiked high on his forehead, his eyes wide.

"Holy shit! How did I do that?" Astonishment rang from my throat.

"Have you ever moved so fast before?"

"No." I shook my head. "Nothing like that."

Something fluttered over Eli's expression. I looked down at the metal wrapped around my wrist, keeping my Fay powers at bay. If they were locked up tight, how did I do that?

"Again," Eli commanded. His face returned back to his usual stony expression.

*Bring it.* I smiled, wanting to crack that stone.

*Be careful what you ask for.*

Eli was a predator. I could feel him studying me, measuring which way I would go, calculating his moves. My brain was doing the same, trying to counter his. The blood in my veins pumped faster. My head became light, my body more aware of his every nuance. He launched himself at me. I darted back and turned to the side, his hands grazing a few strands of my ponytail. I sprung up, silently landing on a table next to the mat getting out of his reach. He quickly adjusted his direction. Faster than I thought possible, he had my leg in his grasp, trying to pull me off the table. Simultaneously, I jumped and caused both of us to tumble onto the mat. My back slammed down and his body fell on top of mine. Our breaths were ragged as we lay there. My tank top was thin enough I could feel every muscle in his torso.

"Impressive," he said, his voice deep and gruff.

Tension filled the gap between us as he stared down at me. My breath became more labored as his eyes turned more and more primal. Sex screamed from them, primitive, wild, raw, and no doubt incredible. It terrified me, excited me, and heat encompassed my body. Yearning crippled the air trying to reach my lungs. His head leaned in closer, his lids lowered with heavy desire. Abruptly, he broke his gaze from mine as he turned away, rolled off me.

My body protested at the sudden absence. I couldn't move. Everything in me screamed for his physique to lie on me again, for him to end this excruciating torture. We were already sweaty, stimulated, and mostly undressed. *Why stop when we're halfway there?*

Eli got up, suddenly looking irritable; he reached out his hand and pulled me up, not looking at me.

I wanted to cry, to hit him. I also wanted nothing more than for him to kiss me, to push me back onto the mat, tear off my leggings, and thrust deep inside me.

"Lesson is done for the day," he said coolly, then turned and was gone before I could even respond.

I groaned.

*Okay, time for a painfully cold shower.*

# SIX

"I'd like to go get some of my own clothes." I walked into the kitchen where Cole was making breakfast. It had dawned on me after the long, cold shower I only had the same clothes to put back on. If I was going to wear some bitch's clothes, I'd prefer them to be mine. "I'd really like my own stuff if I'm going to be a 'guest' for a while."

Cole's eyebrow lifted. With the knife in his hand, he pointed to the kitchen stool at the counter.

"Have a seat. You must be hungry." I stood there for a moment wondering how to respond. "I'm not ignoring your request. I think you can take a moment to eat while we discuss this. Coffee?" he asked.

"Yes, please, yes."

Cole smiled at my dramatic response, "Help yourself. Cups are in the right-hand cupboard next to the sink." He hacked at a raw hunk of meat.

Finding the cups, I poured myself a cup of coffee. "Real coffee. So good." My eyes rolled back in ecstasy after my first sip. "You want one?"

"Yes, thank you. Black."

I brought him the cup and leaned against the island. "Is this breakfast?" My nose scrunched up as I looked down at the bloody juice pooling around the meat. The longer I looked at it, the more it actually started looking good to me. *What the hell? Raw meat looks good?*

"We eat and enjoy lots of different foods, but our preferred food source is raw meat. While we've been here the need has lessened a bit, though," Cole replied.

"From animals, right?" I felt a slight wave of nausea. "Please say it's from animals."

Cole looked at me silently.

"Fuck." I gripped the counter.

"I'm kidding." Cole chuckled.

Nervous laughter erupted out of me. I moved to the stool. "So, before you came to Earth what did you guys eat? Is there a Fae Bambi or something?" Cole's grip on the knife tightened. "I'm sorry. I know I'm not supposed to ask anything about you."

He shook his head. "Silence is an automatic response when somebody asks a question about us." He sighed deeply, but his shoulders were still locked with tension. "Our needs in the Otherworld were different. We were different."

There was something he wasn't telling me. I had a feeling I'd be better off not knowing, which didn't stop me from wanting to. I squirmed in the sudden, uncomfortable silence.

"How long have you guys been around? How old are you?"

Cole rubbed his head with the back of his hand as he paused hacking up the meat. He exhaled before he replied, "I am considered young by our species. I have been around for several centuries."

Centuries? Several? Shit, no wonder when I asked Eli how old he was, he stumbled over the question. He told me he was 24. Think he forgot a zero. Still, this was more than I expected to get.

"How long have you been on Earth?"

"We've been here for a little over eighteen years now."

"Hmmm—that's funny. I guess you guys came about the same time my mother must have smuggled me here."

Something in Cole's expression changed, turning dark and causing a spark of alarm. "Yeah," he retorted quickly. "What would you like for breakfast, since raw meat doesn't seem to be appetizing to you?" I didn't want to confess that it kind of did. Red meat had never been a favorite of mine, but looking at it now, even raw, my mouth watered.

Obviously, he wanted to change the subject, which only made me more interested. If the saying "curiosity killed the cat" is true, I should start meowing. I continued on, "It's evident everyone looks to you as the leader, but Eli seems to look to you as a father figure as well. What happened to his parents?"

Again Cole stayed quiet, veins straining against the skin on his forehead. "All I will tell you is they were killed. I've raised Eli since he was little." He pressed his lips together. "There is a lot about us you don't know and never can. Our past is not anything you need to know about. It will only bring you trouble."

He made it clear the topic was over, and this time I didn't push it. "We also have cereal or eggs." Cole pointed to the refrigerator as he wiped his bloody hands on a cloth.

The thought of eggs, even real ones, sent up a gag reflex. It reminded me of the many mornings I had stolen powdered eggs from a discarded plate near the shelters.

"Do you have peanut butter?" I asked, hopeful. "It's one of my food groups. I've been craving it for weeks. All the convenience stores I went to had already been robbed of it."

A sexy smile over took the dark expression that had been etched on Cole's face. "Oh boy. You and Eli really are going to cause me a lot of grief." He laughed, which only increased his hotness. I could feel a blush sweep over my cheeks. Damn these guys...

"It's in the top cupboard," a deep voice rumbled behind me. I turned to see Eli leaning up against the wall, his hair damp from a shower. "But if you eat all my peanut butter, I will have no qualms about *actually* chaining you in the basement."

Cole's smile grew. "Eli has the same food group ideals you do, once he discovered it here. They don't have peanut butter in the Otherworld."

"Guess I won't be moving there then. That's a deal breaker for me." I headed to the cupboard, pulling out the jar of peanut butter. "Extra crunchy," I read the label with uninhibited joy.

Swiftly, Eli came up next to me. "Like there is any other kind."

He yanked a drawer open and pulled out two spoons. Our eyes met as I took the spoon from him, then I looked away quickly and focused on unscrewing the lid. He dove in as soon as the top was off, taking a massive heap.

"Hey." I dug my spoon in after him and took out a huge spoonful, shoving the creamy, chunky goodness into my mouth. It had been so long since I had actually eaten. If there was a heaven, it was in this little jar of happiness. I closed my eyes in bliss. When I reopened them, I found Eli staring at me, his eyes glowing as they ran over every detail of my face. "This is so good," I mumbled.

A slight, suggestive smile turned up the side of his mouth as he continued to gaze at me. I felt my body heat up, a warm blush attacking my cheeks, my breath catching in my throat. Turning my focus back on the jar, I shoved my spoon in again.

"I don't think so." Eli's spoon crashed into mine. "What did I say about eating all my peanut butter?"

Pulling the jar away from him. "It will be worth it." I took another huge bite, a wicked smile playing on my lips.

"Oh no." He reached out for the container. Before he could grab it, I turned away, slipping it out of his grasp.

"Oh, this is *soooo* good." Dramatically I took another bite, as I stepped backwards away from him.

"You're asking for it. Do not mess with a man's peanut butter."

I smiled. "Good thing you're not a man, then." I knew I was begging for trouble, and I was pretty sure I wanted whatever was coming my way.

Cole chuckled as Eli cocked his head at me, a smirk deepening his features that said I should probably run, which was exactly what I did. I feigned going one way, then pivoted but only made it to the doorway before he caught me. His arm wrapped around my waist, picked me up, and threw me over his shoulder.

"What the hell, caveman?" Cooper sniped at Eli as he walked in. "Never thought *you* would have the need to knock them over the head."

"Well... this one is a little more ornery than the rest." He patted my butt. "Must teach Em her place."

"Hey. Let me down." I tried to wiggle out of his hold with absolutely no results. "Fine. I'm going to eat the rest of your peanut butter." Jar still in hand, I scooped up another bite and hummed happily as I munched away.

"See?" Eli retorted. Looking up, both Cooper and Cole chuckled, amused by the scene in front of them.

"You know, he didn't have the need to knock the girls out before..." I pointed my spoon at Cole and Cooper as I spoke. "Because what's the need if they were already brain dead?"

"Oh man." Cooper howled with laughter. "Think your work's cut out for you with this one." He gave me a high five.

"Don't I know it?" Eli put me back down on the ground and grabbed the peanut butter jar out of my hands. "You're cut off."

I frowned.

Cole placed the knife down and turned his attention to Eli. "Ember would like to go get some personal items from her home."

Eli turned serious. "Do you think that's a good idea? I thought you said—"

"It will be a good time to check on some things." Cole eyed him with a steady look. A message only Eli understood passed between them. "Check out the house. See if anyone's been there."

"Right, yeah. That's a good idea." Eli nodded.

The way they spoke ignited my interest. Something was up, but since it was getting me what I wanted, I decided to ignore it.

"I'll go. We can take Gabbs and Jared," Cooper spoke up.

"Jared needs to get out more. You can treat it like a training exercise for him. He's still a little too hyper to be stealthy." Cole rolled his eyes, but I could see the absolute love he felt for his nephew.

"Cool, I'll go get J and Gabbs." Cooper slipped off the stool and headed out of the kitchen.

I wanted some underwear and a pair of jeans. How did this turn into a whole parade? I glanced nervously at Cole. "I didn't mean for this to be a big deal. I just wanted some of my stuff."

"I understand, but we like to be prepared for any situation. Plus, I want Jared doing more fieldwork. Being a Dark Dweller is not as natural for him as it is for the rest of us."

They treated Jared with kid gloves. Now that I knew they'd come here over eighteen years ago and that Jared was sixteen made me curious. "Jared was born here?"

Cole's expression grew shadowy again. "Yes. His mother was human. He's not quite like us."

Jared was half human and half Dark Dweller. Interesting. I really wanted to know more—curious about this human woman Owen had let in. Had he loved her? Or did he use her to obtain a child? What had happened to her? Theories built themselves in my mind. My mouth opened to ask, but Cole turned his back on me, busying himself with packaging the raw meat. His countenance conveyed to me the end of subject and to not ask more.

I slammed back my lukewarm coffee. I did need my caffeine fix, but now I was wishing the coffee had a shot of whiskey in it.

Everything was going to be fine, right? So, why did I have a deep, sinking feeling in the pit of my stomach?

## SEVEN

A short time later we loaded into Cole's huge SUV and drove down the road. Gabby, Cooper, and Jared argued in back over who was going to carry the bigger knife. Cole had made sure they were all armed, even though they didn't need to be since they were walking weapons. He hadn't given me anything, probably still unsure if I would use it against them.

Eli didn't seem to have the same worry. "Strap this onto your leg." One hand was on the steering wheel as he handed me a sheathed knife. "Since you have the bracelet on, I don't want you to be without protection. But remember that you stab to kill. Don't play nice because they won't, and they won't be stopped for long. You get out when you can and run."

"But if I kill them, doesn't it stop them?"

"You won't kill them."

"Gee, thanks," I snapped. I wasn't expertly trained, but I could kill. *Yeah, if they walk up to the knife and fall on it.* My insecurities mocked me.

"Relax. We'll probably be in and out in seconds."

"Something you probably know a lot about," I muttered as I looked out the window. I could see him turn to me in the reflection. He arched his eyebrow before turning back to the road, shaking his head.

As we drove, I realized I didn't remember anything about what roads we had taken and how to get back. I was exceptionally good with directions, always had been, as if I had an internal GPS. But now my compass felt like it got knocked over. I scrubbed at my head, trying to clear it.

"We have a misdirection device and a protection spell over our land. No one can find us, and anybody who gets near will suddenly decide to go another way." Eli looked over at me.

"So, how do you get back?"

"When we first executed the spell, we provided our names and a sample of our blood so it can recognize us. We are the only ones who know the way. The only way a stranger can find it is if we lead them in."

"So that's why you want to keep me there."

"It's not so much of a 'want' to as a 'have' to," Gabby's voice shot out from the back seat.

"Gabby," Eli grumbled.

"What? None of us really want her here."

"I don't mind." Jared shrugged.

"Oh, shut up," Gabby shot at him. "The fact we are even going on this little field trip is ridiculous. Poor little *bitseach* can't live without her blankie for the night?"

"What is the deal with the girls in your group?" I looked over at Eli. All her comments, even when she didn't know I had heard, caught up with me. "Are they all such catty bitches?"

Eli exploded with laughter.

Before Gabby could verbally or physically attack me, I swung around to look at her.

"Look, I get it, you don't like me. Fine. Whatever your problem is with me, get over it because I've done nothing to you. I don't like this any more than you do. I want to go home. I want my dad back and to see my friends. Instead I get to be treated like some Fae livestock, with my own personal dog collar, constantly being hunted down to be sold to the highest bidder. I've lost everything—my mother, Mark, my friends, my life. So, I'm sorry if I want my own underwear or a favorite T-shirt to get through this. You can continue to hate me. I don't care. All I am asking is you back off for five minutes."

Gabby pressed her lips together. My heart thudded several beats as she considered my request. Then with a sharp nod she sat back, my appeal accepted. The car was filled with an awkward silence. I felt embarrassed by my outburst but was also proud I stood up for myself and won.

"All right guys, we're here." Eli pulled up in the driveway. "Ember and I will go into the house. Cooper, I want you around back. Gabb, you and Jared guard the front. This will be a quick in and out."

Climbing out of the car, I stared at the front of the house. It felt so familiar but so foreign at the same time. I was no longer the girl who used to live here. Hell, I was no longer human. Everything was different, though the same step still squeaked as we walked up. Nothing here had changed, but everything felt strange to me.

Eli pulled my keys from his pocket and unlocked the door, stepping aside to let me enter.

"How do you have my keys?"

"I've had them since the night in the forest. They were in the pocket of your jacket that was torn to shreds." He motioned for me to enter the house.

The familiarity of the place hit me, stabbing into my soul like a dagger. Home. Mark. Seeing one of his jackets hanging from the coat rack and his running shoes at the door, waiting for him to return. Would we ever be able to come back here? Blinking back the tears I turned to head down the hallway. If I let myself have those thoughts, I would end up lying down on the sofa and falling apart. Turning to head down the hallway, Eli's arm came up, blocking me from moving.

"What?" I looked down at his arm then up to his face. "What is it?"

"I don't know, but something doesn't smell right."

"Smell right?"

"I know your odor; I know this house's odor..."

"Are you saying we stink?"

"Everyone has a scent. It's not bad. Yours is a mixture of earth, cinnamon, and camp fire."

"Camp fire? I smell like a campsite?"

"No, of deep, rich, smoldering fire." He looked down on me. "Makes me want to have sex out in a forest next to a roaring campfire."

I gulped so noticeably his lip inched up in the corner. "Ironic, huh? Ember, who starts electrical explosions and affects fires, smells like and is named after fire." I always knew my name was different, but until recently I had never understood it was a key to who I really was.

Eli told me to stay put as he went ahead of me. He skulked down the dark hallway, his body hunkered close to the ground, prowling, reminding me of a jaguar. He disappeared into my room.

"Eli?" I whispered hoarsely.

"All clear," he called back.

I entered my room. Of course, everything was as I left it. The three different tops I had tried on before the party were still spewed across my bed and floor. My books and papers were in messy disarray on my desk next to my laptop. A framed picture of Ryan, Kennedy, and I being goofy sat on my desk. I reached for the picture and held it to my chest. How different things were now. I looked at our silly expressions. We had been so carefree, untroubled, and ignorant then to the Fae world where Kennedy and I were actually considered "normal" girls. As much as we had felt different, we really had no clue how truly different we were. She still didn't. Kennedy and Ryan were always on my mind, but lately more so, especially Kennedy. I felt sick to my stomach at the thought of anything happening to her.

"Grab what you need while I check the rest of the house," Eli said, breaking into my thoughts. He headed out of my bedroom.

Not hesitating, I grabbed my duffel bag and stuffed in clothes, shoes, and basic necessities. I forced myself not to think about the fact this might be the last time in my room. At my desk I grabbed a sketch pad and paused. A sensation scoured over my skin. My internal alarm rang. I wasn't alone. Subtlety, my eyes drifted, inspecting every cranny of my room.

"Eli?" I called out. Silence.

I trusted my internal warning. It had kept me alive while I was on the streets, running daily from Fae and humans. Dropping the pad, I spun around, my feet scrambling for the door. From under my bed, long, white, scaly fingers scurried out and wrapped tightly around my ankle, pulling me back. A choked scream popped in my throat as I fell to the ground. Tugging against the boney hand, which seized me, I stopped as a shape whizzed out of my closet, shut the bedroom door, and closed me in.

I peered up at the individual in front of me. I shouldn't have. I really shouldn't have.

My heart crashed against my ribs. The mere sight of the creature made me almost lose bladder control. It was tall and skinny with pasty, white skin and a bald, patchy head. Veins and scars were lumped around and under the skin. Sharp, pointy ears protruded from its head with red, bulging eyes and a bulb nose. Lining its mouth was what looked like hundreds of needles sculpting down into long thin piercing teeth. Vegetarian he was not.

*Holy crap on ash bark...*

"You look as juicy as I hoped." The monster licked his lips, his voice nasally and strange.

"She does," a voice spoke from under my bed. A similar creature crawled out, letting go of my ankle.

*Oh shit!*

Both reminded me of the Orcs from *Lord of the Rings*. Skinny, needle-mouthed Orcs, except both were dressed in my clothes from head to toe. Mine. It was disturbing and wrong. To see my favorite newsboy cap on the creature that stood blocking the door made me feel dirty. He also wore a scarf, yoga pants, and a sweater. The one from under the bed was in a pair of my sweats with the dress I wore to my last school dance wrapped around his neck. It made me feel sick.

The creature by the door swung my scarf farther over his shoulder. His sharp teeth curved up in a disconcerting smile. "Our odors are disguised by being wrapped in yours."

I stood up moving farther away from the two beings and kept low and ready to fight for my life. Anticipation hung in the air, each waiting for the other to act. Their muscles were coiled and ready to pounce just as my bedroom door burst open, slamming one against the wall. Eli sailed through, immediately putting himself in front of me.

"Well, well, well...look who we have here?" The one by the door straightened himself up and stepped farther into the room. "Elighan, you are the last person I expected to see here. It has been a long time. Thought you guys were dead."

"Had the same high hopes for you, too, Drauk," Eli said stiffly. "What brings you here?"

"Looks like the same thing as you," Drauk sneered as his eyes inspected me like a starving animal. It made me step back. Eli pulled me tight to his body.

Drauk began to laugh. "Look, the poor little lamb thinks she's safer with you. Oh, if she only knew."

"Well, we both know the truth. So why don't you do the right thing and bow out. You know you don't want to fight me." Eli's tone was cold and cruel.

"I will fight you in this case. Do you know what she is? The power I can get from her? I was here first. This one is mine, Elighan." Drauk stepped even closer as the other one pulled out a knife.

"You're making a mistake," Eli warned. "You really think you and stupid there can take me?"

"And you are stupid if you think we didn't come equipped. I smelled that other Fae had been here before. We were prepared. As we speak, my friends are introducing themselves to yours."

Eli stiffened but didn't move from his place. It didn't stop me from detecting his sudden fear for Jared before he locked down his emotions.

"My men and I will have her. With her capabilities, we will be able to fight the Queen. Don't tell me that's not something you want as well? It is a win-win. Revenge on both her kind and the Queen." He looked to be salivating at the idea. "I don't want to fight you, Elighan, but to gain her powers I will."

"Mine," Eli growled so deeply I could barely hear what he said. "You will not touch her."

"Holy shit, you're protecting her." Drauk stood in shock, absently rubbing the scarf around his neck. "Wow, your time here on Earth has made you a pussy. Have you actually forgotten what her kind is capable of? What they've done to you? I would never have thought you would go soft. At one time we weren't so different, you and I. But now? You are not what you used to be."

I suddenly felt Eli's nails grow, breaking through the fabric of my hoodie. "Run to the car and get the hell out of here." He shoved the car keys in my pocket before pushing me to the side. His face was already half changed as he lunged for Drauk.

I couldn't move, engrossed in watching Eli's body transform into a Dark Dweller. Eli had changed only partially in front of me before and in darkness. I hadn't been able to see him change when he fought the Phooka so I'd never seen the whole transformation. It was disturbing, fascinating, and somehow beautiful all at the same time.

Mesmerized, I watched his clothes tear. His body curved and twisted into another shape. A sleek, black creature emerged around the size of a large panther. His presence made everything feel dwarfed by comparison. Every muscle moved tightly under the midnight-colored coat. His jaw was longer than a wild cat's, with razor sharp teeth. His spine was lined with small, sharp, spiked horns. Anyone who got near or fell on them would be no more than a *shish-kebab*. There was also something about him that reminded me of a wolf. But neither panther nor wolf seemed to define him. His movements were graceful and stealthy. A deep, vibrating growl shook the room. Nails, curved like sickles, ripped at the floorboards as he moved closer to Drauk. His eyes flared red.

"Get her, Vek," Drauk screeched over his shoulder to the other, pointing at me. This finally broke my trance on Eli. In a breath, Vek bounded toward me, his hands grappling for me as I darted out of his reach. I turned and ran out the door and sprinted down the hallway for the front door. Grappling for the wall, I skidded around the corner, and my feet slipped on the smooth hardwood. I hit the floor with a thump. Vek was on me the moment I landed, straddling my back. My pulse throbbed loudly in my ears, my body reacting in alarm to the foreign, male body on me. Panic raged in my chest, paralyzing me. I recalled what had taken place the last time I had been in a predicament like this—what the men at Mike's Bar had tried to do to me. This was not quite the same, but my mind had trouble grasping the difference. My body went into defense mode.

Vek grabbed my hair yanking my head back making me whimper in pain. He jarred my head sharply to the side so I could see his face. His lip curled up and the pointed teeth reminded me of a shark's mouth.

"I'm going to enjoy this. I should let you know now I'm a messy eater." His mouth came down clamping on my exposed throat, his teeth sawing their way through my flesh. A bloodcurdling scream came from deep inside me, my body thrashing against him. Blood spurted down my neck, pooling onto the floor. A strange tugging sensation pulled at my insides—my essence being drawn out of my body as he bit down again.

My powers rattled the iron cage it was locked in. I could feel them pushing and throwing themselves against the invisible barrier. A little slipped through, but not enough to really help me.

*Was this the way I was going to die? A buffet meal for a dark Fae?*

Sounding like a wounded animal, I heard myself cry out. Tiny dots flicked across my vision. *Oh Jesus, I am going to die.* A rushed frenzy whirled inside me at that realization. Abruptly, a deep growl tore out of me. My vision narrowed. In a flick of a switch, I was no longer afraid.

I was pissed.

At my rumble, Vek tore his teeth from my throat in time to see my fist slamming into his face, crushing his nose back into his head. A high-pitch squeal echoed through the room as he fell off me. Clambering to my feet, I felt my blood drip down my neck and soak my clothes.

Vek screamed at me in some strange language, but I got the gist—their version of "bitch." All I needed was a cue stick and I'd be back in the bar with Pock. But, unlike Pock who had stayed down, Vek jumped up, lunging for me again. I wheeled back, escaping his long fingers. As he continued to dive for me, I twisted, put my back to him and clapped my arm around his neck. With a sharp yank down, he flipped over my head and onto his back. Instantly lurching, my feet slammed into his chest as I came down on top of him, pouncing like a cat. Without thought, I pulled the knife from the sheath on my leg, sliding it under his jugular. Energy buzzed through me. *Kill prey. My prey. My kill.* This repeated in my mind. I had the sudden urge to let him go, so I could track him down and play with him a bit before I killed him. That sounded fun...to hunt him down and let him squeal like the pig he was before I obliterated him. The desire was so deep in my soul I knew I would do it.

"Let's try this again, shall we?" My voice was playfully sinister. "When I say run, you run, and this time we'll see who gets the other first."

"Brycin?" Eli's voice rang out behind me.

I was so focused on my prey it was hard for me to take my eyes off it. A repeat of my name forced me to turn around and acknowledge Eli, who stood back on two legs in nothing more than a pair of shredded pants. When my eyes met his, his head jerked back and sucked in a hiss of air. He stood there with blood all over him, staring at me. I'd never seen him look so visibly startled before, and something about it made me feel unsure and frightened.

"Ember, move off him."

"Mine," my mouth uttered before I even realized I'd spoken.

"Now, Brycin. That's an order."

I wanted to protest, to declare my rights to the kill. *It had attacked me. I have the right.* But my objections never made it out, feeling the weight of his authority. Once more I looked down on Vek. The longing to destroy him was strong, but Eli's demand was stronger. Bitterly I stepped off of him, standing up, angry that Eli was taking my kill away from me. He walked up to Vek, tugging the knife from his sheath, and leaned down over Vek's body. Vek watched him nervously; the confidence he held earlier had vanished.

"I gave Drauk the same message. Forget you know anything about her. If I see or even sense a hint of you boys around, it will become my mission to hunt each and every one of you down. I will find a way to ensure your death is as painful and slow as possible."

Without fanfare Eli shoved the knife in Vek's gut, pushing it down so hard the knife stuck into the wood floor underneath him. Vek howled with pain before his body twitched and went limp. The wretchedness of this scene made something in me snap. The calm and nonchalant violence happening in front of me created a sick feeling in my stomach. How cold and calculated Eli's actions suddenly seemed, when moments ago I had wanted to do the same. I gasped for air, nausea flushing through me. My body started to shake violently.

*Holy crap, what is wrong with me? I had wanted to hunt down this creature and gut him like a pig.*

Eli turned back to me and pointed to Vek. "We need to move. The knife will only postpone him for a few hours, Drauk will be even less."

"Huh?" I didn't understand. His words seem to jumble in my head. What did he mean postpone?

Eli's gaze truly settled on me. "*Drochrath air!*" Eli rushed to me, his hand going to my neck. Placing his palm on my neck, he tried to stop the bleeding. My blood seeped through his fingers, staining his hand. My body was shaking so badly his hand rattled against the wounds, smearing my blood over my chest.

"Eli!" Gabby's guttural scream from outside froze us. "Get out here now!" Eli pulled away from me and darted towards the door.

It took me several more seconds to react and by the time I made it to the door, he was already outside kneeling on my driveway across from Gabby. A body lay in between them.

Jared.

I could hear Gabby prattling on. "I only left him for a minute." She bit at her fingernails. "He's going to be okay, right?"

My feet stumbled down the front steps, quickly moving to where Eli and Gabby crouched. Vomit burned at my throat as I looked over Eli's shoulder. Jared's torso was torn up, blood and bone oozing out of the strips of the shirt that were left.

"Oh, my God." My hand flew to my mouth.

"Get in the car now!" Eli ordered over his shoulder, gathering Jared into his arms. I stood there frozen, unable to move as my eyes roamed over Jared's form. My stomach heaved.

"Ember, move now," he yelled.

I forced my legs to move and ran to the car, throwing the back door open so Eli could place Jared on the seat. Feeling weak, I clung to the car door, the blood loss was taking its toll, my adrenaline receding.

Cooper raced around the corner. "They're gone, but they'll be back soon with reinforcements," he shouted. "How's J?"

"We need to get him to Owen." Eli placed Jared's limp form on the back seat. Then he turned to me. "You, too." Eli motioned for Gabby to give him her hoodie. For once she didn't hesitate or argue and threw it to Eli. He balled it up and pressed the cloth on my neck. "Hold it there. Tight."

"Come on, we need to get out of here," Cooper urged.

"Grab her bag from the house while I start the car." Eli nodded toward the house. Cooper dashed so quickly up the stairs my eyes could barely follow him. He returned just as rapidly with my duffel bag slung over his shoulder. "All right, let's go."

We piled in the car: Cooper in the far back, Gabby with Jared's head on her lap in the backseat, and Eli and I in the front. The SUV tore out of the driveway, swerving onto the main road at full speed.

"We knew somebody would be watching the house. Why did we even come?" Gabby demanded, brushing Jared's hair off his forehead.

"Because." Eli shot her a steady look through the rearview mirror. His Alpha presence filled the car.

I was curious as well, but his authority also shut me down. Leaning my head back onto the headrest, I tried a different angle, "Are they working for the Queen?"

"No." Eli shook his head. "They work for themselves."

"How did the Strighoul find out about her?" Cooper demanded from the back.

"I don't know."

"What the hell is a Strighoul?" I asked.

"Strighoul are bottom feeders, a cross between a type of ghoul and vampire. They are dark Fae who feed off other Fae's powers. They'll eat humans too, but they don't get much from them. They prefer Fae." Eli looked over at me. "When they consume you, they consume your forces and strengths."

"Vampire?"

"Not in the way you think. They are energy eaters. They are nothing like what pop culture has turned them into. These guys don't drink your blood; they eat you to possess your life force. And I mean they eat every part of you."

"Like cannibalism... okay, wow." So Vek tearing at my throat and Drauk's talk of "having me" were literal, as in a need for dental floss after. The Strighoul wanted to eat me to take on my powers. "Daes are extra tasty, huh?" I tried to joke.

"No. Extra powerful." Eli glanced quickly over at me. "There are only a few select species that cannot be controlled by the Queen and also have that much power. When the Strighoul consume you, they take on those same powers. The powers don't last, but even if it's for a short duration, it's worth it to them."

I cringed at the thought, but I was trying to keep my eyes from closing. It was getting harder to stay awake. Pain throbbed though my body. There was so much I wanted to know, so much I needed to understand, but my lids drooped farther. I gave in, letting sleep come.

*Once again I found myself standing by the waterfall. I didn't like Torin bringing me here. It felt intrusive to something I had shared with Eli, just like I wouldn't have liked Eli showing up at the forest where Torin and I usually met.*

*"Torin?" I couldn't hide my annoyance.*

*"Yes, mo chuisle?" His voice rippled over the air, and my skin tingled as he stepped from the shadows.*

*"Don't call me that." I pulled away still disgusted and upset with him.*

*"What should I call you then?" He moved in closer, his gaze landing on my neck. "You are hurt again."*

*"Is it all that surprising?" I replied.*

*"No, not really."*

*"So, what do you need? I'm kind of the middle of something right now." My words were clipped.*

"I was going to ask you that. It is not me who is intruding."

"What do you mean?" I paused and looked around "Wait—are you saying I'm doing this?"

He nodded. "How?" I was stunned. I knew how to dreamscape?

"The ability is part of your nature; it's who you are. You talk like you have accepted what you are, but your mind hasn't. Stop fighting and you will find more things will naturally come to you."

This was probably true. But would anyone be able to accept they weren't human so easily? My entire life was lived as a human among humans. True I had never felt like I fit in, but I never imagined I wasn't human.

"So, I'm the one doing this?" I repeated.

"Yes, you are bringing me in. You brought me in last time as well. This is your dreamscape, Ember, not mine." He motioned around. I brought him to the waterfall? Chagrin flooded my face. Now I understood why the place was different. This was the spot I had subconsciously picked for a dreamscape? I did not like the implications.

"I was actually in the middle of training," he continued, looking at me acutely. "You are more powerful than I thought. Last night proved that."

"What do you mean?"

"The fact you brought Elighan into the dreamscape, also." A frown lined his forehead. "It doesn't make sense. You should not be able to do that. Your ties to him are too strong."

"Why shouldn't I be able to?"

"You and I are Fay. We have this gift so it is easier to bring each other in, but Elighan is not Fay. He is not even a Demon. You should not have any connection with him. It has never been possible for different species to connect like that. Think of it this way. You and I are on the same frequency. In the human realm you would say we're on the same channel. Elighan's kind are not only on a different channel, but a completely different system. I don't understand how you were able to pull him into your dreamscape."

I decided not to tell him about the blood, that the bonds between Eli and me were more than feelings. Blood had bonded us in a way I was not terribly comfortable with. I rubbed at my face, feeling the strain of everything. Why was I capable of things others found odd? Things I hadn't even tried to do.

"You are bleeding badly." Torin stepped up even closer to me, his hands cupping my neck. I knew I wasn't bleeding here in the dream, but he was able to see through to reality. "Let me help you. I can heal you faster."

I jerked back out of his grasp. "I'm fine."

"No, you are not." He shook his head. "Please, Ember, trust me. I can help you."

Speculation did not leave my face as he reached for me again. Torin's hands moved up my chin and tilted my head back. His lips covered mine, inhaling me as he brought me into a deep, toe-curling kiss. My insides suddenly felt full of light and warmth. A tingling zipped up my spine and through my neck.

"Lucky me. I did land on the porn channel this time. But I think I've seen this episode before." As I broke *away from Torin, I saw Eli leaning against a tree a few yards away.*

*Torin huffed with irritation at the interruption. His hands dropped from my face to my hips, possessively, keeping close to me. It was an unstated claim—his territory.*

"To what do we owe the honor, Elighan?"

*Eli stared directly at Torin's hands. I backed away from Torin, keeping both guys in my eye-line.*

"You tell me? I was driving us back to the ranch when I felt this tremendous pull." *He shot an accusing glance my way.* "It was all I could do to stay awake. Gabby was trying to keep me from falling asleep, but it was eventually too much."

"What? Did you fall asleep driving?" *I looked around. What would happen if he crashed? Would I feel it? Would we wake up?*

"No, Cooper's driving now. I got in the back. They think something's wrong with me, that the Strighoul somehow drained my energy. They don't know it's you wanting to have a threesome in dreamland."

*My eyes narrowed.* "I didn't know I was doing it. I don't know how to manage them. I don't want either one of you here."

"Really?" *Eli shot a glance at Torin and me.* "Could've fooled me." *Eli crossed his arms, a smile playing on his lips.* "I do find it amusing while you are kissing him you are thinking about me."

"*I wasn't thinking about you.*"

"See, you're wrong there, Brycin. It's the only way I can come into these dreamscapes. Your subconscious was thinking about me, wanted me. Not that I can blame it..." He looked at Torin and frowned.

Anger and embarrassment seized me. "You have no idea what me or my subconscious want. I don't know how you got in here, but I can assure you, you were nowhere in my thoughts while I was kissing him."

Eli only scoffed, which made me more furious. My desire to wipe the smug smile off his face took hold of me. I moved quickly over to him, like a bull seeing red. Eli propelled himself off the tree preparing for whatever wrath I was going to bring his way.

"You son of a—"

"Hey now." Torin wrapped me in his arms and dragged me away from Eli. "Calm down mo chroi." He stroked my arm, trying to sooth me.

"I'll calm down when he leaves."

"Then make me, Brycin. This is your dream," Eli said with an edge in his voice as he challenged me. "I'm not here because I want to be."

Ouch. Okay, I felt the zing hit my heart. Setting my jaw in a more defiant line, I glared at Eli.

"Mo shiorghra, I must go. I can feel the Queen near." Torin twisted me around to face him and slowly pressed his lips to my temple. "Until next time."

I heard a low, growling noise from Eli, but I kept my eyes from looking over at him. Okay, time to wake up, Ember. "Wake up," I demanded in my head, squeezing my eyes shut. I repeated it over and over. "Wake up, wake up, wake up..."

# EIGHT

"Wake up, Ember." Someone shook me. My eyes opened to Owen hovering over the bed at the Dark Dweller compound.

Something stirred in the bed next to mine. I spotted Eli lying there, blinking as he came out of the deep sleep. It took him only a few seconds before he shot up. "Where's Jared?"

"He's right here, Eli," Cole's soothing voice filtered across the room. Sitting up I saw Jared in a hospital bed across from mine. Cole rested in the chair next to him. Eli got up and darted over. "He'll be fine. He just needs to rest." Cole patted Jared's arm.

Relief radiated from Owen as he looked over his shoulder at his son. These ruthless killers had such a deep love and devotion for each other, something not many, if any, others were allowed to see. Somehow I had become privy to their inner workings.

"Easy there." Owen turned back around, helping me get into a more upright position. "You have lost a lot of blood today from the terrible gash on your neck. It will take a few days to fully heal."

"Believe me, she's all healed now," Eli said, his voice like acid. He pulled up a chair to the other side of Jared's bed.

I reached to my neck, felt the bandage that covered my wound and tore one corner off.

"What are you doing?" Owen tried to stop my hands, but I got it off before he could stop me. "What the..." Owen's mouth fell open.

My fingers grazed the smooth skin on my neck. "The gash is healed?" My eyes grew wide. "How did I heal already?"

Eli huffed from the other side of the room. Owen shook his head, eyes wide with the same astonishment I felt.

"Eli?" Cole rose from his chair and sent him another nonverbal message.

Eli had barely risen from his chair when I clambered out of bed. "Oh no," I shook my head, rising to my feet. "You are not leaving here. I know this is about me. I will be a part of this discussion whether you like it or not. I have the right to know what is going on."

Cole paused at the door then slowly turned around and nodded. "You're right, Ember. You should hear this too."

"Thank you."

Eli huffed again, loudly.

"What is your problem?" I challenged.

"My problem?" He spun around his eyes narrowed into green slits. "My problem is you. You almost got Jared killed."

"What? Me? How did I almost kill Jared?"

"Eli, this wasn't Ember's fault," Cole said.

"No, I'm not talking about what occurred at the house. I'm talking about what occurred in the car."

All heads turned to me.

Gabby scrambled into the cabin. "Wait. I have to be here for this." Clearly she had been listening on the other side of the door. Cooper followed right behind. She moved to an unoccupied seat beside Jared, settling in. "Okay. Proceed."

I gaped at her then back at the guys. Everyone's eyes bored into me. "I-I-I don't know what you're talking about."

"What are you talking about, Eli?" Cole looked back at him, clearly getting impatient with my lack of explanation.

"Yeah man, what did happen in the car? That was strange," Cooper directed this at Eli also. Soon all eyes turned to him.

"Ember pulled me into a dreamscape."

"What?" They all shouted at the same time.

"That's not possible." Cole shook his head, his hair skimming his shoulders "You must have imagined it."

"No. I didn't imagine it. I know it shouldn't be possible," Eli said, "but she has pulled me into two now."

Stunned silence followed. Owen broke the confounded lull. "This could be an outcome."

"Is that possible?" Cole turned to his brother.

"This is unprecedented. It is hard to know, but, in my personal opinion, I think it is possible."

"This is because of Eli's blood, isn't it?" I blurted out, annoyed how they talked around me. "I can bring him in because I have his blood?"

Owen pressed his lips together and nodded. "That is the only explanation for it. Otherwise you should not be able to do that with him." Owen's voice was calm, though I had yet to see him riled up about anything. He was always so steady and soothing to be around. It was difficult to think of him as a killer, but that might make him better.

"Torin said something similar," I responded, recalling the conversation.

"Torin? As in the Queen's personal knight?" Cole exclaimed looking at me and then to Eli for confirmation.

"Yeah, I guess he's been visiting Ember's dreams for several months now," Eli replied sharply.

"What?" Cole bellowed. "And you are just telling me now?"

"Look, I didn't know until last night. I was planning to tell you, but things have kind of been crazy around here."

"Eli, this isn't something you forget to tell us," Cole screamed. "This is Torin. He is the Queen's right-hand man, and he has had access to Ember all these months." Cole's eyes turned a fiery red. I had spent enough time with the Dark Dwellers to know their basic moods. I had seen Cole mad before, but this was beyond that. He had always struggled to stay in control and not change.

"I've known for barely a day." Eli stepped up into Cole's face. "And no, you don't have to remind me. I am fully aware of the threat he represents."

"We'd lose our only chance," Cole spoke softly to Eli, probably thinking I couldn't hear him. Both remained mute for a moment, staring at each other, before Cole swung around and charged straight for me. I stumbled back a few steps in alarm, but forced myself to stop, holding my ground. "You have to block him, Ember." He grabbed my shoulder roughly. "You cannot let him in. He is dangerous."

"He says the same about you."

"This is not a joke."

"I never said it was," I retaliated. "And it's not like I know how to regulate them."

"Learn," Cole responded, his grip like steel. "You don't know what he is capable of."

"Are you guys reading from the same handout?" I pulled out of Cole's grasp. "He won't hurt me or turn me over to her."

"I don't know if I want to smack you because you're naïve or plain stupid," Eli said, irritation soaking his words.

"You touch me and you lose your most beloved girlfriend there." I nodded toward his hand.

Eli scoffed. "Then I'll train yours."

"I'd like to see you try."

"Enough! Both of you!" Cole bellowed. "We have bigger issues to worry about right now. We not only have the Queen coming for you, but we have to deal with the Strighoul. You may think Torin will not turn you over to her, but I do not share that same certainty."

"Well, I'm not particularly confident you have my best interest at heart either. Oh right, you don't." I yelled back. "What are you waiting for anyway? Turn me over to the damn Unseelie King already."

"Don't tempt me," Eli growled.

"Go ahead. I'm sick of your mind games. I'm sick of being your prisoner. I just want to get away from here and go get my dad." My heart felt tied to my muscles. Barely able to stand under the grief it held. Being back in the house today brought Mark back so vividly into my mind. I had been trying not to think of him because it hurt so much. But smelling the house today and seeing his running shoes in the corner ice-picked my heart.

"Believe it or not, we are trying to keep you safe." Cole gritted his teeth. "There is no where you can run that will be safe for you anymore. I think you know that."

I despised the truth in his words. But today had shown me how easily I could be found. They were watching my house, probably watching my friends. My safety had been instantly conceded the moment I ran away from the Queen, but my friends would not be compromised. Not if I could help it.

"What else is out there hunting me?"

"There are a lot of different beings that could be," Eli snapped.

"Like what?"

"Want me to go through the Fae directory?" Eli's voice rose.

"Well, excuse me if I want to know more. I wasn't given the luxury of knowing this stuff my whole life. I've been aware of this world for five weeks. So why don't you give me a little break here?"

Cole took a step obstructing Eli. "Strighoul, without other Fae's abilities, are more bark than bite and not at all bright. Even so, they are dangerous. They work in herds. By consuming forces of another Fae, they can become lethal, especially the more powerful the Fae. The powers only last in their system for a short time before vanishing. So they go find another victim. The cycle continues.

"If they fed on you, it would be catastrophic. Even after your kind was banned, we saw a killing spree of Daes to get their power. You can imagine the destruction and terror this caused. Daes can't be controlled or glamoured, so when Strighoul ate one of your kind, it took on those traits. The Queen almost lost command of the kingdom. It was a dark time and the Daes were blamed for it."

"Not that Daes don't deserve some of the blame." Eli tilted his head, glaring at me as if it was my fault.

"Eli," Cole warned again.

"What is your problem with Daes? Why do you hate us so much? Because you do, right? This isn't something I'm imagining."

Eli's face grew tight. "Yes, I hate Daes."

"Why?"

"This is a waste of time. You can learn this stuff later. Right now we need to concentrate on how to handle the situation." The air around us became tense and thick. Our gazes locked firmly on each other, and I could feel him purposely seal his emotions and thoughts away from me. I couldn't read his eyes except for the anger glaring from them. He turned away.

"I want to know all this stuff so I can understand what is going on," I exclaimed. "If you don't like it leave. No one is making you stay in here."

"I'll break it down for you then. A Demon, a tyrannical Queen, and cannibal Strighoul—"

"What?" I cut him off. "Walk into a bar?"

Eli's face turned red as blood boiled under his skin. His look was full of every swear word there was. Only my pride kept me from slinking under the bed to hide.

"Relax, Eli." Cole touched his shoulder.

"No. She doesn't get it," Eli yelled. "This is not pretend, Ember. These guys aren't going to stop hunting you. This world is no longer the same. The Pacific Northwest is in shambles and overrun with Dark and Light Fae. Most are here looking for you. Don't think someone like Drauk is going to stop searching. They will figure out who your friends are and go after them. The Strighoul will tear them apart, while the leaders will be dining on you."

The intensity with which he was yelling at me made tears burn in my eyes. My automatic response was to yell back.

"You don't think I understand it?" I screamed. "That I don't realize I've lost everything? That I have destroyed and killed people? My powers have burned down homes, killed men, women, and children. I have turned this area of the country into a version of the Wild West with automatic guns. People are killing each other over cans of food."

I flew at him, my hands shoving into his chest. "Everything I love has been ripped from me. My father is being tortured somewhere in the Otherworld! So don't tell me I don't get it. I get it. I feel the burden of what I've done every single second of every single day." My curled fingers banged into Eli's chest. He stepped up closer to me, his arms still pinned to his sides. His hands balled into fists by his legs. "I destroyed lives!" I continued to pound into him.

Cooper came up to me and wrapped his arms around me, pulling me back. I continued to barrel forward into Eli, my arms and hands thrashing against him. "Calm down," Cooper said. I struggled against his hold, until his murmuring voice penetrated my ear, making me crumple. Cooper gripped me tighter and held me up. Leaning into him, wet splotches soaked his t-shirt. I hadn't even known I was crying. "Shhhh... it's okay," he mumbled.

I let the sobs heave out of me, my body gave out, and I collapsed to the floor. Cooper picked me up like a baby. A slight zing ran up my tattoo as he held me, but it wasn't something my thoughts stayed on. My brain was starting to shut down, closing itself to the pain and agony. Cooper set me back on the bed, tucking the covers in around me.

"Eli, I think you should go." Cole's voice was steady, holding authority.

"No."

"Eli," Cole's voice contained a warning.

"No!" Eli roared.

"Leave now!" It was the first time I had heard Cole's voice raise in anger against Eli. It sent shockwaves through the tiny cabin, making even me quiver under its force, wanting to bow under Cole's order

Eli let out a strangled noise, turned stiffly toward the door and strode out, slamming the door so hard it shook the tiny cabin.

Cole sighed deeply and turned around, then walked over to the bed. "The last time he caused me this much of a headache was during what humans call the pubescent years. What are you doing to my Second, Ember?" I knew the question was rhetorical so I continued to watch him silently as he pulled a chair up to my bed. "I think you need to rest, but I promise you tomorrow I will explain anything you want to know."

"Anything?" I asked, my eyebrows rising up.

"Anything except about us."

*Damn...* he knew what I was angling at.

"You are eventually going to tell me some things, right?"

Cole only shook his head as he stood up. "You really are relentless."

"It's part of my charm."

Cole scoffed, but his smile couldn't be hidden. He only shook his head again and left the cabin. Owen checked on Jared one last time before motioning for Cooper and Gabby to follow.

"Gabbs, are you coming?" Cooper turned back looking at his sister.

"Give me a minute," she replied. She sat in the chair like she had been watching TV this entire time. In a way she had been when watching us—with our crying, screaming, and fighting. It was like a bad reality show.

Cooper looked a little worried, glancing between Gabby and me. He finally gave her a nod and left. Gabby moved to the chair next to me. I didn't have enough strength to do much, but I tensed as she came closer to me. Pulling out a pack of cigarettes from her coat, she tilted the pack, offering me one. I shook my head profusely in refusal.

"I know it's a disgusting habit...blah, blah." She lit up and took a drag. She propped her feet on the bed. "Smoking is one of the human traits I've picked up while living here, and since I won't ever die from human diseases like lung cancer, I say why the fuck not."

"You may not die, but it still causes you to stink, yellows your teeth, and gives you awful breath," I countered.

Gabby's head fell back and she laughed. "Yeah, you're probably right. But the guys I date don't seem to care. They smoke like chimneys, too."

Smiling thinly at her I wondered why she was here. *She doesn't even like me. What does she want?*

The silence between us grew thicker before she spoke. "So... that was quite a show."

"I'm sure you can catch a repeat performance tomorrow evening—if I don't kill him first."

Gabby blew out a glob of smoke with a snicker. "What?"

"Oh, it's just the more a girl says she wants to kill him the more I know she actually wants to screw him." Gabby's blunt words made me inhale.

"What? No, I actually want to kill him. No screwing. Purely killing."

"Right." She scoffed as she settled deeper into the chair. "I've known Eli for a very, very long time. He's like a brother to me and whatever realm it is, whatever species, it is always the same. He has an unbelievable, raw, sexual magnetism. He can drive most women crazy. And I mean it in every sense of the word." She smiled. "I've also known him long enough to have never seen him lose his cool like this about a girl. He's never irrational. I can count on one hand the times he's completely lost it and those were understandable. In all the years, I've never seen him like this."

She took another drag from her cigarette. "Is he infuriating? Yes. Domineering? Absolutely. Also pigheaded, dangerous, scary as hell, and at times cruel. But, to a select few, he is also fiercely loyal, honest, and will protect you with his life."

"To you guys, maybe."

"To whom he considers family," she said. "We may not be a lot of good things, but we are intensely devoted to each other. We have to be for our survival. But Eli's always taken this more seriously than most. He was considered different by our clan, not possessing the usual dominant traits of our kind. Cole's the same way. This made them the perfect First and Second even though the Second technically should have gone to Lorcan, who's older. Eli won the fight. A natural leader. I don't think Lorcan's ever forgiven or let it go. Lorcan is a Dark Dweller through and through. But with Cole and Eli in charge, most of us have seen there's more to us—more than being killers."

Gabby looked off in the distance, her mind a million miles from there, probably in a different realm. I didn't move, not wanting to even breathe. This was the most information I had been given about them, about Eli, and I didn't want her to stop.

She turned back to me with a small smile. "Did you know Cole raised Eli, Lorcan, Cooper, and me? He really wasn't much older than us, but he took us on like his own. He had to take care of four teenagers in a new realm. Talk about one crazy bastard." She giggled. The deep love and respect she felt for Cole was obvious.

She looked down, clearing her throat. "You think we don't have compassion for your situation and maybe it appears that way, but we are all orphans here, too. We know how it feels to lose someone you love because of what you are." Her gaze locked with mine. "We have lost everything, also... our families, our homes. What would you do to get Mark back?"

I knew the answer to that—anything.

"We might not be able to get our families back, but there is hope we could get our home back."

"Why are you telling me this?"

"Because you are different from the others." She paused. "We have a pack mentality, similar to wolves. And like it or not, I can sense Eli claiming you. He's making you part of the clan."

"W-What?" I sat up straighter.

She looked at me and shook her head. "Never mind. I'm babbling. I'm gonna go." She abruptly stood up and headed for the door. "Forget everything I said, okay?"

She didn't wait for my response, just walked out of the room, shutting the door behind her.

# NINE

Sleep did not come. Instead there were tormenting images of the Strighoul tearing into my flesh, watching them rip into my friends, slurping down their intestines like spaghetti. My mind and body strained under all the stress. My growling stomach finally got me up in search of food, though I didn't think I could eat spaghetti anytime soon.

Tiptoeing into the main house, I headed straight for the kitchen. As I reached for the jar of Eli's beloved peanut butter, the one I was determined to finish for the extreme pleasure of pissing him off, murmurs floated to me from the office, freezing me in my tracks.

"Were you able to find anything?" Cole's calm voice was instantly recognizable.

"No. I didn't have much time to really look," Eli's deep voice rumbled. My inquisitive nature took over, and I inched closer to the office door.

"I am certain she found it. It would only make sense she would have disclosed its location to Lily or hid something with Ember." Frustration salted Cole's tone. "I was sure there would be something at the house."

Lily? They were talking about my mom. So their willingness to let me get my stuff had nothing to do with me. They wanted something...

"Well, if there was, she obscured it well. I couldn't feel any magic spells or hexes. Could it be back in their old house?"

"No. She would have made sure, if something happened to her, it would go with Ember."

*What would go with me? What were they talking about?* My mom didn't leave me anything except memories, some photo albums, and a fake birth certificate. Was there something I missed? Could she have hidden something important among my baby books? What could she have left me they'd want?

"I can look again. We can't give up."

"No, we'll keep searching," Cole exhaled. There was a moment before he spoke again. "I still want to discuss the dreamscaping with you."

"Cole, I've told you I just learned about it, too. Believe me I'm not happy about it. I want it to stop more than you do."

My hurt feelings tightened uncomfortably in my stomach, embarrassment sloshing around in my chest.

"We have to get her to stop," Cole said. "But, you're right, we'll talk about it tomorrow. Get some sleep. I'll take first run right now and double check that everything is solid and no spells have been tampered with. I've got a feeling our days are only going to get longer from now on." The shifting of chairs signaled me to move behind the kitchen island.

"I think you're right," Eli agreed. "On the morning run, I'm gonna sweep a little farther out. See if I smell or sense anything."

"Good idea," Cole replied. "But, if you wake me up at four a.m. on your way out, I will kill you." Eli chuckled in response and they said their goodnights.

I tucked myself tighter into a ball, blocking all my thoughts and feelings from Eli. It would be pointless to hide if he could sense me. Fortunately, other things were ruling his mind so he walked through the kitchen and down the hall without even a pause. Breathing a sigh of relief, I made my escape as well and was glad to reach the safety of my room in the infirmary.

I didn't know exactly what they were talking about, but it was clear they were keeping things from me. More lies. More untold truths. This development clashed with the information Gabby had recently confided to me. Earlier, I had a slight shift in my anger, believing I could start to trust Eli...or at least I was beginning to understand him and some of his actions better. Was I wrong?

Between my thoughts and Jared tossing, turning, and mumbling in his sleep, I skimmed the surface of sleep. They had decided to keep him in the infirmary bed instead of moving him to his room, and my roommate was not a quiet sleeper.

The moment the sun came up, I finally fell into slumber. Naturally, that was the moment the door flew open and Eli sauntered into the room.

"Meet me in the workout room in ten minutes," he snapped and walked back out.

*O-kay... someone's cranky today.*

I didn't hurry, taking my time as I changed into my sweatpants, tank, and shoes, relishing the happiness of putting on my own clothes. I hadn't had this luxury in over a month.

Twenty minutes passed when I finally headed to the workout room, feeling only a little guilty when I saw Cole and Owen waiting for me as well. It was strange they were there, but I decided to ignore them and focus on kicking Eli's ass.

"All right, let's pick up from the same place as yesterday morning." Eli stepped onto the mat, wearing grey sweatpants that hid nothing, and a white shirt which fit him far too well.

*So, should I lie down on my back?*

My eyes taunted him. I was in a mood to provoke him after what I heard last night. It was too early in the morning to play nice. Especially with no coffee.

Eli tried to keep up the barrier between us, but I saw his eyes spark red. He must have had to work hard at not showing me these things before. Now that I knew he wasn't human, he was letting go of the pretense.

*Don't worry I'll have you down on your back soon enough,* he goaded.

*It's good to have a dream.*

Eli smirked and crouched down, preparing to fight.

Quickly, I tried to go through what he had taught me the day before. He gave me no leeway. We slowly circled each other, both of us deciphering the other's movements. I stepped in close enough to take a shot at his throat. He leaned back, easily avoiding it.

"Sloppy. Pay attention." He criticized, his voice scrapping over me like gravel.

Irritation scrunched my face as I fixed my thoughts more on the fight. He hunkered down; his fist darted up, striking the side of me. Falling back on my rear at the impact, I gasped for air. He continued to come after me. Using my position, I rolled into a backward somersault, instantly jumping to a defensive crouch.

He was not playing around. His movements were intense and threatening, and my body reacted to the threat. Eyes narrowing in on him, I switched gears. He flew at me. Twisting, I vaulted to the side, out of his way. His arm jutted out, slamming against me. The force threw me off the mat.

Hastily whipping around and making sure to keep him in my sights, I leaped over him. His fist barreled towards me, hitting my hip bone. It stung like crazy but didn't stop me. We started circling again; our eyes locked on each other. His pupils became narrowed slits of fire; the first clue his Dark Dweller was coming out. I answered his change with one of my own. All thoughts receded into the far depths of my mind and instinct kicked in.

I pounced on Eli, taking us both to the ground. As we fell, he grasped my arms. Using the momentum, he flipped me over his head and onto my back as we hit the ground. It took me only an intake of breath before I shot to my feet.

Not seeing him get up or move, Eli was suddenly in front of me. I dropped to the ground, barely missing the swipe from his protruding claws. Socking him in the sternum, my hand screamed with pain, while he didn't even grunt. My punch made no effect on him. He shoved my shoulders, taking me off balance, and I tumbled backwards onto the mat.

"Told you I'd have you on your back eventually." He stood over me.

I wanted to wipe the cocky smile off his face. My legs flew up, and I rammed my feet forcefully into his shins, knocking him onto his butt.

"Asshole." Coughing, my lungs ached as they tried to pull in air. The sharp sound of clapping pulled my attention over my shoulder. Cole walked up to us. I had actually forgotten about him.

"Very impressive, Ember, and with no training. Eli told us about how you fought Vek yesterday."

I shrugged like it was no big deal. It was, though. Yesterday something had happened to me. My temper had gotten the better of me at times. I had been in a few scuffles in my life, but nothing like the day before. Never having trained, I shouldn't have been able to take Vek on like that. Usually, I could barely walk into a room without running into a wall or tripping.

I shouldn't be good. Not like that. Especially with my powers restricted.

"See?" Eli popped up, giving me a solid glare before turning to Cole.

"You were right." Owen shook his head, bewildered. "This is astonishing, completely unprecedented. I need to take another sample of her blood and compare it. See if it has changed."

"You were right about what?" I gazed between at Eli and Owen. No one responded to me. "What's going on?" The men continued to talk and stare at me like a specimen, as though they forgot I could hear and respond to them. I scrambled up off the floor. "Wait a minute. You guys need to stop doing this. I am a part of this so include me in whatever you're talking about. Especially when it's about me. Now, tell me, what is going on?"

Owen blinked at me and finally seemed to snap out of his wondering. "Ember, I need you to keep me updated on any changes you feel or notice, even if it's the smallest, most benign thing."

Suddenly I understood the strange experience I had with Vek. The speed, agility, strength. What I had felt and how I responded to Vek. The instinctual desire to hunt him down and kill him. I had felt possessive of him; he had been my kill. The feeling was pure animalistic.

My Dae powers stemmed from fire and earth. My body was made from their magic, like a current of energy going through my body. This felt more instinctual like a deep-seated, inborn reaction. There was only one thing that could be causing me to feel like this—Eli's blood. It was changing me, and Eli had observed the difference and set this up. This was a test to show Cole and Owen what he had seen the day before. He had threatened me enough today for this new characteristic to come out and show itself to the others.

"You mean if I want to hunt and kill? Like how I took on a Strighoul without any kind of training and would have killed him if Eli hadn't stopped me? Things like that?" Anger flared. My body was no longer my own; I was a science experiment.

"Yes. Things like that," Owen responded. "I understand your frustration and anxiety. But to help you, I need to know every little change you feel."

"How do I know what is different if I don't know what I was before? Nothing about me is the same." I had little understanding of what I was becoming.

Owen pressed his lips together. "This must be unsettling for you." With a tilt of my head, I gave him an exasperated expression. "Will you permit me to extract more blood from you?" Owen pulled out a syringe from his pocket. He had come prepared. My stubbornness wanted me to say no, but I knew I needed to know as much about what was happening to me as well.

I nodded begrudgingly. Shifting my gaze to look outside, I felt the prick of the needle enter my vein. Owen was efficient and quick and filled the vial with my blood. He left as soon as he had it, probably excited to test and examine the changes.

"Eli, come to the office when you have wrapped up here. We have some security issues to discuss." Cole looked over his shoulder as he left the room. Eli nodded.

When the door shut behind Cole, I whipped around, glaring at Eli. Fury expanded my chest in and out swiftly. Once again I felt like an object to him. They did a good job pretending to treat me like a person when all they wanted me was to get back to the Otherworld.

*Like Gabby.* The night before now seemed like a ploy, a way to play with my head. Perhaps even the way she had left, making it seem like she slipped up and told me something she shouldn't, was part of the plan. She had preyed on me, used my vulnerability about my friends, for Mark, and mostly my weakness for Eli, against me. She manipulated me into thinking our stories made us some kind of kindred spirits. Pulling on my heartstrings had really been an attempt to get back into the Otherworld.

I cursed under my breath at my own gullible stupidity. I should have known something was up. Why would she open up and talk to me unless there was something in it for her?

I looked over at Eli, but his stony face held no emotion as he looked back at me. I was an idiot. He wasn't any different from Lorcan. Being a Dark Dweller was his nature. Cold, calculating, and cruel. And I wasn't different to him; I was a means to an end.

"This was a test? Training me so you can study me more? Learn how to use my powers to benefit your needs, like I'm some lab rat?" My eyes narrowed. "Guess I should have known. You don't do anything that isn't for your own selfish reasons."

"Selfish?"

"You are only nice to me or help me when you get something out of it. You don't care if you lie, cheat, or use me to get it," I shot at him. "Why don't you be honest about it? Why do you flirt and act like there is something between us? You can drop the act now. All of you can."

"Act?"

"Yeah, the whole, interested, seducing act. I can see through your bullshit from a mile away now."

*Really? You think so?* He stepped up to me making my breath immediately tighten in my throat.

*Yes,* I countered, stepping up to him, the tips of our toes meeting.

*You think I'm pretending to be attracted to you?* His eyes moved slowly over my body.

Not liking the intimacy of the connection of our eyes, I spoke out loud. "Probably. You get some sick pleasure out of it. The power. Control. But I'm not falling for it anymore."

"You think I can't seduce you?" His eyebrow cocked up, his tone magnetic. This was not a game I should be playing. He could seduce me by breathing and the breathing part was probably overkill. He always could, but lately it seemed even more so. His blood boiled in my veins, calling me to him. I sensed his eyes on me when I couldn't see him, felt him in the air around me when he was nowhere near. I got a buzz when he was near me, and I hated it. I hated I was so weak when I knew it was all a game to him.

"You actually thought you seduced me the first time?" What was wrong with me? Why did I always have to challenge him? My pride spoke before my common sense kicked in, even when my self-respect knew it was a losing battle.

A smile twitched on his lips as he backed me up against the wall. "Is that a challenge?"

"No." I breathed in shakily. "Merely an oversight on your part." I had to concentrate extremely hard on every word, making sure there was no tell-tale sign he was getting to me.

"Funny, that wasn't the way I remember it," he whispered in my ear, his breath hot on my neck. He then lowered his head, his lips only a hair from mine. Everything in my body screamed for him to take me up against the wall. I didn't move. "I know you were listening last night. There's nowhere you can go I don't feel you." The end of his hair tickled my cheek as he leaned in, his lips grazing the curve of my neck. He didn't kiss me or do anything more, but by just doing that, I already felt my legs turning into butter. His mouth and stubble lightly skimmed up my throat, warm breath tickling the sensitive spot behind my ear. Locking my legs, I forced them not to give out. Both of us were breathing more erratically, desire and passion filling the space between us like fire.

"This is you not being seduced?" He growled huskily against my ear.

Turning my head to look at him, I grabbed his biceps, flipping us around, throwing him back against the wall. Sucking in, his eyes flared bright red.

I leaned in, my mouth trailing up his throat. My hands moved up his body, my nails raking up his chest, past his neck and through his hair, causing a small growl to vibrate in his chest. This was no act; I knew he wanted me.

"Seems you were right," I dragged my lips lightly over his, my teeth nipping at his bottom lip, my voice breathless and needy.

"Really?" His lips curved into a smile.

My knee came up hard hitting its target. Eli doubled over in pain, grunting loudly, sliding down the wall to the ground.

"I *have* been dreaming about doing that since I met you." I turned and sauntered towards the door.

There would be hell to pay and a cold shower to take, but I didn't care. It was *so* worth it.

## TEN

Before I had a chance to even think about what I was doing, I marched into the house and down the hallway, throwing Gabby's bedroom door open. The décor fit her personality; it was a nod to the 1970s English-punk era. Her bedspread was black with red, fuzzy pillows. On one wall hung a giant, framed, black and white picture of the Queen of England. Written across her eyes it said "God Save The Queen." Over her mouth spelled out "Sex Pistols." I didn't know Gabby all that well, but she seemed like the type who would hang a poster like that one because of the pure twisted humor she found in that statement.

She looked up from her bed where she was reading.

"You are a manipulative bitch, you know that?"

Her eyebrows rose, but she didn't respond otherwise.

"Were you trying a new strategy with me? Get me to sympathize with you so I'd voluntarily help instead of being forced to?" I took a few more steps into the room.

"It would make things a lot easier." She rolled off her stomach, sitting up.

A scream threatened to escape. I was so sick of being used, and her nonchalant confirmation of this made me even angrier. "You admit you're a lying, deceitful bitch and everything you told me was to get me on 'your side'?"

"Not one word was a lie." She closed her book, setting it down next to her.

"It was *all* a lie."

"It depends on your point of view." Gabby stood up and walked over to me. "Eli is dragging his feet on this. So, yes, I'll admit I was hoping it would convince you to help us. If I had to manipulate, so be it. But I did not lie to you."

"Then what did you mean when you said you could feel Eli 'claiming' me?"

Gabby's eyes darted nervously over my shoulder, away from me. Clearly she did not want to bring it up. Maybe she really didn't mean to tell me everything.

"Yeah, Gabb, *what* did you mean?" A deep, husky voice spoke behind me. Eli's tall form filled the entire frame. His ire slamming into my spine, covering me like a blanket.

She swallowed nervously then laughed, "It was a way to get her to help us."

"You are such a bitch." My eyes narrowed into thin slits. Embarrassment rocked my emotions. I had wanted her words to be true.

Scanning the two of them, I let out a crazed laugh. "You're all so obsessed with the idea of getting back to the Otherworld you don't even care how you get there.

Manipulate, deceive, screw, kill...whatever it takes, right? But you know what's funny? I don't think you guys know *why* you want to go back anymore. I've never heard one of you say what you miss about home or what would be there for you if you got back. It's been over eighteen years! Do you even know anymore?" I pushed Eli into the wall, broke past him, and darted out of the room.

Furious with myself and everything associated with the Otherworld, I rushed out into the forest, needing to be away from everyone. I walked for a bit before plopping down under a tree, where I drew in the cool air.

Earthy scents filled my nostrils as I inhaled, immediately relaxing me. A humming force flickered through me. It was so minute I was sure I imagined it. I looked down at the Goblin-crafted bracelet on my wrist. It weighed next to nothing, but its significance compressed heavily on me.

I stayed under the trees for a long time before the copious fog clung to me, not distinguishing the difference between me and the trees.

When my blood began to fizz in my veins, I moaned. "Go away, Eli. Leave me alone."

"Not possible or likely." A large, dark mass emerged from the mist.

I rubbed at my temples, trying to keep myself from snapping into a million pieces. "Why? Why can't you leave me in peace?"

He moved closer; a smile tugged at the corner of his mouth. "Because you really don't want me to."

The memory of him saying something similar to me in the woods months earlier, before he first kissed me, produced heat, which stung my cheeks and body.

"Oh, I do. I really do." My eyes shot up to his.

Ignoring my words, Eli sat down next to me. His shoulder brushed against mine as he adjusted himself closer against the tree.

"I probably deserved the knee to the groin earlier."

"Agreed."

"Do you feel better now?" His tone held slight amusement.

"I did in that moment." I sighed, no longer feeling any joy from the act.

We sat in silence for a while, watching the fog weave over the ground and plants.

Eli rubbed at his face, exhaling deeply.

"Do you know how easy it would be if I wasn't attracted to you? I want nothing more than not to care about you."

His words only invoked resentment and riled my anger further.

"Gee, I am so sorry. I'm sure you'll get over it."

"Em..." he groaned.

"What Eli? Was that supposed to flatter me? Make me feel better?"

"It wasn't meant to do either."

"Plus, it's probably the blood. Something you will get over in time."

"Bry—" He tried to cut in, but I continued over him.

"I mean, do you even like me? As a person? Or is it completely superficial because I have your blood?"

"Yes—"

"Yes?" I cut in again. "Are you kidding me?" Fire burned deep in me. I rose with indignation. "Why should I be surprised? From the first day you met me, you looked at me like I was a bug under your shoe. Being attracted to a repulsive Dae must make you sick. How do you stand yourself, Eli?"

"I don't." Eli was suddenly inches away from my face. "You have no idea how hard I fight this—fight you. This is my own personal hell."

"Fuck you!" My palms met his chest, half hitting him, half pushing him away.

"That's the problem." He threw his hands up. "That's exactly what I want to do. I fight wanting you every minute of the day. And I shouldn't. I should be disgusted by you, by the mere idea of kissing you. But I'm not. I like you—as a person. You make me laugh. You *constantly* challenge me. I like when you are around and I hate that. You are everywhere and in everything."

"Then trade me. Give me to the Unseelie King. Problem solved. All of them."

"I wish it were that easy."

"You're the one who gave me your blood. I didn't want this connection either."

A growl erupted out of Eli, his hands tearing back through his hair. A sign he was hitting high levels of frustration. "This has nothing to do with my fucking blood."

"Then what does it have to do with?" I screamed back.

"I don't know," he bellowed.

"Does this have to do with your hatred of Daes? Tell me what happened, what occurred to create so much disgust towards them."

He turned away, his jaw gritting together. "You don't understand," his voice was low and cool.

"No, I don't. So tell me."

His eyes swung over to mine. *I can't.*

*Can't or won't?*

Eli sucked in a swig of air, his attention going up to the tops of the trees, not responding for a full minute before he spoke.

"Daes slaughtered my clan. They took away my family and everyone I loved."

"What?"

"Don't think for one moment your kind is a defenseless, misunderstood species. They are not. We aren't the only soulless monsters out there."

"My God, Eli. I'm so sorry. What happened?"

His gaze snapped away from mine. I could feel the shift in his body. He was shutting himself off from me again.

"I don't want to talk about it. I actually came out here to give you this." He moved back over to where we had sat on the ground and picked up an object, I hadn't noticed when he first walked up.

He twisted around, shoving it at me. It took me a moment for my brain to comprehend what he had given me. When I did, intense emotions swelled. "My sketch pad?"

"It's a new one. I wasn't able to grab yours from your home. I know how much you enjoy drawing and thought you might like having one here."

I stared at the brand-new drawing booklet. "You went out and bought me a sketch pad?" My head shook in confusion. Eli shrugged, keeping his eyes on the trees. "Sometimes I really don't get you, Eli."

"Me neither, Brycin."

I felt so disoriented. A moment ago we were fighting, and the next he was handing me a present. A very thoughtful present. He went all the way down to an art store to buy me something he knew I'd enjoy. My heart reacted before my brain could weigh in. I stepped up to him, placing my free hand gently on his cheek, popping up on my toes. My lips met his in a soft kiss. His mouth didn't hesitate in reacting. Heat charged instantly between us, but before I lost all thought, I quickly pulled away. Without a word I turned and rushed out of the forest.

When I returned to the infirmary, Jared was sitting up, showing minimal signs of his injuries. He smiled. His cheerful personality was back in abundance.

"Hey. You feeling better?" I asked.

"Yeah, Dad says I'm healing quickly; not as quickly as they do, but I'll be up soon."

"Good." I sat down in the chair next to his bed. "I'm sorry...this shouldn't have happened to you. It was my fault. I shouldn't have asked you guys to go there."

"Are you kidding?" he spurted. "I actually got to fight and not with a punching bag or with one of the guys going easy on me. I won't lie and say it didn't hurt, but it was the first time I actually was allowed to fight something real."

A laugh of relief erupted out of me. "You're not upset?"

"No, not at all. It was awesome," he replied. "I know these guys protect me because I'm not quite a Dark Dweller. They're afraid my human part will be killed. I'm much more vulnerable than them, but they forget I'm still hard to kill and not a baby anymore. I'm going to be seventeen in eight months. But because I'm not centuries old like them, they treat me like a kid."

"Yeah, but they do it because they love you."

"I know, but I'm grown up now. I want them to start treating me like I'm a part of the clan. Do you know what it's like to have *all* these guys treating you like a kid, acting like fathers, mothers, older brothers, sisters, and uncles? Telling you what to do, never letting you really do anything, always trying to keep you in this safety bubble? I feel like I'm in a prison, and it's making me crazy."

I smiled. "You know, I'm starting to."

# ELEVEN

A little while later Owen came in happy to find both his patients in one place. Being looked over like a lab rat was becoming second nature to me.

"Both of you are healing well. One more day in bed, Jared, and you will be good as new." Owen ignored his annoyed huff. Jared was so full of energy, getting him to sit another twelve hours was going to take a miracle. Owen moved towards my bed. "Ember, I got the results back from the blood I took earlier..." he trailed off, which made me gulp. When a doctor's voice becomes quiet, it was never good.

"What?" I asked. "Is it bad? What's wrong with me?"

"Nothing's wrong with you *per se*." He sat down in the chair next to my bed, his face turning serious. "You keep changing. The combination of your blood and Eli's has morphed your DNA again."

"What does that mean?" A strange feeling came over me. My skin prickled. It was an odd sensation, like I was being watched but not by either Jared or Owen. Rubbing my arms, I let my eyes scan the room.

Nothing. I was being silly; my emotions were just running high.

"I told you before that mixing blood between different Fae species has never been done. Humans, if given the wrong blood type, would likely die. Their immune systems would attack the red blood cells in the donor blood if the bloods were incompatible. Fae can only take blood from the same species or we can die. This has always been the case, until you. I don't know if it is a Dae quirk, which allows this, or if you are just different. But, surprisingly, your own blood has not only accepted Eli's, it has taken it on as its own, creating another strand in your DNA."

"Another strand of DNA?" I blanched.

"Yes. And when you didn't die from Eli's blood, I figured your blood would dilute his until it matched yours. And maybe, only at the beginning, you would show symptoms or traits like ours before going back to normal. You aren't only taking on our traits, but merging your traits and ours into your own special category. You are still Dae, but now you have a strand of Dae and Dark Dweller along with your Dae DNA strand."

Alarm was seeping through my forced-calm exterior.

"Okay, your lips are moving, but all I hear is blah, blah, blah. Dumb it down for me."

Owen cracked into a smile. "You don't need anything dumbed down, Ember, but I'll break it down."

He sat forward, clasping his hands together. "You grew up familiar with human anatomy so I'll start there.

"Simply put, humans have DNA in every cell. Each DNA helix is made up of two twisted strands with twenty-three pairs of chromosomes. Well, Fae anatomy has similar DNA cell structure, but ours are made up of eight strands, plus or minus, depending on the type of Fae you are.

"There have been a few discoveries of some humans having three, sometimes four strands, and studies have shown that humans who have more than two strands have 'special abilities.' They are looked at as medical marvels. Those humans probably have Fae heritage somewhere in their background. There was a time when Fae mixed with unsuspecting humans much more freely." Owen gazed over his shoulder at Jared. Jared looked bored and restless, flipping through a computer gadget magazine. "Jared, for instance, because he is part human, has six strands."

I kept hearing how Jared was half human, but I never heard about Jared's mother. I knew there was a story there. Curiosity won out. "Was Jared's mother aware of what you were?"

Owen bristled. His jaw snapped together as his eyes flashed, his pupils elongating. It was the first time I ever really saw the Dark Dweller part of him. It was more unsettling than seeing it in any of the others. With Owen you could almost forget what he was; with the others that was never the case. Owen obviously had worked hard at hiding his predatory nature.

His reaction solidified there was more to the story and more to Owen than met the eye. What was his story? What caused him to react so out of character? My gut told me it was not a happy story.

"No. She was not aware of what we are." Owen's tone was clear—do not push.

Clearing my throat, I went back to the original topic. "Okay, I am getting everything so far. Humans two, Fae eight. So, what's weird about me?"

"Our DNA can copy itself but does not usually form new DNA molecules. This is where you differ. When I first tested your blood, you had ten strands per helix, which seemed high, but might be normal for a Dae. You no longer have ten."

"How many do I have?"

"You have thirteen."

Stunned, I sat with my eyes and mouth open wide. I heard his words and understood them, but my brain was having a hard time comprehending the information.

*Thirteen strands in my DNA?* Guess I couldn't play the human card anymore.

"They are also different. You have made new DNA molecules."

"What does this mean for me?"

"This is all so new to me, so I am not sure. But your test results show you are extremely healthy and strong. Even more so now." He opened up his hands in a display of bewilderment.

I had barely gotten used to the idea I was a Dae, now I was something different?

Sensing my fear, he quickly added. "Don't worry. You are still Dae. Think of it as you are Dae with Dark Dweller on the side."

"I'm a Fay-Demon-Dark Dweller mix? I am a mutt of the Fae world?" I palmed my face, my head wagging. "Are you kidding me?"

"Afraid not," Owen replied.

"Awesome..." Jared spoke up from the other side of the room. "Ember, the Otherworld's wonder mutt."

Both Owen and I turned to glare at him. His smile grew bigger.

"Not helpful, Jared." Owen shook his head.

"Why? That's so cool. You are even more powerful. You could probably kick anybody's ass now that you have some of our traits."

"Jared," Owen's tone warned. Jared sat back sulking but stayed silent.

What I had done back at my house when I went all psycho-predator on Vek's ass was not a Dae trait. Something else triggered it. My new Dark Dweller gene? But I had felt a spurt of my Dae forces in there. I felt them try to shove through their bracelet barrier. I could still feel them pushing against the iron hold and getting stronger.

"Would being part Dark Dweller counteract some of my Fairy or Demon traits?"

"Counteract?" Owen looked at me curiously. "I wouldn't think so... why do you ask?"

"Well, it's not something I really thought about till now. I assumed it was a Dae quality or maybe every Fay eventually grew immune after a while... but I've noticed the effects of the iron have been wearing off. It hits hard at first, but after a day or so I feel my energy starting to come back. My powers are trying to push through."

Owen's eyes widened. "Fay never become immune to iron." He paused, taking in what I said. "I have no medical experience with Daes, so I cannot say for sure, but as far as I know they don't either. Being only half

Fay doesn't take away the allergy to iron. If this is happening to you, then it is something I need to look into. It could possibly be the Dark Dweller DNA making you resistant to iron, which would make sense."

"Meaning?"

"After Lorcan attacked you, you were not only dying from blood loss but from the toxins in your blood." I nodded for him to continue. "Dark Dwellers carry highly poisonous toxins in our nails. A tiny scrape would render you extremely sick, and Lorcan did way more damage. But it wasn't until you had Eli's blood that your fever went down."

Growing up I never got sick, not even a cold. I didn't know it was because I was Fae. So, the two times I had gotten sick, I had found it odd. Now I understood. Each time had been right after a scratch from a Dark Dweller, first from Eli, the second from Samantha.

"When did you first start noticing your immunity to iron?" Owen inquired.

Trying to recall my past experiences with iron, I leaned back against my pillow. I always thought it was an allergy growing up, so I avoided contact with it as much as possible. Looking back through my memories, I could not recall a time when I was indifferent or could function around it until Lorcan had me in the iron bar cell. I also became used to the cuffs the Queen had on me. I looked down at the goblin trinket wrapped around my wrist. All those times occurred *after* Eli gave me his blood; it was the Dark Dweller blood, which created a resistance to it over time.

I told Owen what I remembered, and this only seemed to confirm his theory. I had changed; it was fact. Eli had altered more than my DNA. He had changed me. I couldn't deny he was genuinely a part of me, rooted in my DNA and blood. It was unclear if it was a good thing or not.

"I also suspect that is how you were able to bring him into your dreamscape."

"But you said only Fay can dreamscape. He's not Fay, and I have his blood, he doesn't have mine."

"That is true. But sometimes things aren't black and white. Magic's certainly not. Your connection to Eli goes beyond blood or DNA."

"What do you mean?"

"Logically, if you are part Dark Dweller now, I should be able to sense you or even communicate with you in my head. I cannot. Dark Dwellers are similar to wolves in that we work as a pack. We can communicate and sense each other from vast distances. I should be able to sense Eli's blood in you, but it's as if your Dae traits are disguising it."

I filed this information into my constantly updated "Fae File."

The room was silent. I looked over at Jared; he had been silent far longer than normal. His head bobbed as he drifted off to sleep. A small smile toyed at my lips. He was like a puppy, all bounce-n-go then falling asleep mid-sentence. Wish I could do the same, I thought, but my mind would not let me rest.

"It baffles me why I can't feel you. Are you aware of my presence?" Owen brought me back to him.

It sounded funny since he was sitting right next to me, but I knew what he meant. I closed my eyes and concentrated on anything that sensed or recognized the blood in him. I felt nothing. No, wait, I did feel something. *Eli.* Even though I couldn't pinpoint his exact location, I could sense he was near—just like I knew he was getting close to me when I was on the run in Seattle.

"He's the only one you feel, right." It wasn't really a question. "Is there anything else you haven't told me yet?"

There was one more thing that came to mind. Something that had always been there but I hadn't questioned too much before. "Almost from the moment I met Eli, we've been able to 'understand' each other." I looked down at my curled fingers, feeling suddenly vulnerable. "I don't hear his voice in my head or anything, and I have to be looking at him. But many times I can understand what his eyes are saying to me. We can communicate without speaking."

"Neither of you thought to tell me this?" Owen sat up straighter in his seat.

"No. At the time I didn't want to think about what it really meant or how it was possible; then it became so natural."

"Eli never brought this to my attention either." Owen pressed his lips together. "You're saying this started before he gave you his blood?"

"Yeah, way before—when I first met him."

Owen sat back in his chair. "This is another occurrence that should be impossible. You should not be able to communicate with him like that at all, especially if it was before you received his blood." We both sat in silence. Owen's mind seemed to be working at a million miles a second. Only the soft snores of

Jared broke the quiet. Finally, Owen shook his head. "Like I said, you and Eli have a connection going way beyond DNA or blood. Some things cannot be explained by logic or science. You two have something no one can define. I understand his struggle now."

Long after Owen left, his words stuck in my side like a thorn. There were so many things that should worry me, but one detail kept repeating in my mind. It was what he said about Eli and me having a connection that went beyond blood and DNA. I always felt drawn to him. Lately, I thought it might be because of his blood, but it was more than that. Even before we had been connected. I couldn't explain it, describe it, or rationalize it. It was there, and I doubted it would ever go away, which terrified me.

I didn't let people in, and I didn't like depending on or needing people. Even with my friends I had always kept up a slight barrier. It kept me safe. But Eli wouldn't stay behind the barriers I put up. Like a ghost, he slipped through my thick walls, leaving me with overwhelming desire for him. With just one image I could recall exactly how his lips felt on mine, how his hands felt on my body.

"Hope those thoughts causing you to smile like that have me naked in the shower and you're scrubbing me down."

My head popped up to see Eli in the doorway, watching me. Humiliation flooded my cheeks a deep shade of pink. A satisfied smile took over his lips. He knew he had caught me. He was not too far from what had been playing in my head.

"Come on." He jerked his head toward the exit. "We are going to test your Dark Dweller skills." Owen had obviously talked to Eli, and probably Cole, about his latest findings.

"Can I come?" Jared said sleepily, his eyes only half open.

"No. You have to keep resting, but I'll take you out as soon as you're ready."

"I'm ready now." Jared sat up, rubbing his eyes.

"Okay, what I meant was, as soon as your dad gives the okay." Eli went over and rumpled Jared's hair.

"I am so sick of being treated like a kid." Jared huffed but settled back into his pillows. He might have been irritated, but he respected the authority of his Alpha.

Grabbing my jacket and shoes, I followed Eli out the door.

## TWELVE

"Are you serious?"

"You can do it." He leaped onto the boulder with grace and ease. "Jump."

"Yeah, right. It's pitch black out here. I'm not half cat, you know."

"Neither am I."

*You sure?* From what I'd experienced, Dark Dwellers had a lot of jaguar-like qualities, except a million times more frightening.

"Come on, Brycin." There was a dare in his tone.

Never one to back down from a challenge, I stepped back and made a running leap. My hands gripped onto the boulder as my feet slipped and faltered over the smooth surface. Right as my fingers were slipping from their hold, Eli's hands wrapped around my wrists tugging me over the peak, stumbling into him. We didn't move, but his hand had moved from my wrists to my waist to catch me. His heat soaked into me, the hardness of his body against mine.

## Fire in the Darkness

Peering up at him, only the moon lighting his features, I licked my lips nervously.

"So, I thought we could do some training up here." Clearing his throat, he stepped back away from me.

I tried to ignore the disappointment. "Up here? It's nighttime. What kind of training were you thinking?" I swiveled around taking in what little elements the moonlight let me see. Trees grew in and out of the boulder graveyard. Rock clusters of different sizes and shapes jutted out from the earth.

"I thought I would test your balance and agility."

"O-kay." My eyebrow cocked up. "Or did you just want to see me plant my face into a rock, which is the more likely scenario?"

"I'm not saying that wouldn't brighten my day as well. But I'm certain you will stay more upright than you think."

"Glad someone has confidence," I replied. "Okay, Master Yoda, show me what tricks you want me to do."

He grinned wolfishly.

"Mind out of the gutter, please."

"Oh, like yours is ever above ground."

"True." I smiled with a slight shrug. "But let's focus on the reason you have me jumping boulders in the middle of the night."

Without warning, Eli bolted across the top and jumped into the darkness. He moved so silently and quickly the only reason I knew where he went was because I had been watching him. "I hope you don't want me to do that."

"I do." The hoarseness of his voice came from behind me, whispering into my ear.

"Holy shit!" I jumped, swiveling to face him. "How the hell did you get behind me so fast?"

"I want you to let go of everything you think you should be and be who you really are." He stepped closer to me, looking more predatory. His pupils had shifted to the diamond shape. He was all masculine and virile, scary and dangerous.

His hand closed down on my hip, pressing me closer to his body. Lust clouded my thoughts. Feeling a little dizzy, my eyes closed. The memory of his fingers sliding into my pussy, the feel of his mouth sucking on my breasts.

Need and desire overtook me. My body leaned into his, my head tilting up, preparing to feel his mouth close down on mine.

When he didn't kiss me, I opened my eyes to see him smugly looking down at me. Heat submerged my face in embarrassment.

"If you want me to kiss you, you have to earn it." In one swift movement Eli spun me around, swatting me on the butt. "Your turn."

"Egotistical much?" I grumbled, but focused on the darkness where he had jumped.

"You might not be able to see in the dark like I can, but you should be able to sense what is around you. Feel it. You have earth powers and are connected to it and now you have Dark Dweller traits. You should feel the earth and see it here," Eli tapped at my temple, "even if you can't actually see it. Close your eyes."

Eyes closed, I breathed in deeply, letting everything go except for my connection to the rocks and forest around me. It took a bit, but eventually I started to absorb my surroundings. They were alive and talking to me—not with words, but with impressions. I could sense the life around me, reaching out to me, creating a 3-D map of the landscape in my head.

"I think you got it," Eli breathed into my ear. My lids rose slowly and then snapped wide open. Trees leaned toward me; tendrils of plants had slithered up the rock. Their leafy limbs were caressing my shoes. "They recognize you and know you are a part of them. Let them guide you." Eli's hand pressed against my back, pushing me forward.

I shut my eyes, letting the earth direct me. I took off and leaped into the black void. Silently, my feet planted themselves on the ground; my body crouched down ready for its next movement. It was simple, as if my body always knew what to do.

Something in me stirred. This was different from what I usually felt when my Dae traits came out. This was more in my muscles and reflexes. I felt like I could jump or pounce on anything. Eli had stated firmly that Dark Dwellers were nothing like cats, but I couldn't deny the feline stealth I felt in my movements.

Eli soundlessly landed next to me. "I think I knew for a while something in you had changed. But the moment I saw you with Vek yesterday, your eyes told me for certain."

"My eyes?"

"Yeah. Normally your eyes turn black when your powers take hold. It was the reason I dragged you away at the Outdoor Adventure course at Silverwood a few months ago. Your friend, Josh, saw them change. I couldn't let him confirm what he saw, so I pulled you away," Thinking back, Josh's reaction made sense to me now. So did Eli's. "When I saw you with Vek, they turned black but this time they also changed shape. Your pupils went vertical."

"Like yours do..." I had become such a freak, even for the Otherworld, which was saying something.

"You wanted to kill Vek. The Dark Dweller was taking over."

"I didn't just want to kill him. I wanted to hunt him down and tear him into little pieces." The bloodlust and desire to track and kill him had coursed through me, twitching my muscles. "It made me giddy; I wanted it so much. Is that what you guys feel?"

He smiled, but there was no feeling behind it.

"Jesus, Eli. I'm a killer now?"

"You'll have to learn how to control it, and I'll help you."

"Or you'll have to command me to stop every time." I looked down at my feet. "I would have killed him if you hadn't stopped me. So... you can control me?"

"I wish," he huffed. "It looks like I can only command you when you get into Dark Dweller state, which listens to its Alpha. Any other time, I can't seem to influence you at all."

Panic rushed through me. The thought of anyone controlling me in any way made me feel antsy and uncomfortable. The power was in his hands, and I didn't like it one bit. I wanted to trust he wouldn't use it for his own good, but I didn't have the luxury.

There wasn't anybody from the Otherworld I could truly trust, who didn't want to use me for something. Except Torin. Torin seemed to be the one person who only wanted to safeguard me. He could have turned me over to the Queen dozens of times; instead, he went against her to keep me safe. But his being her lover made my stomach twist. It felt wrong on so many levels.

And yet Eli had not turned me over to the Unseelie King. Was it only a matter of time?

Needing to escape my thoughts and the panic rushing up my throat, I took off at a sprint, jumping, leaping, and throwing myself through the rock obstacle with speed, grace, and agility. All qualities I never knew I had.

Eli wrenched off his hoodie and came tearing after me. "Don't you think you need a few lessons first on how to be a Dark Dweller?"

"No." I smiled and vaulted for the next boulder. The instinct was in me, teaching me what I needed to do better than anything.

For the next hour we bounded and leaped across the terrain until my overconfidence came and bit me in the ass, or in this case, my hand.

"Got a little cocky, huh?" Eli arched an eyebrow at me. Glaring at him, I picked the pebbles out of my palm. "Let me see." Blood dripped onto his fingers as he grabbed for my hand.

"It's no more than a cut, I'll be fine." I grimaced. Pain shot through my hand as Eli touched the gash. It was more than a cut as blood gushed out. Pride kept my teeth gritted together.

"The cut is pretty deep. Let's have Owen look at it. Don't want it to get infected." He pulled off his t-shirt; his muscular torso glinted with sweat under the moonlight. He tore at his shirt, ripped it into strips and wrapped them around my palm into a tight bandage. This guy had lost a lot of t-shirts because of me. Or maybe he wanted an excuse to take off his shirt. Either way, I was not complaining.

"Looks like you've done this before." My breath hitched, stiffening my words as he knotted the bandage. I drew my eyes away from the closeness of his bare chest and onto anything that didn't make me think of sex. Being around him always caused me to feel exposed and stripped.

"Owen taught us the basics, so when he wasn't around, we could get by. Comes in handy."

"Yeah, I bet." Our eyes caught and locked onto each other. I could feel the tension rise, sucking the air from my lungs. His gaze grew more intense, both of us leaning into each other. His eyes shifted for a second, going cat-like, before he snapped his head back, stepping away from me. When he looked at me again, they had returned to normal.

I needed a distraction, any distraction. "Was Owen always the medic in your clan? Or was it something he became in the Earth realm?"

"Owen has always been our medical practitioner, both here and in the Otherworld. But being here compelled him to learn about human medicine. He's the analytical one, a healer instead of a killer, preferring to patch us up than going on a job. He has never been as comfortable with what we are as the rest of us." Eli grabbed his hoodie off the ground and pulled it back on.

*Damn.*

I shifted my weight onto the other leg. "What happened to Jared's mother?"

Eli's face grew serious. "Jared's mother was human. She never knew what Owen was or what their baby would be. We were not kidding when we told you no one learns about us."

"Was she killed?" Horror filled my chest. They were capable of murder, but this felt different. Killing an innocent woman because you got her pregnant and you had to keep a secret from her?

"Owen met Rebecca when he first started medical school in Seattle. She was a fellow student, and they instantly fell in love. A year after they met, Rebecca got pregnant. She died in childbirth..." he paused, recalling the memories. "She died never having known about us or the fact she was carrying one of us. Her death nearly destroyed Owen. He was able to save the baby, but not Rebecca. Our kind had never coupled or reproduced with humans before. But we knew the rumors. Humans don't usually fair well when giving birth to an Otherworlder. Even now Owen blames himself for her death. After she died, he quit the hospital and came back here to live with us. We all helped raise Jared."

"Oh, God, how awful for Owen...to save your child only to watch the woman you love die because of it." My heart wrenched for Owen, but I couldn't deny the relief I felt knowing they hadn't done anything to her.

"Jared is our family, but he's different. He's half human, which makes him vulnerable. We try to keep him safe, but he thinks we baby him. He's probably right, but none of us could handle it if something happened to him. He's a great kid, unbelievably smart, a computer whiz. I'm talking this kid could probably break into the computers at NASA if he wanted. And he's so easy going and happy, nothing like us."

"You sound like a proud uncle."

"Yeah, but I'm afraid Cooper and I are very bad influences on him." Eli chuckled.

"Yeah, the kid has no hope."

"I would do anything for my family. They're all I have," Eli declared. I knew he meant his plans for me. I couldn't find the resolve to be mad at him for it; if anything, I understood. There was nothing I wouldn't do to get Mark back.

"Why haven't you turned me over yet?" My lashes briefly lowered before fastening on him. His focus bowed away from mine, and his hand flew up to his hair. Mid motion my hand caught his, forcing him to look at me.

"We should get back," he stated.

"No. You are going to tell me. Why haven't you traded me to the Unseelie King yet?" His head went down, watching the ground. "Eli?"

A tiny growl rocketed out of his chest.

"Because."

Waiting for him to continue, my silence seemed to only aggravate him. He did not pull away from my grasp, but let my fingers stay wrapped around his arm.

"I couldn't do it..." He mumbled so softly I barely heard him. With that he tugged away from my hold and walked towards the house.

# THIRTEEN

As we walked back in silence, I trailed a little behind him. He needed space, as I did. My brain was trying to understand him.

We had barely reached the porch when we heard the rumble of motorbikes and the distinct clicks of guns cocking. I froze in terror, but instinct took over Eli as he pushed me down. My head whacked painfully against the wood of the porch as Eli's weight came down on me, covering my body with his. In that instant, a spray of bullets tore through the air around us and hit the house. Glass and slivers of wood showered down on us.

"When I say go, you crawl to the wood pile behind us and hide there." Eli demanded in my ear. I twisted my head a little to see the outline of the stack of wood only a few yards away.

"What are you going to do?"

"I'll be right behind. Now go!" Eli rolled off me and I scrambled across the porch stooping as low as I could. Gunfire volleyed around as he moved alongside me, covering me from another round of bullets. Skirting around the logs, I dropped to the ground behind the wood pile. Eli crawled in behind. His face looked stern. In the darkness it took me a moment to notice the spots of dark liquid seeping through his hoodie.

"Eli, you've been shot." I cried out, fingering the holes in his sweatshirt now soaked with blood.

"Don't worry about it."

"Eli?" Cooper's voice shouted from inside the house.

"We're okay." Eli yelled back, wincing in pain as he did.

"Jesus, Eli, you're bleeding badly." Panic rose in my voice.

There was a lull in the gunfire before the guys came out of the house, guns blazing, shooting back at assailants I couldn't see. When they stopped firing, all you could hear was the roar of the motorcycles speeding into the distance.

"Cooper, you and Gabby run the perimeter. Check on Jared first, Go!" Cole commanded. The two took off toward the infirmary.

I looked over at Eli, his eyes were closed, his face scrunching in agony, his body sliding further into the ground.

"Cole!" I screamed. "Hurry!"

Footsteps pounded towards us as Cole rounded the wood pile.

"*Mac an donais.*" Cole swore under his breath and crouched down.

"Don't fuss, Mom. I'll be fine," Eli's voice was strained as he spoke.

"How many times were you shot?" Cole was upset, but nothing like the frantic state I was in.

"Hello? He's going to bleed to death if we don't do something."

"Em, calm down. Eli will heal. As you know, Otherworlders heal quickly, though he's going to hurt like hell for a while. His body has to work out the bullets." He grinned, but then his voice turned soft. "I'll have Owen look at him later."

"Seriously, stop fussing." Eli pushed himself into a sitting position. "I'll be fine. Now go track down who did this. By their awful smell and the sound of the bikes, there's no doubt it was the SOG."

"Retaliation," Cole responded. "I guess that's better than the other reason. But how did they find us? It shouldn't be possible."

"Retaliation for what?" A falling sensation tumbled my stomach.

"For you." Eli coughed and leaned his head back with a pant.

"Well, that's not entirely true." Cole frowned at Eli. "Remember those guys who attacked you and West a while ago?"

"The Hell's Angels?" Of course I remembered them. I ended up in jail that night because Sheriff Weiss was dying for a reason to put me there, even if I was only defending myself. Pock and McNamm had tried to fight West for me, turning it quickly into a full bar brawl. The night ended with me breaking a cue-stick over Pock's head and knocking him unconscious. Both

McNamm and Pock had assaulted me and had wanted to do more.

The memories even now made nausea snake through my gut, but Eli's reaction to it had been chilling. He never told me the story and I didn't want to know. The two men were now dead, and I knew Eli had something to do with it. I wasn't sorry they were gone, but it probably should have made me dread the Dark Dwellers more. They were ruthless killers, and now I was one of them.

"Well, those guys are in a chapter of the Hell's Angels called the Sons of Glory, a small chapter that has designated this area as their turf," Cole clarified.

"They are avenging the deaths of McNamm and Pock." I murmured. "So, this does have to do with me."

"Retaliation, for one of their own, is the law of the gangs. But they shouldn't have been able to find us. Our property has a spell on it keeping fae and humans from finding it." Cole shook his head as he stood up. "Now, if you'll excuse me, Owen and I must go reciprocate with our own laws." He nodded goodbye to both Eli and me.

"I don't want to know, do I?"

"No." Eli's emotions were strong enough. I could feel he was tempted to get up and follow Cole. It was his job to defend and fight for his family. He hated sitting on the sidelines.

"Don't even think about leaving." Frowning, I sat back down on my rear. "You guys should scare me."

"But here you sit."

"Yes. Why is that?" I demanded. "Is it because I'm a Demon? Why don't I care those two men are dead? Don't I have a conscience or soul or something?"

Eli laughed but immediately cringed, freezing until the stabs of pain subsided a bit.

"Em, you have more of a conscience and soul than anyone I've ever met. You understand people live in grey areas and make hard choices, not because they're evil, but because of circumstances. And you know you could, too." He sucked in a deep breath. "Anyone can. You take the most nonviolent person, and if someone is hurting their child or someone they love, they can kill too."

He was right. I would be capable of killing. If I ever found the person who had murdered my mom or if someone was hurting Mark or my friends—yeah, I could kill. "I really should fear and hate you."

"Yeah, but that would be for other reasons." He shut his eyes again, his force was draining.

Seeing him in so much pain tore at my soul. I had to do something.

"After Vek attacked me and tore a hole into my throat, it should have taken me awhile to heal. When I was in the dreamscape, Torin said he could help heal me faster and then kissed me." I paused briefly, gauging Eli's response. His eyes opened and a deep line scrunched up his forehead. "As you know, my wounds were healed when I woke up."

"Point to this story, Brycin?" He shifted against the wood pile, sweat trickling down his face. "Don't need to reminisce about you and your boyfriend."

"Don't be an ass. He was able to heal me, wasn't he? By kissing me?"

"I wish I could say no, but Fay have healing powers. Like Cole said, Otherworlders heal quickly, but Fay can also use their earth forces. By pulling energy from the earth, they help heal even faster. The force they draw can then be transferred to another. It can be done in a few ways, but kissing is probably one of the best. It invokes the most emotion and passes energy to the person the fastest."

"So, I can do this, too, right?"

He nodded in response.

"You didn't tell me I could do that."

"Sorry, I keep forgetting my Fay handbook at home."

*Eli...* My eyes shot him a warning. He huffed, which made him wince in pain as he looked away. I bit my lip, afraid of what I was about to say. "I can help you."

"I'll heal."

"Before you bleed out?"

He was already starting to slump farther down from so much blood loss and as much as he tried to hide the pain from me, I could feel it in him. It was excruciating.

"Let me help you." I moved closer to him.

He turned his head and looked up at me. "You lookin' for an excuse to make out with me, Brycin?"

*Don't cause me to regret being nice to you.* My eyes held his.

He turned away, conflicting emotions running across his face before he muttered, "Fine."

## Fire in the Darkness

"Don't sound all grateful or anything," I snipped. "You know what? Never mind. Bleed out." I was about to stand up and walk away when he grabbed my arm, pulling me back down.

"Hey..." he muttered. His smoldering, green eyes seemed to draw me back to him.

I swallowed nervously and moved over his legs, straddling him. What was I getting myself into? Did I want him to agree or wish he would say no? Giddy butterflies twirled in my stomach. My feelings hit both happiness and pure fear.

"Okay, I don't really know what I'm doing..." I trailed off.

"Think you'll figure it out." His cheeky smile twitched with pain, his eyes growing a little more distant.

"You're probably right." I laughed nervously. "It's probably instinct or like riding a bike or—"

"Brycin? Shut the fuck up and kiss me."

He gripped my hair, pulling me to him, our lips meeting with force. The feel of his mouth on mine sent fire through my veins. My tongue quickly found his as the kiss deepened. His finger dug deeper into the back of my head, pulling me closer to him. It was never close enough.

Everything in me burned with life, and it took me a while to remember I was supposed to be doing something. Concentrating on the energy zinging in my veins, the light bubbled and danced around in me, making me feel alive. I focused on it. Mentally pushing it towards him, I tried to give everything to Eli.

His body jerked and twitched, gripping tighter to me, his mouth growing hungrier. The hot pulse of his cock pushed against the thin fabric of my leggings, my hips rolling over him with a groan. My skin tingled as his hands moved under my top and up my back, losing myself to his taste, the feel of him rubbing against my core.

The sound of bullets plopped onto the dirt, slick with blood from his wounds. His pain was lessening, being replaced by strength. I continued to kiss him with abandon even when I knew he was fine. That my mission was technically done.

The iron bracelet attached to my wrist was limiting the force I needed to pull from the earth. The fact I was able to pull any at all was incredible. Eli's blood was making me immune to the exact thing they wanted to use to control me. Every day I felt better, a little stronger, strengthening my immune system.

Eli's fingers pushed under my sports bra, pinching at my nipples, sending sparks down my nerves. My hips rolled into him harder, dragging over his erection.

"Eli," I muttered his name, telling him what I wanted. There was no doubt. No reservations. I craved him. Needed to feel him inside me more than I wanted air. He was what I *always* wanted—heat, passion, and desire.

His arms went around my back as he lifted me, shifting me onto my back. His body moved on top of mine. Eli's fingers started pulling up my tank, as my hands tugged at the top button of leggings, his fingers sliding under the fabric, rubbing over the wetness of my underwear.

"Fuck." He hissed, sliding in more, my legs opening for him.

"So, little brother." A voice came from out of the dark—a voice I knew. "I see you're still enjoying the perks of your job."

Eli and I jerked toward the voice. Through the dark shadows I could barely distinguish the silhouette of Lorcan.

Gasping, Eli pulled away from me, getting up to his feet.

"You were always big on the benefits." Lorcan strolled closer.

"Lorcan, what the fuck are you doing here?" Eli pulled me to my feet and stepped in front of me.

"Wow, brother, I can feel the love all the way from here. Missed me, didn't you?"

"Why are you here?"

"We a tad cranky? Sorry, I must have interrupted a little too soon. She not able to get you off? Don't worry. I've heard that happens to some guys."

"Make your point now," Eli responded in warning.

"Whoa." Lorcan raised his arms in surrender. "I didn't come to fight with you or hurt lil' Emmy here. I just want to talk." His cool smile made me reach out and grip Eli's arm.

"Then talk."

"Manners, little bro." He shook his head. "I came here to let Ember know she has a choice, other than being stuck with your limp dick. She can come with me and save her human father's life."

"What?" I exclaimed. My legs were still wobbly, so I held onto Eli's arm firmly.

*Em, he's trying to provoke you.* Eli turned around warning me.

"I'm letting you know you can do the right thing here. Don't you want to save your father? Or do you want to let him be tortured and killed because you're too weak to take his place?"

As I started to rush forward, Eli's arm whipped across my chest, halting me.

"Look at you. All fluffed up." Lorcan jeered, crossing his arms over his chest.

"What do you really want here, Lorcan? You think you can walk away with Ember to leave on the Queen's doorstep like a trained monkey." Eli stopped and a crazed laugh sputtered out of his mouth. "I should have known." He motioned at the shot-up house behind us. "You were behind this. How else would they have known where to find us?"

"Too obvious?" Lorcan sneered. "I needed a distraction. You were supposed to go off with Cole; I didn't figure on you staying here and getting shot. Slight oversight of mine."

"Y-You son of—" I pitched forward again, but Eli continued to block me.

"Need help mastering your *striapach*?"

This time Eli charged and I was the one to yank him back. "Eli, don't. You're right, that's what he wants. He's already tried to get rid of you today so he could snatch me without a fight. But it didn't happen so don't let him now."

Eli stopped, gripping my hand and stepping back.

Lorcan broke into a thunderous laugh. "Are you kidding me? My brother is seriously whipped and on a piece of Dae ass. How ironically pathetic is that? And well, frankly, kind of disgusting. What would our parents have thought about this?"

Eli looked away from me and dropped my hand. It stung, but I was grateful he had listened to me and hadn't tried to go over and pummel Lorcan, no matter how much he was asking for it.

"Eli?" Cooper's voice hollered from around the house. "Where in the hell are you, man? You will never believe whose scent we picked up!" He came running around the corner, stopping short as he spotted Lorcan. Gabby and Jared practically slammed into the back of him as they came hurrying up behind. "Speak of the devil."

"What are you doing here, Lorcan?" Gabby moved around Cooper and sauntered over, coming up beside Eli. The rest of them followed suit. None seemed scared of Lorcan, plainly curious and maybe a little leery.

"You've missed me, too, Gabb. Come on, you know you have."

She crossed her arms in response, glaring at him. "Where are the others?" Gabby nodded toward the woods "Hiding behind a tree?"

"They are here... well, all except West."

"Where's West?" Gabby asked.

"West has been *detained*."

The knot in my chest tightened. The way he said it turned my stomach. If they had killed or even harmed him... My skin became clammy as a hot flash crept over my body.

"What does that mean?" Gabby demanded.

"All I've ever tried to do is help my family, but they keep making the wrong decisions, which only hurts us." Lorcan directed his response at Eli.

Eli crossed his arms, keeping his voice level. "This is what you want? A feud between us? How is that helping the family?"

"It's not what I want, but I will fight you if I have to. I seem to be the only one who hasn't forgotten what this girl means to us." Lorcan looked steadily back at Eli. "I am not the reason we are here, that everything was taken from us. You are. But yet they chose you to be leader?"

The accusation snapped my head over to Eli. He was the reason they were exiled? How? Why?

"What do mean?" Jared's voice broke the tension-filled silence.

Without moving his gaze off Eli, Lorcan addressed Jared. "J, why don't you go back to the house? Let us handle this."

Jared's chest puffed up. "No. I'm staying here. I'm a part of this group, too. How could you do this to us, Lorcan? I thought we were family."

"Things have changed, kid," Lorcan responded. "Your leader here has chosen a Dae over his family."

"Jared, go back to the house." Eli ordered.

"No. I'm not leaving. I'm not a kid. I'm a part of this clan as much as anyone."

"Jared. Now." The Alpha had spoken. Jared swore, kicking at the dirt, but turned and walked towards the house.

"Lorcan, don't be a fool. Don't do this." Cooper stepped closer to Eli.

"Do what? I did this for you guys. I'm the only one who is a true leader here. I sacrificed for you, and this is the thanks I get?"

"Sacrificed?" Eli blurted out. "You have a warped version of what a true sacrifice is, which is why you would never be a good leader."

A deep growl vibrated out of Lorcan's chest. "You are the one with his priorities screwed up." He took a few steps forward. This was going to turn into a fight.

"If I go with you, will you let my father go?" I stepped in between them.

"It doesn't quite work like that. Daddy dearest is the best way to keep you cooperative."

"She's not going with you, Lorcan." Eli caught my arm and pulled me back.

"I think it should really be Ember's choice," Lorcan said, turning to me. "And, I wouldn't be too hasty in saying no. It is more than your father's freedom on the line now."

"What are you talking about?"

"You should know me by now, my pet. I always come with assurances."

The sound of people walking over foliage brought our attention over Lorcan's shoulder. My eyes had grown used to the darkness, but it took me a moment to identify who moved in behind him. My stomach sank. Samantha, Dax, and another guy I didn't know, stepped out from behind the trees, each accompanied by another body. Dax held two.

"Look who I found earlier today posting missing persons fliers of you around town?" Lorcan nodded toward the four hostages.

The world slid out from under my feet.

Standing there, bound and gagged, were Kennedy, Ian, Ryan, and Josh.

## FOURTEEN

My brain could not comprehend the scene in front of me. My nightmare had come to life. My friends were being used against me.

Through their gags I could hear all their shocked, muffled exclamations at seeing me. They were looking at me with the same confused, scared look Mark had shown a few weeks earlier. Their minds were unable to contemplate what was going on or what I had to do with it. The last time they saw me was over a month ago at a party, where I disappeared, never to be seen or heard from again. Now here I stood with someone they thought was in some dangerous motorcycle gang. For all they knew they had become leverage in a drug or weapon deal. In a way, that was the truth. They just didn't know the weapon was me.

"No!" I cried out as my brain began to grasp the scene unfolding before me. Kennedy automatically took a step toward me, but Dax kept a firm hand around her throat. Her body went rigid as he squeezed her delicate neck tighter. Ian was tied to Kennedy so neither could get away from Dax. A powerful, Brazilian-looking man kept a knife tight against Ryan's side, threatening to plunge it deep at any second. By process of elimination, I knew it was the man they called Dominic. Samantha restrained Josh, a giddy happiness on her face as she watched the scene around her.

"Please, Lorcan, let them go. They have nothing to do with this!"

"They have everything to do with it. They have to do with you." Lorcan rubbed his hands together. "I told you. I am a man who likes to get what he wants. No matter the costs."

Eli's body stiffened next to me. "Lorcan, you don't know what you are dealing with here."

"You're the one who doesn't know what he's dealing with. You never have."

"No, Lorcan. *You* don't understand." Eli's attention was directed towards Kennedy. His fear only upping mine. I feared for all my friends, but Kennedy was on a whole other plane. If Lorcan learned what she was, it would be "game over."

"You are not getting in my way, Eli, even if I have to kill you."

The scene was quickly spiraling out of control, and I was the only one who could stop it. I couldn't let my friends be taken like Mark had. Fear flourished in my stomach like a weed, twisting and curling around my internal organs. *Kennedy.* If Lorcan figured out she was a Druid, would he tell the Queen? I couldn't let Ancira find out. Ever.

"I'll go. Please don't hurt them." I progressed to Lorcan, repeating the sentiment. "I'll go with you."

"Fuck. No." Eli growled.

*We don't have a choice.* My gaze shot to him.

*You are not going with him. Don't be stupid.*

"Why? Would it be any different if I stayed here with you?" I voiced, turning my anger on him. "This is all happening because of me." I waved my hand at my friends then to the bullet-riddled house. "I can't sit back and let him take people I love. They are *my* family. There isn't anything I wouldn't do for them." *And what about Kennedy? Are you willing to let the Queen find out what she is?* My stare demanded. The tension of our unspoken words grew.

Eli looked deeply into my eyes. *No, but giving yourself up won't help either. This won't benefit Mark or your friends. The moment she has you, she will torture or kill them. It will only bring them more pain if you go.*

My gut knew he was right, but my heart felt wrong letting any of this happen and for not already going after Mark. How could I let him or my friends be locked up in some dungeon in the Otherworld being tortured as I continue to sit here?

I couldn't.

"You can't go," Eli whispered, his hand lifted to the side of my face.

"I'm sorry. I have to." I pulled away but my eyes pleaded with him. *Rescue Kennedy and the others and keep them safe for me.*

He gave a slight nod. Yanking me into him, he whispered something strange into my ear. The word twisted and curled around my lobe. As his lips finished speaking there was a prickling over my skin and the iron cuff, which had been wrapped around my wrist, silently dropped into the long grass. I looked up at him surprised. I knew what he was doing—what he was giving me back. My dormant forces uncoiled themselves, coming back to life. I felt whole again.

*We'll be right behind you and will come around and strike from the front. I will not let him hurt you.* Eli's eyes communicated to mine.

I went up on my toes, kissing him quickly before turning to face Lorcan again. This time it was Sam who moved forward, her eyes blazing with hatred. The loathing she felt for me was written all over her features.

Taking an unwavering step, I nodded toward my friends. "You have me now, so please let them go."

"Oh pet, I'm not stupid." A smile slithered over Lorcan's features. "They are my insurance you will do what I want. They are coming with us." Lorcan reacted to movement behind me. "Don't think about it, Eli. I will gut her friends right here. You may not care, but you know Ember does."

"But you have me now. You don't need them." My gaze flittered over my friends' terrified faces as they looked between me and Lorcan. Blood froze in my veins upon seeing how scared and confused they were. The fact I now had my full powers back, even though they weren't always consistent, should have all these people huddling in fear of me. I was consumed with rage. But I couldn't do anything until I knew my friends were safe. The inconsistency of my powers might actually hurt or kill them. I couldn't take the chance.

I gulped and looked back at Eli; his face was like stone. My attention filtered over Cooper and Gabby. They all stood there with the same hard, blank look that gave me no comfort, no solace.

"Let's go, my pet," Lorcan whispered into my ear, causing a cold tremor to run through my body. He grabbed my arm and tugged me toward him as he pulled something from his pocket. Immediately, raw iron encircled my wrists. My knees buckled and Lorcan grabbed my arm pulling me back up, pinning me to his side. "Never underestimate me. I am not a fool like my brother. I will always be several steps ahead of you."

"It was great doing business with you," Lorcan retorted, looking directly at Eli. He started to move, but stopped and turned back. "Oh, and don't worry brother, I will take *good* care of Ember. She will get the same service from me as she did from you..."

Panic surged through every fiber of my being at the implications of his words. Eli surged forward, but Cooper quickly blocked him. Lorcan laughed with delight, happy to provoke his brother. Was he needling Eli or would he actually follow through and physically assault me knowing it would be the ultimate disrespect and revenge?

Lorcan moved us through the brush deeper into the dark forest. The other Dark Dwellers disappeared from sight. With every step, my limited energy inched back through my muscles. We were only a few minutes into our walk when someone moved in front of me, blocking my path.

Looking up I saw Samantha's fierce glare boring into me.

"So, we get to take home the repulsive, little whore." Sam looked at me with disgust. "I'm so looking forward to the day you are torn into little bits."

"Oh darn, and here I thought we would be having a girl's slumber party tonight: pillow fights, doing each other's nails, and talking about how Eli would rather touch an abomination than ever touch you." Low and spiteful? Definitely. And it felt good, but I was unprepared for her rage. Her fist slammed into my face knocking me hard to the ground. With my hands bound, I could do very little against her strikes. I swung my arms up, the metal clipping her chin.

"You fucking bitch," she screamed at me.

Dax yanked Samantha back and pulled her off me. Lorcan roughly grabbed me, dragging me to my feet. The moment his hand clutched my back, a searing, white-hot pain raced up the lines of my tattoo—an excruciating pain. I gasped and fell back to the ground.

Lorcan screamed next to me, dropping to his knees. It was clear my tattoo had triggered a similar pain in him. Everyone stood around us, in stunned silence, not sure what had taken place or what to do. Lorcan bent over on all fours and spat before sitting back on his heels. "What the hell?" His voice was raspy, as he stared at me with an expression of bewilderment and fury.

Eli's touch had never caused me pain, only an intense warming sensation and that feeling was lessening over time. Cooper and West had touched me, but it had been barely a buzz. Lorcan's touch was like tiny knives being driven into my flesh. Why did I feel Lorcan's touch so violently and not the others? And why was Eli's touch fading? Less than twenty minutes ago his hands were up my shirt touching my tattoo, but I couldn't even recall if it had warmed or not. He didn't jerk back or act like it had hurt him. But, to be honest, lightning could have struck us and we probably wouldn't have noticed.

"What the hell was that?" Lorcan stood and grabbed the neck of my shirt.

"I-I don't know."

His eyes narrowed in on mine. "You're lying."

Snatching the back of my top he pulled it up, exposing my tattoo. I struggled against him, but Dominic grabbed my arms, holding me in place. Lorcan reached out, grazing the lines of my tattoo. Simultaneously, a cry broke out from our lips. Pain filled my eyes.

"Fuck." He yanked his hand away. "Touch her tattoo," he commanded, motioning to Dominic who still gripped my arms. Dominic's face stayed stoic, but I could see the hesitation in his movement. His fingers slowly reached out over my shoulder. As he made contact with my skin, a small warmness shot up my tattoo. It was so minimal compared to Lorcan's, I almost missed it.

"Hmmm... interesting." That's all Lorcan said, as he dropped my shirt back in place.

"What is it, Lorc?" Samantha asked.

"Nothing you need to concern yourself with," he brushed her off. "Ember, you are becoming more and more fascinating to me by the moment."

"Too bad I can't say the same about you," I snapped. My gaze once again moved to the frightened expressions of my friends. "Please, Lorcan, let them go.

He shook his head.

"Promise me you will not hurt them." I implored, even though I knew his promises were empty. I was desperate for any hope they'd be okay.

"As long as you do what I say, I will not harm your little buddies." He peered over his shoulder at them. "But there does seem to be too many of them. We don't need all of them for you to cooperate."

A small relief filled me if even one of them got away and was safe.

"Which one do you pick, Emmy? Which one means the least to you?"

Relief evaporated. "What do you mean?"

"Which one do you choose to kill?"

"W-W-What? You promised me you wouldn't hurt them!" I exclaimed.

A devilish smile formed on Lorcan's mouth. "I promised you *I* wouldn't hurt your friends. I didn't say anything about them." He nodded toward his group of Dark Dwellers.

Blind terror locked in my chest. "No, please no... I'll do anything."

"I know you will, but I think you need to see what real Dark Dwellers are like. We are ruthless, and we kill. Sometimes solely for the enjoyment of it. Eli has lost what it is to be a Dark Dweller. You should fear us, not want to play house. Deep down, you believe he would never actually turn you over or hurt you. Eli is an insult to our kind, to our parent's memories. All of them are."

*Eli!* I screamed in my head. Where in the hell was he? He said he'd be coming around to strike from the front. They probably had to go way out so Lorcan and the rest of them wouldn't sense them. But his arrival would be good about now. *Please, Eli. I need you.*

"Samantha?" Lorcan motioned with two fingers for Samantha to step up, bringing Ian with her. The knife she held to his throat gleamed under the moonlight. A fear so unfathomable reverberated in my bones, rocking me forward with a stumbling step. He was not bluffing and had just chosen for me.

"Noooooo!" A scream tore from my throat. Dominic had a tight grasp on me, restraining me from moving forward.

"Oh, this is going to be fun," Samantha smirked.

Feeling faint, the world blurred around me. All I could see were Ian's terror-stricken eyes. The agony was too much. I looked away. "Please! Don't do this!" I choked out. All-consuming horror jangled my powers, which were under the iron curtain. I was helpless though it didn't stop me from trying to pull on my powers through a tiny gap in the wall.

"Don't." Lorcan shook his head. "If I sense any of your powers coming out even slightly, I will kill *two* of your friends."

I tensed. He didn't bluff—ever. I looked over at Ryan, and the absolute terror as he looked at his cousin caused me to whimper. Ian and I weren't as close as Ryan and Kennedy were to me, but he had become a good friend over the years. He was Ryan's family, which made him special. He had been out there with them, looking for me, putting up posters. Ian had no idea what world he had become involved with by being my friend. There was no way I would leave his side or not try, with every fiber of my being, to get him out of this. All of them. This was my world we were fighting in now, not theirs.

"Poor, Ember." Samantha's condescending tone crackled up my spine. "All is fair in love and war, little Dae. You take something from me, and I think it's only fair I take something from you." Samantha's green eyes blazed through the night, locking smugly onto me.

"What are you talking about? I didn't take anything from you!" I shrieked.

"Eli was mine, and you took him from me. Your kind took everything from us that we used to be and used to have."

*Oh God... she is seriously insane.*

"I don't know what you're talking about. I didn't take Eli from you. Please, Samantha, put the knife down," I pleaded.

"You think I'm blind and don't see the way he looks at you? Did you do something to him, whatever your kind does? Did you put some magic spell on him, bewitch him? Because there is no other reason he'd be with you. To want you so much. He hates everything about your kind," she seethed out accusingly. "But for some reason you have them *all* falling at your feet. West did, also. In the end he chose you and look what happened to him."

"What happened to him?" I whispered.

Disregarding my question, Samantha rattled on. "I will not sit back and let this happen. I cannot touch you. I am forbidden. But, if I can't hurt you, then I will hurt the very things you love the most."

"*Please...*"

"Sorry, too late," Sam crackled with laughter. Her arm jerked in a fluid motion, the knife slicing across Ian's bare throat, blood spraying across my face as his eyes bulged in shocked fear. His body dropped to the ground with a thud.

An anguished howl tore through my body. My mind immediately shut down, overwhelmed with agony. It was as if a thin slab of glass fell, dividing me from the world around me. My actions and movements felt like someone else's. In my periphery, I saw Ryan fall to the ground, wailing. With his arms bound, he hobbled on his knees through the dirt to get closer to his cousin. I heard myself screaming and calling Ian's name, but I knew he was no longer there. Ian's eyes were still open wide in shock, but there was no soul in them anymore, no light. Blood seeped onto the ground, blending with the night, the earth quickly absorbing Ian's life essence.

# FIFTEEN

My blood sensed the moment Eli was there, but agony kept me on all fours, gagging. Feeling activity happening all around me, it seemed a world away. I crawled on the ground to Ian's body. Ryan was wailing, rocking back and forth over Ian's lifeless form. I pulled Ian's head onto my lap, closing his lids, numbness gripping all my thoughts and actions.

Suddenly a hand came down and grabbed me, carting me up to my feet. Eli pushed me behind him and ripped at my cuffs. No time to get them completely off, so he broke the middle, releasing my hands from being pinned together. Cooper headed straight for Kennedy. He was about to reach her, when Dominic barreled into him, knocking him to the ground.

Still dazed, I had trouble taking in the fight happening around me. Dark Dweller on Dark Dweller. Four against three. But Eli fought like three guys in one. He was staggering to watch. They were all fighting fiercely, but they weren't in Dark Dweller form, meaning they weren't serious about actually killing each other. This only made me angrier. I wanted both Lorcan and Samantha dead.

The atmosphere called to my new Dark Dweller side—the part of me that iron had no effect on. It wanted to join. The shift was subtle, but I knew my eyes had probably changed, going diamond-shaped. I caught sight of red hair as Samantha soared through the air toward Gabby. I locked on my prey.

Pushing past Eli and Lorcan, I sprang, coming down hard on Samantha's back. Not expecting me, she lost balance and fell forward. Rotating mid-fall, she faced me. I grabbed for her neck. Being on top of her gave me a little more leverage. With all my strength I slammed her head back onto the ground. The moist dirt did nothing more than cause her head to bounce. Samantha growled deeply, her eyes flaming. She came up swinging, the contact knocked me across the space into a tree. Gabby jumped back into the fight, grabbing Sam in a chokehold from behind. Eli was right. She had only been playing with me before when she jumped me at Silverwood. My head was fuzzy but quickly cleared. It didn't hurt as much as it pissed me off.

Pushing up, a whimper brought my attention back to my friends. The three of them were bound and gagged, sitting on the ground in a huddle next to Ian. Suddenly Samantha was the last thing I cared about. Rushing over, I plunged to my knees in front of them.

"I will get you out of this. I promise," I yanked off their gags, tearing at the rope binding them.

"What the hell is going on, Em? We didn't know what happened to you. We were so scared you were dead!" Kennedy said wildly. Ryan didn't seem to notice

I was helping him. Josh only stared at me, his eyes huge.

"I don't have time to explain everything right now. I need to get you guys out of here. Are you okay? Can you run?"

Kennedy nodded, standing up. She seemed the calmest of them.

"I can't leave Ian here," Ryan yowled.

"What are you?" Josh asked. His face held no fear, only awe and excitement.

"Josh, your life is at stake here. We don't have time for explanations. I need you to run. Now." I was desperate for them to get as far from me and the Dark Dwellers as possible. Deep down I understood it might be futile, but I had to try. They had been tagged and were now my responsibilities.

"You're a shape-shifter or something, aren't you? You're not human, are you?" Josh was buzzing with excitement. "I knew it. I knew something was different about you."

"I am not a shape-shifter." I grabbed his shoulders. "Josh, I need you to focus. Please, you have to get out of here." Nothing appeared to be breaking through to him. I turned back to Kennedy, the only one who showed any rational thought. "Ken, get them out of here," I pleaded with her.

"What about you?" she asked.

"Don't worry about me. They won't hurt me. They need me too much," I replied. "Now go." The fighting continued nearby as Kennedy gathered Ryan up and pulled at Josh's coat. Finally, Josh seemed to notice her desperate pleas and turned to go with her. They ran and relief flooded me. I needed them to be away from the present danger.

"Lorc!" Dax screamed over to him and nodded at the escaping detainees.

"Get them!" Lorcan yelled back.

"Gabby!" Eli called. Gabby tore off after them. It was a race to get to the prizes first. Seven Dark Dwellers tore after the captives, pushing and shoving past each other to be the one leading the hunt. I had been a fool. My friends had no chance. I joined in the pursuit, ready to put myself between them and their pursuers.

Dax was the first to reach Kennedy. She screamed as he locked his arms around her. Dominic made it to the other two before Eli or Cooper could get there. They pulled out their knives, threatening to slice my friends' throats, which stopped all of us in our tracks. "One more step and Ember has another dead friend."

Dominic struggled to keep Ryan on his feet. Ryan was in no state to fight anything, and Josh didn't put up much of one. He might be skinny and young, but the years of abuse had left him with a quick temper and a knack for fighting. If I didn't know better, I would swear Josh wanted to get caught.

"That was stupid, Ember." Lorcan turned to look at me. "Your friends were cursed the day they met you." He smiled haughtily. "But you actually got us close to our exit. Thanks for that." He then mumbled a word under his breath. A tingling of magic teased my skin. Waves of night air folded and curled in the empty space between two trees.

A gasp came from Gabby. "A door? How? I don't understand."

"I'm capable of more than you could ever imagine. Or ever gave me credit for. You picked the wrong brother." Lorcan snapped his fingers and Dax, Dominic, and Samantha moved toward the ripple with their treasures.

Everything in me snapped. "No!" I screamed and hurled myself towards them.

Eli's arm curved around my waist, pulling me back. Thrashing against him, he struggled to keep a hold on me. "No, Ember."

My outstretched fingers grazed Kennedy's as we both reached for each other. Dax yanked her back and through the opening. Cooper jumped at the opening, hitting it with a thud, bouncing back to the ground.

Out of nowhere, a form came bolting into the space, knocking past me, leaping, grasping for Kennedy. His body hit the shimmering space and fell through, disappearing.

"Jared!" Cooper roared.

Lorcan and the rest of his gang, along my friends, dissolved into the space. Cooper once again sprung towards the opening to no avail.

"Stop, Coop. There's no point. We can't get in," Eli bellowed.

"B-But Jared?"

With a strange sucking sound, the glitch in the air shrunk until there was nothing.

"No..." I reached out for it, but I felt nothing but emptiness.

"They are gone. Jared is gone," Gabby said in shock.

"What the fuck happened? What was that?" I looked around the forest running over trying to find the opening.

"Door to the Otherworld," Eli responded. "There are veils between the realms where you can exit and enter."

"There are more out there? Why haven't I seen them before?" I demanded whipping around to face Eli.

"They are not easy to see. Humans can't see them at all."

"They have Jared!" Gabby yelled, breaking from her stupor.

"How the hell did he get through? How did any of them get through? We're banned; we shouldn't be able to enter the doors to the Otherworld," Cooper exclaimed, pacing back and forth.

"I don't know." Eli shook his head. "But they did. Shit, Lorcan, what have you gotten yourself into?"

"He's working closer with the Queen than we thought," Cooper said.

Gabby paced frantically. "What are we going to do? J's not from there; he knows nothing about being in the Otherworld."

"Lorcan will protect him," Eli responded.

"What? Are you kidding me? Lorcan has traded his soul to that bitch. They will torture him."

"You can say whatever you want about Lorcan, but the one thing he will not do is allow Jared to be hurt. He may want to destroy me, but he loves Jared and will see to it he stays safe."

"I don't know if family means what it once did to him," Cooper responded.

Eli stayed quiet. As much as he was putting up a front, I could sense the anguish he felt over Jared. He felt responsible. "Shit!" Eli pounded his fist against a tree, wood splintered off in large hunks. "Fuck!" The violence he turned on the tree made me step back, in alarm or awe, I wasn't sure. Cooper, Gabby, and I watched him assault the tree. "I've lost Jared and Kennedy. This is all my fault."

His guilt only impacted my own. I let out an aggravated cry, my head falling into my hands, collapsing under the weight of everything. My friends were gone. Ian's dead body lay close by in the forest, his skin sunken and pale and drained of blood. Bile rumbled in my stomach. The pain Kennedy's and Ryan's families would go through, thinking their children had been kidnapped or murdered, overwhelmed me. They'd never know the truth. It would be the same with Mark and me. Josh would probably be presumed to have run away, lost to the streets. Sadly, no one would look for him.

"I am sorry." Eli nodded towards where Ian's body was. "I know it isn't much, but it is all I can give you now." He sounded emotionless. "We have to move. Lorcan will be back for you."

I looked down at the object that had blocked my powers. I should have been able to save them, to stop Ian from being killed, to stop Lorcan from taking the rest of my friends. I failed them...all because of these thin strips of iron wrapped around my wrists. My anguish flipped, seething hatred filling me until there wasn't a breath in me that didn't feel malevolence and loathing. "Get these off of me!" I flailed my hands at Eli. "Get them off! Get them off!"

Eli came over to me. "All right. Calm down."

His words had the opposite effect on me. I had destroyed the lives of the people I loved. Darkness oozed into my soul like crude oil. My need for revenge overflowed my body, spilling out on everything and everyone around me. They were as much to blame for this. The instant Eli entered my life everything in my world had turned upside down, only causing me pain and anguish, leading to this. I not only welcomed the darkness, I opened myself to it, willing it to come to me.

The moment Eli broke me from my bonds I stood up, rage giving me strength. Everything around me shifted and became brighter and sharper. My sadness dissolved into a frightening force of power. I watched as weariness fluttered across Eli's face. He knew he had made a huge mistake. Power swirled around me. A tree nearby abruptly exploded and snapped in half, sending a rain of bark down on us. The forest came alive. I could feel the life flooding into my body. It took my anger and made it its own. Tree limbs started to move, groaning and snapping.

"Ember, no!" Eli's hand reached out for me.

I took a step back. "Don't. Touch. Me." I seethed, malice and anger soaking my words. Eli jerked his hand back.

Cooper took a step toward me, setting off warning bells in my head. They slowly circled, trying to trap me. I knew Eli had another iron bracelet in his pocket—a goblin-made one. He, like all the others, only wanted to contain me. To tame me like a dog. No more. I would not be a hostage any longer.

Damp leaves began to fall down heavily from the twisting branches. Another tree moaned, wood chips cascading around us.

"Ember, listen to me, you haven't learned control yet." Eli kept his voice level as Cooper lunged for me. My arms flew up in panic.

"No!"

Cooper came off the ground and flew back, smashing into a tree. He hit it so hard the redwood splintered in half, falling with a loud crack to the ground. The surprise of the magnitude of my power was short-lived when Gabby leaped towards me. My arms flung up automatically in defense. She stopped in mid-air and flew backward, smashing into another tree. She fell alongside her brother, out cold.

Power surged in me, creating the feeling that I was soaring up into the air. I didn't feel pain or sorrow. I only felt strength. Wild and untamed. Alive. Power sung in my veins.

"You have to stop." Eli's voice brought my attention back. He didn't move, but his voice was enough to create anxiety and confusion. Looking at him caused a burning in my heart. It was something I didn't want to ever feel again. I shut the door to any emotion causing me weakness.

My energy slammed him back into a tree; his feet dangled high off the ground.

"If you or anyone of your group comes for me again, I will not hesitate. I. Will. Kill. You."

He stared at me, his face blank. Ivy and weeds slithered up the tree, wrapping around his legs, arms, and neck, pinning their prisoner in place. The energy from the earth pumped in my veins. The sensation was unbelievable. *Nothing can touch me.*

"Brycin, look at me," he said, his voice soft. But he was nothing to me anymore—just another faceless enemy.

"Shut up," I growled. Another vine of ivy glided up the tree and twined around his neck, reducing his air supply. He gasped. I snapped my wrist slamming his head back into the trunk of the tree. His head cracked loudly against the wood, his body slumping. Something deep in me screamed. Switching everything off, I pivoted on my toes and took off at a run.

My legs carried me away from everything I wanted to escape. If I stopped, it would all catch up with me. *Keep moving* was my only thought as I passed through woods and neighborhoods. The glow of the sky told me dawn had come. The rise of the sun did nothing to take my nightmares away. No monster could come close to the horror I had gone through tonight—what my friends had gone through. And one of them would never see a morning again.

People were rising with the daylight. I didn't care I was covered in blood and dirt, running like a criminal through the streets. But no doubt my appearance attracted attention and alarm. I would expect people to call the police, reporting a mad woman running at top speed down the road, covered in blood.

Because of the people taking advantage of Olympia's weakened state by the ES, police heavily patrolled the streets. But nothing mattered. I didn't see anything in front of me or behind. No future, no past, merely featureless objects standing in my way.

Abruptly, a siren wailed behind me. It only made my adrenaline surge. My Fae side dreaded humans; they only led to discovery. That I was not human was becoming exceedingly clear to me. They were so fragile. The blood on my hands was already thick with victims.

Cutting through someone's yard, I ran from the pulsating red and blue lights. The cop car came to a screeching halt, loud voices screamed after me as I weaved through the yard.

"Freeze!" A policeman shouted behind me. "Ms. Brycin, I'm warning you. Stop now."

It took me a moment to fully comprehend he knew my name. A police officer who knew me by sight. There was only one—Sheriff Weiss. I felt more annoyed by his presence than anything. Would this man ever leave me alone?

"I said stop or I will shoot." The click of a gun finally slowed me down. "You have nowhere to go. So, give yourself up." I stopped, glancing between him and the twelve-foot fence blocking my way. "I finally have you, Ms. Brycin. Don't make it worse for yourself." Weiss motioned with his gun for me to move to him.

I almost wanted to laugh. Didn't he know I was more of a threat to him than he could possibly imagine? He had always feared me. He had known something was different about me. Well, I should hand it to him. He had actually been correct about me for once, but not in the way he had thought.

I used to think someone like a cop could protect me or had authority over me. Not anymore, not in the world I belonged to. There was nothing he could do to stop me. It was the first time I felt the true distinction between a human and myself. The understanding of it consumed me.

"You are such a tiny man." I looked him up and down with a sneer. "But you were right about one thing. I did cause those fires." A mocking smile cast over my lips. "But you will never be able to prove it."

Weiss inched closer to me, believing he had a chance to catch me. Handcuffs in hand, he was about to grasp for my arm.

"Keep dreaming, asshole. This will be the closest you'll ever get to catching me." In a blink of an eye, I sprang, jumping over the top of the fence. I was gone before he could even fathom how I could disappear over a twelve-foot fence in front of him in mere seconds.

At a distance, sirens wailed as I darted through Olympia. He was scouring the city for me, but by the time he followed a lead I was long gone, leaving the city far behind me. Soon the sirens became the only sound in the countryside. I kept running till there were no more houses or people.

Hours and endless miles later, my body began to grow weak, wanting to give into fatigue. Haunting images propelled me forward.

When I reached a creek, my legs paused in their insistent thumping. My brain too tired to think properly, I foolishly tried jumping it. The notion of changing direction or running along it came to me in the middle of my leap. A little too late. Coming up short, I crashed into the rocks and fell back into the rushing water. Battling against it did nothing more than tire my already fatigued muscles. Trying to relax, I let the force of the current wrap itself around me, holding me in its arms and escorting me for a few miles. My lassitude made it impossible for me to fight. The icy water drained what was left of my strength. My head grew uncomfortably heavy, and I slipped deeper under the water.

My lids closed. *You are going to die*, my survival instincts bellowed at me. The lull of never feeling again, to slip under the water and release my tortured soul forever, overpowered any other urge. My body and mind would find peace from all the pain.

Dipping under the blanket of water, I felt a sharp sting slice across my face, scratching me. Jerking up, my head bobbed out of the water, gasping for air. My heavy lids opened to see a large root growing out of a tree, jutting out far enough into the creek for me to grab. With my last speck of strength, I seized the root. It took me several tries, my fingers numb and stiff from cold, but I pulled myself up the tree root onto the bank. My lungs burned as I coughed and sputtered, excess water spewing from my mouth. My brain and body were deadened with cold and exhaustion.

I closed my eyes and curled into a shivering ball, understanding I would most likely die in the forest tonight. I didn't care. There was nothing left in me, and all I wanted was for either sleep or death to declare which one wanted me more.

# SIXTEEN

Daylight streamed down, making me shut my eyes tighter with a groan and pull the covers over my head, burrowing deeper into the soft bed.

I stiffened. Everything came flooding back to me. Visions of Samantha slicing the large blade across Ian's throat ripped across my mind along with his bewildered expression. His face would forever be seared into my brain—his pain, his terror. My heart seized in my chest, and a guttural cry wanted to push its way out; my mind also torturing me with all that had happened the day before.

Sitting up with a jolt, I looked around. I knew I should have been dead from hypothermia or at least waking up on a river bed. How was I in this beautifully decorated bed?

The king-sized bed sat in the middle of a large room. The furniture was modern, but elegant. On one side were large, French-style glass doors that opened onto a large, wooden deck, which overlooked a stunning view of the rolling hills. On the other side were double doors, which probably led out to a hallway. In front of me another door opened up to a bathroom. A large chandelier hung over the middle of the bed, casting rainbows on the wall as the sun glinted through the crystals.

Still taking in my surroundings, I heard a sharp knock on the door. Not waiting for a response, a woman steamrolled into the room. She was dressed in a grey, tunic-style, button-down dress with white tennis shoes decorated with sparkles. She was short with silvering, black hair, a voluptuous figure, and with what would have been a sweet-looking face, if it wasn't for her stern expression right then. She carried a bundle of clothes in her arms.

"*Señorita, usted debe despertar y vestirse,*" the woman rambled on, looking at me expectantly as she placed the clothes down on the bed.

"Huh?" I responded, befuddled.

"*Levantarse.*" She motioned with her arms to get up. I had paid enough attention in Spanish class to understand at least that word.

"What on Earth is going on right now?" I shook my head, feeling like I had stepped into an episode of the *Twilight Zone.*

"Shower, Senorita. Senor would like to see you." The lady spoke in broken English.

*Senor? Where the hell am I?*

The woman pulled down my covers impatiently, nodding towards the bathroom and then down at a pair of terry cloth sweatpants with matching hoodie in a shocking pink. I cringed. A lot of girls loved that color, but I hated it. My entire personality revolted against pink. That's when I noticed I was no longer in my clothes except for my underwear and tank I had worn the day before.

*Oh Jesus... someone undressed me.* "Where are my clothes?"

"*Basura. Muy sucio.*" Her nose wrinkled up in disapproval, like I was a kid who rolled in the dirt solely to annoy her.

*Trash? She threw my clothes away?*

"*Rapido*, Senorita," she tsked me.

I slid off the tall, enormous bed, feeling an awful lot like the princess and the pea. She herded me toward the bathroom, which was almost as big as the bedroom. A huge, white tub sat in front of French doors which opened up onto the balcony; another gorgeous chandelier hung over it.

"*Pronto.*" The lady motioned for me to hurry and then shut the door.

When I was finally alone, I turned towards the mirror. The girl looking back was a shell of my former self. Mud clumped in dried chunks in her ratted hair, looking like a wild beast. Her body was covered with dirt, scrapes, and blood.

The biggest difference was in the face. The normal, glowing eyes were sunken and lifeless. Pain seemed to be etched through her face, like a brand mark. My eyes couldn't stop staring at the dried, red stains on my top—Ian's blood. My fingers slid over the soiled area. A sob gurgled in my chest. I pushed away from the counter, turning away from the husk of the person who looked back at me in the mirror.

After a quick shower, I climbed into the soft sweatpants she had laid out for me. They were blinding to look at, but I couldn't deny the sheer comfort of them. Tacky, but definitely the top-of-the-line tacky. Someone who lived in a house like this could afford to buy the best.

I had barely slipped on the zip-up hoodie and pulled on the cushy socks when the lady headed for a door. "Come, Senorita," she said over her shoulder. I hurried, making sure I was close on her heels. She already felt like my safety base. If I was near her, nothing bad could happen to me, right?

*Please let this be true...*

She led me downstairs to the first floor. My eyes widened as I followed her through the different areas of the house. I had thought the previous rooms were enormous and decadent, but the rest of the house blew me away. It really couldn't be called a house, more like a mansion. It was in the style of an English manor, with old dark wooden beams, huge fireplaces, curved entries, and beautiful chandeliers. But there was a modern, elegant, and contemporary feel in its furnishings and style. It was gorgeous and probably had been on the cover of *Architect Digest*. My mouth hung open the entire way.

*Would these people adopt me?*

As soon as the thought flickered through my mind, betrayal engulfed me. Mark. I took in a gulp of air and pushed him out of my thoughts. The pain was too raw.

The woman finally stopped in front of double, frosted-glass doors at the end of the hall. She knocked lightly on the door. "Senor?"

"Yes, Marguerite?" A deep, sultry voice slid from the other side of the door, making me more alert. I could feel his force through the door. I was not dealing with a human. I should have known. My luck was never that good.

"*Senorita es aqui.*"

"Send her in," the voice spoke again.

I gulped down the instinct telling me to run.

Marguerite opened the door and stepped aside to let me pass. Nodding a polite thank you, I stepped into the room.

I should have run.

## SEVENTEEN

A regal, elegant looking man sat behind a desk with an assured confidence. His tall frame was dressed in a dark, very expensive looking suit. He had black, wavy hair and light olive complexion. I could feel wealth, elegance, and danger rolling off him in waves. I sucked in my breath with a hiss, as his piercing, yellowish-green eyes pinned mine.

*He was a Demon.*

My one eye was an exact duplicate of his. The glowing, odd, yellow color had always made people more uncomfortable than the blue one. Now I understood why. They could sense, without understanding, the Demon in me.

The energy pounding off him and through the room told me he was no ordinary Demon. I hadn't felt this level of power since being in the same room as the Queen.

"So, this is what all the commotion is about." His eyes cut into me, adversely. "You definitely have your mother's looks, if you get past the street urchin look."

My head jolted back. *My mother? How does he know my mother?*

The years of lies came hurdling back. Of course. My mother had been Fae. He probably knew her or, at least, of her. It felt strange to think of my mom as having this secret, this other life and world, which she had kept from me. Every Fae I'd met recently told me I looked like my mother. It always struck me as odd. I didn't really look anything like her. I only resembled her in personality. They apparently saw something I didn't.

"I am so glad I finally get to meet you." The Demon smiled at me. The smile was calculated and full of hidden meaning to which I was clueless. Tensing, I held my ground. "I guess I shouldn't be surprised Elighan tried to keep you for himself. He had a valuable token in his arsenal. Worth a lot in trade."

Only one word slammed into my brain. "Eli?" Was that how I got here? He had finally traded me?

A slight frown creased his forehead. "Yes, Elighan, the Dark Dweller you have grown so found of..." he trailed off, looking at me for a reaction. "His adamant interest in what I thought was an ordinary human made me curious. He is someone I have kept a close eye on over the years. They are a clan you keep on your radar—smart, powerful, ruthless, and *extremely* dangerous. They don't find interest in something unless it is exceptionally important. I soon realized their notice of you was not unfounded."

I dug my nails into my palms, clenching my jaw together in a hard line, forcing back the hollowness I felt hearing Eli's name.

"You've been following me? Who are you?"

"I think you know." Like with the Queen, I already seemed to know the answer to my own question. My gut understood the moment I walked into the room. I was face to face with one of the most formidable dark Fae there was.

"The Unseelie King."

He smirked. "You can call me Lars. Feel honored as only a select few get to."

*Lars was the Unseelie King. Why hadn't Eli or Cole told me that? Why hadn't Torin? This was who Torin wanted me to find and who the Dark Dwellers wanted to deal with?*

Sweat started to tickle the back of my neck. "Thank you, sir."

His smirk grew into a beautiful, half smile. It was not a warm smile. There was something else about him making my gut wrench and my lungs feel as if they were in an iron grip. The instinct to run thumped across my shoulders, down my back, to my legs.

*How do I keep finding myself in these situations?*

He regarded me. "How are you feeling?"

"Um... okay."

*Like crap actually.*

"Good." He nodded. "You did not look well yesterday when we found you. I hope you slept all right? Were the accommodations to your satisfaction?"

This was a tad surreal. The dark and evil Unseelie King was asking me if I slept okay. Once again I felt like a toy being batted around.

"The place is lovely, but you know that. Let's cut the chit-chat here." I crossed my arms.

"Direct and to the point." He nodded, seeming to be pleased. "What would you like to know?"

"How did I get here?" I motioned around. "Did the Dark Dwellers trade me? How did you know where I was? Did you track me down with a Demon spell or something?"

"A Demon spell?" A condescending smile twitched on Lars' lips. "Well, if we had such a thing, it still would not have been hard to find you."

"Demon sixth-sense then?"

"No," he replied. "I didn't use anything like that. You came to us, Ember."

"What?" I stepped back, stunned. "What are you talking about? I passed out on a muddy embankment, not in a bed with eight-hundred-thread-count sheets."

"Yes, you did pass out on an embankment." He leaned forward in his chair. "My embankment, next to my creek, on my land."

*Was not expecting that.*

"And where are we exactly?"

"We are about forty miles southeast from Seattle. I own about two hundred acres." He dipped his gaze out the doors where gorgeous forest lands rolled outside the windows. "It is easier to run my business from here and keep it well-guarded. Nothing can penetrate my lands without me knowing it." He looked back and pointed to the chair. "Please, sit."

I crossed my arms and declined with a shake of my head.

His eyebrow lifted, but he continued on. "It is not a coincidence you found your way here. Intuition brought you here."

"You think I would knowingly, or even unknowingly, come to a place inhabited by the Unseelie King?" I laughed bitterly. "Where I'd be held prisoner?"

"Prisoner?" His eyes widened slightly. "Has anything you experienced so far made you feel like a prisoner in any way?"

"Just because I can't see bars doesn't mean they're not there."

"Fair point." He gave a nod of acknowledgement and then shifted in his seat. "You are not a prisoner here, and you are free to go at any time." He held up his hands, motioning to the outside. I felt like I was missing something. "Go ahead." He nodded towards the door. "You can leave right now, if you would like."

"What's the catch?"

"There is no catch." He looked at me evenly. "And I even promise no one will follow you. But I will not be able to protect you from the others who want you."

"I thought you wanted me...to use me? Wasn't that your deal with Dark Dwellers?"

"There was no deal made with them. Nor did they even approach me with one." He sat back, clasping his hands together. "You could have been. I would have gladly assisted them in their fight against the Queen for you. Now they have lost their bargaining chip. I am thinking Elighan is to blame. It is usually not in a Dark Dweller's nature to love outside their own. But obviously that is not true here."

My head snapped up. This reaction produced a small smile to come across Lars' lips.

"Your feelings for him are written all over your face." His tone was reprimanding. "You have been with humans too long. Your emotions are a weakness. You have no filter, and we must break you of that."

"We?"

"Yes. I want you to stay here and train."

A sharp laugh broke from my lips. "You've got to be kidding?"

"On the contrary."

I had to hold my tongue from saying something smart-ass; he was not someone you got lippy with. Safety and danger teetered in the air, easily swinging in any direction.

He stared into my eyes and pressed his lips together. "I understand you are distrustful. So many have lied to you before."

"Or have wanted to use and destroy me."

"For what it is worth, I do not want to hurt you nor do I want to see you destroyed. Quite the opposite." He looked levelly at me. "Use you? Yes, I suppose I do; but I also want to train you, Ember. I want you to become the powerful warrior and fighter I know you are meant to be."

"But still a weapon in a way—your weapon."

"You would work for me, yes." His blunt honesty was comforting. At least I knew where I stood. "I want to prepare you for the war with the Queen, because it will come. You will need to be able to fight against her."

"And you think you can train me to take on the Queen? Are you nuts?"

"That is yet to be determined."

I looked out the window. Grey clouds were rolling in covering the blue sky. It felt like some kind of omen.

"Why are Daes so hated? What did we do?"

"Do you know anything about Dae history?"

I shook my head.

"How about Fae history?" My response was the same. "Lily really kept you in the dark, didn't she?" He thrummed his fingers on his legs in thought.

Hearing my mother's name always tore at my heart, poking at my suppressed sorrow.

He continued, "I do not recall when or where the first Daes came into existence. Knowing Demons and Fays, it had been happening since the beginning of time." Lars stared off in the distance. "You should probably understand a little Fae history first to really understand where you fit in it.

"The Fae once inhabited Earth's realm. We lived numerous centuries all over the world. The major citadels were in what are now known as Greece, Italy, Turkey, Egypt, and Ireland. Your heritage is Celtic."

At least there was one thing my mother hadn't lied to me about.

"And Greek."

*Okay, that was a new one.*

"Humans eventually came along, breeding faster than space would allow. Our ways were generally ignored by locals until Christianity and the church moved in. Suddenly there was fear, prejudice, and intolerance of our magic. This created hate and soon we found ourselves hunted, strung up, and killed. The need to survive caused Fae to retreat to the Otherworld. The future Queen Aneira, and her sister, Aishling, were only children then."

Aishling. Interesting. One of my middle names. My mom named me after Fay royalty. Probably common in the Fay world. Humans picked their child's middle name from British monarchy all the time.

"It was their father, the King, who made the decision. I don't think Aneira ever forgave him for retreating. She considered it a weakness. To her, humans were beneath Fae; therefore, Fae should not run from them. She also never forgave humans for taking her land. She's had a personal vendetta against them ever since."

Lars got up from his chair and walked to the glass doors, looking out at his property.

"She also resented that Demons and some Unseelie stayed on Earth, living quite contentedly alongside humans. I suppose she felt consorting with the enemy made you one as well. Her anger was set in stone when the former Unseelie King denied her retribution. She had come to him in hopes they could lay down their differences and come together to retaliate against the humans and take over Earth once again.

"Foolish. She had forgotten Demons and some Unseelie need humans to live. We did not want our 'energy source' to be taken away. Humans gave us endless resources, especially the more the population swelled. Interestingly, we found humans were capable of the worst depravities towards each other. Greed, lust, corruption, unbridled ambition. And they call us evil." He shook his head, resuming. "We were quite happy with how things stood. The previous Unseelie King had created a powerful empire here on Earth, ruling comfortably and growing in strength every day.

"When she became Queen, Aneira was too vain to see how dominant the Unseelie King had become. She could not control him like she used to. When she comprehended how much clout he gained, her anxiety turned to hatred for him along with anyone who no longer followed her rule."

"What happened to him if he was so strong?"

Lars turned around facing me. "He was killed. We don't inherit our roles. We take them."

I swallowed nervously as his yellow eyes blazed into mine. I had no doubt that Lars was the one who did it

"As for Daes...when the Queen discovered she could not manipulate them with her glamour or bend them to her will, she started relentless propaganda and smear campaign against them. Aneira still likes giving the impression she is not a ruthless dictator. She would not kill your kind unless it was for the 'safety' of her people. Therefore, she gave the people a reason for the killings.

"With a few set-up incidents, where Fae died supposedly because of a Dae, she easily got a law passed forbidding Demons and Fay from mating. But, of course, like on Earth, making it illegal created it more tempting. And Demons do not like to follow rules, particularly if they can create a weapon against the Queen. Unfortunately, the former Unseelie King only encouraged this, and it got way out of hand."

"You mean Demons were raping Fay women?" I spit out in disgust.

"Yes—though not all did."

He seemed to hesitate before shaking his head slightly. "But, remember, Demons are female, too, so male Fay were raped as well. It would have been a lot more rampant if Daes weren't only produced through an upper Demon and a pure, noble-blooded Fairy."

"Produced? It sounds like raping a Fairy to get a Dae baby was equal to a manufacturing industry."

"To some it was." He shrugged. "It was a dark time and something I halted as soon as I came into control."

"Aren't you a sweetheart?"

"Watch yourself, Ember," he warned. "Be careful not to mistake Dark or Unseelie with evil. There are no good and bad sides here. Light and Dark might work differently, but 'Light' does not mean good, nor does 'Dark' equal bad. Good versus evil thinking is a narrow-minded way to look at it and will only get you killed."

My fingers nervously fiddled with the zipper of the grotesquely pink hoodie.

He cleared his throat, carrying on. "It was said every Dae would eventually lose control—some getting high off their powers and letting it overtake them—becoming insane and killing everything in their path."

"What?"

"This is not entirely untrue. Certain Daes can be too powerful and end up destroying everything around them, *if* not trained properly. But all you need is a shred of truth for something to seem factual in people's eyes. They destroy what they fear or do not understand. Aneira created panic, deciding the fate of your kind. There were some reasons to dread Daes, but it was more because she couldn't master your kind than what you are or what you did."

"Did any Daes live?"

"Very few that I am aware of. Some were smuggled here, raised by humans, to protect them from the Queen. Sadly, most were eventually found and killed. Ultimately, they could not hide their powers for long, especially if they did not understand what was going on. You were one of the lucky ones."

I looked away. Warmth for my mother wrapped around me. I was beginning to understand why she did what she did and why she had kept the truth from me. Her love and strength had kept me alive. It also sounded very similar to what happened to the Druids…what had happened to Kennedy.

Aneira's cruel smile popped into my head. The bitch had taken everything from me. She and Samantha.

*Vengeance...*the word swirled around, enticing me. "My dad, my friends—I can't sit here and let her have them. I have to go after them."

"And how do you propose to do that?"

"I don't know, but I can't sit here and do nothing. I have abilities. She can't control me. I can fight her."

His deep, haughty laugh echoed through the room. "Ember, you would not last thirty seconds against her."

"I don't care. I'm not letting them suffer any longer." I jumped up from my chair.

Lars flicked his wrist and I found myself across the room, pinned to the wall by an invisible force. My lungs fluttered in alarm as air leaked from them.

"You think you can go against the most formidable Fae? You are not even a match for a barely trained guard. You are a baby, untrained and ignorant." He walked over to me, watching me struggle against his invisible hold. Veins in my neck and face swelled as the lack of oxygen gripped me. "Now, are you going to be more sensible if I let you go?" Lars spoke to me like I was a three-year-old. "I have a proposition for you, one that will help you eventually get your human father and friends out."

Black spots dotted my sight.

"I would decide quickly, Ember."

He was right. There was no way I could go up against the Queen. My own fears caused me to panic and act irrationally, but I didn't know what else to do. It would be tough, but I had to play their games to get what I wanted.

"Are you ready to make a deal?" Forcing my head to nod, I dropped from the wall and landed in a heap on the ground, coughing and gasping for air.

*Am I really going to deal with a Demon? Am I that stupid?*

Yeah. I guess I was. It was probably beyond the most idiotic decision ever made, but it was the only way I could see to help my family. I needed help. The Dark Dwellers couldn't get to the Otherworld, and Torin was dominated by the Queen.

Sadly, the only person I could count on right now was a Demon—the Unseelie King. Torin had told me to find Lars, and he knew I needed help fighting Aneira. This must be his way of helping me. I had to trust Torin; there was no other option now.

"Good decision. A fight is coming. You need to be prepared." Lars looked directly into my eyes, sauntered back to his desk, and pushed a button on the phone. Less than thirty seconds later, a firm knock sounded at the door. I pushed myself up, my legs shaking as I leaned against the wall.

"Come in," Lars called out.

The door opened to a massive man who had to be at least 7 feet tall and 400 pounds of solid muscle. My Dark Dweller sense of smell perceived he was Fae. He ducked his head through the doorway as he walked in. Cuts and gashes covered his sour, harsh face. He was baldheaded, with coffee-colored skin, and his meaty hands, the size of baseball mitts, hung at his sides.

My neck had to bend back to take in all of him. He was large and scary looking, not to mention the first unattractive Otherworlder I'd seen. I immediately wanted to cower in his presence.

"Ember, this is Rimmon."

"N-Nice to meet you, Rimmon," my voice wobbled out. He nodded and grunted at me as he moved into the room. For his colossal size, I was shocked at his light steps.

"He is the muscle of our security here."

*Yeah, he looked like he'd be good at that.*

"He is the one who found you last night when he was out patrolling."

"Oh...thank you?" I didn't mean it to come out like a question, but everything about him made me slink back in fright. His head jerked down in response. Not a talker.

"Rimmon, tell Goran we need to double security tonight." Lars walked over to me, and without a word or warning, grabbed my arm, flipping it over. His fingers slapped against a vein.

"What are you doing?"

He responded by jabbing a needle into my arm before I could break loose from his grip, quickly extracting blood.

"Owww!"

He sauntered over to Rimmon and handed him the vial of my blood. "And have Maya reset the wards and incantations to include Ember's blood around the property. We need to ensure they are extremely tight and solid. We might receive some immensely unwanted visitors from now on."

"What the hell? You can't take my blood without asking," I yelled, rubbing my arm.

"I take whatever I need," he declared. "But you should not complain. This will allow you to come and go freely. Without these enchantments you would not be able to even step across the property line without forgetting where you were or what you were doing. We have many levels of wards and spells that deter people from finding this place." This was like what the Dark Dwellers installed around their property. "Last night you set off every security alarm and only reached us because you were mostly unconscious, which was when Rimmon here found you." His glanced over to Rimmon. "You are excused."

Rimmon gave a swift nod, pivoted, and exited the room.

"He's a chatty dude." I turned back to Lars. "And frightening."

"Yes, he is, but that is his purpose, to frighten, terrorize, and unnerve his opponent. For as big as he is, he's also extremely quiet and quick in battle. He's an ideal guard; his presence alone stops most from even trying to attack here."

"Are Demons' looks based on what they do?"

"Not only Demons but most Fae use their shell for their needs. Most of the Dark prey on humans, mentally and/or physically. So, our human forms help us achieve this—whether to seduce, scare, or entice humans into our varying wants and vices."

It suddenly clicked why all the guys in Eli's group were take-me-against-the-wall hot. Their looks were part of their "hunting" equipment. I cocked my head at Lars. "Is this why you look like you do?"

"Yes, but I am a special case," he replied, not elaborating.

"What about me? I'm part Demon." I stepped back to the chair I had being sitting in before being flung across the room. "Do I feed off humans, too?" My voice went higher than I even thought it could. The idea I had to "absorb" human energies to live made me want to retch. What if it was worse than that? Would I eventually have to kill humans to live?

"Relax, Ember. You are also a unique case. You do not feed off humans. A Dae's energy usually comes from the earth or nature. There was a case where Daes took their powers from humans," he said, then swiftly changed the subject.

"As for our deal—you will stay here and train every day. I will decide when you have had enough or when you are ready. You will owe me one favor when asked and, in exchange, you have a home, food, and protection. You will be taught to use your skills and abilities for combat—learning to master them as easily as breathing. Do you grasp what is being offered to you?"

I could feel the manipulation winding around his words, but that didn't stop me from wanting it. I nodded.

"Yes."

"You will not be able to back out of our deal once it has been agreed upon. Do you understand?"

Again I nodded. "I want you to train me." I looked up, determination set on my brow. "I want to learn how to control and use my powers. I'm getting my dad and friends back."

His eyes watched me thoughtfully for a time. "So we have a deal? You live and train here until you are able to manage your skills to help me and to get your friends and father back. Agreed?"

I sucked in some air. "Agreed." As the words came out of my mouth, I felt a pressure of energy swirl over my body. "What was that?" I held out my arms looking for the imaginary source.

"That is our bonding agreement. I do not take deals lightly, and if you sever our contract, repercussions will be severe. From now on you cannot leave when things get tough or you no longer think they are fun. You are committed."

I gulped; my head dipped in acknowledgment.

"Good." There was a slight gloating in his tone. He leaned over to his phone, pushing another red button. "Rez?"

There was a beat of silence before a woman's silky voice came back over the intercom. "Yes?"

"Can you come in here, my dear?" Lars' voice didn't hint at any emotion, yet I couldn't stop my eyebrows from popping up. He ignored my expression.

"You knew all along I'd agree to this."

"There is very little that does not resolve in my favor. If I see a weakness, I go for it. Yours is the love for your family. They are your weakness, which is why you keep losing them."

My fists balled up against my side. Several expletives were about to roll off my tongue when there was a soft knock at the door as it opened. My mouth dropped open as the most beautiful, sexy woman I had ever seen walked into the room.

She looked to be in her late twenties or early thirties and flawless. Long black hair hung to the middle of her back, framing perfectly proportionate features: strong cheek bones, an elegant swan-like neck, and big almond-shaped, dark chocolate brown eyes—maybe part Italian or Greek. She was thin, fine-boned, but curvy in all the right places. She was elegant, classy and sensual.

She made me feel about as pretty as a hairless cat.

*Please say she's a bitch, so I can hate her.*

"Ember, this is Rez." He motioned toward her. "If you need anything, go to her. She is in charge of running the house."

She smiled and nodded. "I hope you are better?"

"Yes, thank you." I was getting used to the Dark being beautiful, but well-mannered and nice? This was a little too much to grasp.

"Rez, Ember is going to be staying with us while training. I would like you to help her get settled. Whatever she needs: clothes, shoes, personal items. Also, if you could introduce her to everyone so she feels at home."

"Of course," Rez replied.

Lars nodded and then moved toward his desk, signaling our dismissal. Rez motioned me to follow as she headed out the door. I had so many questions for Lars, but it was clear he was done with me for the moment.

I got up and trailed after her. She wore a nice pair of black slacks with a creamy white, off-the-shoulder blouse. The outfit was simple but looked incredible on her and made my hot pink sweat suit look even tackier. She would have been a tiny bit shorter than I was without her heels; and like me, she was all legs, though she made having long legs look glamorous, not gawky. She was runway; I was alleyway.

"I'm glad you decided to stay with us, Ember," her voice soothed me. "I think you will like it here. Our home is yours now." She turned around to continue on with the tour. "There are a handful of us who live here. I guess you could say we are a family." It was a strange prospect, the Unseelie King putting on his jammies before going to bed. Demons living in a house together like some reality show, watching movies, eating, joking around. It seemed so human. "We work for Lars, but he gives us flexibility to go out and do *our thing*." She said "our thing" in such a way I knew meant whatever they needed to do to live, which probably meant feeding off humans.

"Can I ask you what you are?"

"I'm aware you know next to nothing about the Otherworld, but it is considered rude and presumptuous to ask. Otherworlders in general are quite secretive and suspicious. Over the centuries humans have made us this way. If Otherworlders reveal themselves or you figure it out that is fine... but never ask. Ever," she stated firmly, and then smiled gently. "Because you were unaware of this, I will answer you this time. I am a siren. You are aware of what that is?"

"Yes." I briefly recounted what I knew about them. Sirens were dangerous mythological creatures, seductresses, who lured sailors to their deaths. Looking at her I had no doubt any man in a boat or in a bathtub would gladly follow her to a watery grave.

"Not everything you hear is true; the folklore was written by humans. They do not have the full truth, only the myths and legends they created."

My mind was still trying to wrap around the fact that sirens were real when she led me into a gorgeous kitchen the size of a small house. It had top-of-the-line appliances, an oversized, double-door fridge, and a restaurant-size stove, all sleek and blending in nicely with the cabinetry. A huge island sat in the middle with its own double sink and built-in chopping block. Stools lined up on the other side. There was a curved breakfast nook with built-in benches on one side and a chandelier hanging over the round table and a walk-in pantry on the other side. It was a gourmet chef's kitchen.

"Obviously, this is the kitchen," Rez motioned around. "You met Marguerite earlier. She is the reason we function here at all, and we could not live without her. She does the cooking and house duties. Sinnie, our house brownie, comes out mostly at night to clean.

Marguerite always leaves a bowl of honey or porridge for her, so please don't throw it out. Sinnie gets offended easily. Also a warning, brownies love shiny or sparkly objects. So, unless you are willing to lose it, don't leave anything out she will be attracted to. I've lost more jewelry that way," Rez laughed lightly.

"Brownie?" I had heard of them but needed to be sure she was not referring to a baked good.

"Oh dear, you are a newbie. Brownies are a sub-category of Fairies, but they are one of the least magical species. They rank with gnomes and hobbits and have limited glamour powers. Humans usually mistake them for a large rat or something of that nature. Although their glamour is thin, humans will turn what they see into something their brains will accept. Being lower Fae, brownies can only turn into creatures their own size and can only use the most basic glamour."

*Rats. Always rats. Why not a fluffy kitten?*

"Household brownies help clean houses at night while you sleep. They are quite shy and not social creatures. Because we are not human, Sinnie will venture out every once in a while in the day, but she usually prefers attending to our rooms when we are not there. She handles the most basic cleaning and tidying and is recently obsessed with making beds. I got up to go to the bathroom in the middle of the night and came back to a made bed. Drives us all a little batty." Rez laughed.

She turned back to the room. "Marguerite does pretty much everything else; she is essential to this house. Lars would probably kick himself out before he'd get rid of Marguerite. She cooks breakfast and dinner, and sometimes lunch, though for most lunches you're on your own. The kitchen is yours to use as freely as you want—snacks, drinks, whatever. I only suggest staying out of Marguerite's way when she's cooking." Rez shook her head, as though remembering a story. "She'll chase you out with a steak knife if you get under her feet. She technically has Sundays and Mondays off, but she never really leaves. We are her family and she prefers to stay and take care of us, no matter how much we tell her to get out for the day."

Rez walked through the kitchen into a huge dining room. A long, modern, oval table with velvet-covered chairs circling it sat in the center of the room, and another stunning chandelier hung from the ceiling. A curved, limestone archway opened up to the living area. A giant, deep grey, velvet sectional, a glass coffee table, and several large chairs sat in front of a glowing fireplace. Heat and energy flowed from it into me. Aware of my connection to fire now, it felt incredible. I couldn't believe I never noticed the strong sensation before.

Rez pushed a button and a flat screen TV the size of a Cadillac came down from the ceiling. "Usually you'll find the gang either here or downstairs in the family room where you can find tons of video games and DVD's. There's also a pool table and a small bowling alley."

She waved me forward, finishing the rest of the house tour. There were two different wings. One held the majority of the bedrooms, each with their own bathroom. The center of the house was the living space, and the other wing included Lars' office and his bedroom that was bigger than an Olympic-size swimming pool. As we walked past the closet, I also noticed it had women's clothes hanging in the closet, which looked like those Rez would wear. *Hmmm—a Demon and a siren playing house? Interesting.*

As for an Olympic-size swimming pool, they had a real one in back—heated, of course. It was installed so naturally it looked like a lake instead of a pool. There was a gorgeous patio with a fireplace and an outdoor kitchen and barbeque grill, which would have made Mark cry. All this overlooked the creek where Rimmon found me, surrounded by the most beautiful, rolling, lush green grounds with flowers and oak trees. There were a few buildings that looked to be stables, more living spaces, and offices off to one side. On the other side was a densely rich forest. It took my breath away. This wasn't a house; it was an expensive spa retreat.

"So how many others live here?"

"There are seven of us who live in the main house. Of course, Lars and I, then there's Marguerite, Nic, Maya, Koke, and Alki. Goran, Lars' right hand, stays out with the rest of the security in the farthest building out there." Rez pointed to one of the large, English-cottage-style, stone buildings.

"So, where is everyone?" I asked.

"Alki and Koke are probably out practicing in our training facilities, which is the building right there." She pointed to another bungalow-looking house. "Nic is most likely sleeping, and Maya is probably working." Rez turned back to face the house. "As you could probably tell, we are self-contained out here. We don't like being dependent on ties to humans if we can help it. We have our own electricity and water."

The Dark Dweller's compound had also been self-sufficient. It seemed to be a Fae characteristic. During my little jog through Olympia yesterday, I noticed most stores were open, generators were giving people electricity, and even some gas stations were open. Life in Olympia was slowly getting back to normal. Seattle was not as lucky.

Rez lifted her hand, touching my arm gently. "I'm sorry. You are probably starving. I'll have Marguerite fix you something. Since we are on our own power out here, we actually have satellite Internet and some TV. We can order you clothes and other personal items and have them delivered. I'm thinking pink is not really your color." She winked.

"That's an understatement." I grimaced down at my outfit. "But I don't have any money."

She let out a musical laugh "Oh, you don't need money here. Don't you worry about it; Lars will take care of everything."

*That is exactly what I am afraid of—someone else controlling me.*

## EIGHTEEN

Marguerite made me a deli-style sandwich bigger than my head. I knew I was already in love with the woman's cooking on my first bite. Whatever she did that made it taste so good, I didn't want to know. She was the type of woman who was stern but full of love and affection. Rez was also easier to be around than I thought. She helped order clothes and personal stuff and even made sure it would be delivered overnight so I wouldn't have to wait. Exhausted and with my tummy full, my lids drooped with heaviness.

"Go take a nap." Rez looked at me with concern written all over her face. I nodded and found my way back upstairs. When I entered my room, the bed was made. I couldn't help but look around to see if there was a twelve-inch woman hiding under my bed.

Sleep came easily enough, but staying asleep was a different story. I woke myself up screaming. I couldn't escape the image of Ian's cold, white face, blood spilling from his neck as his eyes, now black, looked emptily into mine. "Help me." His lifeless hand reached out for mine. His hand then transformed into Kennedy's as her fingers slipped out of my grasp. I woke up sobbing till I was so exhausted I slipped back into another restless sleep. Then the cycle repeated. I woke up screaming over and over.

When I roused once more calling out Kennedy's name, I decided I could no longer lie there caught in that repetitive hell. Carting myself out of bed, I slipped into the hallway. The corridor was dark, but light and voices flittered up from downstairs. Slinking down the steps, keeping close to the wall, I tried to overhear what was being said.

"Do we have a spy in our midst?" A sultry voice spoke behind me making me jump "Let me know if you learn Marguerite's secret chicken molé recipe. Now there's something I'd kill for."

I gripped my chest, twirled around and almost forgot how to breathe. A Spanish god stood on the step above me, smiling down. His smoldering, dark eyes and shoulder-length, silky, brown hair seemed to glint in the dim light. He was built like a gladiator and was probably a walking fantasy of every woman, and many men, on the planet. My mouth kept falling open, no words forming on my lips.

A smile broke over his face. "You must be Ember."

I continued to stand there and gawk.

"I'm Nic by the way." He reached out for my hand. When my brain finally caught up with his words, I put my hand in his. He kept his eyes on me as he leaned over and kissed my hand.

*Did I just step into some romance novel?*

Now that I understood a lot of Otherworlders' physical appearances were based on what they needed from humans, looking at Nic, my brain instantly went to sex. I thought Eli was sexual, but this guy took the cake. Eli had many layers while Nic seemed to have only one—sex. It was a little unsettling.

"Nice to meet you, Nic," my voice choked out.

"And you, Ember." I could detect a slight Spanish accent. "Would you like to venture out of the shadows and come join us for dinner?" He held out his arm for me to take.

*Okay, he had to have taken a Romance Novel Studies course.*

I took his arm hesitantly, but as soon as we entered the brightly lit dining room, I dropped it. Four heads turned our way. I recognized Rez, but the rest of the faces were new.

"Ember, so glad you could join us. I see Nic has already sought you out," Rez said.

"She was skulking on the stairs." Nic tried to grab for a biscuit from the basket Marguerite was putting on the dining table.

Marguerite slapped his hand away. "*Usted muchacho travieso.*" Setting the biscuits down, her tone was full of teasing warmth. Nic laughed and sat down in a chair across from mine. He did look like a naughty, mischievous boy. Marguerite scurried back to the kitchen and soon returned with another delicious smelling dish and then settled herself at the table next to Rez.

"So now you know Nic, but I warn you, keep away from that one." Rez pointed her fork at Nic.

"What?" Nic exclaimed, not looking quite as shocked as he sounded. "All I did was politely escort her here, and I'm already getting attacked? So much for being a gentleman."

"Oh, you are so full of shit." Rez rolled her eyes. A slight smirk hitched up on Nic's lip. There was no doubt he agreed. "Off limits, Nic." She now circled her fork around my head.

"A challenge…the way I like it."

"Nic," Rez's voice went up in warning. "I am not kidding."

"Yeah, yeah, yeah." Nic rolled his eyes, reaching for a biscuit.

"Ember, this is Alki. He will be your main trainer and will teach you combat skills." She pointed at a young, compact, muscular Asian man. He looked to be in his late twenties, but now I knew looks had nothing to do with actual age. His dark hair was cut close to his scalp. His almond-shaped eyes were so black you could not even see the pupils, and if his severe no-nonsense expression gave me an indication of his personality, I probably should roll into a ball and start crying now. He looked like a warrior. I could already feel the torture from his training. I was doomed.

Immediately, I scolded myself. *Remember who you are doing this for.*

"This is Koke and she will be training you in learning to manipulate objects with your mind." She was also of Asian descent. She was stunning and tiny, but size meant nothing in the Fae world. She nodded back; her hawk-like, dark eyes watched me, picking up every detail.

"And lastly, this is Maya. She will be helping with your earth powers." Maya looked to be another no-nonsense housemate. She was tall, regal, beautiful, and extremely intimidating. Her expression was unsmiling and stern. She had eyes that, when they looked at you, made you feel she could see your most inner thoughts. She scared the bejesus out of me. My first thought when I saw her was of Madame Laveau, the famous Voodoo Priestess. Who knew, maybe she was one.

"You've already met Nic." Rez waved her hand in Nic's direction.

"I'll be helping you with—"

"Nic..." Rez cut him off, her eyebrow arching up with a non-verbalized threat. "You will be staying as far away from her as possible." There was something about her tone that went beyond what seemed like normal concern. She didn't know me so why was she so concerned for me? I could see from a mile away he was a player, and I could take care of myself.

"Nice to meet all of you," I uttered.

Other than everyone looking at me warily, the dinner went smoothly enough. I still felt tense and unsure of what I was doing here. They all had me baffled. This was not how people described Demons—sitting around the dinner table, talking and passing rolls to each other. It seemed surreal. Weren't they supposed to be off terrorizing villages and killing people? They seemed so normal, well as normal as Demons and Unseelie could be. And where was Lars? Did he join in these family dinners?

I looked around the table, watching everyone eating the delicious meal Marguerite had made.

"Is this how it is every night here?"

"Not always, but Marguerite," Rez nodded her head at Marguerite and smiled warmly at the woman, "likes us to eat as a family when we're all here." It was clear Lars was in charge, but when it came to the house, Marguerite and Rez ran the show. Rez represented the business part of the house, and Marguerite, the heart and soul. "For some of us our 'jobs' keep us away for a night or two a couple times each month; others, like Nic, go out most evenings, but his hours are late night."

I realized what would keep a siren away for a while, and I had a pretty good idea what would keep Nic out all night as well. I didn't fully understand about the others but knew better now than to ask. I wasn't at all sure I wanted to know anyway. Ignorance might be bliss in this case.

After returning to my room, relief at being alone only lasted a few minutes. Ryan's howls of anguish and Ian's frightened face haunted me every time my lids closed. Staring at the ceiling, the minutes crawled by. The softness of the bed could not draw me into sleep. The nightmares of reality penetrated every dark corner. Desperate to talk to Torin, I tried over and over to contact him but with no results. I needed to know my friends were okay—that he would watch out for them.

Hours passed and nothing. Sighing, I swung my legs over the bed and stood up. It was right then I felt the tug. It was so commanding and strong I couldn't stop myself from plunging into it. My body fell to the floor, comatose.

"Torin? Torin, where are you?" I yelled the moment my lids lifted. We were back in the forest where he usually pulled me. His favorite spot.

"I am here," he murmured behind me.

I hopped up, turning to face him. "They have my friends, Torin. Samantha killed Ian. Are they okay? You didn't answer me. I tried to contact you."

"Calm down," he soothed. "I know what has transpired. I was there with Her Majesty when your friends were brought in so I had to ignore your calls."

"Lorcan took them... Samantha killed Ian... She killed him..." Emotion took charge of my mouth, words spilling out, spouting out the horrible truth again.

His arms wrapped around me, pulling me into his warm, strong body. "I know. I am so sorry," he mumbled, kissing the top of my head.

I tucked farther into him, seeking his solid, protective form. "I've lost everything. My friends, my family, my home. I can't... Ian's dead. Ken, Josh, Ryan, my dad..."

"I know." He held me tight.

"I have to get them out. I can't sit here. I have to get them out. They shouldn't be there. I will trade myself."

"No." Torin pulled away; his hands gripped tightly to my arms. "Ember, you cannot let her have you. She will only use you to kill more innocent people. She wants Earth back and will not stop until all humans are either dead or enslaved. If you give yourself over, you will not only destroy those people you love so much, but all those innocent human lives as well." His deep blue eyes focused intently on mine. "Do you understand? You cannot give her what she wants. It will be even *worse for your family. They will be the first she kills. You staying away is their only protection. Do you hear me?"*

*My head fell forward, agony and defeat weighed heavily on my shoulders. I was so ready for people to stop using logic on me. Plus my deal with Lars kept me from acting on a foolish whim. Feeling helpless, I tucked my head back under his chin, seeking comfort.*

*"Tell me you understand," he pleaded.*

*"I understand."*

*Torin pulled me into another tight hug, his lips like feathers against the top of my head. "Do not scare me like that. You cannot afford to act irrationally. When it is time, I will help you. Okay?"*

*I nodded against him. "Why didn't you tell me who Lars was?"*

*"I can only tell you what her bonds allow. The Queen has exceedingly tight rein on me."*

*Something in his statement made me sad. His life was not his own; his freedom was not his own. He pushed and bent the rules as far as he could for me. There was a connection between us I could not deny, and it scared me.*

*"Why would you choose this life? You're almost a slave."*

*He exhaled. "It is an honor. My father was her father, the King's, First Knight."*

*My eyebrows hit my hairline.*

*"No, Ember, it's not what you're thinking. That is something the Queen turned it into." He looked away with guarded embarrassment. He was a sex slave. He had no control over his own body and how it was used.*

I shuddered. I had no doubt she probably brought her authority and sick need for dominance in the bedroom as well. "I was destined to be First Knight, but I worked hard at it for you."

"For me?" Surprise widened my eyes.

"I knew being her knight would come with 'consequences,' but it also came with opportunities—the skill and ability to find you." Words took the wrong way back down my throat. I was speechless. "I do not really want to discuss this topic with you." He had moved away from me, more guarded.

"Do you love her?"

Torin stopped, his face becoming a stone fortress. He spun away, his back facing me. Many tense seconds passed. With a huff of air, he lowered his head. "I did. Once. A long time ago."

Jealousy gnawed at me. But then how dare I ask that? His answer was going to upset both of us in some way. Would I rather him be sleeping with someone he hated? Did I secretly hope he would be pining for me the entire time instead of living his life?

"I'm sorry. It's none of my business." I fidgeted with the end of my ponytail.

"That was the past. Now I have found you, and you are my present." He faced me again.

Panic constricted my chest. Barely seconds ago, I felt upset he hadn't been yearning for me the whole time, and now I wanted to bolt for the door.

I was so messed up.

"I need to know my friends and dad are all right."

"I promise I will watch over them and will not let anything happen."

*Warmness grew in my chest.* "*Thank you.*"
*He bowed his head in recognition.*

"*I want so badly to see them. To see for myself they're okay,*" *I said, twirling my hair tighter around my finger.*

"*You can do that.*" *Torin stepped up to me, brushing a strand of hair behind my ear.* "*Your abilities go further than simply dreamscaping. Your mother had an extraordinary gift of being able to dreamwalk. I have no doubt you have the same gift.*"

"*Dreamwalking?*"

"*You can turn your dreamscape location to where they are. Dreamwalking is different from dreamscaping. It takes a great deal more energy since it happens in a real place and time. I came to be in poor health the first several times I did it.*" *He rubbed his stomach.*

"*In poor health?*" *I asked, and then laughed when I realized what he meant.* "*You mean you threw up?*"

"*Yes.*" *He rolled his eyes at me.* "*Now, let's focus. Dreamwalking is also different since you cannot interact with anyone. You will be a ghost to them. They will not be able to see or hear you.*"

*All the times I wished to see Mark, I could have?* "*Why didn't you tell me I could do this before?*"

"*My apologies. It wasn't something that crossed my mind.*"

*The Dark Dwellers had the same response. All of them had grown up in the Fae world with knowledge of this stuff. They didn't understand what it was like to be me and not to know.*

"*Can you do this, too?*" *I asked.*

## Fire in the Darkness

"It was not a gift I was born with, but the Queen has bestowed some of her abilities on me. They allow me to bring her in so she can see what I am seeing without physically having to be there. Her Majesty finds this quite useful in her dealings."

"You mean she could be watching us right now?" I scrambled back from him.

"No. I can feel when she is there. She has a heavy presence, and I can always feel her when she is trying to get in. Do not worry. She is not aware of our meetings."

"O-kay." I felt uneasy. "So how does this work?"

"I will control this first dreamwalk, thus you can see how to do it. It can be a little disconcerting I warn you." His hands came up to my face, brushing over my lids. "Close your eyes. Otherwise you will get dizzy."

"And throw up all over you?" I smiled. He only cocked his head in exasperation. I closed my eyes.

"Now focus on their faces. You can choose any one of your friends since they are all together, or Mark."

Mark was my first stop. My thoughts zeroed in on him, remembering his smile and laugh, the way he had teased me in the morning or had called me Sunny D. A few seconds later a strange wooziness came over me, and it did take everything I had not to be sick.

"Okay, you can open them," Torin's voice spoke gently in my ear. My lashes flew up.

The sleek, dark wooden floors and stone walls glimmered under the floating fire-bulbs and flickering fireplace. The room was large, but void of furniture or anything personal besides a bed, table, and one chair.

*The chair was scooted close to the fireplace and occupied by a familiar form.*

*"Mark," I cried, rushing towards him. He did not look up or react.*

*"Ember, he cannot see or hear you," Torin responded.*

*Right. My mouth clicked shut. No point in calling out to him again, but I couldn't stop myself from going to him. With a relieved cry, I crouched in front of him, taking him in. He looked similar to when I had last seen him. Even though it had been a month and a half, there were still bruises and cuts healing on his face.*

*"Has he been hit recently?" My fingers went to touch his face, disappearing as they touched him. Okay, creepy.*

*"No. I promise you he has been treated well enough since he has been here. She will only hurt him when it benefits her. And, as you see, she has put him in one of the vacant castle rooms. He is not in the dungeon."*

*"If he hasn't been touched, why is he covered with cuts and bruises?" I longed to be able to touch him, to feel his arms around me in a bear hug. He was dressed in the same clothes and dried blood coated his collar. My gaze skimmed over him from head to toe. His body looked healthy enough so at least he wasn't being starved.*

*"Those are the wounds he obtained on the mountain that night." Torin remained along the wall, keeping to the shadows. "Remember time works differently here in the Otherworld. Not much time has passed compared to what you have experienced in the Earth realm."*

*The time thing was hard to really wrap my brain around. It had been almost two months for me and, to look at him, it seemed like it had only been two hours.*

"Oh, Mark." *My eyes started to water.* "I am so sorry."

*Mark stared at the fire; his eyes watched every lick and curl of the flames. Sorrow sunk deep in his eyes. He may have been physically healthy but not mentally. His agony tortured me.*

"I will not rest until I get you out of here. I promise. I love you." *Wiping the tears from my cheek I stood up, my resolve strengthened.* "Let's go. I also want to see my friends."

*Torin held onto me. Closing my eyes, I pictured my friends vividly in my head. Another whooshing, a feeling of extreme nausea, and we were in a room similar to Mark's. My four friends were here, along with four beds, four chairs, and one table.*

"Why didn't she tell us?" *Josh exclaimed. He sat in the windowsill. Gaping metal bars lined the window, wide enough for someone to slip through. They were probably more for looks as the tips of the trees outside the window indicated they were several stories up.*

"What would she have told us? Would any of us have believed her anyway?" *Kennedy sat on the bed; her legs folded under her.*

*Jared sprawled out on another bed, looking around the room.* "Guys, she hasn't known for long. She found out less than two months ago, right before the ES. Not that she would have told you. Humans aren't supposed to know about us. I shouldn't even be telling you this stuff, but it seems a little pointless now."

*"I don't care. She's supposed to be our best friend, Ken. She should have told us the truth. Didn't she trust us?"* Ryan piped up from the chair. *"Ian's dead because he was helping us hang flyers, to find our missing friend. If we had only known..."* Ryan started sobbing, his face in his hands, his shoulders shaking.

My guilt and anger began to suffocate me, spreading out to include Lorcan and the Queen. There was no forgiveness for what had happened to Ian. He shouldn't have been there. He never should have been involved in my world.

Kennedy rose from the bed and knelt down in front of Ryan and pulled him into a hug.

*"I know you are hurting, but Ian's death was not Ember's fault."*

Ryan continued to sob on her shoulder. *"Really, Ken? Where was she for the last month? Where was she when we were so scared and worried over her disappearance? Then the ES hit. I thought she was dead—gone forever. But, no, we find her with the Riders of Darkness, living this whole time with Eli Dragen."*

*"Hey, guys."* Jared sat up. *"Ember wasn't shacking up with us on some vacation. She was practically being held a prisoner there. After she caused the ES, she was on the run in Seattle, being hunted daily... so give her a break."* I had felt that Jared and I bonded over the days we spent together at the compound, and this only confirmed he had my back. He had grown into someone I really cared about. Like family.

That warm fuzzy quickly got squashed. *"She what?"* The entire room bellowed.

"She was the one who caused the Electrical Storm? Are you serious?" Josh shot up, wide-eyed, from his relaxed position.

Jared's flustered expression made me burst out laughing. Good luck with that one, I thought.

"Oh yeah, right... you guys didn't know." He then gave them a quick rundown of what he knew. I kept interjecting with what "really happened" much to Torin's amusement. Knowing they couldn't hear me didn't stop my trying. They would have kept drilling Jared, but after a while he put up his hand. "Guys, that's all I know. You'll have to hound her later."

The bitter memory of that night rotted a hole in my soul. It was the turning point of my life—and thousands of others. With the help of a young Fae boy, who was the equivalent of jumper cables, the Seelie Queen harnessed my powers and destroyed Seattle. All to pick a fight with the Unseelie King—Lars.

"Damn... this is all so insane." Josh shook his mop of blonde hair. "The girl I was building garden frames with a month and a half ago can level cities. She's like a walking superhero from a comic book."

Kennedy was kneeling in front of Ryan. He had stopped crying, but his face was carved with pain.

"I wish she had trusted us enough to tell us," Ryan muttered.

Reaching up, Kennedy rubbed Ryan's arm soothingly. "Would you have believed her if you hadn't seen it firsthand? I don't blame her. For any of it. This is not something you can confess without people thinking you're nuts. She was already fighting that."

*And just wait, Kennedy. You will be joining me on the list of nuts. My eyes closed briefly in fear. Please don't let the Queen find out what she really is, I chanted in my head.*

Ryan snorted, "Yeah, I guess. We always sensed something was different about her, but this..." Ryan rubbed his head. "I feel like I don't know who she is anymore. Our friend is not human. Oh God, my brain hurts again."

"What is Em exactly?" Josh directed his question to Jared. Jared pressed his lips together. His natural reaction was to stay silent. "Come on, man. We know she can explode things and take down cities. What will it hurt to tell us?"

Sitting up, Jared sighed. "Fine." You could tell he didn't want to talk. "She's a Dae."

"A what?" Josh replied. "What the shit is that?"

"She is half Fairy and half Demon."

Kennedy's hand went silently to her mouth.

"A Demon? Are you kidding? She's seriously a Fairy and a Demon?" Josh exclaimed.

"But it doesn't mean she's bad." Jared immediately turned defensive. "Demons aren't always evil. Ember's cool. But Daes are illegal in the Otherworld. Ember technically shouldn't be alive and that's why she was hiding with us. We were protecting her. Like I said, Ember wasn't lounging on some beach. She stayed away from you guys on purpose. She didn't want you to get involved because she knew it was dangerous."

Josh scoffed, "Too late for that."

The room went quiet.

*Josh stomped his feet onto the stone floor excitably. "Holy shit... this is insane. The Otherworld actually exists. What would all my counselors say now? They thought I was wasting my life with the videos, World of Warcraft, and now I am the one going 'suck that, bitches'. Wonder if I can actually kill some real trolls."*

*Kennedy, Ryan, Jared, and I stared at him with our mouths open. Josh was taking this way differently from how I imagined he would.*

*"Ember, your Earth night is coming to an end. We have to go," Torin said kindly.*

*Nodding, I scanned my friends once again. I missed them so much it hurt. "I will get you guys out of here," I vowed to them, and then turned, letting Torin lead me away.*

*We were back in the forest where our first dreamscape took place. Without words, I went up to Torin and wrapped my arms around him. He gave me more than he could ever know, even though seeing and hearing them hurt more than I imagined. To know my family was all right meant everything to me. They were being treated better than I thought. The urge to rescue them was still strong, but it was clear to me it would be foolish to rush in. I would do this right, with a plan.*

*Torin pulled me in tighter. "I am glad it helped."*

*I tilted my head back. "You have no idea. Thank you, Torin."*

*"You are welcome." His eyes lowered, locking onto my mouth. Suddenly aware of how tight and close our bodies were, tension filled any sliver of space left between us. I couldn't deny I was curious to know what it would feel like to have his lips on mine again. "I*

*would do anything to protect you and keep you safe. It is my job."*

*The warm feeling vanished as my head lurched up. I stepped out of his hold. "Your job?"*

*"Yes." His eyes narrowed in confusion at my sudden mood alteration. "I told you, now that I have found you, you are my priority. Since the day you were born, it was my job to protect you. Now I can. You are mine, Ember. We are destined."*

*So many aspects of his words bothered me. His romantic, sweet words earlier seemed to sour in my stomach.*

*"Why do you keep saying we're destined? It's freaking me out. No one controls my life. I decide. I am nobody's to own, and I am not your job." I crossed my arms.*

*A pained expression creased his forehead. "It is something I want to do. I only want to keep you safe and protected."*

*"I can take care of myself. You cannot guard me from everything, nor do I want you to. I don't need a protector; I need a partner."*

*"I cannot stop my desire to do what is proper. To do my rightful duty."*

*"Rightful duty? Who says stuff like that anymore?" I shook my head and took a deep breath.*

*"We were intended for each other before you were even born. You are my betrothed."*

*"You're what?" I sputtered in disbelief. "Did you say betrothed? Like in marriage—an arranged marriage?"*

*"Ember, please, calm down."*

"Calm down? I've had to process a lot of crap lately, but this one might push me over the edge. Did time actually stop in the Otherworld? Are you still using the 'Beginning of Time's Handbook'? Arranged marriages. Are you kidding me?" My voice rose higher.

"It's not like that. We are noble. The god and goddess brought us together. Most Fae can marry whomever they want, but you aren't most Fae. Your bloodli—" He stopped, dread filling his face. "She's coming."

With that I was shoved back into blackness. When my eyes popped open, I was on the floor in my room at Lars' compound. The bed, only feet away, was perfectly made. Sinnie had struck again.

I had been betrothed to Torin? Was that before they realized I was the devil's spawn? My mom had been extremely independent and raised me to be as well. Was it something beyond her control? If I wasn't a Dae, would I be marrying Torin right now? I cared for Torin. It wasn't him I had the problem with. It was the fact I had no choice in it.

Huffing, I got up, climbing back into my crisp, clean sheets. *What did Sinnie do, starch and iron them while I was unconscious on the floor?* Plopping back into my pillows, I pulled the covers over my head.

My life had been a constant revelation—in a continual state of change. I knew we would have to fight the Queen. I needed to be ready for what I knew was coming—both mentally and physically. But there was so much I couldn't prepare for. After everything, why did I feel the worst was to come?

Stacey Marie Brown

# NINETEEN

The morning came faster than I wanted. Well, if you could call it morning—the moon, still suspended in the sky, told me it was not a time I should be up or functional. "Roosters would find this time of morning offensive," I whined when Alki barged into my room, blinding me as he flicked on the lights. I preferred the night. I wasn't surprised Demons were nighttime creatures. My hatred of mornings and night owl preference had established itself at a very early age. Unfortunately, training for a war did not follow my bedtime preferences. I needed to bring this up at the next Otherworld council meeting.

"This is when training starts. Get up. Dress now. I will be waiting downstairs," he barked at me before he left.

Sleep had not come easily for me. I felt as if I had just fallen asleep when Alki came barreling into my room. Now I pulled a pillow over my head. I would not even last a week if this was the time I had to rise every morning. Wonder what would be the punishment for backing out of a Demon deal?

Images of Mark and my friends invaded my head. *You selfish bitch, get up.* The disgust at myself for even teasing about quitting—just because I didn't want to get up early—produced enough anger to get me out of bed, dressed, and downstairs within minutes.

"First training so you will not eat." Alki motioned me to keep moving for the door.

I wasn't exactly hungry yet but couldn't stop myself from asking why.

"Because it will be wasted. You will only throw it up," Alki responded.

I knew I shouldn't have asked. Training was going to be even worse than I imagined.

Two hours later, I was pretty sure I had greatly underestimated that sentiment. Military training would have been like going to a spa compared to this. Alki was relentless and appeared to enjoy causing extreme pain a little too much. Maybe this was his "vice." I wouldn't have been surprised.

He had me running up hills, stairs, through mud, doing sprints, and long distances till I threw up. Then he started me on weights until my arms and legs could barely move. And that was only the warm-up. Next we started on my first lesson in martial arts. Within the first hour alone, I had already contemplated quitting about twelve times.

By the time Koke and Maya came in, I had thrown up four more times, all bile and a tiny bit of the power drink he allowed me to have.

I spent my lunch break trying to find a way for the sandwich to make its way to my mouth—without moving my arms because they ached so much. Not an easy feat. After lunch, Maya worked on my earth powers, but Alki was in charge of my overall training so he remained, pushing me to my limit.

"Concentrate," he commanded.

"I'm trying."

"Ember, you must not only be able to connect with the earth but be able to regulate what it gives you. It has no filter. You have to become the filter," Maya spoke sharply. English was not her first language, and she pronounced each word carefully.

"I'm filtering. I'm filtering. I am filtering all over the place." I rolled onto my back, rubbing at the headache pounding in my temples.

"Sit up. We are to go again." Maya sat on the ground across from me, her legs folded. She was in baggy, brown cotton leggings and a loose-fitting shirt. Today her short hair was wild and natural, sticking out over the leopard-print scarf wrapped around her head like a headband. Her skin was a rich caramel color. She was gorgeous, full of confidence and strength, and definitely commanded attention. Even though she was connected to the earth, I could sense her powers weren't always used for good or for healing. She could probably take down countries with a tiny curse, destroy crops with a hex, and turn a cheating husband into a snake. I had to be careful around her.

"Wouldn't it be better if we were in the forest or something?"

"No. You won't always be touching nature. You need to learn how to bring it to you without having to feel it."

Exhaling air, my head fell back and my lids closed.

"Open yourself to it. It knows you, recognizes you. It will listen if you command it."

Energy from the earth buzzed at the tips of my fingers. Earth and life were everywhere. There was a forest outside the door; I simply had to reach out to it. Feeling the force dance around, I called it to me. A spurt of energy struck me, almost electrical, but within me.

"Let it stream through you, but bridle it." Maya's words entered my ears.

Sweat beads gathered at my hairline. Squeezing my eyebrows together, I tried again, more forcefully. Too forcefully. A rush of energy slammed into my body, trying to get in all at once. My system couldn't take it. With a roar, it burst out of me and into the room and everything in its path. The lights erupted with a surging explosion. Everyone dove for cover. Alki pulled Koke under a table, while Maya scrambled under another one.

"Control it, Ember," Maya yelled.

It was too late. Loss of control spiked my adrenaline with fear. Sparks grabbed onto the electrical force filling the area. Flares of energy and fire popped and burned through the room.

"You're letting your fear dictate," Koke screamed at me from under the table.

Shit, yeah, I was. This kind of power was terrifying. But I had no idea how to fight my fear and regain command.

Another ball of fire slammed across the room, hitting the wall heater.

"Oh crap" was all I could utter.

A loud boom ripped through my eardrums. Suddenly the room exploded. Walls were demolished, exposing the daylight. I went flying through the air. Chunks of wood, shards of glass, and fragments of plaster flew past me in a tornado of intensity. I heard bones crunching as my back hit the grass yards away from the burning building.

Feeling woozy, it took me a couple of tries to sit up. When I did, I almost fell back again. The wooden shed where we had been working was a burning mass of lumber although there actually wasn't much left to burn. It had been blown to bits.

Quickly, I looked around for everyone. Alki, Maya, and Koke were sprawled in different areas across the lawn, covered with blood. Struggling to get up, I half crawled over to their bodies. Maya was the closest. Deep gashes covered her face and body, and her eyes were shut tight.

"Maya? Are you okay?" I gently touched her.

She grunted out some unintelligible words.

"What?"

Maya's eyes slowly opened and shifted to mine. "I was not sure I liked you. Now I know. I definitely do not." She was serious, but it still made me snort—probably more out of relief she was okay enough to be considering whether she liked me or not.

"I second that." Koke struggled to sit up. Blood covered almost every inch of her body as well.

Alki stayed on his back, but his voice was nonchalant. "We will have to continue to work on your skills in this area. I do not feel you have gotten a handle on them yet."

There was a pause. Then crazed laughter came from the rest of us. I flopped back on the ground. Stunned and dazed, I heard alarmed voices coming from the main house, heading for us.

"Aren't you the little fire-starter?" Nic said from the doorway of my bedroom later that day.

Too exhausted to move, I grunted in response.

Nic chuckled. "Yeah, I heard you pretty much destroyed the training room and almost took out three Fae in the process. Good work."

Even though they would heal quickly, I felt awful for hurting Koke, Maya, and Alki. Okay, maybe not Alki; he had enjoyed torturing me too much.

"Lars wants to talk with you. He's waiting for you in the library. Find the strength as he is not a patient man."

I just wanted to be left alone for five minutes to sleep. Possibly forever. Was it too much to ask? Willing my body to move, I groaned while trying to sit up. Every muscle in my body screamed in protest. I could not decide what hurt more. Between the blast, the weights, and the running, my entire body hurt equally.

"Let me help you." Nic's mischievous smile appeared. Too tired to fight him, I let him help me stand and walk me downstairs. I even ignored when his hands dropped lower on my back than necessary.

"Ember, please join me," Lars greeted me.

"Thank you, Nic, but I think she is capable of handling it from here."

Nic nodded and gave my butt a squeeze, before walking out the door. It took too much effort to glare at him so I stepped into the room. A gasp came from my lips. In front of me was a beautiful, floor-to-ceiling library stocked full of books.

*I found my happy place.*

The room was located in the turret. Windows curved with the rounded room and covered an entire wall two stories high, letting in tons of natural light. A large window seat was built-in, a dream spot for a reading nook with every other inch covered in books. A catwalk above my head held even more book-lined shelves. A door told me there was access from upstairs. With nerdy ecstasy, I sighed.

Lars sat at a table in the middle. This was the first time his presence didn't command my attention. My gaze was focused on all the books, dying to devour them.

Lars cleared his throat, "I have found your ignorance of the Otherworld appalling. So, besides your training with Alki, you will be schooled in matters of history, language, and geography of the Otherworld." Lars clasped his hands on his lap. "Since you know next to nothing—and your understanding of this information is highly important—I will personally be handling your education."

My stomach clenched. Something told me I would soon be wishing for Alki's trainings instead.

Lars pushed a book towards me. "Sit."

Painstakingly, I lowered myself down into the chair; my arms trembled as I pulled the book towards me. "What is this?"

"Our history," Lars replied. "Our events are chronicled differently than human history books, and they are not exactly the most consistent, but at least we get it accurate. I'll want you to read this." He tapped the cover. "But tonight I want to give you a brief rundown of Dae history. Little has been recorded." He tapped his fingers on the table in thought. "I will assume you know nothing. Why she kept you so ignorant I will never know. She shouldn't have hidden you; she *should* have brought you to me."

"Do you mean my mom?" I sat up straighter. "Why would she bring me to you? And who are you to judge? She did the best she could." I crossed my arms in a huff.

"You really do have your mother's stubbornness." Lars shook his head and began his history lesson.

For the next fifteen minutes he rattled off what little information was known about Daes. Most of it I had already learned. But there were a few things new to me. "Is every Dae different depending on their parents?" I asked.

"Yes. The particular power and strength of a Dae depends on the parents' abilities." He leaned back in his chair. "Combining a noble-blooded Fay with a full Demon is not the only thing making Daes so powerful. Mixing Daes with Light and Dark creates powers so strong most can't handle them. Daes tend to 'short-out'." He paused. "You, Ember, not only have all these powers in abundance, but you inherited the rare combination of mind, fire, and nature powers from your parentage. You are even unique in the Dae world. I am sure you have experienced the ability of what humans call psychokinesis and pyro-telekinesis?"

I nodded. One of my first vivid memories was when I was three. Mom and I were out shopping, and there was a stuffed dog I really wanted. Mom had said no, took it from my hands and put it on a top shelf out of my reach. I was really upset. I couldn't understand why I couldn't have the stuffed animal. I recalled looking back up at it and wanting it so badly. All of a sudden it was in my hands. When mom turned around and saw it back in my arms, she screamed my name and tore it out of my hands.

Now looking through clearer eyes, I realized she had been more scared someone saw what I did than anything. She had never cared before what people thought, but that time had been different.

When I got upset electrical devices went on the fritz. But the huge fire, which almost burned down my first high school in Monterey, clued me in that there was more to it. I had tried to ignore it, but now I knew. It had always been me. I had blown out our Christmas lights when I was ten, I had caused a "strange" dining room fire at a restaurant when I was seven, and I had started the fire in the little old lady's house where we lived when I was four.

"You inherited not only powers but also your physical appearance from your parents. Daes became easy targets because of that. A Demon's eyes are a yellow color. Noble Fay have blue or purple tones. Eyes became the easy tell-tale sign of a Dae because they have one of each. Some, like you, also had the distinguishing feature of the two-tone hair."

*Huh?* My mom had orangish-brown colored eyes. If she was Fay, why didn't she have the violet-blue color? Her hair also had been more auburn than the bright red of my streaks. She had been hiding from the Otherworld. Did she change her hair color and wear contacts? Or maybe she glamoured her hair and eyes so she would remain better concealed to keep Fae from finding her? What else did my mom change to keep us safe?

"Can Fae glamour others besides themselves?"

"No." Lars shook his head. "No Fae can. Even the most powerful Fae only have the ability to glamour themselves and inanimate objects."

I took this in. My mom couldn't change my looks, so she changed hers to hide us the best way she could. There was so much more I wanted to know about her. "Since my mother told me nothing, what do you know about my Fay side?"

"Well, as you know, you have the ability to absorb and use the energies from nature and the earth, hence, the debacle today. You have an abundance of power and no aptitude to use it."

*Ouch, that stings.*

"Even though your earth power comes from the Light side, it actually is much more dangerous. The earth contains unlimited energy and tapping into it can destroy and kill you and others if you don't know how to use it properly."

For example—an hour ago.

*And Seattle.*

Nature had always soothed me and made me feel strong, as if it wanted to give me everything it had. It knew me—was part of me. To know those abilities could destroy as easily as they could heal and create was frightening. Was this the power I felt taking over me and consuming me? There were times my power had hurt people, like today. Or when I had hurt people while on the run like those kids in the Red Cross shelter who got hit with the bake cart when my fear got the better of me. How much worse it could have been if I had taken on more power. I had harmed a lot of people, but now I really understood they had gotten off easy. I could have killed them. A chill curled around me, causing me to shiver.

Lars must have noticed the concern in my eyes. He replied, "We will help you manage it."

I looked away. "My mother was part of the noble court." It was more statement than question. I knew she had been. She had to be Fay to have created me, but it still didn't feel right. She was so real and down to earth, wearing jeans and t-shirts, loving motorcycles and blues music. When I had met the Queen, she had not been at all how I pictured a noble Fay to be.

"Yes," Lars nodded. "She was one of the most beautiful women in court, maybe anywhere. Definitely the most loved. She had many admirers, which her husband hated. He was an enormously jealous man."

"My mother was married before?" Another secret she had kept from me. Another detail that felt wrong.

"Fay nobility do not have the luxury of marrying for love."

I had heard something like that. Perhaps escaping to Earth was not only to save me, but her as well. Was she a victim of an arranged marriage also? Even if Torin was everything I might want in a husband, if I even wanted to get married, which I didn't, no one should be forced to marry. It was strange to think of myself in that world—in the elite noble class. *Me, noble? Yeah, right.* It felt as false as thinking of my mother as one.

"Obviously, her husband was not my father..."

"No, he was not. Be grateful for that."

"Not a nice guy, huh?"

Lars pressed his lips together, giving me enough of an answer.

"Did you know my real father—the sperm donor?"

Lars grimaced. "Your mother's affairs did not interest me. We have other details to discuss now."

"He raped my mother, didn't he?"

Lars got up from his chair. "Ember, this is not the time."

"Did they love each other?"

"Ember, I said enough." His tone alerted me to stop talking.

Grumbling, I slumped back in my chair, my arms crossed.

"Sometimes you act so much like one of those human, teenage girls." He rubbed his forehead.

"Well, up until a few months ago I thought I was."

"You are not. You need to start remembering that." He jammed a book back onto the shelf. "You are a mortal of the Otherworld, powerful, strong, and feared by most, including the Queen."

"What does that mean?"

"I will not say you are immortal, as you could die. But Fae live thousands and thousands of years."

"Thousands of years? H-how is that possible? That can't be..." I stopped talking, my brain trying to wrap around this new information.

"This is the problem. Even now you do not think of yourself as one of us, but as a human. You are not one of them." He said "them" with obvious superiority. "You are nothing like them; you do not have their weaknesses. We do not die so easily, and we age very slowly."

"How slowly are we talking here?"

"Just as time is not the same in the Otherworld, neither do we mature at the same rate. Years are not the same to us as they are to humans. It takes us centuries to age even a little. What is equivalent to a human decade is barely a few hours to us. If we stay in a certain area for a time, most Fae use glamour to age their looks, so humans do not get suspicious." He headed for a bookshelf.

"But we can die? How?" I demanded.

"Our physical make-up is different from humans so we don't die from anything like diseases, gunshot wounds, or old age. That's not to say it wouldn't hurt like hell if you were shot or you wouldn't prefer to die if a semi-truck hit you, but we won't actually die. We would eventually heal, but we are not invincible. We can die on Earth by fire or decapitation, and also weapons made in the Otherworld can kill us here. In the Otherworld we can die much easier—from our own diseases, weapons, and eventually old age. But that is not something you will need to worry about for several thousands more years."

He continued to scan the bookshelf. "There's a secret no Fae would freely tell you because it is their ultimate weakness. As I do not suffer the same concerns, I will. Two times a year the realms collide, Earth and the Otherworld. Fae are extremely susceptible during those times, maybe even more than humans. They can die by the same means as a human but also by Otherworld means."

"When are those times?"

Pulling out a book, he flipped it open to a page and set the book down in front of me. "The first time that our realms bleed together is Samhain. You probably know it as Halloween. It is when we celebrate the end of the 'lighter half' of the year and the beginning of the 'darker half.' Beltane is the other, which is at the beginning of May. It is the beginning of the light half of the year, the exact opposite of Samhain. The barrier between Earth and the Otherworld comes down. When the veil is that thin, the magic is tremendous. Humans who are 'sensitive' can even feel it."

Halloween had always been a strange holiday for me growing up. All my friends loved getting dressed up and going trick-or-treating, but I had always felt unsettled and itchy, sensing I was missing something. The younger I was, the more I remember being aware of the tingling force humming in and around my body; the older I got, the more I denied it.

My mom had always pushed me to go out with my friends on Halloween. She rarely forced me to do anything, but she had purposely urged me toward normal, human activities. Now I knew why. She had known I felt the surge of our realms colliding and wanted to keep me from asking questions or figuring it out on my own. Maybe she was afraid I would start experiencing my powers. It was strange to think, during all those years, I had felt the energy of the worlds meshing, its power.

For so long I had hidden in the shadows, afraid of why I felt so different. But now I wrapped myself in the darkness, finally knowing where I belonged.

"So when the walls come down, we can die more easily?"

"Yes, Fae become very susceptible during that time, except for the rulers of the Otherworld. Neither the Queen nor I follow the same tenets. We do not die by the same means other Fae would. As ruler you have the extra luxury of knowing you are not so easily expendable."

"Oh, that's convenient," I muttered derisively.

"That is a benefit of being the ruler," Lars replied smugly. "There are more threats on us. We should not be as easy to kill."

"Is it you or is it the position that offers this?"

"The position. If I were not the Unseelie King, I would be subject to the same means of death as you. Being a monarch does not make me indestructible, though, as the last Unseelie King found out." His fingers skimmed along the bindings of the books. "The Queen is the same. Only one thing can kill her—a particular weapon." His hand stopped on a section of books. He tugged at the binding of one and a short sector of book spines peeled away. To anyone who didn't know better, they'd think they were normal books. But it was a shelf of fake books to cover up what was behind—a safe-like box. I stared at him, intrigued, waiting for him to resume.

"I presume you haven't heard of the four treasures of *Tuatha Dé Danann*. This book is the only one left of its kind, and it took me great pains to obtain it." He took a key from his pocket and opened the safe, pulling a book thicker than Rimmon's neck from the strongbox. Lars gently placed it on the table between us.

The book was bound in a soft, thin leather, or what I assumed was leather. It was from the Otherworld so it could have been unicorn skin for all I knew. Gold calligraphy was etched deeply into the cover. It looked so ancient and aged I could hardly decipher the writing on it. It took a moment to realize it wouldn't have mattered anyway since it was written in a language I didn't understand.

"What is it?" I stood to get a better look, my fingers reaching out to feel the edging of the book. Lars cringed but let me touch the soft leather. The moment the tips of my fingers connected with the buttery cover, energy zipped up my arm. Jerking my hand back, air slipped between my teeth. "What the hell?"

Lars smiled. "Our books are alive, taking and absorbing our knowledge. They can feel and experience people's energies, especially a book this old. This one is wise enough to know if someone wants to use it for good or bad."

"What do you want to use it for?" I looked up at him.

"Only a fool would be ignorant enough to think they could handle *this* book with an agenda." Lars caressed the cover, smoothly opening it. "You respect a book like this. It will let you in and confess all its secrets, if you are quiet enough."

The lure to touch it again was too much. Giving in, I let my fingers glide over the pages. Its life-force pulsed in my hand, as if introducing itself to me. I let it read me. An eagerness and excitement pulsed off the pages the longer my skin stayed in contact with it. "That is really weird," I laughed.

"I think it knows what you are. What you will be."

I pulled back, my gaze leveling at Lars. "What do you mean?"

"Before I get into that, let me finish the history lesson."

Knowing this wasn't going to be a simple lecture, I sat back down.

He sat down, continuing, "The *Tuatha Dé Danann* came to Ireland to be instructed in the magic arts, Druidry, knowledge, prophecy, and magic. They brought four magical items with them: The Cauldron of the Dagda, the Stone of Fal, the Spear of Lug, and the Sword of Nuada, also known as the Sword of Light.

"These magical items have been lost over time, and there has been a hunt for these treasures for centuries. Most Fae believe these items are a myth, a story that has been passed down. It is quite similar to how humans continue to hunt for the Holy Grail." He paused, watching me drink in the bits of knowledge he was giving me. I was always a history buff, but this was even more fascinating. "Except ours is not a story. These treasures exist."

My eyebrows popped up. "And you know this because?"

"That is not important. But there is no doubt they do exist, and you have a tie to one of these items."

"I'm tied to one? How?"

Lars clasped his hands together. "If you would let me continue, I will explain. You need to learn about only one of these items now, which is the Sword of Nuada—the Sword of Light—Nuada's Cainnel. This means a glowing, bright torch, and it is the most desired and by far the most powerful. The legend of the Sword of Light states no one has ever escaped from it once it has been drawn from its sheath, and no one can resist its power.

"For centuries the Queen searched for the sword. She tracked it down, but when she sent her First Knight to acquire it, someone else had gotten to it. Aneira learned a Druid helped hide it, putting a concealing enchantment on it. Enraged and terrified, she killed and tortured hundreds, maybe thousands, of Druids to find who took it. When that did not work, she figured if all Druids died, the curse would end, so she annihilated the entire Druid race. The curse did not break."

"Oh my God..." I trailed off. Kennedy. Is this what happened to Kennedy's people? Why her real parents hid her from the Queen? Eli had told me a little of the tale, but getting the full story was much different. But how did this all tie to me?

"The Queen fears the sword and will not rest until it is found. She is afraid of anything she cannot dominate." Lars opened the book and carefully flipped through the pages. "Another, stronger reason exists for her fear of Daes and the Sword of Light." He stopped, landing on the desired page. "A prophecy."

"A prophecy?" *Of course, there has to be a prophecy.*

Lars turned the book towards me, pointing at a page. I leaned in farther to see it better although it was pointless since it was in a language not known on Earth.

His finger skimmed down the page, and he muttered to himself before he found what he was looking for.

"Here it is—

*By one of the Light, Darkness will take its revenge.*

*A bloodline that cannot be repressed will rise to power.*

*A descendant will take the throne.*

*Blood will seek to kill you.*

*She who possesses the Sword of Light will have the power.*"

"O-kay, what does it mean?"

"Well, as usual, prophecies can be interpreted in many ways. Only a few types of Fae exist who the Queen cannot dominate, but only one species is both Light and Dark—a Dae. Her fear of Daes is not only because they can't be glamoured or controlled. Aneira is convinced a Dae will kill her with the Sword of Light and take the throne. Is this true? I do not know for sure.

"Prophecies are abstract and unclear on purpose. Either way, the Queen has found an excuse to kill your kind. I feel she has shaped the perceptions of Daes through propaganda and lies. If she got her people scared enough, they would start demanding the Daes be 'taken care of.' She then presents herself as a Queen who cares and protects her people by handling the danger.

"Only a select few know of the prophecy. I made sure I was one of those. It is my business to know what others are hiding."

I had a feeling his business thrived off of blackmail, deceit, and shady dealings.

"Okay, so she murders all the Daes because she is afraid of what she thinks the prophecy is telling her that she will be killed by a group she cannot control, which is both Light and Dark, wielding the Sword of Light, and they will take the throne. Did I miss anything?" I couldn't deny it made sense why she was frightened of us.

Lars replied, "Remember, perception and truth are two different things." Lars leaned in closer to me. "You, Ember, fit the prophecy more than you know. Aneira has been after you since your birth. Her need to take revenge will soon be outweighed by her fear and the desire to see you dead. Her lust for control has kept you alive—for now. I feel this will be coming to an end soon."

He didn't have to tell me that. I could feel my life had an expiration date. The only thing I wanted to accomplish was to see my family safe and the Queen dead before my death. That was enough.

# TWENTY

"Again, Ember." Alki moved into the first stance, his sword raised and waiting for me.

I gripped my hilt tighter, trying to lift it up. A small whimper escaped my lips. We had been training non-stop for the last three and a half hours, and there wasn't an inch of me that didn't burn in agony. Alki was relentless with my training. At the end of each session, I could barely move. On several occasions I actually fell face first into my dinner. One time it was soup. I swore I could smell beef broth for a week.

Even after months of training, it never got easier. Probably because he kept adding different and harder challenges, switching between physical fighting and mental control, both extremely exhausting. I always thought I wanted to be practicing the other form, until I was.

"You think your enemy will wait for you to raise your sword?" When he hit mine, it flew out of my hands. "Come on. Again."

"I need a break." I bit my lip, suppressing overtired groans.

"No. No break."

I picked up my sword and lunged at him. His sword clanged with mine as he blocked my move. I spun around, and my sword sliced through the air as it headed for his side. He twisted, escaping my blade. We circled one another, parrying each other's moves.

"Bend your knees; keep close contact with the ground. Only video games and dead fools flip and jump around. You are unable to switch direction quickly if you are in the air. You must be ready to move and change course in a split second," he reminded me as we moved around each other. "Be fully aware of your enemy and surroundings. Death can come from anywhere at any time."

I had heard the same spiel every day, but it was worth thinking about constantly. My awareness of my surroundings had magnified since these lessons began. It frightened me how unaware and vulnerable I had been before. Now I could never relax. I was so highly in tune it bordered on paranoia. I had, on a handful of instances, flipped Marguerite on her back when I thought someone was sneaking up. The older woman would get up, shake her head at me, tsk as if I had just left my socks on the floor, then continue on to wherever she was going. I adored her.

"Focus, Ember," Alki yelled at me to get my attention as he lunged. I parried and riposted, our blades colliding. He encircled his blade around mine, twisting the sword out of my hand. The loud clang as it hit the floor erupted off the walls. I jumped back. My eyes never left him as I reached for my dagger in my boot, the one Eli gave me. I had cut a space between the leather and the lining to keep it safely tucked away and easy to grab.

Alki had taught me, early on in our training, never to be without a weapon of some kind. There were several times he had snuck up on me in the library or kitchen that had me so paranoid I slept and took a shower with it. Now it was like a piece of jewelry that I never took off. It felt naked without it.

Alki spun and lunged, almost prevailing, but I retreated in time, gripping the handle of my blade tighter. I spun to the side and carved my knife down to his legs. I tapped the blade against his calves, mimicking slicing the back of his legs to render them useless.

"Ha!" I victoriously yipped, but as he fell to his knees, he twisted, stabbing his blade towards me, my victorious celebration evaporating.

"Never count your enemy out until they're dead." He shook his head and got back up on his feet. "But better."

"Wow, was that actually a compliment?" I gasped, trying to catch my breath.

"Compliments only soften you and will not help you survive."

I groaned and flopped onto the ground, sweat dripping down my face. "Feeling good about myself would make me more confident, therefore, a better fighter." He sent me a dubious look. "Do you ever relax? Do something because it's fun?"

"Yes."

"And what would that be?" I propped myself on my elbows, my eyebrow cocked.

"*Ninjuitsu.*"

I fell back with laughter. "That's so sad."

"I am a Demon, Ember, not human."

"Most of the others here seem to have fun, you know, on their days off from eating children."

"Not me."

"Yeah, I gathered that." I sighed and with great effort pushed myself off the ground, stuffing my dagger back into my boot. "We done?"

"Yes, for today."

I gave Alki a bow of respect, picked up my fallen sword, stowed it in the chest, and high-tailed it out of the room before he changed his mind.

The few stairs up to my room were extra torturous to my aching muscles this evening.

"Ember, there you are," Rez's voice came from behind me. I turned to look over my shoulder. Her long, dark hair hung loosely around her stunning face as she stared up at me from the base of the stairs.

"I just finished training and was going to go soak my body in the tub until dinner."

"Lars wants to speak with you now."

"Rez..." I pleaded.

She looked at me debating, and then sighed. "Fine, I didn't see you. But you'd better hurry before he hears you are back."

"Thank you." I pushed myself up the stairs, hobbling quickly to my room.

I locked the door behind me as soon as I entered and headed straight for the tub, stripping as I went, leaving a trail of clothes behind. I looked around as I waited for the tub to fill. I considered this my room, but nothing in it was really mine. That's what I liked about it. Nothing made me hurt, nothing invoked the memories I had locked away, and nothing here reminded me of my old life. It was blank and void of emotion—the way I wanted it.

It had been over five months since my arrival. And every day I spent submerged in training, reading old history books and texts of the Otherworld, finding out what little there was about Daes, and learning about my powers. Nothing of my old self survived the day in the forest when Ian was killed. I gave up drawing, writing, or doing anything creative, which used to give me joy. Joy had lost its meaning. I tried not to think about Mark or my friends locked away in the Otherworld. It only caused my volatile feelings and emotions to surface—emotions I did not want to feel. Every day that I didn't go after them piled more guilt and frustration on me. The deal I made with Lars also kept me from being imprudent. The repercussions of breaking a contract with a Demon were probably too awful to think about. I didn't know how to get to my friends, and Torin was being extremely elusive about helping me.

Instead, I buried my feelings and focused on learning about my powers—powers I once thought of as dark. Dark held a different meaning to me now. It was not good or bad, but neutral, only good or bad by your intent. The kind of focus I needed let little else in, like thoughts and sentiments. I was usually too exhausted at the end of the night to think of anything more than sleep.

This night was not one of those. My mind couldn't fight the thoughts. Stepping into the tub, my muscles melting in the hot water, I sighed, laid back and tried to relax. The silence finally let my mind wander to a time when I was happy. When I had friends and family. The world and I had both changed so much.

It had been over six months since the ES, and Seattle was slowly rebuilding itself. About three months ago, the phone lines went back up and electricity returned to the area. Neither of the Fae compounds I had lived in had suffered from any of these outside problems.

The Seattle area, and much of Washington, would never be the same. The wounds had been too extensive not to leave huge, ugly scars. The death toll had been 5,673, a number embedded in my mind. I had to live with this every day. And those were only the bodies accounted for. There were many who were considered "missing." The truth was their bodies had probably been burnt and might never be recovered.

Speculation about me—that no hospital even had reports of my birth—added fuel to the rumors. I had disappeared that fateful day in April, as well as Mark, stumping everyone. The paper said records showed he had gotten off the plane in Portland from Japan; eyewitnesses spotted him getting into a uber before vanishing without a trace.

The media had gone ballistic when the police found blood in my house and on the driveway. The coroner only added to the mystery when his reports came back stating the type of blood was unknown and wasn't even human blood. He was right. It was blood from me, Jared, and Vek, the Strighoul.

Newspapers and the Internet kept me apprised of my own disappearance, as well as my friends' and Mark's. I was suspected of murder. The fact Weiss had seen me running covered with blood was unquestionable proof of my guilt. Papers went crazy with the knowledge I was still alive and might be responsible for the disappearances. Weiss only encouraged these rumors. He accepted no other theory. It probably chafed him he had yet to find my friends' bodies. He couldn't lay the full charges at my door and have my picture splashed up on America's Most Wanted list. I had no doubt I was on the wall in Olympia's police station. Weiss would never be able to fulfill his dream. He would find no bodies. No proof. There was only one body to find, and the Dark Dweller's land was well warded. The cops would never discover Ian's remains.

I couldn't imagine the pain and confusion my friends' families were going through. Every day of not knowing had to be unbelievable torture. Someday, I hoped my friends could get back to their families. They had lost so much. Suspecting something was unusual about me, they never imagined how much my differences would affect them. I had to stay strong and believe I would get them out.

I had visited them only a few more times in the dreamwalks since the first time with Torin. It was painful and negatively affected my concentration. With Alki you only had room for one thing to be in your head. Fighting. My attention lacked on the days after a dreamwalk, and I paid for it. Between my heart hurting and the extra time he held me at the gym to get my fighting sequence down, I went to see them less and less.

Eli was another subject I tried to stuff so far down it would take a crane to dislodge. Funny thing about passion, it could easily turn into hate. The lies, the deception, even my desire for him only increased the rage I felt. He wouldn't leave me in peace, mentally or physically. I could feel him sulking around the outskirts of the property, letting me know he was there, without crossing the wards. No one besides me picked up on his presence, but I couldn't ignore it. It was raw and primal. I was conflicted in the need for him and the desire to punch him. And not in the fun, kinky way.

Torin was the only one I looked forward to seeing—my link to my friends and father. We had only able to dreamscape a few times because he felt the Queen hovering close to him. He was afraid she would discover our secret, and his paranoia grew each day. He was glad I had found Lars, but at the same time he was very uneasy with me being among the Dark. No matter what the Queen did, Torin would always remain faithful to the Light.

I personally didn't trust either side, but if the Light Fae were the so-called good ones, then I was fine with being on the "bad" side. The Light wanted to destroy me; the Dark only wanted to make me stronger. I didn't know how corrupt or nefarious Lars really was, but killing or using me to destroy Earth was not in his plans. I no longer feared or hated my Demon heritage. There had always been a dark part of me, but it was now something I desired.

Light was blinding; it burned you. You did not see the true darkness hiding inside it. Dark was sensual and luscious, something you wanted to dive into, like melted chocolate.

Torin saw the changes in me. He never said anything, but I could tell he did not like how easily I accepted my Demon side, allowing it to grow stronger every day. He'd never admit it, but I could sometimes sense his true feelings about my Demon part. It secretly appalled him.

"Ember, are you in there?" Nic pounded on my door.

Tempted to remain quiet, hoping he'd eventually go away was futile. "Yes," I sighed. "I'm in the bath."

"Well, get out. Lars wants to see you right now."

He always wanted to see me "right now." I rubbed at my face, irritated. All I wanted was ten minutes to myself. Was it at all possible in this house?

"Ember?" Nic's voice rose. "Do I have to come in there and drag you out myself?"

*"Holy fuck that would be a bad idea,"* one side of my brain commented; while the other side screamed out, *"Yes, please."*

Nic was trouble—a gorgeous, sexual, bodice-ripping-fantasy kind of trouble. I had no doubt he would be an incredible lover. But he was bad news...really, really bad news. That's what I kept telling myself anyway.

"No. I'm coming." I scrambled out of the tub. The threat of him coming into my room while I was naked gave me much more vitality than I thought I possessed. I dressed as quickly as possible, throwing on a pair of sweats and a hoodie. My hair was wet when I opened up the door. Nic leaned against the frame.

"It would have been much more fun if you had let me come in and get you."

My stomach fluttered as the Spanish god looked down on me with an expression that would cause most women's panties to drop.

That's what you get with an Incubus. He had been easy to figure out—a Demon that seduces humans and steals their life force through sex. Being Demon myself I was more or less immune to his power of seduction, which was the only reason I wasn't tearing his clothes off right then. As two Demons, we could have all the fun we wanted and no one would be mentally or physically hurt. But as much as I wanted it at times, I didn't let it go beyond flirting, though he often made me question my decision. The person who now stood before me was plain Nic, which was enticing enough. I pitied and envied the men and women whom he seduced. Talk about going out with a smile.

"Next time I won't ask." His eyes glinted, lowering his mouth really close to mine.

"And next time you'll get a shuriken in your gut."

"You know I prefer it rough." He winked at me, stepping back and starting down the hallway.

Since my nineteenth birthday, a few weeks back, both my hormones and powers had gone off the charts. Rez explained that my Fae body was now coming into its own, discovering its power. For me it also meant my sexuality. Damn if that wasn't off the charts, too. Rez figured, because no one really knew much about Daes, my Demon side might cause more extreme levels of emotion, which meant it wanted to feed. Lars had told me Daes fed off the energy from nature and magic.

All I knew was my hyperactive hormones craved sex, power, and energy all the time. This caused my powers to become even more volatile and sporadic. Let's just say there had been a lot of cold showers lately.

"Stop holding yourself back, Ember. Don't deny what you want. It's who you are." Nic whispered in my ear before disappearing down the stairs.

I stood there locked in place, desire rocking through my body. I breathed in deeply, gathering myself, and tried to think of dead bunnies and scary clowns before heading after Nic.

Living in a house full of Demons and dark Fae wasn't bad at all. We actually had a lot of fun, which shocked me. They liked who they were and made no apologies, and I was one of them. It could be easy to forget what they were. While at the house, they stayed in their human forms, they ate dinner, cracked jokes, and watched way too much reality TV. I didn't want to think that most of them probably got off on seeing human debauchery at its highest form.

I was comfortable in my new home, content enough in my surroundings to try to ignore the emotional memories of my old life.

Once at Lars' office, I knocked softly. "Come in," Lars called. Opening it, I stepped inside. He sat behind his desk, looking unbelievably handsome and elegant. I was sure his suit cost more than most people's cars, but I didn't want to think about how he got his money.

Lars visited the newly built, nonflammable, training bungalow whenever he was around, checking on me and how my instruction was going. We had our study lessons, but they had grown sporadic. He left me on my own to read 900-page books. Lately he had been gone a lot. When he was home, he was usually in his office. I would never describe him as a warm fuzzy, but there was a difference lately in how we interacted. There were brief moments when I saw something resembling kindness or fondness in his eyes; usually I figured I had imagined it.

"Have a seat." He nodded towards the chair in front of his desk. "There are some incidents I need to tell you about."

Keeping silent, I waited for him to continue.

Lars sat up in his chair. "I have spies keeping tabs on what is going on at the Seelie court. I learned a few days ago, through one of my infiltrators, the Queen has discovered you are with us."

I breathed in. "What does this mean?"

"That means she'll send someone here, demanding you be handed over. If I don't, she will declare war."

Gulping down my fear, I realized the time had finally arrived.

"Actually, her messenger arrived yesterday." His expression fluttered with annoyance at the memory. "I sent my answer back loud and clear."

I had a disturbing notion of what it meant. The Queen was minus one messenger.

"Why didn't you tell me yesterday?"

"I didn't want to interrupt your training session. There was nothing you could do, and it would only keep you from concentrating on your task, which is more important. If you want to survive this battle, you need every second of training possible."

Although I felt stunned by his revelation, I couldn't actually fault his logic.

"I will keep information from you until you need to know it. I want your full focus on training and managing your powers, and I want to ensure you and I both do everything to keep you alive." There was the slightest hint of emotions in his words. "We will double your training to get you prepared. I would rather you not die in the first five minutes."

*And there goes the "almost" nice moment.*

"Yeah, *that* would be embarrassing," I scoffed.

He shot me a displeased look. "Go have some dinner and get a goodnight's sleep. You will have a long, exhausting day tomorrow. I have already informed Alki of the plan."

A small whimper broke from my lips. I left the room torn between crying and wanting to run like hell out of this place.

Relieved that Nic wasn't waiting for me, I left Lars' office with a strong need to be alone. Darting through the kitchen, I grabbed a slice of pumpkin bread Marguerite had made earlier, then headed to the coatroom to get my thick, winter jacket and boots. Tugging them on, I took off into the cool, night air.

Foliage crunched under foot as I drifted through the forest. The late autumn moon broke through the hazy mist, giving the trees a sinister feel. Strange that Christmas was less than a month away. Last year at this time I was heading into finals at Olympia High, thinking about graduating and colleges. Well, that would never happen. Instead I lived with a Demon and trained for a battle with the Seelie Queen in a war between Light and Dark.

*Yep, exactly like college.*

My stomach churned with all the information trying to settle into my brain. A war was coming—a war I had little hope of surviving. What would happen to my friends and Mark? I needed them to be out of the

Otherworld and safe. This was the only outcome I would accept. My thoughts helped me keep a steady pace through the trees, walking along the property line. Some days I was so tempted to cross it, jump the wards, and run. After five months, Lars' 200-acre compound felt like a jail cell. I missed being free to do what I wanted, going to a movie, shopping. Anything. I was desperate to get out.

Training had instilled in me that even while in my deepest thoughts, my body was constantly aware of its surroundings. I sensed I was no longer alone. The blood in my veins hummed, alerting me. I continued to walk close to the spelled border, weaving through the looming timber, wispy tendrils of vapor licking at my ankles. Fog crawled over the ground and wrapped around the trees. The blood under my skin tingled, triggering a shudder up my back.

Stopping, I swiveled around, air caught in my throat. A hazy outline of a man stood about 25 feet away on the other side of the property line. His green, cat eyes burned through the darkness. My heart smacked against my ribs and my insides twisted into knots. Mindful he posed no real threat, I still was cautious. His glower slowly moved over me, his eyes and face full of dark emotion. My body was aware of every inch of what Eli scrutinized and even more aware of the effect he still had on me. In comparison, my hormonal lust for Nic seemed mediocre at best. Air no longer pumped in and out of my frozen chest. Our eyes stayed locked on each other for several minutes and my body trembled. Then, abruptly, he turned, dissolving into the night as if he had never been there.

Eventually, when I came to my senses, I took off at a run for the house. I threw open the door, not stopping to take off my shoes or jacket, ignoring Nic as he called out to me. I bolted up the stairs, slammed my bedroom door, and checked the lock three times before backing away from it.

I sensed Eli had been around for a while, but seeing him was different. The last time I saw him was when I threw him against a tree before bolting. Why was he appearing to me now? Was it to prove he could find me? Didn't he know I was aware he had found me a long time ago? Was this some kind of game or message? What did he want me to get from seeing him, looking like some warrior god, besides scaring the bejesus out of me?

Sinking back onto my impeccably made bed, I curled up into a ball in the middle of it. Something in the corner of my eye caught my attention. Standing at the furthest corner of my bed, hands on my pillow looking as if she was fluffing it, was a tiny woman about a foot tall. Sinnie. She had hair so blonde it was almost white and huge, light blue eyes. Her face was old and worn, but she was prettier than I expected. Her features looked Norwegian or Swedish.

"Hello." I looked at her, trying to be as nonthreatening as I could. I didn't want to frighten her. She only blinked at my greeting, continuing to watch me suspiciously. "Sinnie, right?"

It was a few moments before her teeny head bobbed up and down. "Been watching you." Her voice was small, but hardy. Not completely sure how to respond to her, I slowly sat up, moving so glacially as to not scare her. "Not sure about you. But, in time, I will decide."

Okay. At least she was upfront about it. "Well, I appreciate you giving me a fair appraisal." *Is this a job interview?*

Her nod was quick, like I should be grateful for her generosity. She gave my pillow one more pat and in a blink of an eye was gone.

"My life couldn't get any weirder." I flopped down on the bed. Sinnie had kept my thoughts briefly away from Eli, but once again, alone in my room, his haunting image circled my heart and thoughts. I stared out the sliding glass door into the impeding darkness.

"Ember?" Rez knocked softly on my door. "Did you want some dinner? I brought a plate up for you." I didn't respond but continued to stare out my window fixated on the idea he was out there, perhaps watching me now. Apprehension filled me. "Okay, well, I will leave it here, if you want it later." She placed something in front of my door, and I could hear her quiet footsteps moving down the hallway.

It caught me by surprise that a Demon, like Rez, could torture and feed off humans, mentally and physically, but to her own be so caring and nurturing.

I went to my door, my stomach suddenly yowling with hunger. I grabbed the plate of food, peeking under the lid. The smells wafting up my nose only made my stomach growl more. Bacon-wrapped beef tenderloin with baby red potatoes and asparagus. Did I say how much I loved Marguerite? I hopped back onto my enormous bed and devoured my meal, not bothering with cutlery.

Once my belly was happy, I got ready for bed and crawled under the blankets. Sleep found me quickly, but my dreams were filled with death and destruction, burning bodies and screaming. Restless and wide awake at three a.m. my mind began to wander.

Missing my friends and my dad, I decided to try a dreamwalk on my own. Torin usually helped me, but the last time he let me control it and stayed for support. Pretty confident I could do it, I let my mind relax and concentrated on my friends.

Mark was hard to visit. Not because he was harder to dreamwalk, but because every time I saw him he was either sitting in the chair staring absently at the fire or pacing the room. Frustration and sadness were etched deeply into his face. It hurt to look at him, to see his pain. He appeared so lost. He was probably wondering how many signs he had missed, how many times he had brushed things off not wanting to *really* think about them.

The last time I had come to him in a dreamwalk, Mom's and my names were being muttered under his breath. It broke my heart. Discontinuing seeing him for a while was the only way I was able to focus on my training. The training that would help get him out.

Jared and Kennedy were the easiest for me to lock on. I figured it was because they both were "special." Kennedy might be human, but she still was magical. It was in her genes. Jared was almost effortless as we were connected. Eli's blood in me could zero in on Jared with precision. Securing myself firmly against my headboard, vertigo spun my head. It had only gotten slightly less stomach turning, possibly because I knew what was coming.

*The room and the position of my friends hadn't changed much since the last time I had dreamwalked. Josh sat in the window, one leg on the floor, the other up on the sill. Ryan was lying on his bed, Kennedy sitting next to him, and Jared sat in a chair.*

*Kennedy's body gave a tiny spasm, her hands going up to rub her arms.*

*"What the hell was that?" Josh laughed.*

*"I don't know... I just got the chills or something." Kennedy continued to rub at her arms, looking around the room apprehensively.*

*Jared stood up from the chair. "Yeah, me too. Must be a draft in here." Pulling the blanket off his bed he went over to Kennedy, wrapping it around her shoulders. "That better?"*

*"Yes, thank you." She smiled up at him, but he continued to stare blatantly at her. "What? Is there something on my face?" Kennedy started wiping at her cheek.*

*Jared shook his head. "No, you have really nice skin and cute freckles."*

*My friend's face flushed with embarrassment. Her cheeks turned a deep pink and her hand flew up to her glasses, adjusting them nervously.*

*"Uh... Thanks."*

*Josh looked at both of them and shook his head while Ryan continued to lie there, in a zombie-like state. His crying had stopped, but now he had gone numb. I remembered the same stage after losing my mom. It was the brain's way of coping when the endless agony kept ripping at your insides.*

*The clinking of a key in the lock turned their attention toward the door. A guard stepped into the room. Like all Fay, his beauty was almost painful. Short, dark hair was slicked back, emphasizing high cheekbones and glittering blue eyes. Broad and tall, he looked younger than most soldiers I had seen. He looked to be around our age, which meant he was probably several hundred years older than us.*

*He shot my friends a warning look before three higher-ranking guards followed him in. They appeared a little older, but still so fair it didn't seem to matter. My senses held no power while dreamwalking so I was as surprised as my friends when the Queen stepped into the room. Normally, I could feel the magic emanating from her, but I was a ghost with no real bearing in this world.*

*Sweeping into the room, her fashionably-cut dress brushed the floor. Jared and Kennedy stood on ceremony, but Ryan and Josh stayed seated. Ryan still looked more unconscious than alive, while Josh stared at her open-mouthed and boggled-eyed.*

*No matter how many times you saw her, the response was always the same—bedazzled bewilderment. Her unearthly beauty and presence were awe-inspiring. She had flawless alabaster skin. This set off her fiery red hair, which fell in silky waves down her back. She stood tall and proud. Confident. When she looked at you, her eyes were an intriguing blue-violet color that drew you in. She was exquisite, captivating, and sensual. This made her even more dangerous.*

*Her gaze flittered over the room, touching lightly on the fireplace and window. Her face clouded with a far-away expression. "I used to play in this room as a* child. My sister and I would hide from our mother and nannies in here." With a tightening of her jaw, her emotion flipped to anger. "Now it's being used to hold the abomination's little, human friends. I'm sure there is irony in there somewhere."

Jared stepped closer to Kennedy.

"Well, some human friends."

She closed in on the pair. Her hand reached out to touch Kennedy. I felt as if hot lava were being poured down my throat. Searing heat gripped me, making tremors run over my skin.

Oh God, did she know about Kennedy? Without thinking I darted for Kennedy, ready to intervene. No matter how many times Torin had stressed to me it was heedless, I still couldn't stop myself from reacting. I grabbed Kennedy's arm, trying to pull her out of the way. Kennedy's flesh rippled with goose bumps where I had touched her. Her gaze locked on Aneira. She shivered, but didn't move. Had I caused that? Could she feel me? She had complained, along with Jared of a chill when I had first arrived. Were they sensitive to my manifestation? If they could feel me, could the Queen? This concern had me stepping back out of the Queen's reach.

"Well, aren't you a pretty, little thing." Her form towered over Kennedy's tiny frame, and her fingers clasped Kennedy's chin with a firm grip. "Is this why the little half-breed here is getting all protective of you?" Her eyes stayed locked on Kennedy's face, but her disgusted tone was directed at Jared. "Protect the precious humans against the Seelie Queen. Yet, we are the ones in hiding."

*She ripped her fingers away from Kennedy's face, which snapped to the side like Kennedy had been slapped. Jared stiffened. The Queen's guards took a protective step towards the Queen who waved them back.*

*"Don't worry. This baby Dark Dweller will do nothing. He is all fluff with no bark or bite. I did promise Lorcan I would not hurt you, but I didn't promise I wouldn't show you into manhood." She roughly patted his cheek, leaning close to him. "You will probably enjoy it."*

*Kennedy sucked in breath with a hiss.*

*"Awww, your girlfriend is getting all jealous. Isn't it sweet?" The Queen's tone was light but full of venom. Her gaze went over the room, landing on Ryan. "Why is he lying there? He should stand in my presence."*

*The guard, who first entered the room, moved forward. "He is ill, my lady."*

*"Oh, is he now?" She stared disapprovingly at the lump lying incoherent on the bed. "I guess I still have enough enticement for Ember if he dies." Aneira turned away from him and took notice of the boy who now stood by the window. "And what about you?"*

*"You're gorgeous," Josh muttered, watching her with complete fascination.*

*A superior smile pressed on Aneira's lips. "Flattery my boy? Smart."*

*"You are like those hot character chicks in the World of Warcraft," he said. Josh's expression held reverence and worship. I wanted to smack him to wake him up. She was not some anime in his video game. She was cold and cruel and could kill him with a snap of*

*her fingers. Reality was not hitting him the way it should.*

*"I am sure that is a compliment?" She swayed closer to Josh, captivating his attention on her body and face.*

*"Yes... oh yeah... totally," he babbled.*

*The Queen cringed at his words, but forced the fake smile to stay enticingly on her mouth. "You are tall for a human. Young, but strong for your age. You could almost pass for one of my soldiers."*

*Warning wiggled in my chest as I watched her. What was she doing? Aneira was shrewd. She could work people to get what she wanted. Flattery and compliments would not work on Jared or Kennedy, but they would work on Josh. And by Josh's expression, she understood that. Probably from the moment she stepped into the room, she had known everyone's weakness. She had assessed them as soon as they had been brought to her. What was her game plan? I knew her end game was getting me, but what was she going to do with them to achieve that?*

*I didn't have to wait long for the answer.*

*Aneira turned back to the room, demanding all eyes on her. "Since you have been utterly useless in helping me find your friend, I may have to entice her to come out and play. At the end of this week, any one of you need to give me the information I seek, or she will have one less friend." The Queen swooped back down on Kennedy. "Starting with you. I sense something special about you. When Ember hears your dead body has been delivered back to your family, I believe she will come out of the woodwork." Aneira's voice was seductive and alluring.*

Without another word, she departed the room with the same sweeping superiority as when she entered. Her three minions followed suit. Only the young guard stayed, his head bowed as she exited.

Everyone stood silent until Kennedy sobbed, tears plummeting down her cheeks. Jared immediately pulled Kennedy into his arms. "Shhh... it's okay. Everything will be all right."

"H-how? How will it be all right?"

"She's trying to scare us into talking." Jared pushed her hair away, cupping his hands around her face to look at her. His fingers brushed away the train of tears rolling down.

"How can you be sure?" Ken whispered.

"I promise I won't let anything happen to you," Jared declared.

Jared sounded sure, but I was not. Going crazy in my spirit form, my arms and legs were frantic with movement.

"There will be nothing you can do," the guard across the room stated.

Jared frowned. "We'll escape. Jump out of the window if we have to."

"You think the window isn't charmed? You might be able to slip through the bars and you could probably manage the fall, but the moment you slide through them, the entire castle will be alerted."

The fact they were talking so openly with the guard about escaping stopped my hysterical tantrum, taking more notice of him.

"The charm will not stop you from running away. It only sets off a warning alarm, which unfortunately will go off right away. But I can see how someone might still be able to run into the forest and through a door to Earth before they are caught."

It almost seemed like he was encouraging them to take this route. What the hell was going on? Was this guard on their side?

"Otherwise, I hope you are all comfortable."

"Yeah. Awesome. Cold stone is so inviting." Jared's tone was full of sarcasm.

The guard nodded. "It could be worse. The dungeons are most unpleasant. They stink like rat piss." There was amusement to his words. I think deep down this boy actually had a sense of humor.

"Seriously, dungeons?" Josh said. It was the first time he had spoken since the Queen's departure. "This only continues to get better. It's like in the movies and video games. Do you guys hunt and kill trolls?" Josh hopped up, pantomimed a stabbing gesture.

"Kill trolls?" the guard repeated. "No. They are rude, dreadful creatures, but we do not hunt them. They stay away from us, and we do the same."

"So, what do you kill? Goblins?" The guard stared at Josh with an incredulous expression. "What? Come on, you have to hunt down and destroy some kind of evil monsters," Josh said.

"Yes. Humans." The guard turned away from Josh, but I could see Kennedy and Jared biting back their laughter. Yep, there was a sense of humor in there. The guard focused on Ryan. "How is he doing?"

"I am sorry. I will try to get you more substantial human food and maybe have the medic look at him."

"Thank you, Castien." Kennedy nodded at him as a soft moan came from Ryan.

"What did he say?" Castien asked, worry across his face.

Kennedy's face reflected her pain. "He said, 'Ian.' I think he keeps replaying Ian's death in his head. What he could have done to save him."

Gut-wrenching guilt and sadness washed over me. I had to go, to run from the pain I had caused. Focusing back on myself, the whooshing sensation came over me.

When I awoke, fresh tears were trailing down my cheeks. I scrambled out of bed and headed down the long corridor to the other side of the house, pounding on Lars' door.

"Em?" Rez's voice was sleepy as she opened the door.

"I need to talk to him. Now," I demanded. Without hesitation, Rez backed into the room as another form filled the doorway.

"What is it, Ember? I had just fallen asleep." He wrapped his robe around him tighter. It was not unusual for him to go to bed after three in the morning. He would have preferred to be completely nocturnal, but his business didn't allow only night hours.

"I need to get my friends. Aneira is going to kill them."

He briefly shut his eyes. "Meet me in my office."

Five minutes later I sat across from Lars, giving him the rundown of the night.

"You never told me you have been dreamwalking," he growled. "Do you know how dangerous it is? What if she sensed you?"

"But she didn't. And that's not the point now. I need to get them out of there. My father, too."

Lars sat forward in his chair. "Like hell it is 'not the point.' You were lucky. Aneira is so self-absorbed and narcissistic she has stopped seeing what is in front of her face. But you will *not* do it again. She has extraordinary powers and could have followed you back through the dreamwalk if she had been aware."

I pressed into the chair with disbelief. Had Torin known she could do this? He had never mentioned she could follow me back or even be aware of my presence. Was this an oversight or something he didn't know? Had he known and kept it from me? How well did I know him and why did I trust him so explicitly? Could this all be an act?

"So what exactly did she say?"

Closing my eyes, I tried to recall her exact words. "*At the end of this week, either one of you will give me the information I seek or she will have one less friend,*" I repeated the Queen's words.

He leaned back. "You have time then."

"What do you mean I have time?"

"The end of an Otherworld week could be a year here on Earth. Your friends will be fine for a while. And as for you, you are not prepared to face her. You need more training. Remember, I will tell you when you are ready and when you can leave. It is not time yet."

A snarl curled my lip. I wanted to fight him and tell him to fuck off, but then I felt a weight come down on me. Air pushed out of my lungs and my bones felt crushed under the pressure.

"That is the burden of your binding contract. You agreed to the terms, Ember." He waited a few more moments, until my eyes began to water under his power. "Now it is time to go back to bed. You have training in the morning, and I think you will want to work even harder. You are still unremarkable in any skill set. You need to vastly improve before you can rescue your friends and step-father." Lars got up and departed the room, leaving me gasping as the heaviness lifted from me.

"Bastard," I mumbled before heading back upstairs to my bed, which was, of course, newly made.

# TWENTY-ONE

My eyes burned as I stumbled down the stairs the next morning. Alki had already pounded on my door twice, threatening me, before I finally got up. Sleep had been hard to come by. All my thoughts were on Mark, Kennedy, Ryan, and Josh. The Queen had made an obvious threat, but my underlying fear was of the Queen finding out Kennedy's secret. There were things worse than death, and I feared if the Queen discovered she had a Druid on her hands—the last living Druid—death would be the easy way out for Kennedy.

"You have fifteen minutes before you will be in the training room ready to go," Alki barked before he walked out and slammed the kitchen door.

I had been trained in the art of fighting, whether sword, *ninjuitsu*, *pankration*, or *bataireacht*, an Irish form of stick fighting. I was mediocre at best across the board. Alki was determined to get me up to satisfactory before the week was out. Maya and Koke begrudgingly worked with me. But they did help me learn to regulate both my fire and earth powers with my mind. Several times I had started a fire in the new training room so they quickly decided to move me outside. Whatever I splintered out there, Nic cut up and used for firewood. For only training five months, I thought I was doing pretty well, but no one seemed happy with my skill level. Lars least of all.

Since not many Daes had survived, this was as much learning by trial for them as it was for me. The only things I had going for me were my speed and agility. Again, I decided against telling anyone about my Dark Dweller blood. It felt wiser to keep it to myself.

"Alki is such a warm fuzzy in the morning." I sighed, heading over to the coffee pot. I pulled out the largest coffee mug in the house and filled my cup. Suddenly, a flash of Mark and me in our kitchen, going through our usual morning banter, rushed into my head. I swallowed the tight lump forming in my throat.

Marguerite eyed me and shook her head as she flipped an omelet in the pan she was holding. "*Mi querida*, are you all right?" She spoke over my shoulder.

"Yeah, I'm fine. Breakfast smells delicious, Marguerite." I took a deep breath and turned around, making sure my memories and pain were tightly secured again.

"You must eat. You need your energy, *mi dulce nina*." She scooped the omelet onto a plate and set it down on the table. "*Muy flaca*."

"*Gracias*." I smiled. It amused me she called me "my sweet girl." Being Demon, even half, seemed like it should disqualify me from that term. But it didn't seem to stop her from hugging and cooing over me. She was human but knew what we were. She was one of those rare people who had the "sight." Instead of being terrified of us, she ran the household, feeding and loving us as if we were her own. She had been working for Lars since she was a teenager, and he treated her very well. I guess she preferred sticking close to the monster she knew, one that would never hurt her, than being unprotected and taking her chances with the monsters she didn't know.

I pulled out a stool, diving into the eggs and melting cheese, consuming half an omelet and two cups of coffee, all of which I feared I might see again later after a hard training session. Marguerite rushed me out the door since I was already late. *Great.*

Alki tortured me in ways I didn't think possible. It was Fae army boot camp. He had me practicing things like sword and stick fighting in the mud after running up hills and doing sprints for two hours. I'm not above admitting I had a few tantrums during the day, but I pressed on.

When Koke came in, Alki mixed my physical combat with mental fighting. Fireballs once again threatened the roof, so we moved outside. The earlier rain saved the lush lawn from becoming crispy and blackened. I fought Alki in ninjuitsu-style with a stick, as Koke urged me to use my mind to take the weapon from him. Maya joined later, adding the nature element. This was when things could get dicey. Fortunately for all of us, my control was getting a little better. I hadn't blown up a building in days.

After seven long hours, I passed out from sheer exhaustion and awoke two hours later in my bed. Lying there with my eyes closed, I heard my door creak open, followed by the familiar sound of feet sauntering towards my bed.

"Nic..." I grumbled without having to look and pulled the sheets over my head.

He slipped under the covers, scooting himself close against the curve of my body. He had done this frequently in the last three months, usually in the morning after getting back from an Incubus night out, which I really tried hard not to think about. It never went past snuggling with us even though he desired more and he wore little clothing.

"Isn't it too early for you to be out seducing and taking life forces of unsuspecting victims?"

"I wouldn't call them victims. Believe me they are willing, and I leave them incredibly satisfied."

"And barely alive."

"A technicality." He snuggled in closer to me, his warm breath tickling down my neck. Nic was pure Incubus, always on duty; although I think he enjoyed the chance to be close to someone he couldn't kill.

"I'm exhausted, Nic." I dug my head farther into the pillow, trying to ignore his warm, tempting physique.

"Then let me do all the work," he mumbled against my ear, kissing my neck.

I fought back a deep, happy sigh wanting to escape, to forget everything happening in my life—even if it was just for a few minutes. He felt so good and was breaking down my will power bit by bit. Soon I'd be left without any, which was exactly what he wanted. What was I really fighting? I was nineteen, single, and extremely horny. All. The. Time. It was either a really bad time to have a Spanish Incubus god in my bed or a really good one.

Even if I kept thinking of someone else when I was pleasing myself.

Like everything else, I pushed my thoughts way down, not wanting to deal with them. I knew what was holding me back, or more like *who* was holding me back.

Nic was next to me, yet it was the thought of Eli that flushed me with heat. Desire for the dark dweller made me furious with myself. Anger made me do stupid things sometimes.

I rolled over to face Nic, my hand reached up to bring his face to mine. He made a shocked sound. Our lips met with a softness I hadn't expected. I suspected Nic would be a good kisser. He had to be, right? It was part of his job description.

*But wow... I mean w-w-wow...*

I could see how easily he'd have defenseless humans giving him everything, solely to keep him kissing them. A Demon is naturally prone to surrendering itself to the so-called seven "deadly sins," especially desire. Demons were gluttonous in sex, and I felt my Demon side winning the battle. *If he's this good at kissing, imagine how the sex will be,* a voice inside me commented.

I rolled over, straddling him as we continued to kiss, the intensity leaping bounds in a single second. His hands moved up under my shirt, making my skin feel like butter. If this was me being immune to him, I was in serious trouble. His hands pushed inside my sweats, cupping my ass, pulling me in closer, rubbing me hard against his erection. There was a logical, responsible part of me telling me to stop; he wasn't the one I wanted to be with. My "who gives a crap" part won out. I was young and single. My logical side got bitch-slapped unconscious.

We were in heavy make-out mode, rolling and fumbling around. Our shirts and pants already on the floor and both of us were only in our underwear, his cock pressing so hard against, I whimpered under the friction.

"Nic." I was asking for more. His fingers started to yank at my underwear when there was a firm knock on my door.

"Ember, I know you're resting, but Lars wants you in the library in five minutes," Koke's voice came through my door.

*Resting... right.* Nic put his hand over my mouth as a giggle tried to escape.

"Also, I can't find Nic. Do you know where he might be?" The serious way she said it told me she wasn't joking.

"Uh—no. Have you checked the garage? You know how he likes to tinker with his little boy toys," I replied as I stared at him, a grin on my lips. He returned a look, which told me revenge would soon be coming.

"Thanks. I will look there."

"Tinker with my little boy toys?" Nic scoffed after Koke departed. His eyes glinted. "I'll show you tinkering..." He again started kissing me deeply, his hands running all over my body.

I knew I had to stop now. Someone else might be sent up here, who probably wouldn't knock.

"Nic, I have to go." I pulled away from him.

"Yeah, yeah, Lars is waiting." He frowned and moved off, falling to the side of me. "But don't think you're getting away from me so easily. There will be a continuation of this."

Smiling, I sat up, tugging on my shirt, not bothering to respond. I was insanely attracted to him. Any living thing in this realm, or any realm for that matter, would be.

My lust was into it, but my heart wasn't. It was easy to forget when you were with Nic, but I knew my feelings were somewhere else.

Standing up, I gazed down on the olive-skinned, ripped, half-naked man in my bed. I really hated my damn, stupid heart.

Yanking on my jeans, I pulled my hair into a ponytail. "Remember, Koke's looking for you," I said over my shoulder as I left my room.

# TWENTY-TWO

The next couple of days were intense, bordering on horrendous. But I loved how strong I felt in my body and my powers. Physically, I had changed quite a bit over the last five months. I had always exercised, but this was different. I was becoming a weapon; my arms, stomach, and legs toned and cut. My powers were developing slowly, but in the last few weeks I had felt them blossoming in strength, and my control of them was becoming firmer. There was still a long way to go, but fewer things had gotten blown up. Always a positive.

The thought of my friends and family being held captive in the Otherworld helped me focus harder, especially with the death threat looming over. Obtaining control over my gifts was the only thing I wanted. I didn't like the idea of annihilating any more towns, turning myself into a version of the Mad Hatter, or killing my newly found, and very dysfunctional, family.

Like a kid in a growth spurt, the escalation of my powers gave me a bad case of growing pains. Though I was exhausted and got plenty of exercise, my legs ached and itched to move. Every night I took a walk trying to ease the sore muscles.

The temperature had dropped into the low 30s, unusually cold for this time of year, but I had to get out. Bundling up, I ignored the biting cold clawing at my face. Propelling myself farther and farther into the forest, I wound my way through the endless trees, following the creek to the property line. I no longer could see the lights from the house or the smoke from its chimney. My hand touched a large ash tree—my usual stopping point. The property line ended on the other side.

A sudden rush of energy whirled within me. My eyes quickly surveyed the space around. Tense and on guard, my blood zinged through my veins. The hair on the back of my neck tingled. My respiration quickened and created vapor visible in the cold air around me.

"Why don't you stop hiding behind a tree like a crazy stalker and come out and face me?" I declared. My anxiety vanished. Why should I be afraid of him? He should be afraid of me now. I was not the same girl he had known five months ago. I may not have perfected my abilities yet, but I was still a force. There was a reason Fae feared Daes. I would no longer quake in front of others. He would see I held no fear of him now.

There was rustling across from me. Eli stepped out.

"I wasn't stalking you."

"Oh really. What do you call it?" I crossed my arms. With head held high, I crossed the ward line. Here the fences were invisible, but stronger than any walled fortress. Lars had put my blood in with the wards so they knew me, and I could cross without them going off.

"Observing." His eyes moved slowly over my figure.

Damn, he looked hot. His hair was a bit longer and his stubble a little thicker around his jaw-line since I last saw him. He wore jeans, a grey hoodie, and his motorcycle boots and jacket. His physique filling them all out to perfection.

"Is it really still considered 'observing' if it's been over four months now? I have felt you slinking around here since July."

He looked at me with a frown. "I found it best to keep an eye on my adversaries and know what they are up to." He crossed his arms staring me down.

"You're bordering on restraining order territory," I said. "Lars has this place spelled and guarded up the wazoo. How did you even find me?"

"My blood is like a GPS system in your veins. Even against a deterrence spell, I will always find you, Brycin."

"Well, congrats. You found me. Now leave."

As soon as the last word left my lips, he had me pinned against a tree, his hands holding my arms above my head. Air pushed out of my lungs in a sharp rasp. Our eyes snapped on to each other's for several deep breaths.

"I think I'm having the strangest sense of *déjà vu*," I griped.

"You'd think I'd remember to bring a rope and a muzzle with me." His voice was full of venom. "Next time I won't forget."

"Believe me, Dragen, there will be no next time," I fumed, my teeth gritted. His breath fluttered across me, slipping down my neck as he breathed in and out angrily. "Unless you like being thrown around like a ragdoll, you'd better get your hands off me," I threatened. I could feel my powers ready to respond. I was keeping them in check but that only fueled my agitation.

"Do your worst," he challenged me, moving in closer to me.

I didn't move. The closeness of his body made my breath quicken. We both stayed there, staring each other down, the tension consuming us. Spikes of heat thrashed inside me, causing me to tremble under his gaze.

"Look, I came here for a reason. I know you've seen Jared and the others. I need to know they're okay."

Blinking, it took me a moment for my brain to add up his words. "How do you know I've seen Jared?" Eli let my arms go, turned away from me, and ran his hand through his hair. "How do you know I've seen them?" I demanded again.

"You think you stopped pulling me into your dreamscapes?"

Ice and fire moved up my chest. "What?"

"I'm always there. I just didn't show myself. Thought it would be better, for both of us. I'm not able to go into the dreamwalk with you, but when you returned to the dreamscape, I heard you guys talking."

Speechless at this discovery, it took me time to find my voice, but finally I muttered, "He's fine. They all are. Jared's actually taken the lead. Well, he and Kennedy seem to take turns. They're a good team."

"The Queen hasn't figured out what Kennedy is?"

I shook my head. "No, not so far." I decided to leave out the bit about the Queen's threat against Kennedy. He could not help me, and it would only cause him frustration and worry.

Eli sighed, his relief palpable. "Good." His respite lasted briefly before his face turned hard and impassive. "Well, I'll let you get back to your boyfriend." He turned to leave.

My heart hurtling itself almost through my chest. *Don't go!* I thought, but responded, "Boyfriend?"

"Well, whatever Demon you've been getting hot and heavy with."

"You were watching me?" I shrieked out. "Through my window?"

"Observing."

"Not funny. Call it what you want, but it's creepy, pervert." I shot at him, fury turning into cold, controlled anger. "And he's not my boyfriend or a demon. He's an incubus and I'm using him for sex. Enjoyed watching us? Actually seeing what true pleasure is on my face."

Eli was in my face in a blink, slamming me against the tree. Bark broke off into pieces as the tension around us intensified.

My powers seeped to the surface, no longer suppressed.

"Pleasure? That's what you called that?" His brow lifted. "Pretty sad if you think what you felt with him is pleasure. If it was, he'd have those training wheels off already."

"How do you know he hasn't already?"

"He hasn't." Green eyes held mine firmly. "Admit it Brycin, when you slip your fingers into your wet, dripping pussy, feel yourself about to orgasm...all you are imagining is how it felt when it was my fingers deep inside you."

Sucking in sharply, it was like he could see right through me, peeled back my fantasies.

"Believe me," I seethed. "I'm not thinking of you. You make me sick."

"Yeah, you've said something like that before."

"I meant it then, too." I pushed him. He didn't even budge.

"I don't doubt you did." He reached around my head and ripping the band from my ponytail, letting my hair fall loosely around my shoulders and down my back.

"Don't touch me." I spouted angrily, but I didn't move, my body pulsating with tension.

"Stop me."

As he moved in closer, I could feel the heat resonating off his body. He paused for a moment, waiting for me to act on his words. I didn't. Grabbing the back of my head roughly, he tugged a handful of my hair back so I had to look up at him. Breathing in shakily, conflicting emotions of hate and desire raged inside me. Fire burned in his pupils, making him look even more feral.

We stood there for a moment glaring at each other, the air taut with tension.

"Fuck you," I seethed.

"Gladly." He yanked me to him, pressing his body into mine, his lips coming down with a savage hunger, crashing hard into mine. I felt dizzy; my need for him was desperate and raw. His hand curling into my scalp as I pulled him to me by his belt loops. We were both fierce and demanding as we kissed. Biting. Tugging. Wanting.

Emotions took over. Fear burnt to a crisp in my veins. Desire thumped through me, my core pulsing with craving, needing him inside me. The difference between Nic and Eli was night and day. I could easily stop with Nic and walk away.

Eli I couldn't.

Pushing his jacket off his shoulders, it hit the ground. His arms went up as I grabbed the hem of his sweatshirt, ripping it over his head. His bare, muscular arms wrapped back around me the instant they were free of his clothes, pressing me nearer to him. My hands moved over every curve and ripped muscle of his torso, along his sides, down his abs to his crotch. A low, animalistic growl vibrated from Eli as our lips separated for a second to catch our breaths. But even a second was too long for me.

I pulled his face back to mine taking his lower lip softly between my teeth, slightly tugging at it. Eli groaned and grabbed my hips as he lifted me up. I wrapped my legs around him, my back slamming up against the wood. He tilted my chin back grazing his teeth down my neck. Shivers of ecstasy rippled through me and I let out a low, deep moan as I slid down his body. Desperately I undid the buttons on his jeans and felt him with my hand. Fuck. He was huge. Gripping him firmer, my brazenness surprising both of us. Eli watched my hand slide up and down, my thumb rubbing through his pre-cum.

"Brycin." He growled, his eyes were flames of desire so intense, I forgot where I was for a moment. His lips met mine with such raw passion my pulse quickened. He broke away, yanking off layers of my clothes. The fact I was braless didn't go unnoticed by either one of us. The freezing temperatures dulled my burning skin. I barely felt the tree bark gashing into my bare skin when he brought his mouth to my neck moving down to my breasts, licking, sucking, and nipping at my nipples until my pussy throbbed, making me moan.

Holding me with one arm, he took us to ground, laying me on our clothes. They were the only barrier between me and the frozen ground, although I couldn't feel anything except his body on mine. As Eli unbuttoned my jeans, pulling them off in one tug, I hauled his down over his hips, taking his cock in my hands. My mouth watering to taste him.

"Fuck." He hissed. I knew my cold fingers burned into his skin making my touch even more electric. His hands ran over me, kissing and touching every inch of my body.

"Em?" He stopped to look at me. I knew what he was asking, but there was nothing I wanted more.

My fingers grabbed his hands, bringing them to me, and hooking them around the sides of my underwear. My answer was clear. He slowly started to pull them down—painfully slow. My breath heaved quickly in and out, while every nerve ending felt like a live wire.

Stripping me bare, he sat back, his fervid gaze moved sensually over my curves, before a sexy smile tugged at his lips, mumbling something in a language I didn't understand. I cocked my eyebrow in question.

"It means beautiful." His hand ran from in between my breasts to my stomach then lower.

"Same back at you." My voice was husky as I looked him over; he was unbelievable. This sexy, hot man was looking at me with such desire in his eyes. He slid an arm underneath me, tilting my hips up towards him. I gasped out loudly when his mouth kissed my inner thigh, slowly moving up, his tongue slicing through my folds, arching my back. He licked through me again, sucking on my clit.

"Fuck!" A tree exploded nearby, bark ripping off, flying in all directions, as my energies crashed into it. Pushing my legs wider, he devoured me like a beast, low vibrating growls hummed against my pussy, only hurling air through my lungs as I cried out. He devoured me, escalating me with every lick and nip, until air no longer reached my lungs.

"You taste so fucking good. You are all I want to eat." His fingers joined and his thumbed rolled over my nerves as he bit down slightly.

I screamed out, everything exploding inside and outside of my body.

Time was irrelevant, and I had no idea if it had been minutes or hours when he finally crawled up from between my legs.

"Damn..." I heaved, trying to draw air into me lungs

"And just think, I'm not even close to being done." His crooked smile caused another rush of desire to pound through me, which I didn't think was possible so quickly after a mind-blowing orgasm. But, with him, my desire knew no bounds. He pressed his forehead to mine, his warm hand cupping my face, letting out a breath. In that tiny, little moment I could feel the solid walls I had built up over the last five months crumble. All the emotions waiting on the other side flooded out. I tilted my mouth, kissing him deeply. It took a moment before our lips were ravaging each other again. He moved up farther, aligning us.

"You sure?" he asked me quietly.

"God, yes," I replied, I tipped my hips into him. He leaned down, kissing me deeply as I wrapped my legs around him. He pushed up slowly and entered me.

A cry bellowed from me, every nerve lighting and singing in bliss.

"Fuck. You feel so fucking good." He pushed in a little more. "So, fucking tight."

I moaned, waiting for the pain I had heard about, but it never came.

"You're not human, Em; you're not built the same. Fae are made to fuck." He growled into my ear. "And demons, dark dwellers, and fairies are the most sex-crazed. So you are truly *fucked*." He bit down the sensitive part of my neck, thrusting all the way to the hilt.

"Oh gods," I cried out, his size filling me so much I could hardly breath. Pleasure shook my bones. "Oh fuck!" I wanted more. I wanted it hard. "Eli…"

"What do you want? Tell me." He kept himself still as I clawed and bucked against him.

"You...so fucking deep inside me." I begged. "Fuck me! Hard!"

He let out a deep growl, his hips slamming into mine, dragging me over the ground, hitting every nerve on the way in and out, making my eyes roll back. My body moved with him, our hips cracking together trying to get even closer. Gasping and clawing, I squeezed my legs tighter around him, feeling him hard inside me, adrenaline pounding in my ears, my breath coming quicker as he pushed in deeper, our pace picking up. I felt dizzy, my body shaking, crying out as he fucked me relentlessly. Every time his hands touched my tattoo, he sucked in at the pain, going harder, only shooting more energy through me.

"Eli!"

Things creaked and popped around us, our magic slamming into everything, bits of trees falling on us like rain. It continued to escalate until I felt like my body was going to explode. Every muscle in me began contracting, and we rocked even more fiercely, groaning, nails digging, before an explosion tore through me, my eyesight blacking out, feeling like I was torn from the universe.

"Fuuuuccck!" He bellowed as I clenched around him. He pushed himself even deeper than I thought possible, crushing his pelvis into mine almost painfully, leaving my body twitching and trembling violently as his hot cum spilled into me, ripping another orgasm through me. His body sagged against mine and we laid there several moments in silence, breathing heavily, almost frozen in pleasure, our bodies trembling.

Eli muttered something huskily in my ear in his language, then pulled my face to his, kissing me deeply.

I didn't want to be the fool. His track record with women was pretty consistent. I didn't want to think I was different, but I couldn't help it. I felt that he loved me in the way he touched and looked at me, the unexplainable connection, which made our hearts beat simultaneously. Against all odds and realms, we had found each other. I knew what I felt for him, something I had been feeling for a while.

He slipped out of me, positioning himself on his side next to me. I continued to lay there looking up at the twinkling stars filtering through tree leaves, or what was left of them. I closed my eyes taking in the sounds of nature, feeling it reveal in our energy, throbbing underneath me in reverence. Eli's steady breath, his hand running softly over my body, tracing every curve.

"I didn't come here with this intention." He traced my breast.

I turned my head, opening my eyes. "Sure you did. You're a guy and, well, you're you." I smiled, watching his face scrunch up with denial and offense. My hand reached up to touch his face. "I'm kidding."

"I can't deny that from the moment I met you, it was always somewhere in my subconscious." My eyebrows cocked up. My fingers traced his features. "Okay, there was nothing subconscious about it." He laughed against my hand, the vibration tickling my fingers. Our eyes caught each other. He put his hand over mine and pressed it to his lips, making my breath hitch. It was such a small gesture, but for some reason it made me fall even more. I could feel something come over him as he continued to look at me.

"What?"

His eyes darted away from mine. "You know, Brycin, I am not built to show or talk about emotions."

"Really? You?" Still keeping his eyes off me he sighed, his demeanor changing. "What, Eli?"

He rubbed at the space in between his brows, "I will never be the guy who talks of poetry and brings you flowers. That's not who I am."

"I know. I wouldn't want you to be. That's not who I am either."

He rubbed at his face, almost in frustration. "I can't fight you anymore, woman. I will follow you anywhere in the world, if you ask me." It wasn't his words that affected me; it was the way he looked at me as he said them.

Tears filled my eyes, knowing how hard even this was for him to say, as I struggled with the same problem. I had put up so many walls around my heart, but now he had broken through them all. Not able to respond with words, my throat closed up with emotion.

I pushed myself up on my elbows. Leaning over I kissed him deeply, pushing him back to the ground, my legs swinging over him. Eli was hard in an instant and I realized I was far from done. The demon/fairy/dark dweller hormones had been flicked on with endless supply of energy.

"Ride my cock, Brycin. So fucking hard." He clutched my hips, driving my pussy down his dick, making me scream out. But I did what he asked. With everything I had.

More than once.

Even though I was sure I was getting frostbite, every time we would start to get dressed, we wouldn't get far before our clothes were back on the ground, while we took turns lying on them or being up against a tree.

I was sore, exhausted, and completely exhilarated.

"I really have to go," I mumbled against his lips, as I leaned over him.

"You've said that for the last hour and a half," he replied, gliding his hands up my backside.

"I only semi-meant it those times, but now I really mean it. I have training in a few hours. And Rimmon will be patrolling the property line soon. Not even you want to be caught by him." I kissed him quickly and got up, grabbing my jeans.

"Yeah, I've seen him."

"Going back with no underwear or bra. Class act, Em." I grabbed my sweatshirt from the ground.

"Brycin, you didn't come with a bra."

"Right," I nodded, stopping my search for the nonexistent bra.

"Which I'm not complaining about." A sensual smile tugged at his lips as he laid there watching me.

"No." I shook my finger at him "Don't do that. I have to get home."

"Do what?" The crooked arrogant smile was still on his face.

My eyes narrowed. "You know perfectly well what."

"It wasn't me the last three times."

"No, but you were the six before." I pulled my shirt over my head.

*Was nine times in two hours a lot? Maybe a couple of those had actually overlapped.*

A chuckle came from him.

"For humans, yes." He pushed himself up, heading over to me, his dark brown hair falling in tousled layers around his face, my lower region again tingling with desire.

"You sure you can't read my mind?"

"I can't, but I could see you trying to do the math." His body touched mine. "We aren't human, we don't tire easily...and between us two? It could be centuries before we resurfaced." He looked down at me, tucking a strand of my hair behind my ear, sending thoughts of lust through me. He lowered his head, his lips finding mine. I could feel my craving for him start to dominate my body. We started diving into each other again, his hands going for my recently buttoned jeans.

*Oh yeah. I am in serious trouble.*

"I have the strangest feeling I might be intruding—again," a voice came from behind us. "Darn my timing. I seem to come at the most inopportune moments."

## TWENTY-THREE

I whipped around to find Lorcan there looking at us with a half-amused, half-disgusted expression on his face.

Eli's arm pushed me behind him. "Funny, I don't feel it's by chance at all."

"You think I want to watch you offending our family's memory by screwing your little pet Dae there?" The insult burned through my skin. Eli's arms curled around me. It was to comfort me, but also to keep me from attacking Lorcan. I could. I wanted to. But something kept me from acting.

"What do you want, Lorcan? Or are you nothing but a voyeuristic prick?" I retorted.

"You better keep this one on a leash, bro." Lorcan nodded towards me.

Before I could respond, Eli rushed forward, slamming Lorcan into a tree. His teeth were bared. "I'm starting to think of fewer reasons to keep you alive, Lorc. I think I would get to the point and fast before I decide there are none."

"Easy there. I've come to talk."

"I don't think you ever come just to talk. Though I think you really do love hearing the sound of your own voice," I snapped and stepped up to the guys.

Seething hate pulsed out of Lorcan's eyes. His repulsion for me was acute. "I've come to see if you've changed your mind."

"You're kidding, right?" I crossed my arms. "If you think I will ever go willingly to be the Queen's pawn, you are sorely mistaken. You can't bully me anymore. You've run out of my friends and family and things to threaten me with."

A cruel grin spread over his face. "Have I?" Lorcan turned his gaze back onto his brother, a strange look passing between them. Eli's jaw clenched and his arm dropped away from Lorcan's throat as he stepped back from him.

*What was that look for?*

"I figured that would be your answer." Lorcan shrugged. His mood was too light for me to believe this would be the end. He turned to Eli. "I think it's time Ember learned what you really are—what you're really capable of."

"What is he talking about?" I looked over at Eli. His body had gone stiff, his face remote and detached.

"Lorcan..." Eli's tone warned.

"You know I've been the only one who has ever been truly honest with you, Ember. My brother would rather you didn't know the truth before he fucked you." He sauntered closer, putting himself in between Eli and me. "Now he's got another notch on his belt. Not that you were much of a challenge. Actually, I guess that's not fair; you held out a little longer than most of his conquests." Lorcan's words were like ice in my veins.

"I'm warning you, Lorcan. Stop. Now." Eli took a step forward.

"What, little brother? Don't you think Ember should know the truth?"

"The facts always get lost in your version of the truth." Eli's fists were clenched, and the nerves around his jaw convulsed, looking ready to pounce.

"Oh, that's amusing. I just thought she should get to know the real you. Do you really believe she would have been so willing, Eli, if she'd known the full truth?" Lorcan tilted his head to look over at Eli. "Yeah, I don't think so either. But that's my brother. Fuck them first before they get wise."

The ice had moved up to my lungs, making it hard to breathe. "What are you talking about?"

"Do you want to tell her or you want me to?" Lorcan grinned. It made me nauseous.

"Why are you doing this, Lorcan?" Eli spoke low and gritty.

There was something Eli did not want me to know. I could feel him; feel his emotions rumbling under his aloof façade. Anger was the strongest, but there was something else. Fear? Sorrow? Neither one was an emotion I usually associated with Eli. Betrayal started to gurgle up. The blissful happiness I had felt earlier grew into a huge, cold lump inside.

Ignoring Eli, Lorcan continued on. "Okay, so me then?" Without a word, Eli lunged for Lorcan. It seemed the desire to silence him for good was overpowering.

"Stop!" I sent my powers out, binding Eli in place. It felt wrong, but intuition nagged at me. I had to know what Eli didn't want Lorcan to tell me. "I want to know what's going on."

"Believe me, Em, nothing he says will help you. Now let me go!" He thrashed against the invisible barrier.

"Oh, I think this will help her decide once and for all which brother to trust."

Eli stood helplessly locked in place. "Please, trust me on this."

My gaze went between the brothers, hesitating. I wanted to—I really wanted to—but something told me this was important. "I'm sorry. I want to hear him out."

Eli's lids closed. Fury and other emotions slid over his face. Then his face turned cold. *What did I do?* It was too late. I had to know.

Lorcan's smug, Cheshire-cat smile took over his lips.

"Don't get cocky, Lorcan. I didn't say how long I'd listen to you or that I wouldn't kill you myself," I shot at him. "So, talk."

The smile fell from his face, but the cocky gleam in his eyes didn't. "I feel it is my duty to tell you the truth so you have all the facts. I think if you knew the realities about what he's done, you'd be a lot more willing to see him for the real monster he is. At least I've always been upfront with you."

I crossed my arms over my chest, trying to keep back the floodgate of fear humming beneath my skin. "Yeah, you're a real upstanding character. Now get on with it."

"This is the last time I ask you to leave this alone, please," Eli begged.

Shaking my head, sorrow in my eyes as I responded, "I can't, Eli."

"Let me go. I won't stop him."

Unbound, he backed away, resigning himself to his fate. As much as he didn't want me to hear what Lorcan had to say, he wasn't going to stop it. This went against his character. He was doing it for me. My heart twisted in my chest, which made me wish I had let Eli stop Lorcan. Whatever was coming wasn't going to be good.

A gratified smile curled up on Lorcan's lips. "She's a smart one, Eli. Even now she knows not to trust you completely."

Eli had turned unresponsive again.

"I'm sure you are aware in the Otherworld we were killers, but I don't think you know what that really entailed. We were one of the only types of Fae not ruled or under the thumb of Seelie or Unseelie power. We were what you call mercenaries, loyal to no one but ourselves." Lorcan's eyes glinted with memories. "That creates an impeccable killer. It was what we were created for, why we existed. We were unbiased as to who or what we killed. No remorse, no feelings either way. We were executioners and were exceptional at it." Lorcan's chest puffed out with pride.

I looked back at Eli, feeling dizzy and nauseated. I knew they weren't innocent. They had told me on several occasions they were killers, hinting at their past, but my brain had never fully wanted to comprehend it. How soulless did you have to be to kill only for money, for power?

I looked down at his curled fists. It felt strange that a short while before those hands had been moving over my body, full of animation, life, and affection.

"But there was one job that changed things," Lorcan continued. "We were to kill someone who had betrayed her own kind, who had forsaken everything for her child, a baby who should never have existed. An abomination that should have been destroyed at birth."

My chest locked.

"This woman's family was quite high in the ranking, and they would not allow this kind of humiliation, this kind of treachery. She and the child were to be killed." Lorcan's gaze burned into me as he paused. "We were hired for a huge sum to take care of this problem. We knew the child would be easy enough. The woman on the other hand was known to have incredible power... but we were born to kill.

"Things didn't go as smoothly as we hoped. The child was not there, and the mother had somehow known we were coming." Lorcan's eyes shot over to Eli. Something passed between the two of them, but I couldn't distinguish what. "Your mother put up a fight, I will say that. She was powerful and didn't go easy."

My legs barely kept me up. I recalled what the coroner had said: *It looked like a wild animal had torn her apart.* He'd been so close to the truth; she had been torn apart by a Dark Dweller.

"I don't think it will be a surprise to you to know who was there, the ones who went in and killed your mother?" Lorcan tilted his head towards Eli, a mocking tone skating through his words.

A sledgehammer to my heart and gut would have felt like a feather compared to how the last bit of information hit me. The world around me started to feel hazy, tilting slightly as I turned to look at Eli. His face was stone, but a deep sadness echoed in his eyes.

"Is this true?" I asked, my voice catching in my throat. "D-Did you kill my mom?"

Eli's lids dropped down, his gaze looking away from mine.

"Eli?" I pleaded "Please, tell me what happened."

He continued to look away from me. It was all the answer I needed. Everything in me wanted to scream out it wasn't true; he couldn't have possibly done it.

"How could you?" I whispered out hoarsely. Black spots began to dot my vision. "After everything that has happened between us? Was this all some kind of sick joke to you? Was I? I mean, what kind of person does something so cold and cruel?" I shook my head, still in denial. "When I told you about her death the day on the bridge, you knew the truth all along." I gulped, feeling wetness sliding down my cheeks. "You could have told me a more thorough version of the story. You slept with me, knowing. At any moment we were together did you ever think about telling me the truth?"

The devastating betrayal had me grasping for any hope, anything to tell me this was not true. All I had to do was look into his face, to feel his essence, to know it was true. "Was this why you were exiled from the Otherworld? Because you killed my mother or because you didn't kill me?"

"Em, it's not wha..." Eli finally spoke.

I cut him off. "It's not what, Eli? Did you or did you not kill my mother?"

"It's not that simple."

A crazed laugh burst from my lips.

"Oh, I think it *is* that simple."

I suddenly realized I was standing between two murderers. I knew Eli and the Dark Dwellers had killed before, but this was different. They were responsible for all my pain and anguish.

"You would have killed me, too, if I had been there?" Again, I already knew the answer to the question, but it had to be said out loud anyway.

Lorcan replied instead, "Yes, that was the plan. You were never supposed to exist. We were setting right a wrong. Revenge only made it more pleasurable."

I swallowed. "Revenge? Revenge for what? What did I ever do to you?"

"It's more of what your kind had done."

"What did my kind do to you?"

"Enough, Lorcan," Eli growled behind me.

A malicious smile crept over Lorcan's lips. "Do you want to know when Eli knew he helped kill your mother and you weren't some random Dae he chanced upon?" Lorcan tapped at his lips in mock thought. "How many months has it been now, Eli? Since the day you got her out of jail?" Eli had bailed me out of jail back in April. A little over six months ago. "I gathered then who you were, too, but it wasn't till I touched you did I realize your mother had put a curse on us."

"A curse?"

"You had the truth of her murder in your tattoo." Lorcan nodded toward my back. "It isn't some random symbol, Ember. The tattoo is your family crest, but it would also reveal to you who her killers were, the true threats."

My hand automatically went to my ink. The recollection of when Eli touched me for the first time, the zap of electricity that shot through the lines. His reaction when he saw it. He had realized who I was and what my tattoo meant. I shook my head, embarrassed how I'd thrown myself at him, begging him to stay.

My next memory was of the excruciating pain when Lorcan had touched me. It had been a warning—my mother telling me who had killed her. There was little doubt Lorcan had been her main executioner. His touch-initiated, knee-crippling pain to run through my tattoo.

Eli's effect for some reason had diminished over time, but it had not begun that way. Eli's touch had also caused discomfort, but not like Lorcan's touch. I had no idea why Eli's had lessened. It was probably because I shared his blood.

I had felt a small buzz with every Dark Dweller, but nothing compared to Lorcan or Eli. Eli had been involved with my mother's death; he was my mother's other murderer. His hands were red from her blood.

"You fucking bastard." I shuddered with fury.

"Em—"

"Don't! Don't you dare speak right now. I could kill you so easy." Even as the words left my mouth, I knew I wouldn't. I thought if I ever came face to face with my mother's murderers, I would have no problem seeing them swing from a rope. Against my desires, my Dark Dweller side could not hurt its own. Especially its creator. Eli had turned me into one of them. I could not destroy him as much as I wished it.

Feeling sick just looking at him, I turned back to Lorcan.

"I dreamed up this tattoo. I got it after her death. How could it be a warning?"

"Fay powers go beyond death. She probably sent it through the dream. The curse was locked in your family seal, which you now have tattooed on your back." Lorcan paused and then a deep guffaw barked out of his throat. "How disappointed Mommy must be in you, Emmy. This is a little more than fraternizing with the enemy, isn't it?" Lorcan leaned casually against a tree. His satisfaction at being the one to tell me was clear. "Not a very good daughter all around, are you? Sleeping with your mother's killer and leaving your dear ol' papa to suffer. You could have saved him, but now it is too late.

"Too late? What do you mean too late?"

"Oh, another detail Eli didn't tell you?" Lorcan tilted his head with false empathy. "If humans eat or drink Fae food, they can never eat human food again. Fae food cannot exist in Earth realm so either they go back to Earth and starve to death or they stay permanently in the Otherworld. Either way they are never quite right again."

"What?" I looked over at Eli. His head turned away from me. "Are you saying Mark and my friends are stuck in the Otherworld...forever?"

"Kennedy and Jared will be okay," Eli said softly. The voice, which minutes before had been telling me I was beautiful as he made love to me, now made me want to throw up.

Lorcan eyed Eli before shaking his head. "I thought you were keeping something from me, Eli. I knew something was different about her. She smelled different. What is she?"

Eli and I disregarded Lorcan's question. "So, my dad, Ryan, and Josh won't be able to return."

"No. If any of them eat Fae food, they can never live on Earth again. If they come back to the Earth realm, they will die painful deaths. Some struggled and ended up killing themselves. Some returned to the Otherworld. Nothing can be done to change this," Eli answered.

I could barely breathe. "They've been there for months. How could you not tell me this before?" My eyes narrowed in on him, showing my swelling frustration.

"To them it has only been a couple of days," Eli replied. "If the Queen is smart, she will hold off feeding them Fae food. She needs them as leverage."

"That is a big if," Lorcan taunted.

My stomach churned with bile. I couldn't absorb everything—my mother's murder and finding out Mark and two of my friends were probably stuck in the Otherworld. Ryan's family had already lost Ian. I could not let them lose Ryan as well. I couldn't fail any of them. Mark was all the family I had, but because he was being used to trap me, I may have already lost him.

"I am sorry, Ember." Eli pressed his lips together.

"Sorry?" I sputtered out. "Are you kidding me? Did you just say you're sorry? Really?"

Rage and disgust blinded me. Energy pummeled my veins and tore out of me. A tree next to me shook, vibrating with tension. A popping sound was the only warning before it exploded. I felt my powers taking over, deadening me to all but revenge. Chunks of a tree flew out wildly, some headed towards Lorcan and Eli. I was focused and deadly. Sharp stakes drove into their skin, making them roar with pain.

A vindictive laugh clawed its way from the depths of my soul. I watched their bodies wriggle with pain as more and more fragments of wood penetrated their skin. They'd picked the wrong girl to mess with.

It took me a few moments, through my narrowed vision of hate, to understand all the howls of pain were coming from Lorcan. Eli took his agony in silence. He had dropped to his knees, his arms at his side, surrendering to the shards of wood as they plunged into his body.

Deep down a feeling gripped at my subconscious. It made me hesitate—falter from my emotionless oasis. But it didn't last long, and soon I was back to where I felt nothing. No remorse. Anger took control of my soul. I wanted him to wither in agony, to feel all the pain he had caused me. How dare he take this away from me, too.

My eyes locked onto Eli's. The words in his eyes broke through my wall.

The thousands of tiny spikes still directed at them dropped to the ground. I took off, escaping the torment and misery of staying near Eli any longer. I needed to run from the voice telling me that I had fallen in love with him... I had fallen in love with my mother's killer.

Fire in the Darkness

## TWENTY-FOUR

Most of me wanted to curl up in a ball and collapse under the weight of the agony. The pain was almost unbearable. But I had to keep moving and not let myself reflect on what happened. My mind desired action. The only thing I could think to do was save Mark and my friends—if it wasn't too late. I wouldn't give up if there was still hope. That wasn't an option. I had waited too long, allowing others to convince me to postpone rescuing them till I was deemed "ready." I was willing to risk whatever punishment breaking the Unseelie King's oath would bestow on me. I was ready now but I needed help, and there was only one person who could provide it.

"Torin!" I screamed into the darkness. "Torin, I need you."

He was the only person I could trust now. Why hadn't I seen it before? He had always been there for me, had warned me against Eli, and I hadn't listened. Torin had been my rock from the beginning, only wanting to keep me safe. Even if he couldn't act on it because of the Queen, my happiness was always his first thought. He told me he would help me get into the Otherworld. He had to.

"Torin!" My voice ripped through the air—pained, enraged, and broken.

There were minutes of nothing before the pull slammed into me, knocking me off my feet, crashing me to the ground. My eyes closed as I fell into a deep sleep.

"Ember? Are you hurt? What is going on?" The words rushed into my ear as my lids lifted. Torin kneeled next to me.

Sitting up quickly, I asked, "Torin, did you know that E... that the Dark Dwellers killed my mother?"

He stilled, staring at me with wide eyes, before slowly standing up. His head lowered. "Yes."

"You didn't think to tell me I was living with the men who killed and butchered my mother?" My voice pierced the night air, wild and desperate.

"I could only warn you to stay away."

I bolted up, my arms lashing and whirling through the air. "Is there anything you are allowed to talk about?"

"I am sorry, mo chuisle mo chroi. She has bound me on many matters." He frowned and shook his head.

"Why? Why would she constrain you on my mother's death? Or about the Dark Dwellers?"

Torin kept his gaze off me. His back ridged. "I am not allowed to speak on such matters."

*The aching hurt gnawed at my stomach. I had to push it away; I had to focus on what I could change now.* "Has my family eaten Fae food?" His eyebrows furrowed. "Tell me. Have they had any Fae food? I need to know now."

"No. They haven't. I have given them some processed human candy bars they seem to consider food." Torin shook his head. "Is this the only reason you beckoned me? Ember, it was exceptionally dangerous for you to call me. She has spies everywhere watching me all the time. She is always hovering close to me now."

*I knew it had to be safe now or he wouldn't have come to me.*

"Why didn't you ever tell me about what would happen if they ate Fae food?"

"I didn't think it would help you if you knew," he paused, turning back towards me. "The Queen is not foolish. She understands what would happen if they eat our food. She'll use this as a threat to hold over your head."

"Yeah, but if she plans to kill them or turn them into slaves why would she care?"

"She is calculating and understands their worth as bait right now. To lure you to the castle is her only desire."

"That's why I called you. I am coming to get them. I can't wait till she kills one of them or decides to feed them Fae food." I crossed my arms in defiance. "I am coming. Tonight."

"Absolutely not." Torin shook his head.

"This isn't up for debate."

*"No, you're right, it's not."* He crossed his arms mirroring mine. *"You're not coming."*

Tilting my head, a smile of insolence twitched at my lips. *"I can do this with or without you. Either way I'm going in. I can't stay away any longer. I'm done waiting."* I worked my expression into what I hoped was stern determination. *"It would be better if you helped me. Safer. I might make it out alive if you did."* It was evil of me to manipulate him, but a girl has to do what a girl has to do.

He gave a cry of strangled frustration and rubbed his forehead. *"Ember..."*

*"Please, Torin. I won't be able to do this without you. I have to get them out. Don't you understand that? My family needs me, and I'm not going to leave them there any longer."*

He groaned again and lapsed into silence. Eventually a deep sigh came from him. *"All right, I will help you, but we are going to do this my way. You will do everything I tell you."* I nodded vigorously. *"I mean it, Ember. If I tell you to get out, you get out. Understand?"*

With plans set during the dreamscape, I woke up with my face planted in the dirt. Dawn ignited the trees with a twinge of deep pink. Reality felt harsh in the stark presence of day. The soreness between my legs would not let me pretend last night had all been a dream. More like a nightmare.

"Ugh." I spit out the loose dirt, which had made its way into my mouth. Brushing my face and body off, I stood up, calling out to Torin, "Okay, I'm ready."

Nothing.

"Hello?" I belted out, twisting around in a circle. The only way into the Otherworld was through one of those doors to their realm. "I need your help, Torin. I don't know how to get in. Where the hell are the door thingys?"

I listened for a few seconds when the fluttering of bird wings caught my attention, sending my gaze up into the trees.

"Hello? Torin?"

Nothing.

Another small bird zipped in, dodging close to my head, making me duck down. "Hey!"

The soft sound of a giggle made me pause. Did that bird laugh at me? Turning to locate it, another one dive-bombed me. Bending, I tried to get out of its path. Too late. Tiny feet dragged across my head as it tried to land on me. Its legs tangled in my hair, skidding across my head pulling some of my hair out as it plummeted to the ground.

"Ouch!" I shouted at the same time a strangled cry came from the small bird as it collided with the earth, its legs entwined in strands of my hair. "Dammit!"

It struggled against the binds. Standing in shock, I looked down at the creature. A familiar glow of glamour hummed around the bird. The sound of cackling laughter snapped my head up. The other bird-creature landed softly on a branch near me. This time the glamour stripped away. In the bird's stead was a tiny man, all of six inches high, with wings.

*Oh my God...a pixie.* Many hours of studying Fae mythology allowed me to easily identify them. But coming face to face with Otherworld creatures still bemused me.

"Nice landing, Simmons." One of the tiny men chuckled. I followed his attention back to the other tiny guy who lay crumpled at my feet.

"Hey, my legs got tangled in the mop up there. It wasn't my fault."

"Riiiight. Neither was the time you crashed into the berry bush, or the time your head goosed the leprechaun or the time you nosedived—"

"All right. I get it."

"Or the time you collided with the bunny, or the time you side-swiped the Oak tree, or—"

"Stop." I put up my hands. My neck was getting whiplash from looking back and forth between those two. "Who are you? What the hell is going on?"

They looked up suddenly as if they'd only just noticed me.

The one on the branch whistled, "Yo-ho. Looky here, Simmons. Sir Knight Uptight told us she would be a lovely lady. Too bad she's already been paid for."

"I don't think she's a harlot, Cal," Simmons replied. His tiny fingers pulled at the hair twisted around his ankles.

"I can't imagine how else he would get her."

"He didn't pay for her, Cal."

"No? You think she came willingly? Then she's a stupid floozy."

"She's not a harlot, Cal." Simmons yelled back. Finally breaking free of my locks, he joined Cal up on the branch.

"Whoo-ey. She is a pretty thing. I like 'em tall. Strange eyes and hair but I can overlook that. How much?" Cal directed his question to me, crossing his arms over his pirate-like jacket. Underneath the jacket was a Woody Woodpecker t-shirt and a pair of jeans. His feet were bare.

"Juniper crackers, Cal. She's not a strumpet," Simmons sighed. He was dressed in a 1960s fighter pilot outfit. I once had actually owned the Ken doll that had come with that uniform. Both must have raided a little girl's doll collection. "I am Simmons of the Blue Guardians, but most call me Captain Simmons because I am the best flyer in the kingdom." He puffed up his chest proudly as he introduced himself to me.

"Ha. You can't even fly to the next limb, let alone the next tree, without crashing." Cal laughed.

"That is false and a great insult." Simmons puffed up even more. "And I was talking to the lady, not you." He turned back to me.

"I-I'm Ember."

"And I am Calvin, Calvin of Smokey Wood Forest." He gave me a stiff formal bow.

I couldn't stop the smile curling my lips. "Nice to meet you both."

"Well, Ember, we have been appointed to lead you safely into the Otherworld," Simmons said with pride.

"Yeah, Todo said you were an escort."

"In *need* of an escort, Cal, not *is* one." Simmons shook his head in exasperation.

"Todo?" I looked questioningly at the two pixies.

"He means Sir Torin, my lady," Simmons replied.

"Torin sent you?"

"Sent us? Like he could order us to do anything. Huh! We were obliging enough to listen to his request and accept." Cal flounced about. "And I only did because I thought there would be a harlot waiting, and she would be so grateful for my help and so overtaken with my charm and handsome looks..."

"We were ordered, my lady, by Sir Torin. I am honored to do my duty." Simmons stood up tall and saluted.

"Oh, please. You came for the girl, too."

"That part didn't hurt, my lady. I will be honest," Simmons responded, still in salute position.

"Well, I thank you both for whatever reasons you came." I bit back the giggle popping around in my mouth. I sensed that Simmons might be sensitive if I didn't take him seriously. "Show me the way to the Otherworld."

# TWENTY-FIVE

I must have been through a similar type of door once before. There was no other way Torin could have gotten me on the mountain above Seattle so quickly—right after I leveled it. But I had been so out of it, I scarcely recalled the event. What I did remember was that it was like walking through a thin layer of invisible gelatin. You couldn't see it, but you could feel the barrier between Earth and the Otherworld push and rub against your skin as you broke through it.

Torin told me once you had to know what you were looking for to see the openings between the two worlds. I would have to take him at his word because I didn't see anything different when Cal stopped and pointed towards a gap between two trees.

"Am I missing something?" I looked at him and then to the air in front of me.

"How can you miss it? The door is right there." Cal pointed at the empty spot again. When I gave him a slight shake of my head and shrug, he sighed heavily. "You are still looking through your human vision.

Somewhere inside, my lady, you don't believe stuff like this really exists."

A need to argue came immediately to my mind, but I swallowed it back. I thought I gave up on using logic to figure out my new world, but deep down I clung to the fear if I really let go, I could never go back.

I nodded and closed my eyes, letting my anxiety dissipate around me. When I reopened my lids, there was a glimmering space in front of me. I had seen Torin come out of one and my friends being taken through one, but I hadn't seen it like this before—vibrant and dynamic. The air rippled and danced in shimmering waves, glowing and glinting under the sun rays. It was beautiful.

"Wow," I muttered.

"See, my lady? You had to let go of who you think you should be and be who you are." Simmons' words felt like ice in my veins. Someone else had once said that to me. *Eli.* It was a punch to the gut. I swallowed back the pain.

"Now, step through." Cal motioned for me to venture ahead. I nodded but stayed rooted in place.

"Would you like me to go first, my lady?" Simmons offered, noticing my lack of movement.

"Please."

Simmons flew in front of me and disappeared. Biting my lip, I took a giant step. A slight pressure slipped across my skin as I stepped across the threshold. With that step, a force came down on me. The same powerful weight I had felt in Lars' office hit me tenfold.

I fell to the ground crushed under the gravity. Severing contracts with the Unseelie King was discouraged. It felt as though something sharp chewed at me from the inside out while a million-ton weight pressed down on me. The blinding pain my body and mind felt was the consequence of breaking the transaction. Dealing with the ramifications of my disobedience with him later would be a whole other problem, but right then pain was the only thing I felt or thought about. Twisting in agony, crying out, I wished for death to come, to be swift and take me from the excruciating pain.

"My lady! My lady!" Cal and Simons buzzed around my ear as I continued to wail and flay around in torture.

Then as fast as it had come on, it snapped off. Breathing heavily, I lay on the ground, trying to pull my thoughts back into my brain.

"My lady, are you all right?" Simmons flew around me.

"Not when I meet up with the Unseelie King," I said sitting up.

"Excuse me, my lady?"

"Nothing. I'm fine now. Sorry about that." I blinked. I blinked again. Taking in the scenery around me, my mouth fell open. The basic terrain was similar to what I had left, but everything else about it was different. It reminded me of when you first put up a Christmas tree. It's bare and simple, pretty in its own way. But as soon as you put on the lights and ornaments, the tree is breathtaking, shimmering, and magical. That was the difference between the Earth realm and the Otherworld.

"Oh my..." I uttered in amazement, standing up. My dreams didn't do this place justice. Colors were so vibrant and unreal I had to shield my eyes until they adjusted to the brilliant glow. The grass on the rolling hills was a lush, vivid green. The trees swayed under the light breeze; the flowers on their branches bounced and bobbed under the sparkling sunlight. Butterflies as large as birds fluttered around me. I jumped back when a bunny the size of a dog hopped across my path. Various birds, all different colors, shapes, and sizes, glided through the forest. A deer that didn't stand any taller than a house cat nibbled on a plant. Its eyes watched every move I made.

It was a bewitching fairyland. I could feel the life brimming around me, in the earth and trees. Everything was moving and breathing and was aware of me. I could sense the trees and animals taking me in, connecting with a part of my soul.

"It is tasting you, my lady." Simmons buzzed close to my ear.

"Tasting?"

"Smelling you, tasting your essence. It remembers people and determines who is foe or friend."

"Good pick-up line. Need to remember to use it next time," Cal noted to himself.

I smiled, shaking my head. How strange to feel comfortable so quickly with two pixies and an enchanted forest. I exhaled in relief—I had finally come home. The trees and flowers swayed and rustled around me. The animals were more obvious. Some slunk down, backing away from me, while others moved in closer.

"Interesting," Simmons remarked.

Fire in the Darkness

I looked over at him. "What's interesting? Why is everything reacting like that?"

"I think, my lady, it's because you have a tremendous bond with the earth. You are your mother's daughter, a true Fay. Your mother was one of the most commanding earth Fairies ever known, and they can feel the same force within you. You are connected to them, to earth, to the animals, and they understand that," Simmons paused. My stomach dropped; I could feel the "but" before he spoke it. "You are also a Demon and can destroy them in an instant. Fire is nature's number one enemy. They feel the strength of the darkness in you as well. You are their best friend and worst enemy, death and life, all rolled into one and, they don't know how to respond."

I could never knowingly hurt animals or nature, but I knew better than to say this out loud. If my dreams or even my experiences taught me anything lately, it was that I was capable of things I never imagined or thought I would do. I turned back toward the forest.

"Come, my lady. Sir Knight Torin is waiting for you." Simmons motioned forward. I followed behind. The animals watched me closely as I passed them.

The pixies zipped through the forest at a neck-breaking speed. We passed by thatched-roof cottages and dwellings that reminded me a little of hobbit homes built into the hills. Extravagant tree homes dangled from above. Soon the castle appeared in the distance. It reminded me of Mont St. Michel, the castle in France my mom and I had visited one summer. It was elegant and ancient, forbidding and detached.

The closer we got to the castle the more inhabited the area became and the more I itched to touch the knife

I had stashed in the lining of my boot. It had been there the night before, when I had been with Eli. He had never suspected it was there secured in my boot.

Knowing what I knew now, would I have used it against him? I gripped my hands into tight fists, trying to push back the burning flashes at the thought of him. The betrayal, the humiliation of sleeping with him, falling for him, and then finding out he helped slaughter my mother. On the verge of being sick, I quickly turned my thoughts back to the present problem.

I had other worries right now, like sneaking into the lion's den. The Queen wanted me, and I felt like I was handing myself over to her on a silver platter. Torin had told me of a secret passage into the castle. There were several, but the one least guarded was the sewer system. It would lead me where I needed to go. It would have helped if I could glamour myself and sneak into the castle that way. Of course, it was another thing I had yet to perfect or even do well.

Cal and Simmons stopped at the edge of the forest, the castle looming in front of us. "Okay, from here on, my lady, you must do everything we say. Guards and wards are everywhere, and we will be able to see and sense them before you do."

I nodded, finding it impossible to speak.

"We are going around to the side where the river runs and the sewer tunnel starts," Cal explained as he pointed. Nodding again, I wiped my sweaty palms on my jeans. What the hell was I doing? How did I think, for even a moment, I could pull this off?

The thought of my family pushed back my fear. There was nothing I wouldn't do to get them.

It felt like hours, with a couple close calls from patrolling guards, but we slowly made it to the tunnel. Moss and ivy grew thick, covering the trench, disguising it. If I hadn't been looking for it or, actually, if the pixies hadn't pointed it out, I would never have seen or smelled it.

"There is a spell on it. The Queen isn't stupid by any means. She knows this is a direct way into the castle so she has placed several concealing spells on it, but pixies aren't affected by her wards. She doesn't seem to worry we will do anything against her. Pixies are not worth her time, except as spies," Simmons said.

"Well, the snobby bitch should never have underestimated us," Cal snorted.

"The spell doesn't do anything but keep it hidden. The wards will go off. But no one ever thinks to look towards the sewers, probably thinking it has its own warning system."

I had already known this as Torin had explained to me about the wards and what to stay away from. Pulling my knife from my boot, I hacked at the overgrowth, making a hole big enough to squeeze through. Cal fluttered down onto my shoulder. "Okay, girly, this is your last chance to run. It's do or die from here on out."

"I'm getting my dad and friends out. There is no other option for me," I said.

"You are a fighter, my lady. A true solider." Simmons drifted down to my other shoulder, his foot slipping as he landed. My hand quickly caught him and tucked him up in my hood.

Cal gaffed shaking his head. "Can't even land on her shoulder."

"Shut up."

"Both of you shut up," I hissed back at them. Cal grumbled, but he also settled into my hood. Taking a deep breath, I hunkered down and started crawling through the smelly sewer.

The stench of rotting compost and feces hit me immediately. On this side of the wards, reality saturated the air. Dry heaves lurched from my stomach. Using my sleeve as a mask over my nose and mouth, my eyes watered as I continued to gag. In spite of it, I pushed on. Turning back was no longer a choice.

## TWENTY-SIX

A stick, a spark, and voilà—a pathetic excuse for a torch. It wasn't a flashlight, but it worked. We ambled through the duct for hours, or what felt like hours. The smell and sewage dissipated as we crawled into an underground passageway. Eventually sporadic fire bulbs donned the walls, suggesting we'd reached areas inhabited by Fae.

Being vigilant I kept to the shadows, trying to keep my footsteps silent. The pixies were the hardest to keep quiet—tiny, flying balls of endless energy. Cal could stay quiet, but he could not stay on my shoulder for too long without buzzing ahead or getting distracted. Simmons sat on my shoulder obediently, but couldn't stay quiet. At first I had been thankful for not being alone—that swiftly changed.

"Simmons, why don't you fly ahead and keep a look out for me. Let me know what's coming."

"Aye, aye, my lady." Simmons zoomed off, sounding grateful for having a duty to fulfill.

Sometime later both pixies tore back down the hallway towards me. "My lady, my lady, some soldiers are coming this way."

"Damn." There were only two dim fire bulbs along the wall providing barely enough light to see. But there were not enough shadows and nowhere to hide, just one long, uninterrupted corridor. The bulbs were going to have to be enough distraction.

Backing against the wall, I slid down, pressing myself as far as I could get into obscurity. Cal and Simmons flew behind me and hid. The Dark Dweller in me became still, ready to strike. My focus turned to the fire caressing and swirling around in the glass.

The men's voices grew closer. Timing was everything. *Oh please, this has to work. Otherwise I am so screwed.*

"Did you see the new water fairy serving today?" One of the men spoke.

"How could I miss her? It looked like two garden gnomes were under that sweater. I could not stop staring."

Focusing, I tuned out the two men as they gabbed about some hot, Fay waitress with huge boobs. *Men.* Their footsteps turned the corner, and they appeared to be engrossed in their conversation but would soon see me.

I squinted my eyes and let my emotions funnel to the lights. The fire inside the bulbs flared hotter and pushed at their clear confinements, catching the attention of the guards. The room glowed brighter.

*Now Em!*

With a shattering crack, the two bulbs exploded. Fire was unleashed, sending fragments of glass flying out in all directions.

"Ahhh!" Both men turned away burying their heads under their arms. The flames licked the air close to them before sizzling out. The hallway was plunged into darkness. They could see nothing, but my Dark Dweller and Dae abilities did not leave me vulnerable. My eyes adjusted quickly to the blackness, my powers recreating the space clearly in my mind.

Alki's unrelenting training kicked in. Jumping up, I swung my foot up in a karate kick, connecting with the face of the first guard. There were sounds of his nose breaking when my foot made contact. He fell back with a pained scream. The guy next to him could barely get into a defensive pose before I spun around, my fist smashing into his throat. He put his hands to his neck, coughing and sputtering. Crouching, I whipped my leg around and took him off his feet and onto his back. Both now wheezed and groaned in pain. Quick and efficient. Even Alki would have been proud.

It was actually hard to knock someone out cold in one hit. Eli had taught me that. But, if you cause the body enough stress, it will do it for you. Unable to cope with the pain, the body will shut down to start the healing process. That's what I was counting on now.

I came down on top of the first man and rammed his already broken nose with the sharp part of my elbow. Cracked bones ground under my arm. He screamed out in pain, until his body reached its limit and his head fell to the side, unconscious. Leaning over, I kicked out my foot knocking the other guy in the head; the blow took him out, too.

Breathless, I rolled off the man. *Holy shit!* I wasn't sure if I was proud of myself or was going to be sick.

"Jumpin' Juniper, my lady!" Simmons came hovering over my shoulder. He had relit the torch, passing a dim glow over the two men.

"Damn. Remind me not to piss you off." Cal landed on the chest of one of the guards poking at him with his plastic sword. "You cracker-crumbled his ass."

A flicker of remorse swooped in but quickly evaporated. I was too close now. It was unfortunate they came along, but my actions were necessary. This was the first time I had used my fighting skills in a real situation. Although Alki did treat most of our training as real, this was different. The strenuous work he put me through had been worth it, and I had controlled my powers.

Pulling at the dagger hanging off the guard's belt, I slipped it in my other boot. It would always come in handy. My legs shook as I stood up. "Come on. We have to keep going."

A short time later, I found what I was looking for. Torin had described it perfectly. We had come to an area that splintered off into three different paths, but I didn't care where they went because I wouldn't be taking any of them. In the corner of this area, crates were piled up, nearly touching the ceiling where there was a trap door—my path. It would eventually lead me to the side of the castle where Mark and my friends were being held. Sucking in a breath, I grabbed onto one of the higher crates pulling myself up. They smelled of soil, spices, and chickens—probably food crates. My cat-like qualities really helped me keep my balance as the wooden crates wobbled and teetered.

## Fire in the Darkness

"Almost there, my lady. You are doing so well." Simmons, my own personal cheerleader, rallied behind me.

"Thank you," I said through clenched teeth, my arms trembling, my foot trying to find a place to safely secure itself. Cal was already standing at the top with a look on his face that probably said, "What is taking you so long?"

Finally, I reached the top with only a few slips. Moving close to the ceiling, I pressed my hand to the cutout stone. It begrudgingly shifted under my hand. It was heavy, and I strained to move it. I managed to slip it over a bit before getting a better grip to slide it all the way over. Torin had said the passage led into a vacant room. Let's hope he was right.

Pushing off the crates, I struggled through the opening. My arms locked against the stone floor as I tried to hook my waist onto the ledge. I knew if I could get myself up that far, I could wiggle up the rest of the way. Sweating and huffing, I finally got my legs pulled up through the hole. Crawling away from the opening, I flopped down. I was so ready for a nap.

"About time," Cal snipped.

I ignored him and looked around. I was at ground level of the castle, which was an improvement from the sewer where we had started. The room was small and empty except for more crates stacked against the walls. The distinct aroma of food filtered into my nose. I must be near the kitchen.

I took another moment before standing up. "Okay guys, this is where things become very risky. I want you to promise me no matter what happens you will stay hidden. You will not fight or create a fuss if I am caught. This is my quest, not yours. You deny any association with me. All right?"

"But..." Simmons puffed out.

"No," I said firmly. "Simmons, this is for your safety. Please do this for me. I need to know you guys will be all right. I might need you later. This is a direct order."

Simmons went straight and rigid. With a proper salute, he agreed. "Yes, my lady."

Gazing over at Cal, I tilted my head waiting for him to respond. He huffed, "Yeah, yeah... whatever."

Pressing my ear against the wooden door, all I could hear were muffled sounds: pots banging, China clinking, and people talking. *Okay Em, now or never,* I said to myself, then reached for the handle of the door. Cracking the door an inch, my eye was the only thing exposed. An enormous kitchen lay out in front of me. On the farthest wall, which felt like half a soccer field away, was a stone fireplace. The opening was at least my height and four times as wide. There were racks and pots hanging off poles. Between the fireplace and me were endless tables, storage areas, and other culinary objects.

There were only three people in the kitchen cleaning up. They were all at the far end, but I had to be extra careful not to attract their attention. Going low, I slipped carefully through the slight opening and darted for the doorway closest to me, hiding behind tables as I went. With a sigh of relief, I got through the entry without detection.

My relief was premature. Twenty soldiers stood with swords drawn and guns and arrows pointing at me. The man standing right in front was fueled with rage as he looked at me. His nose was red and blotchy, trying to heal itself from the damage I had bestowed on it a little while ago.

"*Téigh trasna ort féin,*" the man barked roughly at me. It didn't take a genius to know he had probably told me I needed to get very limber and intimate with myself.

"Back down, Quilliam," a voice said from the back of the group. I knew the voice. Torin pushed through the horde of men, a haughty smile playing on his lips.

"Wow, your stench could be smelled all the way down the hall." Torin waved his hand in front of his nose.

"W-what?" I stuttered.

"You smell, Ember."

My lids constricted into a glare. "Traveling through a sewer will do that."

"Yes. It will." He tilted his head. "You should have entered through the front door. Save time and my senses. Either way, did you really think I would let you walk right in and take your family?"

Swallowing, I looked at the man who had promised me so many times he would protect me.

"I am the First Knight, the Queen's knight. She will always come first with me; my loyalty is to her. Deceiving you was quite entertaining, though." Torin strode forward, gloving his hands. I knew what it meant.

Stepping back away from him, my body bumped into a solid form. Craning my neck, I saw it was a man with a bruised neck, a lump on his temple, and a glare that could turn a person to stone.

*Crap! Crap! Crap!*

Guard number two clamped down on my shoulders. Torin pulled a pair of thin iron cuffs off his belt. "You aren't known for your good behavior." He slipped the handcuffs over my wrists. I was getting really tired of this cuffing business. My legs gave out as the iron weakened my powers. His arms gripped me firmly, holding me up. Not having strength to struggle against his hold, I let myself fall against him. When my iron levels started to even out, he placed me firmly on my feet.

Hatred spewed from my eyes. "This whole time you have been playing me?"

He shifted, crossing his arms. "You really made it a little too easy."

"Sir, the Queen is requesting your presence in the Great Hall immediately." A young guardsman stepped into the mass of men, looking directly at Torin.

Torin didn't take his gloating eyes off me as he replied. "Thank you, Castien. Tell her we are coming presently." With a nod, the boy turned and disappeared into the throng. "Let us go, Ember. We cannot keep Her Majesty waiting."

# TWENTY-SEVEN

The soldiers stepped aside as Torin escorted me down the hall. The men I had beaten up nailed me with a shoulder or a foot as I passed them, grumbling Gaelic insults in my ear. My fear kept me from feeling or hearing anything except my own heartbeat.

Guards standing at the door bowed respectfully to Torin, opening the door for us. He gave them a quick nod, his hand on my lower back, and pushed me forward. Twisting away from his touch only made him laugh.

As we stepped into the room, I couldn't hide the awe that flooded me. The Great Hall was exactly that. It was similar to the Throne Room where Torin and I had dreamscaped one time. This was the size of a football field and equally tall. Windows filled one entire side of the room and overlooked the brilliant blue lake below. Fire-encased bulbs dangled from the ceiling lighting up the space like thousands of glow worms. I took in everything, calculating and assessing.

"Well, Torin, it is about time. I was beginning to worry you let this loathsome creature slip through your fingers once more." The Queen's expression was lofty and beautiful. It took me a moment for my eyes to adjust to her beauty. She was so stunning and so ethereal that it was hard to take her in. Today she wore a gorgeous, one shouldered sheath dress that followed the contours of her thin body to the floor. The fabric was so thin and lacey her skin looked like it was inked with a delicate design appearing through the dress.

"I will not disappoint Your Majesty again." Torin bowed his head, but she didn't seem to notice, her eyes searing into me.

"I love when the prey plays so easily into my hands. Did you think Torin was on your side, my dear?" Her lips parted in a thin smile. "That he would go against me and help you?" A breezy laugh floated out of her as she stood up. Servants and guardsmen instantly rushed to her. Without moving her eyes off me, she waved her hand for them to back down and continued toward me. "He was using you this whole time. I told him to get close to you to win your trust and, like I imagined you would, you fell for it. We planned this, and the whole time you thought he was helping you. You are such a fool. He is mine and is faithful to me."

My gaze snapped over to Torin. His jaw locked tightly, turning his cold, unemotional face toward mine. "Did you really think I had feelings for you? A Dae? You are revolting. My Queen needed you, and I will stop at nothing to please my Queen."

An impish smile curved the Queen's lips. "And he does know how to please me."

"It was all a lie?"

"I found it laughable how easy you fell for it." His sneer looked wrong on his face.

"Y-You are sickening."

"No dear, you are the one who is nauseating. And your odor is even worse." The Queen grimaced as she stepped closer. "Actually, it suits you." She smiled cruelly.

Gulping, I couldn't keep my eyes off her. She was stunning, powerful, and extremely scary. She was my height and, therefore, could look directly into my eyes. A strange cloud seemed to pass over her features as she assessed me.

Her hand reached up to my hair. I flinched back, but she didn't seem to notice or care. For some reason I didn't feel like she was really seeing me. Her hand slipped through my hair and softly rubbed one of my red streaks between her fingers. Her focus became even more distant. She was not here with me, but lost in some past memory I was not aware of. Keeping my eyes on her, I watched as her hand moved up and cupped my face. Vulnerability and an unbelievable sadness flooded her face.

She whispered something so softly I couldn't make out what she said. There was something about the way she said it that made me react. My movement finally broke her trance. Her hand jerked away from my face and anger filled her body. Fury shot from her eyes as she looked me up and down. "You are a disgrace to Fay blood," her voice seethed. "You should not have lived. You took everything from me!"

A palpable energy saturated the room, making it hard to breathe. Her anger was so palpable I could feel it digging into my skin. Silent tension kept even a single breath from being released. The Queen looked around suddenly aware of being watched by her people. She snapped back into her usual cool, controlled demeanor. Taking a step back, she yelled, "Guards, take this *thing* down to the dungeon." She swished her hand at me and pivoted, heading to her ruling seat.

"My Queen, permit me to take her down." Torin took a step forward. "I feel the need to see this all the way through. I want the honor of locking up this atrocity myself."

Turning back to face Torin, the Queen stared at him for a brief moment before a small, cruel smile hinted on her lips. "If it will make *my love* happy." My stomach rolled at her words. Her tone had me feeling I was missing something.

"It will, my lady."

"Then by all means take her," the Queen replied.

"Thank you, Your Majesty." Torin grabbed my arm as he gave another bow to the queen.

"Get away from me!" I screamed as I looked back at him. "Don't touch me."

"Like I want to." Torin looked me up and down with revulsion. Hurt flushed through me. No matter what, I couldn't stop his callous tone and gaze from ripping through me. Tugging me roughly by the arm, he quickly rushed me out of the hall. Neither of us spoke as he pulled me through the corridor, down the long descending stairs, and among the dark, dingy hallways leading to the dungeon.

Stopping at the door he abruptly turned me to him. With gloved hands he unlocked my irons, looping them back onto his belt. Then taking another key from his belt he opened the entry to the crypt.

Rows and rows of cells lined the way, disappearing in the murky shadows. The heavy, wooden door creaked with weight as he pushed me through it. As soon as we were in, I whirled around to face him.

"Well..." Crossing my arms, I took in his stony expression. Slowly a grin turned up my mouth. "We did it."

His features softened and suddenly I was in his arms, his warm lips kissing the top of my head. "I hated every minute of that."

"Yeah, but it had to be this way. You said so." I shifted under his embrace to look into his eyes. "Do you think she bought it?"

"Definitely. She would never dream I would betray her, and technically I did not. I told her of our plan. It was the truth."

"Part truth. Thank the gods she did exactly what you thought she'd do."

Our plan was based upon Torin knowing her so well that he could predict, down to the most minuscule aspect, how she'd react. Though I hated that he knew her so intimately, I couldn't deny it had been extremely helpful in this case.

Turning, I looked at the tiny, cold cells lined up down the long corridor. Scatterings of dirty straw sparsely covered each cell floor. A set of chains hung off each of the back walls.

"Home sweet home," I said dryly.

"Just for the night," Torin replied. "We will have you, your dad, and friends out soon. I promise."

I nodded, my eyes locking on the set of shackles.

"You trust me, right?" Torin's gentle hands gripped my arms. "You know I'd do anything in my power for you."

He pulled me to him and his warm lips found mine in the dim corridor. My first instinct was to push him away, but he held me in tighter, his lips hot and passionate, consuming me with emotion. Like floodgates, all the emotion I kept locked inside—the hurt, the fear, the loneliness—came pouring out. I kissed him back with desperation and need. He was my only link to safety, to my family and friends, to my escape, to anything I knew. Passion and desperation are strong motivators. Heat sizzled in my veins as his mouth moved over mine. I longed to escape from this harsh reality, to let him help me forget Eli, to forget all my pain.

"Oh, this really is precious," a voice tinkled out of the dark, full of saccharin. "Young love always is, but young love renders you stupid. You become careless..."

Torin and I sprung apart, whirling around to the shape emerging from the shadows. Queen Aneira stood behind us, followed by several soldiers. Her eyes on Torin.

"You are a fool. You thought you were being so careful, so meticulous with your little planned rendezvous with her. I knew you would hang yourself eventually; all I had to do was provide you with a little rope and be patient. In the meantime, you would lead me directly to her."

She continued to move forward, her gaze never leaving Torin. "My dear how much you have hurt me. I have given you everything. Loved you." Her voice held no emotion as she stepped up to him, her fingers gliding softly along his face.

Torin had become still as stone, jaw and emotions locked down hard.

"Nothing?" Aneira nettled him. With no response from Torin, she sighed. Her voice then turned icy. "Kill her."

"No!" A protest immediately came from Torin. "Your Majesty, you don't want to do that. Please, hear—"

"You. You of all people dare ask me for leniency?" She spit at him. Her face twisted into fury. "You, who betrayed me? I gave you everything, and you deceived me for this monster? How could you? Is it because you were promised to her years ago? This was not what was meant for you. You were promised to a true Fay, not this abomination. You were meant for me."

"My Queen, you don't understa—"

"Stop," she demanded. Magic flared through the room, zeroing in on Torin. Pain and anguish distorted his features, bringing him to his knees under the pressure. "You have no rights anymore."

"Guards, dispose of them both," the Queen ordered.

Overcome with terror, I could feel my powers rise to the surface, but there was too much iron in the room for them to work properly. The Queen did not suffer from this same weakness. Being Queen she probably could handle higher amounts of iron before it affected her like the rest of us. Good to be Queen.

"My Queen, please listen to me. You do not know the whole truth," Torin exclaimed through gritted teeth.

It was taking every bit of his strength to fight against the Queen's painful hold on him.

*Whole truth? What was he talking about?*

"What whole truth?" The Queen echoed my thoughts; her voice was tight and barely able to utter the sentence. All she wanted was to kill us right then, to see her betrayers destroyed, not to listen to words. But Torin seemed to have some kind of hold over her that prevented her from gutting us right there.

"She is a Dae..."

Annoyance flickered over her face. "I know that."

"No, but that is not all she is."

My head jerked over to look at him. *"What are you doing?"* I said into his head. Torin and I had always been able to communicate in our heads. It wasn't the same thing I experienced with Eli. Torin and I could communicate without looking at each other.

*"Trust me,"* he pleaded.

Did I really have a choice at this point? It would be death now or later. I voted for later.

"What do you mean? She can't be more than that. She is either a Dae or she is not." The Queen's patience was waning and her previous admiration for Torin would only go so far.

"She also has the blood of a Dark Dweller."

Her audible gasps echoed through the room.

*Oh. My. God... No!* I had never told him. How did he know?

His eyes met mine. *"I dreamwalked in on you and the Dark Dweller doctor talking about it."*

"You what?"

## Fire in the Darkness

*"I am sorry. I wanted to make sure you were safe. I overheard him telling you."*

My memory recalled that evening with Owen—the moment I had felt someone watching me, the chills. It had been Torin. It was the same reaction Jared and Kennedy had when I dreamwalked on them, perceptive to the spirit form visiting us.

The Queen stood in shock for a few moments before her voice wavered, "T-That is not possible."

"It is, Your Majesty." He looked up at her. "It was my plan to tell you this all along."

My eyes widened. He said to trust him, but my past record of people betraying me was consistent. I found it hard to fully believe this revelation wasn't solely to save his own ass.

The Queen lifted her fingers and the pressure in the room eased. Torin climbed back up to his feet, standing tall and proud.

"Torin, I cannot foresee what game you are playing or why you would lie to me since you know I can easily find out the truth of this claim."

"I assure you I am not lying."

The Queen cocked her head, taking in Torin's genuine demeanor. "Thara? Come forward."

A girl who looked all of sixteen came forward. She had long, flowing, dark hair, deeply tanned skin, and dark, almond-shaped eyes. She was elegant and majestic and looked like a descendent of *Pocahontas*.

"Yes, Your Majesty?" The girl's soothing voice seemed to slide into my bones, immediately calming me.

"Thara, could you please verify what Torin said is true?"

Thara bowed her head and walked up to me, closing her eyes. She didn't touch me or do anything except take a deep breath. My skin tingled and I knew, like the forest, she was "tasting" me. I stayed frozen, watching her.

She stepped away from me and reopened her eyes. "Yes, Your Majesty, he is speaking the truth. She has Dark Dweller blood in her. Her body has adapted and taken on some of their traits." Thara smiled at me, which was warm and somehow comforting.

"How is it possible?" the Queen mumbled to herself in disbelief. "No Fae can take the blood of another species."

"Remember she is no ordinary Fae, my lady; she is a Dae."

The Queen took this in, the wheels of thought spinning in her mind.

Torin looked over at me. *"You are safe from death, mo chuisle. Do not be afraid. She will not kill you now."* His voice spoke softly into my mind.

My defensive walls instantly cracked. I should have known Torin would do everything and anything in his power to keep me safe. My heart warmed as I looked at him. Love was never a word I said or admitted easily. I kept myself guarded and protected from it. But in time, there was a possibility I could find myself falling for him. He must have seen something different in my eyes because suddenly his own glinted with hope and... love.

A slow, seductively dangerous smile spread over the Queen's face. "Torin, I will not forget your duplicity, but in time, if you keep proving yourself like this, I might come to forgive this transgression."

"Yes, Your Majesty," Torin looked pained as he uttered the words. He would take whatever came his way. All because of me.

"Guards take him to my chamber and tie him up. I will see he is properly punished."

A boulder plummeted into my gut. "What? No!" She would torture and abuse him.

*"Ember, let it be,"* Torin said firmly into my thoughts.

*"No Torin, I can't let you do this."*

*"You don't have a choice. I can handle it. I can handle anything if I know you will be all right."* Grief filled my entire body. This was so wrong and twisted. Disgusting. I felt like I was going to throw up.

The guards circled around. He held up his wrists as they clamped on iron cuffs. It took everything I had not to fall to the ground as they led him out. He kept his head high; his form was tall and proud even as he was being led away to humiliation and abuse.

*"Stay strong. You will stay alive as long as you are useful to her. I love you, mo chroi,"* he uttered into my thoughts before he vanished out the door.

Tears freely fell down my face now. How did our plan turn out so wrong?

"I am so glad I did not kill you. You will be even more useful to me." She clasped her hands together, her fiery mood simmering into giddiness. "Dark Dweller blood mixing with a Dae? Who would have thought?" Her delight was clear. "Oh, the things I will be able to do now."

This time the Queen escorted me, hauling me down the rows of cells. The dungeon was dark and smelled of urine and feces. One of the guards pushed me into the far cell and pulled gloves off his belt, sliding them on, before reaching around me for the chain hanging on the back wall, a manacle dangling from it. He bent down and slipped it over my ankle, locking it in place. Then he did the same with one of my wrists. I instantly felt my energy being pulled from my body and my legs give out, falling onto the stiff, smelly straw.

*Damn iron.* It always took a few minutes before my body accepted the shock and relaxed into it. After that I could function somewhat, but the first part was a bitch. I swallowed through the flash of pain. I hated feeling so helpless and vulnerable even for a short time. I held up my shackled wrist. "To keep us slaves well behaved?"

She smiled smugly. "There was a reason Torin wanted you down here. But if he thought it would be more than a little reunion, he was sadly mistaken. Sorry, Ember dear, nothing down here can help you. I think my favorite prisoner is way past that—seemed a little broken the last time I tried to play with it."

Aneira nodded at the guard and he slammed the gate. The bars rattled, the reverberation hurting my teeth. Something at the other end of the cell stirred. I wasn't alone. They locked me up with another prisoner.

"I do hope you enjoy your time with us." Aneira turned and swept out of the room.

When the room emptied, my prison mate's head rose up. Glare from the little light that was in the cell reflected in the eyes. It reminded me of when your car headlight catches an animal's eyes. They nervously assessed the space. Sensing there was no immediate threat, the form sat up. The chains clinked and scratched across the floor and against the walls. By the simple movement I knew it to be a woman. The figure was too delicate and small in stature to be a man.

"Hello?" The voice was quiet and groggy.

"Hi," I responded back, hauling myself up into a sitting position. The pain of the iron began to fade.

"Did they just bring you in?" she asked, her voice so quiet. I couldn't stop feeling like I recognized the voice from somewhere else.

"Yeah. Guess I should not have checked the Dae box at immigration."

The woman went quiet for a moment before I heard her whisper, "Oh, holy crap on ash bark."

My stomach plummeted and chills rolled over my flesh. There was only one person I knew who had ever used that phrase—but there was no way. No way.

"What did you say?" I demanded.

"No, I can't believe this...you aren't supposed to be here. That was the whole point," the lady mumbled to herself.

Fire and ice seared through me. My legs began shaking but somehow I got to my feet. Shadows were thick, but my eyes were slowly adjusting. I didn't need to see, though; my heart and gut knew.

The woman in front of me was a shell of what I remembered, but it didn't keep me from seeing who it was. This was too much, my body quaked underneath me.

"Oh, my God." My throat felt tight as I whispered out, "Mom?"

"Yes, sweetie, it's me."

My legs collapsed under me.
*My mother was alive.*

## TWENTY-EIGHT

Air no longer moved in and out of my body easily. I stared at the outline of my mother with a numbness that cut off all thought. If I blinked, I was afraid she would disappear, an apparition created by hope and memories. My vision took in a hand reaching for me, the chains rattling. They sounded far away, muffled. The hand grazed my shoulder, but it didn't feel like it was touching me. It was as if I was not present in my body.

"Holy ash bark. You have grown up into such a beauty." She continued to ramble on about my looks, height and how old I had gotten, but it was all buzzing in my ears.

"Breathe, Ember." Both her hands moved to my shoulders, gripping me. Her orange-brown eyes stared into mine.

With a sharp inhale everything came back into focus. Warmth from her hands soaked into me. She was real. "Mom," my voice squeezed out, emotion choking me.

"Yes, my beautiful girl. I am here." Her arms wrapped around me, pulling me into her.

I broke. Hot tears spilled vehemently down my cheeks. Nothing made sense. Once again my world had turned upside down. But the deep joy I felt at her being alive was almost too much for me to take. I crumbled in her arms, sobbing like a child.

My mom was alive.

She kept her arms tight around me and rocked me as I continued to cry. "Shhh. I'm here," she whispered over and over, her hand running continuously through my hair, soothing me.

It took a long time for me to stop crying or for any thought to enter my head besides my mother was breathing and holding me like I had wished and dreamed about for so many years.

"I don't understand," I hiccupped out. Sobs ricocheted through my body.

"I know. I will explain all in time."

Pulling away from her arms, sitting up. "No, tell me now."

She bit her lip and looked out of the cell. "I'm sorry I had to leave you. The soldiers were getting near, and I needed to protect you."

All of a sudden some anger and hurt bowled over the joy I had felt a moment earlier. I had lived almost seven years thinking she was dead. Every day the images of her shredded, tangled body robbed me of any sanity I had tried to salvage. She had left me. She had left Mark. Alone.

"You were dead. I saw your body." The words fervently spit out of my mouth. "I was the one who discovered you. How do I even know you are my mother? You could be glamoured to look like her. The

Queen set this up to mess with me, huh?" I looked around ready for the Queen to come from out of the shadows, laughing at my gullibility.

"Ember, it's me, I promise you." She extended her hand out to me. I yanked my hands away from her reach. "I had to do it. I am *so* sorry, but it was the only way to keep you safe."

I stood, anger causing me to move away from her.

"Safe? Letting your twelve-year-old daughter discover your remains, lose her sanity, and grow up not knowing what she was or capable of, is what you call safe?"

"Compared to the other choice, yes. I did what I thought was right. I had to keep you protected no matter what."

"What could be worse than that?"

My mom sighed, sorrow deep in her eyes. "The Queen."

"But she didn't find me until recently. You supposedly died almost seven years ago. In a different realm."

"Time and space mean nothing here." She sat up on her knees, the weight of the chains straining out from the wall. "From the day I snuck you out of the Otherworld, she has been hunting us. I did my best to keep protection spells around you. I even tried to block your gifts, but you were too powerful and every once in a while, especially when you were young and didn't understand, they would come out. I couldn't always keep them at bay. If an 'incident' happened, we would move to a new place and start all over again."

So many things about my childhood seemed clear. The reason we moved around so much. Why after something strange would happen she would panic and have us packed up, leaving within a day. The reason my powers hadn't showed up till after my mother's "death," when the protection spells were broken. She had done it all for me. She sacrificed having a real life.

"It wasn't until I met Mark I realized I wanted both of us to have more of a life than the one we were living. Mark brought love and stability to both our lives. You and I were always tight, but he made us a family with a real chance for you to grow up and be normal. I hoped, with him being human and my protection spells, we could have a good life."

"But we aren't normal. Mark would have aged—eventually died. We wouldn't. I think he would have noticed eventually." The logical part of me still doubted this was my mother and thought it was all an illusion.

"With love you do not want to think about how things will end. I loved him so much. I would have glamoured myself, appearing like I was aging with him until he died. You would have slowly continued to age. I guess I was hoping he would not notice there were only slight changes in you." Her voice choked up. Thinking about Mark must be painful for her.

"Why didn't you tell me?" I asked. "Were you ever going to?"

"Eventually, I knew I would have to. I wanted to keep the truth from you as long as possible. Then it was too late."

"But why? Don't you think I would have preferred knowing the truth? I always knew I didn't fit and I wasn't quite right."

"You would have been treated much worse in this world. You could have been killed." Her lips went white as she pressed them together. "Plus, I know you, Ember. Telling you would have meant certain death for you. You are too inquisitive, which is a good trait in most cases, but not in this one. Your need to know what and who you were would have been too overwhelming. There would have been no way of stopping you from trying to find out more. The Queen would have found you instantly.

"You must be angry with me, but I did what I did to keep you safe. The less you knew the better. I won't deny some of it was selfish. We were finally able to stay in one place and live a life I never imagined possible."

I couldn't fully let go of the anger and resentment I felt, but I also understood why she did it. She was right. I would have been too curious to stop searching and discovering the world I was meant to belong in. I would have been found and killed.

"There were a few close calls. Several times we were almost discovered. The Queen was closing in, and I knew it would be only a matter of time. I could not risk leading her to you. I encountered Torin in Canada when I was doing my research. I didn't want them anywhere near you so I turned myself over. Unfortunately, that meant leaving no question I was dead. I did not want even the slighted hint I was still alive. If you came looking for me, which I knew you would if no body was found, you'd be even more unprotected."

The trip to Canada, the conspiracy theory I came up with about her death had been wrong. The truth had been much more convoluted and crazier than I could have ever imagined.

"The house in Monterey had a protection spell on it. I hoped between it and living with Mark you would stay hidden. I should have known Torin would not stop until he found you."

"But how could you do that to me? Do you know what it was like seeing your mutilated body on our back porch? The nightmares, the therapists, medication...all because I couldn't see anything but images of you, torn into shreds."

Lily pressed her lips together, agony filtered across her face. "I didn't know."

"What do you mean you didn't know? How do you think I'd react to seeing that?" I pushed farther away from her.

"No, I mean I didn't know how my death was staged. My connections, who were living secretively on Earth, set it up for me. As fellow Fae they understood the body had to be glamoured to appear to be me, but not enough to be clearly identifiable. They took care of everything. No details were given to me." Her eyes watered up. "I am so sorry, Em. I know nothing I can do will make it up to you nor can I ask for your forgiveness."

"Was it the Dark Dwellers?"

The words came to my lips before my mind realized that thought had been humming under the surface the moment I saw my mother. Why had Eli and Lorcan told me they killed my mother? Did they mean they had helped her look like she had been murdered? None of this made sense. Knowing Eli really hadn't killed my mom lifted a weight from my soul. Rubbing at my head, the hurt and betrayal were riding high. There were so many things I wanted to know, countless things unanswered.

"The Dark Dwellers?" My mom jerked with surprise. "Why would you say that? How do you know about Dark Dwellers?"

Her reaction told me they had nothing to do with her faked death. My confusion only intensified.

"No reason." I shook my head and hurriedly changed the subject. "As much as I'd like to discuss every detail of the things you kept from me my whole life, we actually have more pressing issues to focus on."

Hurt showed clearly on my mom's face, but she nodded. It was upsetting to see her pain, but my own was too raw to let it go. Most of me wanted to lay my head on her lap like I used to and forget the world outside of us existed.

"The Queen has taken my friends to use as bait." I paused, taking a deep breath.

"I am so sorry Em—"

"That's not all," I interrupted. "She has Mark as well."

The moment of stunned silence broke into an anguished cry. "What?" The complete and utter dismay on her face only confirmed not one bit of her time with Mark had been faked. Her love for him was deep and concrete. At least that aspect of my life had been true. "Oh my God! She has Mark?"

I nodded in confirmation. "I came here to get them out. Torin and I came up with a plan...which didn't exactly work out."

"Oh Mark, nonono... he can't be here. If he eats Fae food..." She rambled on, not listening to me.

"Mom!" I shouted. She snapped her head up to me. "Please, I need you to focus. Torin has assured me he is all right for now, but we have to come up with a new plan."

She blinked and then a small smile crept onto her mouth. "When did you grow up?"

"Seven years ago..."

"I can't believe I've been gone so long." Sadness resounded in her eyes. "I missed you growing up." She shook her head, taking in the information.

"Well, right now we need to come up with ideas to get out of here." I sat down leaning against the cool, stone wall, pushing the years of questions and feelings back into the locked box in my heart. Now was not the time. Nighttime was closing in on the Otherworld, darkening the cell in a murky haze. The only light came from the single glass fire bulb hanging from the ceiling. Cool air seeped through the tiny windows. Shivering, I hunkered down deeper into the foul straw.

"I am going to try to contact Torin. I need to know he is okay."

"You two have grown close?" She looked at me curiously.

"Umm—yeah, I guess you could say that. He has been there for me and saved my life a couple times. It's hard not to feel close to someone after that."

"Do you love him?"

The question stopped me in my tracks. "Uhhhh..." I faltered. "Love him? I care about him a lot. He's a wonderful guy. Everything I would want."

"But..."

"There's no 'but'."

"Ember, I am your mother. I know you and I know there is a huge 'but' in there. Is there someone else?"

I clenched my teeth. "You've supposedly been dead for the last seven years of my life. You don't know anything about me anymore."

Wounded, my mom looked away, blinking away her tears. A few moments of tense silence hung between us before she cleared her throat. "You're right. I don't know. Nothing I can say can take away the pain I caused."

Resentment and guilt wrestled in my chest. "This really isn't the time to talk about this."

"No, you're probably right." She broke off, before speaking again. "He's in love with you. So be careful."

"How do you know he's in love with me?" How would she know? Unless he came down here and told her, there was no way she could know.

Mom looked away, "Oh, I'm just gathering."

My forehead creased suspiciously, but pushed it aside. *More important issues at hand, Em.* Settling myself against the wall of the jail I closed my eyes.

*"Torin?"* I called to him in my mind.

For the next fifteen minutes I tried to contact him to no avail. There had been other times when he didn't answer, yet I could at least feel a presence of some kind, a feeling he heard me. Almost like receiving a busy signal. He wasn't available, but I knew he was there. This felt more like the cord had been cut. There was nothing, and it unsettled me. Something was wrong.

"Shit!" I banged my hands onto the stone floor in frustration.

"Nothing?"

"No. Something's not right. The Queen's done something to him." I closed my eyes briefly and hoped he was okay. The thought of the Queen hurting him made me ill.

"Now what?" Mom looked down at the chains attached to her arms. "I am useless having been down here so long. I can barely stand."

I pulled at my handcuffed wrists. How in the hell was I going to get out of here without Torin's help?

"Shit!" I yelled again.

"I really wish you would hold it," a small voice said above my head.

Whipping around, my gaze landed on two pixies standing in the tiny, barred window. "Cal! Simmons!" I exclaimed.

"Seems, my lady, you have gotten yourself in a terrible bind." Simmons nodded toward my chains. "Cal was sure you would need our help so we stayed close by." Simmons stood like a solider ready for duty.

"Cal?" I felt both surprise and affection that he chose to stay near—just in case.

"Don't get all mushy on me. I expect payment for the services rendered," Cal responded abrasively.

A smile came to my face. "And what would the payment be?" He didn't fool me for a minute.

"Endless supply of juniper juice. A new sword." He tugged at his plastic cocktail garnish stick tied to his waist. "And maybe...a kiss," he gruffly threw out.

"Done, done, and done," I agreed.

His eyes lit up before he looked away. "Okay, fine. We'll help the harlot."

"Harlot?" My mom spoke up with a laugh.

"Hey. I've had to make a living somehow, Mom." I arched my eyebrow at her.

Her lips quirked up, her voice proud. "That's my girl."

The warmth spreading through my chest brought a smile to my eyes. It reminded me of the old times, the way she and I had teased and bantered, the years we missed. I looked away from her.

"Okay, let's get this show on the road." I clasped my hands together firmly. "First, we somehow need to get these cuffs off."

"Oh, my lady, you greatly insult us." Simmons flew down and, with only a tiny slip, perched on my knee. "We are prepared for duty."

Simmons pulled two bobby pins from his belt. Cal came down, plopping on my arm and took one of the pins from Simmons. In a matter of seconds he had worked the metal into the locks, wiggling it around, and freed my wrist and ankle from the shackles.

"You guys are unbelievable. Thank you." I rubbed at my freed wrist, the weight of the iron peeling away from me instantly. "Oh, that is so much better."

They hopped over to Mom. Her cuffs were a little harder to get loose as they had been on a lot longer than mine. The metal clenched together with its greedy bond. Finally, after several minutes, hers plunked to the ground as well.

That was when I saw her chains were not just energy suckers. They were torture devices. Each cuff was lined with teeth, small spikes that embedded into her skin. She cried out in pain as they tore away from her wrists. Aneira had tortured her by draining her energy and driving rods into her skin.

I looked forward to killing that bitch.

Mom crumbled back against the pile of straw. From the little time my powers had been pulled from my body, I knew the immense emotion she must be feeling after that constant torture.

I wanted to go to her, to hug her but struggling emotions held me back. She needed a few moments to adjust. If what everyone told me about her earth powers were true, it had to be overwhelming to have so much crash through you at once. She quieted down and took a deep breath, her head turned up in my direction. "Okay, I am ready."

I nodded to the pixies. "So, you guys think you can work the same magic with the door locks?"

Simmons' puckered face told me I had insulted their capabilities again.

"Sorry. Please, precede, Captain Simmons." I motioned toward the door. I thought adding 'Captain' would help with his hurt pride. It worked like a charm; he glowed with satisfaction, fluttering toward the locked cell door.

"No matter what size the man, their egos need to be stroked," my mom mumbled.

I snickered and looked at her, nodding. It was so easy to fall back into our old rapport. It hurt how much I'd missed her, how long I had wanted my mom back in my life. The years after her "death" had turned me hard and defensive. My heart had been shredded so many times, I guarded my feelings. My mom and I had a long road to recovery. It wasn't really easy to accept she was alive and everything was okay and back to normal. Life didn't work that way. I didn't work that way.

With a loud crack and whine of metal, the cell door swung open. I winced, hoping the walls of the dungeon locked in noise as well as it did its prisoners. There had to be guards close by so I stayed watchful of every nuance of the large underground.

Taking the lead, I slipped out a knife from my boot. We crept down the dimly lit chambers, weaving through the labyrinth of the prison. We turned down a wrong path, and I was about to turn us around when something stopped me. A figure slumped in one of the cells caught my attention. Another prisoner. I peered closer; something about him seemed familiar.

Recognition hit me like a rock. Horror clogged my throat.

"Oh my God."

Unable to stop, I rushed to the bars, pushing through the pain the iron bars caused me. I didn't care. I fell to my knees as my arms went through the bars, grasping the man's face.

"You know I can never resist when you call for me like that, darlin'." His voice was forced and gravelly. Pained.

"West... oh God!" My gaze took in his wounded, damaged body. His neck was ringed by a spiked-lined collar, cutting into his throat every time he swallowed or talked. "What happened? Why are you here?"

He swallowed, a trickle of blood sliding down his neck. His eyes darted up to mine. Sorrow, pain, and anger rolled around in them.

"Lorcan."

My eyes closed briefly in understanding. I had always hated Lorcan, but now fiery abhorrence consumed me. Protectiveness of West made me want to tear at the bars, to shelter him, to keep him safe. *Family.* The notion tore through me followed by a guttural growl.

"Ember?" My mother's hand reached down to my shoulder, her voice unsure. With a protective snarl, my gaze flashed up to her. Her hand went to her mouth and she stumbled back with a gasp.

"Whoa, darlin'..." West said bringing my attention back on him. A strained smile twisted on his face. "It's okay. I'll be all right." Dread gurgled in my stomach as I looked at him in pain. I couldn't be reassured. Another small rumble came from my chest. West placed his hand over mine. "I'm thinkin' Eli's blood did more than just save your life."

It finally hit me what everyone was freaking out about. My eyes and actions had become full Dark

Dweller. Looking down, I took in a deep breath, trying to calm my instincts.

*Shit!*

I recognized right then Eli was not someone I could easily walk away from. No matter what he did or didn't do, he was a part of me. There wasn't a piece of me that wasn't intertwined with him now. Even my freaking DNA.

"Ember?" My mom's voice broke me out of my thoughts.

"I'm okay, Mom." I looked up at her.

"What the hell happened? What happened to your eyes? Who is he?" She pointed to West. I could tell she already sensed what he was but needed me to actually confirm it.

"This is West...and he's a Dark Dweller."

It took her a moment before motherly instinct took over. "Get away from him!"

"Mom...you don't understand."

"All I need to know is that he's a Dark Dweller." Her voice was severe. "Now get the hell away from him!"

"No," I responded.

"No? Did you just tell me no?"

*And I'm back to being five again.* I turned back to West, ignoring her rant.

"Mommy is pissed, darlin', so you probably should listen to her. You guys need to get out of here."

"I am not going without you." My jaw set firmly.

A pained smile formed on his mouth. "I always knew I liked you, but you can't help me. These spikes stop me from changing, and the collar is spelled so it can't be undone even with a key." He took a jagged breath. "Go while you can."

"West..." I reached up touching his cheek again. I heard Mom suck air angrily between her teeth.

*Wait till she learns about my full connection to the Dark Dwellers. That'll be fun.*

"Please, go."

I bit down on my lip. I couldn't help him, but it was hard to leave him. Against all odds, he was my family now. My blood made him so, and I protected my own. "I'll be coming back for you. I will not leave you here."

"Somehow I know you won't. You are one of us now, aren't you?" His eyebrow hitched up in curious amusement.

"Yes," I nodded. "I am." This was not something that would ever go away. I was part Dark Dweller and proud of it. More than I thought I'd ever be. Giving his hand a squeeze, I pulled back, and stood up.

"Until we meet again." West leaned his head back against the wall, giving me one of his infamous grins.

"Until we meet again." I winked and then I herded my mother down the dark corridor, Simmons and Cal on our tail.

"Think we got more trouble on our hands with this one than we planned on, Simmons," Cal said from behind me.

"Why, Calvin, for once I think you are right."

# TWENTY-NINE

"The only way we're going to get through this castle and to their rooms undiscovered is if you guys go ahead of us. You can hide in the shadows and warn us if anybody is coming. This could get really dangerous," I whispered to the pixies.

"When we were trying to find you, my lady, most were retiring."

"Well, that's a little good news." I sighed. "Now go."

Simmons saluted me. "Aye, my lady. Your wish is our command."

"But why can't the wish ever consist of me lying next to a rambling brook with a glass of juniper juice?" Cal grumbled, but took off after Simmons.

"You've been in the Otherworld for a short time and already have two pixies at your command." Mom's head wagged back and forth. "Impressive. Pixies are usually self-absorbed, isolated creatures. They rarely help others or even other pixies."

It was strange to hear my mom talk about the Otherworld. It was odd to associate her with this world; she had hidden that life from me so well for so long.

A tiny figure zipped back into the room. "The soldiers guarding the dungeons are directly on the other side of this door and are snoring. Cal insists they are not pretending, but I recommend going forth with caution, my lady." Simmons' advice lingered in my ear.

"Thank you, Simmons. I will take it into advisement." Gripping the knife tighter in my hand, I tiptoed through the door inching it open until I could pop my head through.

Exactly as Simmons reported, the soldiers were sound asleep, their deep snores echoed off the stone walls. Mom and I crept past them. Room by room, hallway by hallway, this strategy played itself out. The castle was quiet and a minimal number of people were around, which was very helpful.

My newly found Dark Dweller attributes helped. Being slinky and quiet seemed to come naturally to me now. I was also surprised how quiet Mom could skulk. It seemed part of her nature, too. Both of us easily kept to the shadows, undetected by the few we did run across. The real problem was getting past the guards who protected my friends' and Dad's rooms. From my dreamwalk I had a general idea where they were. I sent Simmons out to case the outer windows of the castle.

"My lady! My lady!" Simmons came hurling down the hallway a few minutes later.

"Shhhh!" I held a finger to my lips.

"They—your friends—are in the last room down the hall on the left," he whispered excitedly.

"Any guards?" Simmons had probably awakened the entire castle by now.

"Only one. The Queen obviously feels your friends are a very low threat."

Drying my sweaty palm on my jeans, I re-clenched the knife I had been holding in a death grip.

"Okay, here is the plan: We get my friends out first. Cal and Simmons can take them into the forest while Mom and I find Mark. Then we'll all get the hell out of here." My voice was strong and direct, but I knew how flimsy the plan was. They knew it, too, but they all nodded, too scared to think of all the things that could go wrong.

The guard near their room was also asleep, which seemed odd. I thought we had lucked out with the first guards being asleep, but this was beyond lucky. Glancing up at Cal, my brow furrowed.

"So, they had a little help going to sleep. Indict me." Cal crossed his arms.

"I think I owe you two kisses now." My smile widened at Cal.

Six inches of pixie flushed red from head to toe. "What makes us drunk causes you big Fairies to sleep like babies."

"Cal, I am so loving you right now."

He only turned redder.

We moved closer to the passed-out guard. Recognition hit me as I stared at him. I couldn't recall his name, but I knew it was the beautiful guard who had come into the room in my dreamwalk. I had respected how well he treated my friends. He did not seem to believe they were beneath him, as so many other Fay thought of humans. He reminded me of a younger Torin, proud and honorable, but who would go against the Queen if he believed she was wrong.

Cal flapped down to where the keys were hooked on the guard's belt. I clenched my teeth and held my breath as Cal slowly pulled the keys off. This could go so bad so quickly. The young man stirred, but his eyes remained shut. Cal flew to the door, twisting the key in the lock. With a click the lock turned over. We all froze and looked at the guard, waiting for him to awaken. I knew from here on we would have to be swift and methodical in our movements and choices. When I slipped into the room, my finger was already at my lips telling them not to react.

Kennedy was the first to see me. She jumped off the bed about to say something, but stopped when she saw me shake my head. Josh and Jared followed suit, standing quietly. When we were all in the room, I closed the door.

Kennedy was in my arms before I could even blink. "Em... I knew you'd come."

I pulled her close, hugging her tightly. "I don't work without you guys." My heart realized how much I had missed her.

"Ryan and I feel the same. We don't function without our spice." She squeezed me then pulled back. That was when I noticed that Ryan hadn't moved even an inch.

"What's wrong with him?" I took in Ryan's labored breathing and perspiring, white pale skin.

"We don't know. He was fine but suddenly became really ill," Kennedy responded.

I moved closer to him, and my mom came to my side. She laid a maternal hand on his head. "He's burning up."

"What are you doing here, Ember?" Josh's tone was tense.

"Josh..." I walked over and threw my arms around him. Stiffening under my grasp, he patted my back uncomfortably. Josh and I always had a touchy, relaxed relationship. It was clear he no longer felt comfortable around me.

"Em." Jared took me in a bear hug. His arms felt like they bulked up a size since I saw him. "So good to see you."

"You, too, J." I stepped back, knowing I had to tell him something he would take badly. Blurting it out was the only way. "West is here."

"What? West?" Jared reacted. "What do you mean West is here?"

"He's locked in the dungeon, and I couldn't get him out." My hands reached out to Jared knowing his impulse would be to go to him. "We will come back for him. I swear to you, Jared, we will get him out."

"How did he get here? I don't understand."

He was a smart kid, but denial was a strong seductress. Tilting my head, I said only one word. "Lorcan."

He shook his head back and forth rebuffing my answer, then stopped. The certainty of it washed over him. "Fuck," he swore. I could feel him holding back the scream he wanted to belt out. His hand took a swing at the wall. Blood poured instantly from his knuckles.

"Jared, stop!" Kennedy exclaimed, rushing to his side. She took his damaged hand tenderly into hers.

I sat down on Ryan's bed. Sweat soaked his clothing and his cheeks flushed a bright red as fever ravaged him. Glimpses of consciousness flickered across his face.

"Ryan, I have to get you out of here." His eyes opened for a second before shutting again. "Please, I need you to sit up."

"You won't be taking him anywhere," a voice spoke from behind me. The entire room swiveled around with a start. The guard we had snuck past now stood in the doorway.

"Castien, please..." Kennedy stepped towards him, cautiously. The name finally connected with his familiar face.

"Ryan is too ill to move. You will kill him if you try to take him to Earth. Humans do not take passing through as easily as Fae do. If he was healthy, I would not object, but he is not. I will not allow you to remove him from the premises." Castien's tone held a protective note in it.

"What?" I couldn't help from blurting it out. I felt confused. He wasn't turning us in? He was not screaming down the hallway for the Queen or more guards?

"We can't leave him behind," Kennedy exclaimed.

"If you take him, he will die. If he stays, he will be a prisoner but will live. I will make sure of it."

Looking around the room, Mom and I had the same dumbstruck expression on our faces. The others did not. This was not as much of a shock to them as it was to us.

Looking down at Ryan and back to Castien, something clicked. "You like him," I smiled.

"Ryan is special. I will keep him safe," Castien replied, neither confirming nor denying. "Now, if you are going to sneak out the window, you better do it now. The wards will go off instantly, but I will try to delay them as much as I can."

A small chuckle escaped my throat. This night could not get any stranger. Leaning down I kissed Ryan's head. "I love you, Ry. I will be back for you, okay?" Ryan only mumbled something incoherently, sound asleep. Castien took this moment to exit the door so we didn't have long.

"I'm going to jump down first. Ken, you jump next, then Josh. I'll catch you guys." Jared motioned Kennedy to move to the window, then looking at me. "When they're down I'll start for the woods. You'll help get your mom down?" I nodded. Jared climbed onto the sill, pushing through the bars.

"Jared?" His head turned around to look at me. "Keep them safe. Simmons and Cal will show you where to go. Follow them."

"What are you doing Em?" Uneasiness filled his tone.

"Going after my dad. I won't leave Mark here."

He watched me before he reluctantly nodded. The next instant he was gone, vaulting out the window. Several seconds later we heard a soft whistle. Kennedy crawled onto the ledge. Instead of jumping she sat there, shivering as she gazed down. I remembered she was scared of heights. "Ken, I love you, but if you don't jump, I'll push you." She took a deep breath and then plunged into the darkness. Josh was next, but he also hesitated at the window.

"Josh, we don't have much time. You have to jump now." I moved to him.

"I-I don't want to."

With an agitated breath, "I am sorry if you are scared. I get it, but you have to go." My hand pushed him to the window.

"I am not scared," he yelled at me, anger flushing his face. I took a step back.

"Josh, honey, I am sorry to push you into this, but you are going to have to jump. Now," my mom spoke, her voice sympathetic but firm. Josh grunted and with a heavy sigh climbed onto the windowsill and leaped.

"Good work." I bowed my head in appreciation.

"Takes a mother's firm hand." She smiled. "Now, you get your ass up there."

"Did you not hear me? I am going after Mark."

"No, you are not. I will go after him. You need to get out of here. I need you safe."

"I don't care. I am not leaving without you or Mark!"

Cal flew through the window. "Uh... there is a slight problem with that. The wards must have sounded because the guards are aware of your escape and are heading this way. I'd get both of your asses out of the window now!"

We could hear yells and commotion from down the hall. Getting closer.

"Go!" Cal's arms waved vigorously in my face.

## Fire in the Darkness

Hesitating for one more moment before I hopped on the ledge and leaped into the rich blackness of the night. Flying through the air felt incredible, giving me a buzz of adrenaline. My senses distinguished the landscape around me targeting where to land. And being part Dark Dweller helped my body land on all fours soundlessly. My mom's soft impact followed mine. The fact she was so weak and still tried to keep up with me reminded me of her strong character. Against popular belief, Fairies can't actually fly. She could have hurt herself, but without complaint she followed me and did remarkably well.

"Oh, there you are, my lady." Simmons circled my head. Pixies on the other hand were born to fly. Simmons just had a slight problem with the landing part. "I have been dutifully on lookout. The coast is clear."

"Yes, but it won't be for long." And with that, a drum-like sound penetrated the night—the warning bell. Our window of opportunity was closing with each wailing clang coming from the castle.

"Run!" I screamed.

Simmons waved us forward. "Follow us. We know a good door for your escape." Cal was already taking off for the forest.

"Go-Go-Go!" I pushed everyone forward.

Josh didn't move. "Josh what are you doing?" The way he looked at me caused icy dread to fill me. I knew what he was going to do. "Josh, no!"

"I'm sorry, Ember." He shook his head. "There is nothing for me back there. This is where I belong. I always have. I'm meant to be here."

"No. You're not. You are human, Josh. You have friends who care about you." I could see in the distance soldiers beginning to swarm out from the castle like ants. "Josh, come on. This place is not like your video games. This is real. You can't go back if you decide this isn't fun anymore. I am your friend. I want you with me; I care about you. You have more than you think back there. Please..." I held out my hand.

His jaw was set with resolve as he backed away from me, then he turned and ran straight to the guards who were coming after us. He held up his hands in surrender. They quickly surrounded him, and he disappeared in the throng of uniforms.

"Fuck!" I yelled. I didn't want to give up on him but, somewhere deep inside, I knew I had already lost him, forever. There was nothing I could do now. I ran away from the threat heading my way.

The stars shone so radiantly I saw the outlines of my family merging into the forest. Following them, I came to the tree line and turned briefly to see if we were being pursued. We were not safe by any means, but the soldiers, who were occupied with capturing Josh, did not see where we went. I almost felt safe when movement in a castle window stopped me dead in my tracks. Mark stood a floor above where we had jumped. He couldn't see me, but seeing him changed everything.

"Mark!"

My plans to get him free were crumbling in front of me. I never planned on leaving him, but the situation had changed. Frozen in my spot, my heart wrenched in my chest. I could not leave him, but how was I going to get to him now? With no thought, my body started back for the castle.

"Ember, no!" Jared grabbed me around my waist and stopped me. The army of men hearing my cry had begun to move in our general direction.

"I have to get Mark," I screamed, fighting and struggling against his hold.

Jared swung me around to face him. Taking my shoulders, he shook me. "Ember, you can't help any of them if you are captured. Mark will be okay. You know she will keep him alive. Do you understand me? You cannot help him now."

I had heard it so many times now, but it didn't get any easier. Leaving my loved ones behind didn't sit well with any part of me.

"I know..." I admitted, although there was an unspoken "but" hanging in my sentence.

"No. You cannot hesitate. The best thing is to leave them. It is the only way we can eventually get them out. You think I want to leave them behind? Ryan or West? West is my family, but he would be the first to tell me to get my ass out of here."

Jared had matured into a leader. He was not the same hyper kid I met only a few months back. He had grown into a man.

Nodding, we all started to move deeper into the forest. My head turned to see my mother standing there, agony written on her features. "Mom, come on. Let's go." I gripped her arm hard, tugging her to follow me.

"I am not leaving Mark here." Mom shook her head, trying to fight against my pull. I was stronger, but her resolved determination made it hard for me to gain any real ground.

"You think I want to?" I shot back as I rushed her along. "He is my dad and the main reason I came here, but Jared's right. What kind of help will we be to him if we're dead or locked in jail?"

"Ember, you don't understand. He shouldn't even be here. This is my fault. I should have known from the start I was putting his life in danger. But I was selfish and wouldn't give him up."

I had always blamed myself for Mark's situation. I now understood something I hadn't thought about before. "Do you think if Mark knew the outcome, it would have stopped him? He loved...loves you more than life itself. He would have chosen this. He would never give us up, no matter the outcome, and we will do everything we can to get him back. He wouldn't want us to be martyrs. He'd want us to fight."

Mom's resilience faded away. "Damn, you've grown up into an amazing person. Mark did an exceptional job, not that you weren't already incredible. I always knew how lucky I was to have you."

"Let's save the family bonding for later, okay?" My gaze drifted over her shoulder. It was pure torture for both of us to leave Mark.

When the Queen's soldiers shouted behind us, we ran toward Kennedy and Jared. The dark shielded us as we all slipped farther into the dense forest.

"This way, my lady," Simmons called, zipping through trees. We followed behind, trying to keep up with his rapid pace. Adrenaline propelled my body forward. Glancing behind, I saw Jared had fallen back. He stuck close to Kennedy, his arm wrapped around her, helping her keep up with our inhuman speed.

An object zipped by my head. "I made enough noise so they think we went to the other door. We need to hurry. They will come through here soon," Cal called out. Relief fluttered in my chest, but it was too soon to relax.

"Here is the door, my lady. Hurry, let's get you through before they figure out which way we went." Simmons stopped at a disturbance of air. This time I could see the portal clearly; I had finally let go and accepted what I was—every part of me, including the Dark Dweller part.

Turning, I waited for Jared and Kennedy to catch up. "Go!" I waved them on. Without hesitation, Jared clung tighter to Kennedy and took her through the space, vanishing.

"You go first. I need a moment," I said to Mom as I nodded up at the pixies.

"Make the moment fast," Mom directed her gaze to Cal and Simmons. "Thank you. I am forever in your debt."

I determined from their deep sighs that Cal and Simmons took this as a big deal. "You are most welcome," Simmons replied.

Mom gave me a quick smile. "See you on the other side." And then she was gone.

Hesitating, I stared up at Cal and Simmons.

"What are you waiting for? Go." Cal motioned towards the entry.

"I just want to say thank you also..." There was so much I wanted to say. "You risked so much... I-I don't know..." Words weren't coming to my brain.

"My lady, it was our honor." Simmons gave a slight bow. "Now, do not take this wrong, but please get out of here so it won't all be for naught."

"I still owe you those kisses, Cal."

"And juniper juice," he added.

"Of course." Smiling, I gave them a nod then disappeared through the wavering space.

The exit plunked me into Earth's realm. I blinked a few times from the bright sunlight. Jumping from night into day was a bit unsettling. Looking around I realized this was the spot I had been before. It was the same place the Queen had brought me to destroy Seattle. High up in the Olympia National Park, Seattle loomed far in the distance. Squinting, I walked up next to Kennedy, Jared, and Mom as they stared at the city below. My eyes took in the landscape below, but my mind would not accept it.

The ruins of Seattle were gone. The skyline was dominated with newly erected pristine metal. The hazy sun glimmered off the new buildings as new construction soared up into the sky. Modern high-rises clustered together in the heart of the city, thinning out as the circle spread out. The Seattle landmark, the Needle, was gone, but cranes filled the space, bringing up beams of steel. Rebuilding.

Disbelief resonated deep in my core, keeping me immobile. When I left, Seattle had just restored the electricity and was beginning to clear out the rubble. Now the city stood before me, reconstructed. Looking over at Kennedy and Jared, they shared the same astonished expression.

"What the hell?" Jared looked back at the city in awe.

Kennedy looked even more dumbfounded. She was shaking her head back and forth, not accepting the reality sprouting in front of us. "I-I don't understand. This can't be possible."

"Clearly it is possible." A deep voice rumbled behind us.

We all jumped, whipping around, assuming defensive stances, ready to fight the threat hiding in the forest. But my blood sizzled through my veins with a familiarity I knew could only come from the nearness of one person.

Eli's figure stepped out of the shadows.

Air ripped through my lungs as I tried to suck in a breath. His head was shaven. His jaw was lined with stubble. The scar across his face seemed more defined. It all added up to his looking even more dangerous and threatening. Circles darkened the bags beneath his eyes, making him look like someone walking the high wire of instability. He was still so ruggedly beautiful and hot my stomach and heart fluttered harshly within. Uncomfortable with the notion he could evoke such a dramatic response from me, I looked away. Despite all the lies and the betrayal, my body still desired him beyond reason.

Only days earlier we had lain together under the stars. My desire now was involuntary because it went against everything my head was telling me. I knew they hadn't killed my mother so why would Lorcan tell me they did? What kind of sick joke was it? Though Eli hadn't murdered my mother, I was still leery of him.

Besides the new look, there was something about him that was hostile and foreboding. Something had changed. I recoiled back, feeling the ominous, dark mood emanating from him.

Jared's reaction to him was the opposite of mine. "Eli!" His face broke out with a huge, giddy grin as he ran to Eli who took him into a brief hug.

"Good to see you, J." His voice held little emotion. This was the normal way he acted towards outsiders, but to Jared... Something was definitely wrong.

Eli's eyes took in the group then snapped onto the woman next to me, nodding in acknowledgment. "Lily."

"Elighan," she responded with the same guarded reproach.

"You guys know each other?"

A strange smirk crossed Eli's lips. "We go way back, don't we?"

"That we do." My mom held her ground, but I could see her trembling. Whether it was out of fear or anger I couldn't tell. The pure abhorrence they held for each other was evident.

"Of course you do." Aversion filled my tone. "Why would you lie to me? Why would you and Lorcan say you killed my mother when you didn't? Why would you do that?"

Eli stepped closer, his fists clenched, his muscles tight. "I never actually said I did. You said I did. But if you really want the truth—"

"Ember, this is not the time or place for this," Mom interrupted, stepping between us. Her eyes glared viciously at Eli.

Kennedy stood staring at the new construction unaware of our little tiff. "How—how is this possible?"

Eli's fingers went up to his shaved head, absently running through his nonexistent hair, a habit he hadn't seemed to break even without hair. "A lot of things can get done in time."

"In time? I've only been gone for a couple of weeks," she said.

An icy smile tugged at Eli's lips. There was something wild and unhinged about him, which made me not trust him. "Maybe in the Otherworld, but remember time is not the same there as it is here on Earth."

Taking another look over her shoulder, she looked at the resurrected city. "What are you saying? How long have I been gone?"

"I'm saying you have been gone for more than a few weeks." A dark smile thinned Eli's lips, addressing Jared and Kennedy. "It has been over four years now." He then looked at me. "You have been gone almost three."

"What?" All except my mother exclaimed in unison. We struggled to understand his words. Jared had been raised knowing about the time difference between realms, but experiencing it was different. It was very surreal. What felt like a day or so to me was really three years. Three years of my life had gone by without me.

"A lot has taken place while you guys were away." Eli leaned up against a tree, looking directly at me. "I couldn't feel you. I couldn't sense you at all. So I figured you were either dead or had done something exceedingly stupid. Seems it was the latter." His fuming, volatile anger was barely concealed beneath the surface. "But I am not the only one you should be worried about, Ember. Since your disappearance, you are number one on the Unseelie King's most wanted list."

Kind of figured that one was coming. *Is there a list I'm not on?*

I turned to look down on the city, which once had turned into rubble by my hand. This time I knew it had been a warm-up to the real battle that was coming. This time it would be more than a city in the path of the destruction.

Between the Light and Dark there was me—the Fire. Either I would light the way or burn it to ash.

*Thank you to all my readers. Your opinion really matters to me and helps others decide if they want to purchase my book. If you enjoyed this book, please consider leaving an honest review on the site where you purchased it. Thank you! Want to find out about my next release in the Darkness Series? Sign up on my website and keep updated on the latest news.*

www.staceymariebrown.com

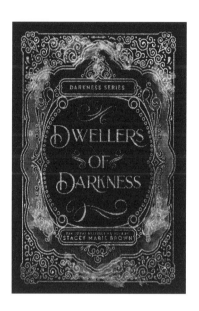

## Dwellers of the Darkness
(Darkness Series Book #3)

Three years have passed in Earth's realm when Ember and her friends finally return from the Otherworld.

Eli feels her the moment she steps back, and the beast is far from delighted. Believing for the last three years she was dead, he has become violent and cruel in her absence.

Eli's anger isn't the only thing she should fear. Ember is at the top of the Unseelie King's list after breaking her oath with him. No one breaks a vow with King Lars without severe consequences.

And Ember will pay.

As tension for war mounts between the Seelie and Unseelie, the pressure to find the only weapon which can kill the Seelie Queen, the Sword of Light, takes them to the high cliffs of Greece…

Where betrayal follows her.

But is Ember the answer to the location of the sword? Is she the one to fulfill the prophecy?

As usual nothing is ever what it seems.

**Book 3 Available Now!**

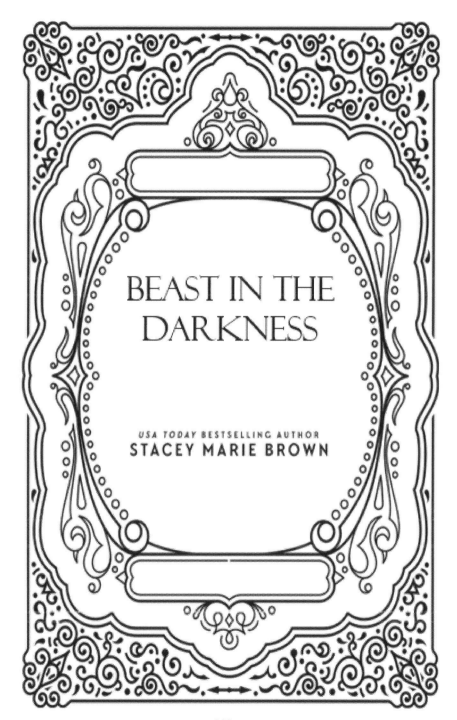

Fire in the Darkness

**PLEASE NOTE**: Eli's Novella takes place between Books 2 (Fire in the Darkness & 3 (Dwellers in Darkness). So please read Book 1-2 first as there will be spoilers. This takes place in the period of time Ember is gone.

Also bonus Eli's pov scenes from Book 1(Darkness of Light), and Book 2 (Fire in the Darkness)

This is a work of fiction. Any references to historical events, real people, or real locales are used fictitiously. Other names, characters, places and incidents are the product of the author's imagination and her crazy friends. Any resemblance to actual events, locales or persons, living or dead, is entirely coincidental.

This book is licensed for your personal enjoyment only. It cannot be re-sold, reproduced, scanned or distributed in any manner whatsoever without written permission from the author.

Cover Design by Creative Paramita
Copyright © 2013 Stacey Marie Brown
Published by Twisted Fairy Publishing
All rights reserved.

# BEAST IN THE DARKNESS
## *An Elighan Dragen Novelette*

## CHAPTER ONE

The tree pressed hard into my back as I leaned into it. The solidness of it eased the pain that stabbed over every inch of my body. My fingers wrapped around the last wooden dagger which lay entrenched in my skin, grunting as I tugged it out. Blood trickled out the dozens of holes where I had already removed the wooden spears. I had deserved each one and let them impale deep into my body without a fight.

Lorcan had not felt the same. He yowled and fought every one of them which burrowed in. He took off moments after Brycin had. Caused mayhem and left. What he was good at.

Nothing about my night had gone to plan. Good and bad.

Barely an hour ago, my cock had been deep in her. Happy. It was the first time I had ever felt that way while fucking a woman. Emotions I never felt before.

The feel of her fingers still ghosted my skin.

*"I will never be the guy who talks of poetry and brings you flowers. That's not who I am."*

*"I know."* Her thumb ran over my bottom lip. *"I wouldn't want you to be. That's not who I am either."*

*I looked down on her.* Ember's lips were swollen from my mouth, her skin bruised and showed bite marks, my cum still dripping from her pussy, her cheeks flushed, her eyes glowing bright.

*Fuck. She was so fucking beautiful.*

*I could feel my beast rumble with possession, marking her as his.*

*"I can't fight you anymore, woman."* I shook my head. *"I will follow you anywhere in the world, if you ask me."*

*Her response was to straddle me, kissing me deeply, my dick going instantly hard.*

*"Ride my cock, Brycin. So fucking hard."* I gripped her hips, driving up into her pussy while wrenching her down on me.

Her loud moans still pierced my ears, the feel of being inside her.

It was the truth when I told her I would follow her anywhere. I realized when she left the ranch a few months back, I didn't like her not being around. Wanting and missing someone was completely alien to me. Fae, Nymph, Water Fairy, even human, I had always enjoyed their company, but not much thought went into them after we fucked. This one . . . this one had been different from the beginning. I had hated her at first for it, trying to continue to deny my feelings for the Dae. That was no longer possible.

Showing myself to her tonight hadn't been a premeditated plan to bed her. Actually it was one of the last things I thought she would do. Hit me, yell at me, throw me into a tree . . . well, all those things had happened, but I didn't expect my dick to be in her while she did them. Her slight innocence on what to do, didn't take away from her strong desire to be free, inhibited, and unrelenting. It completely undid me.

Then Lorcan changed everything. All the trust she had shown me earlier disappeared—transformed to hatred and a look of utter betrayal.

"Fuck!" I yelled up at the night sky. Everything was so screwed up now. Her revulsion of me was clear. Who could blame her? When you hear the guy you just slept with killed your mother, it kind of changes things. There was so much Brycin didn't know. So many lies were tangled and woven together. That's how the Fae were. Secrets were the law we lived by. Truth held great power in the Otherworld. We traded, negotiated, and dealt in secrets. We also kept them. We had to since the day the Seelie King took the Fae into hiding in the Otherworld.

I sat there till the sky began to lighten, recalling what had happened and what I could have said differently. It probably didn't matter; the outcome would have been the same. In the end she would have left.

Forcing myself to stand, I wanted to see her once more, even if I only saw a glimpse of her through her window. It would be enough; it would have to be. The thought of seeing her roll around again with the Incubus had me growling. Not that I had the right anymore. Hell, he was probably better for her than me. I needed to walk away from her. It was better for all of us.

I hobbled towards the spot where I could see her room. She was near, my blood in her thumped like a GPS. I seemed to be able to feel her farther out than she could feel me. That helped me find her in Seattle and how I found her here.

I took a step and grunted. The punctures were healing, but still stung like a bitch. It would hurt to shift, but I'd heal faster in my Dark Dweller form. I was about to turn when a sharp ripping pain ran through my veins. My knees gave out and I crumbled to the ground. It was like knives slicing at me from the inside out. Then it dissipated and everything went cold. Silent. I gasped for breath, feeling an emptiness I had never known before.

*Ember.*

When I first gave her my blood and I felt our connection humming between us, it bothered me. It was intrusive and intimate. Then it became white noise in the background. I grew used to it. Now it was a part of me. How I knew I was alive. Because she was alive.

Now I felt nothing.

That only meant two things. She was suddenly out of my range, which would be strange since I felt her near just a minute ago.

Or she was dead.

"BRYCIN!" I roared, my legs pushed me up and forward. She couldn't be dead; there was no way. Then the thoughts started rolling into my head. *What if Lorcan found her and something happened? Would he kill her? Or did she finally have enough?* No, Brycin would never kill herself no matter what happened. It was not who she was. She was too strong for that. She would try to kill me first.

I ran not knowing where I was going, but hoping with one more step, I would feel the blood dance inside me again.

Instinct kicked in as my adrenaline hit uncontrollable levels. My body responded and I let the call of the beast take over. My spine curved taking me down. My clothes shredded as the beast formed. Throughout my change I never stopped running. Hours went by, even when the sun grew high in the sky, I didn't stop. I trailed the outer rim of the Unseelie King's property, moving out in intervals.

It was only in extreme cases we stayed in our Dark Dweller form. It was too risky, but I didn't care. Her smell was easier to track in this shape. I could smell her scent out beyond Lars' border, but I couldn't tell how recent it was.

Hunger and fatigue did not stop me. The only thing which did was hearing the Demon and his minions leave the safety of his property to go looking for her also. My hopes she remained somehow safely back in her room in his compound vanished.

She was gone.

A roar so deep within me thundered against the mountains, shaking the surface below.

## CHAPTER TWO
### Three years later

The fumes of cheap whiskey burnt up through my nose as I took another swing. My reflection in the cracked mirror taunted me. A week ago I was the one who had thrown someone into it, causing the break. I guess I should be thankful Mike had let me back in tonight. The other guy had been an asshole, and deserved what he got.

Now a huge, angry guy in the fractured mirror stared back at me. His shaved head, scarred face, hard expression, and extremely taut shoulders looked like he would snap your neck like a toothpick. I barely recognized myself. My Dark Dweller nature loved it. I was back to who I was supposed to be—a killer—something to be feared. That fucker, Drauk, was right. I had become a pussy, gotten soft living here on Earth. *She* had turned me weak, making me all human-like, with feelings.

Just thinking of her now had me reaching for my triple shot of whiskey. I slammed the rest of it down my throat and wiped my mouth with the back of my hand. I could feel the killer in me building again which put me in a fighting mood.

"Another one, Mike." I tapped at my glass.

He frowned and grabbed the whiskey bottle. He was never one to cut anyone off. If the money kept coming, he kept pouring. Last week he had cut me off. I guess I couldn't blame him I trashed his bar. Someone called the police and once again, for the seventh time this month, I had been arrested. When I escaped Weiss' feeble cuffs and ran off, he had put a warrant out for my arrest.

I knew tonight's crowd. No one would call.

"I don't want no fights in here," Mike grumbled as he poured the dark liquid in my glass.

I grabbed the cup and held it up. "I won't start any fights," I replied back. *With anyone that doesn't deserve it,* I thought to myself.

Mike huffed, shaking his head.

He knew if it was deserved or not, you got in my way or irritated me, my fist found a way to your face. Gulping down another burning swallow, my adrenaline picked up. Oh yeah, the Dark Dweller was pawing at the surface, ready and willing, for someone to come up and start something.

"How'd I know I'd find you here?"

I looked up into the broken mirror, a warped image of Cooper stood behind me.

"Because you're just brilliant like that," I retorted.

Cooper's hand pounded down on my shoulder. "Yeah, that must be it." He sat on the stool next to me and held up two fingers. "A beer, Mike."

"Pussy." I scoffed as I tilted my glass back.

"Hey, one of us has to be clear-headed enough to get you out of whatever mess you're gonna get yourself into." Cooper took a swing of the beer Mike had placed in front of him. "Our *Second* sure as hell won't be sober, so I guess that means it has to be me."

A growl only Cooper could hear came from my chest. It wasn't the first time I heard comments about me falling down on my job. There was a time I cared about my role as Second. I had wanted it then. No longer did I feel that way. I just wanted to be left alone. It still bugged me, though, because I hated being reminded, I failed. Again, it all stemmed back to her.

"You better be careful. Weiss has a hard-on for you. Take it easy tonight."

My glass clinked on the wood as I slammed it down. "You think I should be afraid of that asshole? He's a measly *human*. What the fuck do I care? And when hasn't he had it out for me?"

Cooper's eyes darted around. My outburst had his panties all in a twist. He was still a little apprehensive because, on a few occasions, usually in the middle of a fight, I had started to shift in front of the humans. Most of the time I got so drunk I hadn't remembered it the next day. But really, so what? They saw my eyes and claws turn, but they had been drinking, too. They wouldn't actually believe it happened.

I gave up on caring awhile back.

"We have a run tomorrow. Cole would like you sober enough to do the drop, if that's at *all* possible." Cooper no longer hid his annoyance with me. Cooper and Gabby were the only ones who were honest to my face. Cole had tried. We had even got into a huge physical altercation a year ago. We both beat the shit out of each other and walked away even madder than we were before. He mostly ignored me now. His focus was trying to get Jared back from the Otherworld—if the kid was even alive anymore.

I took the last gulp in my glass, letting it burn down my chest. If only it would take away all my failures, starting with what happened to my parents. Then to how I let Jared get past me. I should have stopped him, protected him. Sadly, I needed to shield him from his own uncle. Another mistake had been killing Lorcan. Because I didn't have the strength or will power to kill my own brother, I had lost two of my family.

We had stopped feeling West over three years ago and assumed he was dead. Either Lorcan had killed him or got him killed. West should never have left with them. He hadn't known how far Lorcan would really go in his pursuit to get back into the Otherworld. None of us really did. Now West was gone.

Because of Lorcan, we had lost Jared, too. Jared was part human so he didn't have as strong an internal connection to the Dark Dweller as the rest of us did. *She* had been my only connection to Jared. Through the dreamscapes, which she had brought me in on, I would learn she would see him and her friends in her dreamwalk. The night she disappeared she had told me Jared was all right. That was three years ago. We didn't know if he was all right or not anymore.

All these things piled on top of my biggest regret. I didn't know if it was for letting her in or letting her slip through my fingers. It didn't matter anymore. For two years I had searched for her. There wasn't a place I hadn't venture to, thinking maybe if I went a little farther she would be there. I went crazy tracking her.

I only turned human if I needed to talk to someone; otherwise, for two years, I had mostly remained in my Dark Dweller form. I slipped from town to town through the night, living on fresh deer carcass. Even a year after returning home, it remained hard for me to stay in my two-legged physique. The Dweller did not want to go back. It wanted out and it wanted to kill.

"I think I can handle a drop." I tapped my glass on the bar, trying to get Mike's attention. This was a precarious time for me: still sober enough to feel my raging anger, but drunk enough to act on it. I wasn't adequately numb yet. A few more drinks and I'd hit that blissful place where I didn't feel or care. Sleep hadn't offered peace to me in years. Drinking myself into oblivion was one of the only ways I found it.

"Cole is expanding a deal with the Apocalypse Riders. A few of them want to go with us for the drop tomorrow. To have it known we have their back. They've had some trouble with the Portland Hells Angels."

My mind immediately flashed back to Puck and McNamm, two ex-riders of the club. Cooper must have forgotten. He would never intentionally bring up anything related to her anymore. I had flown off the handle too many times when they had. The thought of Puck's and McNamm's hands anywhere on her body still made me see red. Good thing they were already six feet under, because the pain I would inflict on them now. They had made it out easy. The killer in me wanted them alive again, just so I could hunt them down and tear them apart bit by bit. Slowly.

Glass shattered breaking around my hand.

"Jesus Christ, Dragen!" Mike yelled from the other side of the bar. "You want to add that to your tab as well? If ya ever pay me, that is."

I dug into my pocket and pulled out my wallet, slapping a hundred on the counter. "Here. Will that shut you up, old man? Now can I have another fuckin' drink?"

Mike's eyes narrowed. He had always respected us, giving us more leeway than he gave others. I think deep down Mike sensed something different about our group and had a healthy fear of us. I knew I had been pushing that line with him. Just another thing I didn't care about.

Cooper rubbed his face as Mike swept away the broken glass and then filled a new one with brown liquor.

Cooper turned and faced me when Mike got out of earshot. "We're all done with your shit, Eli. We've given you space, but seriously it is time." He stressed the last three words. "I don't know what happened with her, but I can guess . . ."

It was instantaneous. Fury roared under my skin, pushing me up and off my stool.

Cooper sighed. "Jesus man you need to get it together. You are completely unraveled. *She* is gone Eli. You need to deal with that."

They had stopped saying her name some time ago. Owen had ended up flat against a wall with a broken nose one night when he referred to her by name.

*Ember Brycin* . . . two simple words evoked a torrent of emotions. The absence of her in my veins still had not eased. You'd think by now I would be back to how I felt before I gave her my blood. But, like I changed her DNA, she seemed to have changed mine. Now I only felt emptiness where she should be.

To be fair, the night I hit Owen was the night the Unseelie King had tracked me down. He had never officially dropped the reward he placed on Brycin's head for breaking her contract with him. I figured he put it there so he had others looking for her as well. They came up with nothing. He told me it was pointless to keep searching for her. If the Unseelie King couldn't find you . . . you were probably dead.

That was the night I officially understood she was gone. For good.

"Fuck sake, Eli, calm down. I won't bring her up again." Cooper kicked at my stool. "Now, sit the hell back down."

Air filtered roughly through my nose as I breathed out. It took me several moments before I calmed down enough. As I sat back down on the seat my phone buzzed in my pocket. A slightly trashy, but beautiful, dark-haired brunette showed up on the screen. Her lips puckered in a kiss.

I clicked it off and shoved it back into my pocket. In my current mood I had no doubt I would end up knocking on her door later this evening. But no matter what, she could never fulfill me or the Dark Dweller which raged inside. Only one had ever appeased the animal. Though nothing would ever tame it; there was only one it truly craved. One it would never have again.

"Will you answer her so she will stop calling me, looking for you?" Cooper nodded towards the phone in my pocket.

I frowned and took a sip of my drink.

"Natasha is coming tomorrow so you better deal with her."

My frown deepened. She was only interested in her father's dealings when they involved me. I still recalled the night Natasha had kissed me at that bonfire party when I was looking for Brycin and she had seen us.

That was the night everything changed. Good and bad, our connection solidified. Became more than I was expecting.

Natasha had been convenient and easy. I had never led her to believe I was in it past the fucking. She always seemed to want to make me the guy who would change for her. I wasn't the first guy she screwed in hopes he'd eventually fall in love with her, but she seemed most determined for it to be me. I had always been upfront and honest, but she only heard what she wanted. That wasn't my fault. She was a good lay; desperation to claim me had her open to anything, to try anything. I used it to my benefit. Compassion was not a Dark Dweller trait.

Cooper turned back to his beer at my non-response. We drank in silence. Tonight the alcohol was not calming me down. My shoulders hunched up and my muscles twitched. The beast was hitting itself against the man-form I contained it in.

I stood. "Come on, let's ride." Being on my bike was sometimes the only other way, besides drinking, to quiet my inner monster for a while.

Cooper stood and slapped another bill on the counter. "Thanks, Mike."

Mike gave us a nod, and I could smell the relief he felt at our departure. My presence seemed to cause an air of tension, sensing at any moment I could violently turn. Humans seemed to feel the thin line of sanity I was walking.

We went outside, my steel-tip boots kicking up dirt in the parking lot. My legs straddled my black beauty.

"Where to?" Cooper hopped on his baby, next to me.

"Let's just ride."

He nodded in understanding. This is what we did when we needed an escape. No destination. No thought. Wherever the road took us.

The tires squealed as I pulled out onto the pavement, my engine revving high. The moment the wind brushed over my scalp, I felt better. I had shaved my head in one of my agro moments. The severe look suited me better now. People had always feared me, but this only made them know, instantly, I was not someone to mess with.

My wheels flew over the asphalt. The high speed wasn't enough tonight. The bike's odometer shook, trying to reach the red. My hand twisted the throttle until it could no longer turn. The distance between Cooper and me widened. For miles I pushed it, barely staying on the road.

Red and blue light came out of the darkness, swirling behind us. I knew who it was. He was out searching for me. This only upped my recklessness. *Well, he found his man . . . let's see if he can catch him.* I sneered, almost willing Weiss to start shooting at me. The fact I wouldn't die from his bullets only made me want to push the envelope more. What did it matter?

"Pull over." A voice came over the speakers on top of the police car.

My answer was to flip him off.

*He has a warrant out for you. You really want to piss him off?* Cooper said through our link. Most had given up communicating with me through our link. Pointless when I ignored them.

*Let him try and catch me,* I replied back. *You're a Dark Dweller, Cooper, get some fuckin' balls.*

The sigh through our connection was loud. I knew him and, no matter what, he would follow me down this road. We don't leave brothers. Cooper hit the gas and came up even with me.

*Come on, it will be fun.* I egged him on.

*If my bike gets impounded again . . .* Cooper trailed off in warning.

*Stop being a baby.*

"Pull over immediately," Weiss' voice came from behind us.

*Ready?*

*Yeah . . . sure.*

We both punched our gas pedals and the bikes lurched forward. We glided around the curves. The cop car losing pace as it tried to round the bends.

*Too easy.* Just as the thought came out, I spotted two police cars blocking the road in front of us. Guns drawn as they hid behind their open doors.

A gun shot rang through the air.

"Shit!" Cooper yelled. The bullet ripped through his tire. His wheels came out from underneath him. He fell to the ground, cracking his shoulder. His bike skid across the pavement as he rolled. The motorcycle continued to slide, causing sparks to fly, crashing into the bumper of the police car.

"*Ciach ort!*" I hit my brakes, curving in front of Cooper. My brother was down; my defenses to protect him went up.

"Freeze!" One of the cops yelled.

Ignoring him I reached down for Cooper's injured arm. He was out. "Wake the fuck up!" I nudged him with my foot. Panic rose in my chest. The beast danced at the surface.

Weiss' vehicle halted close behind us, blocking us in a tighter circle, only pushing my instincts into a higher gear.

"Stop, Mr. Dragen. Do not move!" Weiss pointed his gun as he climbed out of the car.

My head turned to him, a roar involuntary coming out of me. Weiss stumbled back a little, shaking his head. I knew my eyes had flashed red. I could feel the heat rising in my skin, shifting, and my nails beginning to grow, my back hunching.

Learned instinct still wanted me to hide my true self and push the change back down. Everything else in me didn't care. I could tear through these guys in seconds without the other knowing. Why did I pretend they had the upper hand?

When Weiss looked back, he re-gripped his gun, swallowing hard. Like every human he dismissed what he saw.

"Let's not make this hard. You are surrounded. If you surrender without a fight, I'll be sure to make a note in your report."

I laughed. My nails were still longer than normal, and they dug into Cooper. The pain woke him up. He groaned, using my arm to pull himself up, he saddled in behind me.

"I am going to fuckin' kill you later," he mumbled.

"Let's get out of here first." Again my own words rubbed me wrong. Why was I running from them? What could they actually do to me?

"Mr. Dragen, I said don't move. I will shoot you."

A sardonic grin crept up my lips. "Oh, please do." I climbed off the bike.

"What the hell are you doing?" Cooper took the handles, procuring the weight of the bike from me.

"Giving the officer what he wants." I held my arms out wide. "Go ahead." I tapped the middle of my chest.

As I stepped toward Weiss, his finger seemed to itch to pull the trigger. "What happened to Ember Brycin, Mr. Dragen? She's been missing for three years. The last time I saw her she was covered in blood and her friends had gone missing."

My boots froze mid-step.

"Did she finally turn against you? See you for what you really are? Is her body, along with her father's and her friends', buried in a shallow grave on this allusive property of yours?"

It was like an axe had been driven into my chest. His theory once again was way off, but his words, of her being dead, hit too close to home.

I heard Cooper swear. My back started to curve again, and my clothes began to tear. A menacing growl vibrated my vocal cords. Cooper revved the engine turning the bike towards me.

From there everything went sharply south. Cooper's movement had the other two officers shooting at us. My slightly altered shape, high-tailing it for Weiss' throat, had him firing. I felt each and every bullet dig into my skin, and I welcomed the pain.

Cooper sped up next to me.

"Get on," he screamed.

I hesitated. The need to tear the sheriff's throat out was so strong. I needed to kill, to have his blood dripping from my teeth.

*NOW!* The volume from Cooper's link split my head, breaking my bond to kill Weiss. Another bullet plowed into my side. With a roar I turned instead and began to run down the side of the mountain. My hands and legs becoming more equal in length as my body changed. My clothes ripped completely away as the beast emerged.

With one last look over my shoulder, I saw Cooper pop a wheelie and break past Weiss, knocking him to the ground. The two other officers shot at the back of him, but the bike disappeared before they even got back to their cars.

Turning back, I tore through the forest. A roar bellowed from me again, filled with anger and guilt. Once again I had screwed everything up because someone uttered her name. She was dead, and I not only hated her, I resented her ever coming into my life.

## CHAPTER THREE

The morning light brought no clarity or cheerfulness. I craved darkness. Most of the time I slept until nightfall.

I rolled over with a groan, rubbing at the healing scars where each bullet sunk into my skin. I had to remain in my Dark Dweller form most of the night to help heal faster, but the bruises and soreness were still raw and painful.

My mind rolled over the events of the night before, remembering Cooper lost his bike in the ordeal last night. *Fuck.* I leaned against the headboard. He was gonna be so pissed. I'd have to buy him a new Harley next time we got paid.

"Eli." A fist pounded on my door. "Get up, it's time to go," Gabby said through my door.

Right. The drop.

"I'll be out in a minute." I snarled, swinging my legs over the bed. I stood, rubbing my bare ass as I walked to the dresser. I yanked it open and looked for my least dirty jeans in the back of my drawer.

My fingers stopped on a t-shirt, and I caressed the fabric with the familiar paint stains on it. Even though I knew I was alone, my gaze still darted around the room. If anyone caught me . . .

No one knew about this. No one ever would. It was the last thing I had of her.

## Fire in the Darkness

The bank had just taken possession of her house when I snuck in. Her smell was rich and thick through the house. It had taken me to my knees the first time I had entered. The crushing pain of her loss had made it hard to breathe. My brain kept thinking that she would walk out of her room at any moment, put her hands on her hips, and ask what the hell I was doing there?

Then the slight stink of the Strighoul and a mix of Vek's and Ember's blood, stained on the wood floor, would remind me. The smell and sight of her blood had me exiting the house. I swore to never go back. But the need for her, to be near her again, if only by her smell and possessions, pulled me back. I'm not sentimental, but I found myself stuffing the paint-stained t-shirt she slept in, her sketch pad, baby book, and a few other keepsakes into my bag. The bank would sell or donate it all, glad to get rid of it. It would be gone forever. Brycin would officially disappear from my life.

I stuffed her shirt farther back in my drawer and snatched a pair of jeans and light weight t-shirt. The summer in Olympia had been unseasonably hot. Usually it stayed pretty mild, but it was as if my personal hell had come to life.

Shading my eyes from the glaring sun, I walked out on the porch. Cooper leaned against the rail; his arms crossed.

"Hey man . . . I am so . . ." I was stopped when his fist smashed into my face. The force took me to the ground, blood gushing from my nose.

Cooper stepped on either side of me, grabbing my shirt. His fist poised to punch again. "If you ever do something like that again—I will *challenge* you."

To "challenge" me meant he would fight me for my position in the clan. It didn't have to be a fight to the death, but it got close enough. If I lost, it would be worse than death. I would lose my position and any authority I had. Becoming the bottom of the rung. I didn't think Cooper could take me in a fight; I was sure he knew it, too. But that made it even worse. Even if he knew he'd lose, he'd rather challenge me than continue under my authority. I never imagined losing Cooper's respect. It hit me hard.

"You got it?" He tugged at my shirt again.

"Yeah. I got it." I let the blood trail out of my nose, my eyes locked with his.

"You scared the fuck out of me last night. Reckless and stupid. If you had done that to anyone else but me, this wouldn't have been a warning this morning."

I took in his words and dipped my chin in understanding.

He opened his palm out to me. I grabbed it as he yanked me back up.

"You owe me a bike, fucker."

"Yeah, I do." I patted his back.

"Hey girls, if you're done making out can we go?" Gabby yelled from the cab of Cole's SUV. The merchandise was already packed in the back.

"Cole's letting me take his bike today. So we got Gabby covered front and back."

I nodded and headed out for my bike, pushing on my sunglasses.

There was a long scrape on the side of my bike. "Dammit," I mumbled, rubbing at the chipped paint.

"You're lucky that was all. I just skimmed Weiss' door." Cooper climbed onto Cole's bike. "You know they are gonna be out in full force looking for us. We need to be on guard today." Cooper slipped on his helmet. We didn't wear them often. But today, hiding our faces was a good plan.

"Let's keep off of any main roads or ones he knows we use." I grabbed my helmet and slid it on.

Cooper nodded and started the engine.

I swung my leg over my bike, which fitted me perfectly.

*Just like Brycin.*

The thought was already out before I could squash it. Plenty of times I had thought about her on the bike with me. Her back pressed between the handlebars, her legs wrapped around me, the engine vibrating and humming beneath us as I rode her deep.

My dick went hard at the thought, tightening with need.

"Eli?" Cooper's voice broke into my fantasy.

I looked up at him.

"Let's go man." He hit the gas and took off down the road, following the SUV.

With a deep breath, I pushed all thoughts of her back down and followed them. She had been leaking through too often lately. It had to stop. My teeth ground together, my resentment of her building even higher. She did this to me. She was something I should hate anyway. Her kind. Her name. Everything. I would not let some woman, especially a Dae, turn me into such a pussy. She was dead. She had affected me enough in life; I could not let her reach out from whatever grave she was in as well.

At a stop light, my phone buzzed against my leg. Natasha's face stared back up at me.

"Yeah?" I answered.

"Hey baby. Where are you?" she purred through the phone

"We're on our way. Be there in five." I hung up.

She really was a good screw when I desired one, but I needed to end it. She would always want more, and I felt nothing for her.

We pulled up in our designated meeting spot near an abandoned warehouse in an area which I even considered dodgy. The moment I climbed off my bike and the helmet was off, Natasha had her arms wrapped around me, her lips devouring mine.

"I missed you last night," she whispered in my ear.

I pulled back. "Uh, yeah, something came up."

Her hand moved down my chest, she looked quickly over her shoulder. The group was not looking in our direction. Her hand crept lower.

"Did you miss me?" Her fingers slide down my pants.

"Natasha, not now." I tried to step back, but her fingers wrapped hungrily around my cock. It reacted instantly. Memories of the fantasy with Brycin, I played out in my head earlier, flooded back.

Having her in my head, and not the girl standing in front of me, sent anger through my limbs. I grabbed Natasha shoulders and stepped her back. "I said not now."

My dick was not pleased with me. Even though it never seemed to be fulfilled with Natasha, she was at least a release.

She bit her lip. Pain flashed quickly through her expression before she forced her mouth into a smile and winked. "Sure. Later."

"Dragen." Bobby, the leader of the Apocalypse Riders, sauntered over to me. "Haven't seen you in a while. Good of you to come."

I shook his hand. "Been busy."

"I am looking forward to this partnership. Hope we'll have more future runs with you guys. Take over some of the leg work."

Since Lorcan had left, taking more than half of our group, we couldn't do as much. Apocalypse was a new club and wanted to start making their mark. We needed men; they needed our status. It was a mutual collaboration.

Natasha's hand again filtered across my ass. "I'm sure our partnership will be very gratifying."

Bobby pressed his lips together at his daughter's not-so-subtle insinuation. My reputation with women was no secret around the biker community. He knew he couldn't stop her from seeing me, but as a father, he hated it. He and I both knew his little girl was gonna get hurt.

"All right, let's get going. The drop off is an hour away." I clasped by hands together. "Bobby, I'd like you and two of your men to ride in front with Cooper and two others to ride in back with me. Gabby will be in the middle."

Bobby nodded. "Sounds good." He went back to his men getting them organized.

"I'll ride with you." Natasha turned to face me, her arms wrapping around my middle. No matter how long it had been or how many times Natasha had touched me, my first reaction was always to push her away. Even though we were both getting what we wanted out of this, I knew why.

She wasn't Ember.

And somewhere in my gut, being with Natasha, felt like I was betraying Brycin. We had never claimed "rights" on each other. Hell, before I fucked Brycin, she had been playing around with an Incubus asshole. *I'm free to do who and whatever the hell I want.* I growled in my mind.

"You're frowning again." Natasha stood on her tip toes and kissed me. I didn't fight it. Nor did I fight her riding with me. I didn't have it in me. If I wasn't angry, I was numb. Those seemed to be the only two emotions I felt anymore.

As we rode out, Natasha's need to capture me through sex was relentless. It was the only way she thought I would fall for her. If she was good in bed, I wouldn't be able to stay away from her. Girls like her didn't understand that sex was just sex to us. We could always find it somewhere else. It was the *girl* who made us want to come back, not the pussy.

Natasha was nice enough but boring as hell. She wanted to please me too much to ever risk challenging me. There was nothing to talk about. Not that I felt like talking to anyone lately. The only thing which got her huffy with me was my lack of commitment to her. She would get all pouty and irritating. I would just leave and in a day she would be calling, begging me back into her bed. Brycin would have been furious at the way I was treating her or the fact I was taking advantage of Natasha's insecurity. She would kick my ass across the state and back.

I grinned at the image of Brycin all huffed up, pushing at my chest, as she laid into me. Her two different eyes would glow bright with anger. The vision was so crisp and clear I almost imagined I could smell her. The deep rich campfire scent, mixed with earth and cinnamon.

A hand pushed at the button of my jeans, bringing me back to reality. My cock was starting to get restless. The beast in me needed to let off steam. But I pushed Natasha's hand away. I had a job to finish. I was already in the doghouse with my family. I needed to complete this job without incident . . . then my dick could take over.

My patience and my mood were hitting violent territory by the time we got to the site. The beast had taken over so much it was hard working past the basic needs of sex and food. Everything in me was taut and stressed as I tried to keep my mind on the transaction. Usually when those basic things were ignored, I was easy to enrage. Okay, I had been easy to rile since the day I had lost her.

I looked at my phone. Cole had put in it the combination to the shed where we were dropping off the merchandise. I went and unlocked it, as everyone else started unloading.

Suddenly, agony crippled my body, dropping me like a brick to the ground. Fire ignited in my veins, zipping the blood through my body so fast my sight went black for a moment, locking me in place.

"Eli?" I heard Natasha come to my side.

I groaned as the pain flared up higher, my breath halting in my lungs, causing my body to tremble, needing to shift.

"What the hell is wrong with him?" Gabby dropped down on my other side.

"I don't know." Natasha fluttered and screeched around me nervously. "He just suddenly dropped!"

"Eli?" Gabby called my name, but my mouth couldn't respond.

Slowly the burning sensation eased back, like a fire being turned down low. Gulping, I heaved in air, feeling sweat trickle down my face.

As the pain faded, I noticed something filling the vacancy I had inside me for years.

*No way—it couldn't be.*

But there was no denying it. The feeling of her had been so engrained in me, there was no way I could ever forget it. It was like everything around me had returned to color. I felt life sizzling in my veins.

I felt her…

She was alive.

Instinct took over, blinding me to anything around me. A desperation to go to her. To see if what I felt was real.

Shoving myself up to my feet, I pushed past the two people in my way. Voices yelled at me, but I didn't hear anything but the pounding of my blood in her, calling to me.

I went for the first thing which would take me to her. Yanking the door open to the SUV, I jumped in, tearing out of the gravel lot, heading me in the direction, I could feel her, before anyone could stop me.

Like it always had, the closer I got the more the feeling of her pumped through me. I followed the blood link taking me up into the mountains, where the road ended. I was out of the car running. Soon I could smell her . . . and others.

*Holy fuck...Jared.*

My world stopped when I spotted Brycin through the trees. She still wore the same outfit I had last seen her in, down to the dirt-stained tank top, the one we had relentlessly fucked each other on.

She still smelled like me, like sex. It was as if no time passed for her at all. As if it we stepped back in time three years.

It hit me all at once, seeing her with Jared and all her friends, who were prisoners in the Otherworld.

She hadn't died.

She was in the Otherworld this whole time.

Anger flared in my chest, realizing she had been fine, not one thought spared for me while I had lived three years in hell.

She stood there looking down at the cityscape of Seattle below in confusion. Next to her was Jared, Kennedy, and someone else.

Fuck. Lily.

She was alive.

I couldn't come to grips that after fucking me for hours, Brycin just headed to the Otherworld on a whim? How the hell did she even know how to get in? No plan or thought, she went in to the Seelie Queen's territory without help? It was the most idiotic, stupid, reckless thing to do. But what made me proud, which only pissed me off more. She did it. She got them out.

She had been an idiot, but she didn't need me. *She never has,* my mind quipped back. My chest trembled with ire. She stood there, dirty and bruised, looking gorgeous and a badass, smelling like me, and not realizing, and probably even caring, what had happened to us in her absence.

The beast in me roared and wanted nothing more than to take her right here—claiming what was mine. Pounding into her over and over, until I marked her as mine.

Locking down my muscles, I tried to ignore the need for her dancing in my veins, only adding to the part which loathed her very existence. I resented the effect she had on me, and what I had done and been like the last three years. I had felt guilt over West and Jared, but she had been the main reason I had lost respect with my clan and almost lost my place as second. I had been a wreck, barely hanging on to my sanity so I could survive.

And there she was. Like nothing happened.

Resentment filled my chest, stirring me to move from my spot.

*I could snap her neck and it would all be over—for good.*

"What the hell?" Jared exclaimed, looking down on the city. He had been born and raised on Earth and never experienced the time difference between the worlds. His hand went up touching the lower back of the petite, Kennedy. His touch far more intimate than friends.

Kennedy shook her head. "I-I don't understand. This can't be possible."

Seriously, they had been locked away in the land of Fairies, and they were gawking at the newly built city?

I gripped my hands into fists, trying to push down the storm of emotions whirling in me. "Clearly it is possible."

They all jumped, whipping around. Ember went down in a defensive stance, ready to fight. Then her head cocked to the side, her eyes widening with awareness as she looked around wildly. She felt me now.

I stepped out of the shadows.

She gasped, her eyes running over me, taking me in. Her cheeks flushed, unconsciously licking her bottom lip as she looked away from me. Her breath shortened. I affected her. Good.

"Eli!" Jared bounded over to me. A goofy, elated grin appeared on his face. His arms wrapped around me and I stiffened. It was automatic. To see the kid safe was all I wanted, but now he stood in front of me, I found it hard to show him. All emotion except anger had been turned off for so long I didn't know how to respond to his hug.

"Good to see you, J." I gave him a pat and pulled back.

Ember's eyes were on me, watching my every move. My eyes boldly met hers. Whatever she saw caused her muscles to tense up and take a small step back. She was wary of me. I knew she could also sense something was off about me. The beast was now more of who I was than the man.

My gaze drifted over the group, landing on Lily. Muscles underneath my shirt tightened.

"Lily." I addressed her coolly. She was not someone I had expected or ever wanted to see again.

"Elighan." Her voiced wasn't as guarded as mine. Emotion trickled through, hinting at her hate.

Ember's eyebrows merged further down her forehead looking between us. "You guys know each other?"

Unfortunately, we did.

I smirked, "We go way back, don't we?"

Memories of the last time I had seen Lily flashed through my head. My jaw crunched together, blocking them.

"That we do." Lily pushed back her shoulders, reminding me of Ember. She defied her fear with rebellious disregard.

Brycin shook her head. "Of course, you do." Resentment filled her tone and eyes. She understood it was another secret we kept from her. Her eyes flashed bright as they landed on me. "Why would you lie to me? Why would you and Lorcan say you killed my mother when you didn't? Why would you do that?"

There was so much she should never learn about me.

Lily's eyes penetrated into mine with accusing hatred, which only infuriated me more. Lily was no innocent here. Stepping closer, my fists balled at my sides. "I never actually said I did. You said I did. But if you really want the truth . . ."

"Ember, this is not the time or place for this," Lily cut me off. Her vicious stare didn't move from my face.

*Ah.* None of us were being truthful then. She wanted to keep our past a secret from Ember as much as I did.

"How . . . how is this possible?" Kennedy still stood staring at the city below, seemingly oblivious to the friction around her. But, I didn't buy it. Granted she seemed to be genuinely confused about how a city had become fully rebuilt in what, to her, felt like a few weeks. But, it wasn't the complete reason. She was too sensitive, her abilities too strong. She was trying to defuse the tension, breaking up our conversation.

That was fine with me.

"A lot of things can get done in time," I said.

"In time? I've only been gone for a couple of weeks." She looked back at me, baffled.

Oh, this little tidbit was gonna be fun to share. None of them had a clue how much time had really passed and what had happened in their absence. "Maybe in the Otherworld, but remember time is not the same there as it is here on Earth."

Kennedy took another glace below. "What are you saying? How long have I been gone?"

"I'm saying you have been gone for more than a few weeks." I was enjoying this a little too much—the beast relishing the cruel game. I wanted them to feel the harsh reality of time being taken from them. I pointed my gaze at Jared and Kennedy. "It has been about four years now." Then I turned to Ember. I wanted her to feel my anger the most—what I had been through while she was there. "You have been gone almost three years."

"What?" All reacted except Lily. She understood. She had grown up moving between worlds.

Another part of Brycin's disappearance hit me. Why had I never thought of it before? Of course he would have been a part of this. Torin. This whole time she had probably been with him. He was who she probably had run to after being with me. There was no other way she could have gotten there on her own. He would help her. He'd do anything for her. Their connection to each other was another dagger in my side.

"A lot has taken place while you guys were away." I leaned up against a tree, looking directly at Brycin. I couldn't seem to keep my eyes off of her. Everything about her enticed me and pulled me in. Everyone else seemed to almost disappear when I was near her. She looked up; a muddle of emotions reflected in her beautiful eyes. How could one person affect me so much? Someone I should hate. There was no logic, just emotion. I had come to resent her for making me so weak. For needing someone so much, especially when we were doomed from the start. Fucking her or killing her were my two strongest desires. Maybe it would give me peace to kill the very thing which tortured me. But this time, her death would be by my hand.

Rage trembled in me.

"I couldn't feel you. I couldn't sense you at all. So I figured you were either dead or had done something exceedingly stupid. Seems it was the latter. But I am not the only one you should be worried about, Ember. Since your disappearance, you are number one on the Unseelie King's most wanted list."

That spiteful part of me was rewarded. Brycin's eyes widened as she took in the information. Fear and defiance crossed her face.

In that instant I wanted to kiss her.

I was split in battle: one instinct wanted to destroy my weakness; the other wanted to wrap my arms around her and protect her from the world and the things that would hurt her.

How long before that thing was me?

# DARKNESS OF LIGHT BONUS SCENE
## Chapter 5 from Eli Dragen's POV

"Have a seat Mr. Dragen." The officer motioned to the chair. There was a slight irritation to his tone. Officer Paul had dealt with me on numerous occasions.

With a resigned sigh I dropped down. Paul tugged the handcuffs off his belt and locked my wrist to the chair, which only made me smirk. I was amused at the flimsy piece of metal they thought could hold me down.

"I will be back." He tugged on the metal making sure it was secure.

"Yeah. I think I know the routine by now."

Officer Paul gave me a bemused huff and turned, leaving me in the small confines of the waiting room. It reeked of human smells, bad coffee, and the hint of cleaning products. The scent of the police station was something I was used to. I should be. I had already been here twice this week. For the month, I was hitting about eight visits, so far. Sadly, that was not a record for me.

It was frustrating. I could easily outrun the sheriff. Actually, I could out do him in anything, but Cole was adamant about us not using our abilities in public. Standing out or bringing any more attention to us was something he embedded daily into our brains.

Except I was never one to listen.

I had difficulty staying out of trouble. My entire personality stirred up people and trouble. Only Cooper was close to my number of arrests and that was because he was usually with me when I was causing a disturbance. West got in his fair share, but that fucker had the knack to charm a nun out of her knickers. His arrests ended with a slap on the wrist and a verbal warning most of the time. Lorcan was too sneaky to get caught. If I cared, I could have probably gotten away, too. I just didn't. It was sick, but I kinda enjoyed pissing Sheriff Weiss off. Especially because he could never find anything to really hold me on. I wasn't stupid.

Sliding down further to get comfortable, the hard plastic chair creaked as I shifted in my seat. These seats were too fucking tiny for me. I pulled a book out of my back pocket. The cops liked to leave me sitting for a long time, and I had learned early on to bring something to read when I went out.

Most of my arrests were connected with Mike's Bar and some asshole thinking he didn't have to pay up what he lost a game of pool. Because I appeared so young, some thought they could fuck with me, didn't have to play by the rules. They didn't like some "young punk kid" taking their money. All of us in my club appeared young to the human world. It hadn't taken long for us to earn respect of most of the bike gangs around. But there was always one or two who thought they could take us. It never got old showing the pricks how wrong they were.

Tonight's arrest was one of those times. The guy was in intensive care, and I was handcuffed to a chair in the police station. I already knew there would be no charges made against me. That was not how the biker world worked. Our common enemy was the cops. We dealt with each other on our terms.

In less than an hour they'd release me. I just had to be patient and wait it out.

Flipping to the dog-eared page, I started reading. Even as I let my mind escape into my book, my body was aware of every single thing in the room: every person, every noise, every smell. My instincts were always on, ready to act. Nothing in here was a threat . . . not to me.

Then that all changed.

I smelled them before they entered. An assault of smoldering fire, cinnamon, and the soft scent of earth went up my nose, intoxicating my brain. There was also another scent, like rich soil and olives being baked in the sun—what you'd imagine Italy or Greece to smell like. My head spun as I took another breath. It felt like a tsunami of tequila was poured into my head and chest. Tequila was known as the fight or fuck drink. I wanted to do both.

My gaze lifted, peering under my hood, seeing what Otherworld threats had just walked in.

I was shocked to see only one girl, all her scents throwing me off.

Her striking features had my dick responding immediately, going rock hard. She turned her back to me as she put her money into the coffee machine, her firm ass taunting me. My eyes locked onto her, running over every inch of her body. Her long black hair hung to her waist and was striped with flaming red streaks. She was tall and a little slimmer and more athletic than I normally liked. But her body seemed to be demanding for me to put my hands on it and to explore every inch.

*Fuck.*

Shaking my head, I looked away trying to break the spell the girl had on me. The endorphins she was putting off struck every nerve in my body. I wanted her bad. This never happened to me before. At least not this potent. I pulled down my hoodie further, blocking the bulge that was building up in my pants.

During our time on Earth, we had run into lots of Fae. Most were Dark. We tended to leave each other alone and go our own way, but I could feel this one was different. I couldn't get a sense of Light or Dark from her. That was not a good thing. There was only one kind of Fae that I knew who were both, and they didn't exist anymore. There weren't Fae around this area we didn't already know about. Was she just passing through?

I edged deeper back into my hood, bringing up my book to cover my face. To outsiders my body appeared relaxed and calm. I was anything but. My muscles constricted, ready to strike.

She glanced over her shoulder towards me. Yeah, she was aware of me, too. When she turned, her eyes drifted over to me, halting the air in my lungs.

*Holy shit.* She had two different colored eyes.

It took everything I had not to react. I clamped down tighter on my book, feeling my claws pricking at the surface. *There was no way . . . no fucking way.*

This girl was a Dae? She had the traits—the two-toned hair and eyes. Explain why I couldn't get if she was Light or Dark. Because she was both.

She seemed naively unaware of her surroundings. Clueless to the danger her kind derived. Hunted and slaughtered. There was no way a Dae would just be out walking around, free or unguarded. But I could smell no protection spell on her. Didn't she know what she was?

No. I had to be wrong. It was well known, even to us stuck on earth, there were no more Daes alive. All had been found and eradicated.

And if somehow this one escaped, I would gladly amend that. A Dae was the reason we lost most of our clan. My family.

The girl grabbed her coffee and a magazine and then sat in a row of chairs perpendicular from me. Her gaze quickly found its way back to me. She was trying to be sly, looking like she was reading her magazine, but I could feel her eyes burning into me.

Deep-seated hate and anger burned up my esophagus like acid. The desire to leap over and rip her into shreds consumed me. The beast inside was telling me I was not wrong. This thing was a Dae. My beast part growled, licking its lips to taste her blood. What her kind stood for was everything I despised. Every time she looked over at me, my instinct was to attack her. The killer in me was locking on its prey.

I shifted in my seat to break the link between the beast and its target. The girl jumped up defensively, her coffee splashing over the rim of the cup onto the floor.

So the Dae wasn't as dense as I thought. She could sense the threat. But she wasn't that bright either. If she was, she'd be running for her life right now.

She mumbled something to the onlookers and kneeled down to clean up the spill on the floor. Her skin was like ivory, and I could see the slight embarrassed blush her cheeks. A few freckles were also sprinkled over her nose. The flash of me handcuffing her, bending her over an officer's desk, my cock slamming deep into her, raced into my head. My dick twitched in longing.

*What the fuck?* I hastily shut that fantasy down.

Fury at my own traitorous thoughts heated my body. It itched to act and to get out of this room before I did violent acts to this girl. Fuck or kill her and only one of those I would let myself do.

She sat back down, readjusting herself with the magazine in one hand and what was left of her coffee in the other. It took only a few seconds before she was sneaking glances at me again.

Getting women to notice me was never my problem. If anything, it sometimes became a nuisance. But I liked to fuck, and they liked to fuck me. This one watched me with the same interest, but there was also something more in her attentive eyes. There was a defensiveness and irritation, but what got me was the curiosity. It was like she knew I was somehow different but didn't understand why. Could she not know about Fae? Could she be that ignorant?

"Look up," I heard her mumble to herself. No one else would have ever heard her, but I wasn't like everyone else.

I wanted to be disgusted by her voice, by her demand. It only made me want to do what she asked.

*Hell fuckin' no.* My head automatically shook slightly in response. I could feel the heat of mortification flood her body, flushing her cheeks. Then it swiftly changed to anger and gradually hurt.

Her emotions were blatant and open, like a human. She couldn't possibly have grown up in the Fae world. Hiding what you felt was something you learned from birth. You gave nothing away. Emotions were a weakness, and we would use them against you. One thing Fae knew how to do was hide secrets and feelings.

This girl was a walking diary.

Officer Paul strode into the room and headed for me. Relief showered down on me. I needed to get away from this girl before I did anything I'd regret.

"Okay, you're free to go, Mr. Dragen. You know the drill. Sign the forms and you can leave." Paul unlatched the cuff around my wrist.

I saw the girl's eyes widen as she watched me get un-cuffed. Her fear spiked, and the sound of her pulse thumped in my ears. She had no idea of true terror: the fact my teeth and claws wanted to tear into her flesh to take revenge for what her kind did.

I stood, keeping my head deep underneath my hood. I was enjoying her fear and playing with her. The girl's gaze moved up my body, and her hands balled tightly in her lap. I almost stumbled as her fear shifted into another emotion. Endorphins filled the room and pulsated with desire and need. My beast part responded, but not in the way I thought. It roared, clawing to get out…wanting to take her. I usually didn't care when a woman noticed my arousal. She was different. She was a Dae. She should only disgust me. I would never let this abomination know she got me so hard it hurt to walk or even breathe.

*Never.*

As I walked by her, I tilted my head just enough so she could see my mouth. This Dae would know fear.

I smiled.

I knew that with a certain smile, I could have a woman begging me to fuck her; with another I could make most people back off and stay clear of me. But with this smile I could make the most hard-ass prick pee themselves in fear. Without knowing truly why, they could sense their life was about to end.

By the way she froze when I walked by, my message had been conveyed.

*Good.*

Just the way I like it.

If I ever saw her again outside of these four walls, she was dead.

# FIRE IN THE DARKNESS BONUS SCENE
## Chapter 2 from Eli Dragen's POV

*Fuck.*

That was my only thought when I saw the Dark Fae follow her into the shipyard. My legs had never moved so fast. My body wanted to change—the Dark Dweller in me screaming to get out and protect what was mine.

*No, not yet.*

Cole and Cooper were climbing the rafters. Literally, to get the drop on them. I was the distraction. Phookas were not dumb, but they were greedy and quick to act. I would have to use that to my advantage.

I slipped up to the cargo door, peering in. Even in human form, both men resembled a mountain goat. Phookas could change into several shapes: a dog, rabbit, and sometimes a small horse. But they usually had a dominant form. It wasn't hard to figure out which one was theirs.

"Move it." The taller, bigger one behind Ember pressed a gun firmly against her head. Her face was strong and definite. This girl was the most stubborn pain in the ass I'd ever met. My lip tugged up in a grin. Even defeated Brycin would not go down willingly.

The metal of the gun reflected the little light being let in from the top windows as he jabbed it again into the back of her head. A growl started to vibrate in my chest. I squeezed my eyes shut. Damn that fuckin' woman. She was gonna make me do something really stupid just because I couldn't keep my shit together.

With a deep breath I stepped into the doorway. It took everything I had to not lose it and tear those two goats into pieces. I had not spent this long keeping her alive for her to be snatched away now.

Seeing her again, this close up, was my own personal hell. I had watched her for over four weeks, keeping most of the Fae that hunted her away, but I never got too close. If I did, she would take off. Through our blood bond she could feel when I got near as I could feel her.

The second, smaller Phooka, pulled out iron cuffs from his pocket and was about to put them around her wrists.

"I don't think you want to do that." I leaned casually on the door jamb. I could take these two down in a matter of seconds. The only thing that stopped me was the gun. The bullets were Fae made, coated in iron or goblin metal. She would die. Suppressing another growl, I crossed my arms over my chest.

"And my night only continues to get better and better," I heard her say as she sighed with annoyance. Here I was trying to save her ass, you'd think she'd be a little more grateful. But no, not Brycin.

I scoffed. "Is this how you treat your savior? Your liberator, your rescuer, the redeemer?"

"Oh, hell. Are you and your ego done preening?" she sassed back. I loved provoking her. She got all puffed up. But I was a sick motherfucker—I liked getting her all riled up. Actually, I enjoyed it even more when she pissed me off. Those were the times I wanted to put my cock deep into her and never let it see the light of day again.

"Knight-in-shining armor then?" I offered up.

"Please. Goat-boy here is more likely going to be my knight-in-shining armor than you." She pointed to the guy holding the handcuffs. She was dirty, her hair ratty and limp. She had cuts and bruises everywhere visible and dried blood around the edges of the holes in her clothes. She looked like hell. And all I wanted to do was lay her on that concrete and fuck her till we were *both* scraped up, bruised, and bleeding.

I shut away the images. Those were only gonna get me to act rashly. I had to concentrate.

"Ouch," I responded. I kept my focus on her, but I could see Cole and Cooper moving above the two Phookas' heads. "Now you're just trying to be mean."

"You haven't seen me even get close to being nasty." She crossed her arms. This was foreplay for me.

"Threat or promise?"

"That is a pro—"

"What the shit is going on?" The man behind her finally spoke. The ugly asshole was getting angry and edgy. "Who the hell are you?"

"Someone your mommy told you not to mess with." I was looking forward to this. Most Dark Fae have gotten used to us being gone from the Otherworld. They were getting lazy, sloppy, and arrogant. But our name still caused so much fear it got me giddy. I wanted him to fully see me. Know who he was dealing with.

I stepped out from the shadows. A small gasp came from Ember, her eyes gliding down me. I could hear her heartbeat from where I stood. The blood in her veins rushed frantically around. Good to know I could still affect her.

"This is our take. Get lost." The Phooka was trying to play the tough guy. I could smell fear start to rise from his pores. This was too much fun.

"I don't think so. You have something belonging to me, and I'd like it back now."

Ember stiffened at my words, her face going hard. Anger flared through her. It was all directed at me. I knew Lorcan had gotten to her—had told her that I was actually using her so I could turn around and trade her to the Unseelie King. There wasn't anything about that statement that wasn't true. I had been. My family came first. That's what I was telling myself anyway.

Somewhere along the way Brycin got under my skin. To be honest, it was way before I gave her my blood. What a stupid fuckin' move that was on my part. Yeah, she affected me before, but I could have walked away, right?

I was finding it impossible now.

My blood flowed through her, calling to me. I had my fair share of seducing and being seduced by Sirens, Succubi, Demons, Tree and Water Fairies, and even a few humans. All were very memorable times. But nothing compared to the pull I felt with this one. It was like she wrapped my dick in a spell and could lead me anywhere. I craved her. I felt listless and off when she was gone. This only pissed me off. Made me resent her.

I didn't need anyone. Especially a fucking Dae.

"Sorry, we found her first. She's worth a big reward, and we're gonna be the ones to cash in." The Fae behind her pointed the gun at me. Iron didn't affect me, but Fae-made bullets did. Not that I would let him know that.

"You really think that's going to stop me?" I nodded toward the gun. Even if they shot me, nothing would stop me from getting to her.

"It would hurt like hell and slow you down enough."

"No more than a pinprick." I smirked.

*Okay, we're in position,* Cole said through our link.

I kept my eyes zeroed in on the two Dark Fae. If either even adjusted a hair, I would know about it. I saw Ember's gaze go briefly up to the rafters then quickly drop back down acting like she didn't see a thing.

*Good girl.*

I then let my body shift, my clothes ripping from my body. I enjoyed this…watching genuine fear show on people's faces when they realized what I really was, having a few piss themselves.

"Holy shit! You're a Dark Dweller," the main Phooka exclaimed, wiggling the gun in my direction. "The Queen led us to believe you were all dead."

"Sorry to disappoint," It was getting harder for me to talk as my body continued to change. My spine arched up, the daggers popping out of my skin. The spikes were poison-tipped. One touch and you'd be praying for death.

The Phookas were getting panicky. Not a good thing with them. I knew my eyes must have flashed red because the Phooka with the gun started to shake. The gun went off, the bullet hit several inches from my feet.

Cole and Cooper jumped, changing form mid-drop. Right as they landed on the men, Ember fell to her knees getting out of the line of fire and out of the Dark Fae's grip. She crawled away from the fighting men, heading for the exit. She was going to try and get away from them . . . *and me.*

I wasn't the only one who noticed her escape. The Phooka with the gun pointed it at her retreating frame; his finger squeezed the trigger. Rage burned through me, tearing a growl deep from within me. I crashed into him just before he shot, the bullet going into the wall beside her, close to her head.

A roar billowed the room, my anger zeroing in on my prey.

The Phookas dropped their human form. Growing their own lethal spiky horns. Their goat bodies were bigger and stronger. But we were even larger, tougher, faster, and much more deadly.

*"Eli!"* Cole's voice in my head, snapped my lock on the goat. *"We got them. Go get her! Now."* They didn't need me. They barely needed both of them. This was child's play for us. Still I craved to kill them. It was painful to turn away, but I had get Brycin before she got too far.

I transformed back into my human physique. In either form I could feel her. I knew exactly where she was.

At a full run I dove through the window. The shards of glass tore into my bare ass—stinging like hell. Glass rained down as I collided into her, taking us down to the ground. Using my body as a shield from the glass, I landed firmly on her, my naked body covering hers. She immediately started thrashing and grinding against me trying to get free. My dick was suddenly awake and growing hard against her.

"Stop fighting me." I ground my teeth. She needed to stop right now, before I ripped those tattered jeans off her and made her really thrash.

Feeling me against her she went still. Her stunning, two different colored eyes fastened on mine. I didn't care that she could feel me stiff against her. It caused her heart to flutter faster and that only made me want to fuck her more.

She started wrestling against me again. "Let me go."

"Try again."

"Get off of me."

"Nope, not that one either," No. I was perfectly happy here.

"Do you have her, Eli?" Cooper yelled from inside the building.

Dammit. Guess fun time was over now.

"Yeah." I sighed.

Cooper came out and I ignored the smirk and shake of his head. "Yep, I'd say you definitely do."

He had accused me many times since she had come into my life that she had me rattled. That I lost focus. Lost my way...

Half of our clan left with that same notion, following Lorcan. I couldn't deny she both irritated and excited me. I wanted her, but I could not have her. I could never have her. I was the succeeding Alpha in our Clan. I would do my duty in the end. I always knew it would wind up like that. She was a Dae. Everything I despised. Because of what she was and my past, I should have killed her the moment I met her.

"Get. Off. Of. Me. Now!" she snarled at me, a flicker of desire under her words.

This only made my dick harder.

My job had to come first. With a huff, I stood up, pulling her up with me. Her gaze drifted down to my cock. He eyes widened and then quickly glanced to the side.

"You're naked."

"And you're observant." I muttered close to her ear. I needed to stop. I was Second in Command. I would not let this little Dae get the best of me. I had a job to do.

Grabbing her arm, I yanked her around the corner where our black Cadillac Escalade Hybrid sat. "Now get in."

"Are you kidding me?" She jerked against my grip. "You think I'm going to get into the car? I'm not going anywhere with you."

"It is not a choice." I didn't have an option either. I had to trade her. She would become the Unseelie King's problem and no longer mine.

Keeping her might be what I wanted, but even I wasn't a fool to go against a Demon King.

# Glossary

**A ghra**: Gaelic for "my love."

**Bitseach**: Gaelic for "bitch."

**Brownies**: Small, hardworking Faeries who inhabit houses and barns. They are rarely seen and would do cleaning and housework at night.

**Ciach ort**: Irish for "dammit" or "damn you."

**Cinaed/Cionaodh**: Irish meaning "born of fire."

**Dae**: Beings having both pure Fairy and Demon blood. Their powers and physical features represent both parentages. The offspring of Fairies and Demons are extremely powerful. They are feared and considered abominations, being killed at birth for centuries by the Seelie Queen.

**Damnú ort**: Irish for "damn you."

**Dark Dweller**: Free-lance mercenaries of the Otherworld. The only group in the Otherworld that is neither under the Seelie Queen nor the Unseelie King command. They were exiled to Earth by the Queen.

**Demon**: A broad term for a group of powerful and usually malevolent beings. They live off human life forces, gained by sex, debauchery, corruption, greed, dreams, energy, and death. They live on earth taking on animal or human form, their shell being the best weapon to seduce or gain their prey.

**Draoidh**: Another term for "Druid."

**Drochrath air**: Gaelic for "Damn it" or "Damn you."

**Druid**: Important figures in ancient Celtic Ireland. They held positions of advisors, judges, and teachers. They can be both male and female and are magicians and seers who have the power to manipulate time, space, and matter. They are the only humans able to live in the Otherworld and can live for centuries.

**Fae**: A broad group of magical beings who originated in the Earth Realm and migrated to the Otherworld when human wars started to take their land. They can be both sweet and playful or scary and dangerous. All Fae possess the gifts of glamour (power of illusion), and some have the ability to shape shift.

**Fairy (Fay)**: A selective and elite group of Fae. The noble pureblooded Fairies who stand as the ruling court known as the Seelie of Tuatha de Danann. They are of human stature and can be confused for human if it wasn't for their unnatural beauty. One weakness is iron as it is poisonous to the Fay/Fae and may kill them if there is too much in their system. Also see "Fae" above.

**Gabh suas ort fhéin**: Gaelic slang for "Go f*ck yourself."

**Glamour**: Illusion cast by the Fae to camouflage, divert, or change appearance.

**Gnome**: Small humanlike creatures that live underground. Gnomes consist of a number of different types: Forest Gnomes, Garden Gnomes, and House Gnomes. They are territorial and mischievous and don't particularly like humans.

**Goblins**: Short, ugly creatures. They can be very ill-tempered and grumpy. They are greedy and are attracted to coins and shiny objects. Will take whatever you set down.

**Incubus**: Male. Seduces humans, absorbing their life force through sex.

**Incantation**: An incantation or enchantment is a charm or spell created using words.

**Kelpie**: A water spirit of Scottish folklore, typically taking the form of a horse, reputed to delight in the drowning of travelers.

**Mac an donais**: Gaelic, for "damn it," literally meaning "son of the downturn"

**Mo chroi**: Gaelic for "my love."

**Mo chuisle/Mo chuisle mo chroi**: Gaelic for "my pulse."/Irish phrase of endearment meaning "pulse of my heart." Can also mean "my love" or "my darling."

**Mo shiorghra**: Gaelic for my "eternal love."

**Ni ceart go cur le cheile**: Gaelic for "There is no strength without unity."

**Ninjuitsu, pankration, or bataireacht:** Forms of martial arts. Bataireacht is Irish stick fighting.

**Otherworld**: Another realm outside of the Earth realm where the Fae inhabit.

**Páiste gréine**: Gaelic for "child born out of wedlock."

**Pixies**: These six-inched Fairies are mischievous creatures that enjoy playing practical jokes. They are fierce and loyal and have a high "allergy" to juniper juice.

**Pooka/Phooka/Phouka**: Irish for goblin. They are shape changers that usually take on the appearance of a goat.

**Pyrokinesis**: The ability to set objects or people on fire through the concentration of psychic power.

**Seelie**: The "Light" court of the Tuatha De Danaan meaning "blessed." This court consists of all the noble (pure) Fairies and **Fae**. They have powers that can be used for good or bad, but are thought of as more principled as the Unseelie. However, "light" does not necessarily mean "good."

**Shefro**: A type of male Fairy.

**Shuriken**: Traditional Japanese, concealed, hand-held weapons that are generally used for throwing.

**Sidhe**: Another name for the Fae folk of Tuatha De Danann.

**Striapach**: Gaelic for "whore."

**Strighoul**: "Cannibal" of the Fae world. Consumes the flesh of other Fae to gain their powers. Will eat humans, but prefer Fae.

**Technokinesis**: The ability to move an object with the power of one's thoughts.

**Téigh trasna ort féin**: Gaelic swear word with the approximate meaning of "Go screw yourself."

**Telekinetic**: The power to move something by thinking about it without the application of physical force.

**Tuatha Dé Danann (or Danaan)**: A race of people in Irish mythology. They are the earliest Fae/Fairies.

**Unseelie**: The "Dark" Fae of the Tuatha De Danaan. These are considered the un-pure or rebels of the Otherworld and do not follow the Seelie ways. Nocturnal and have powers thought to be more immoral. They can also use their shell to seduce or gain their prey; however, "dark" does not necessarily mean "bad."

**Wards**: A powerful, magical spell primarily used to defend an area and is supposed to stop enemies from passing through.

# About The Author

USA TODAY Bestselling author Stacey Marie Brown is both a PNR and Contemporary Romance writer of hot cocky bad boys and sarcastic heroines who kick ass. Sexy, cheeky, and always up to no good. She also enjoys reading, exploring, binging TV shows, tacos, hiking, writing, design, and her fur baby Cooper. Loves to travel and she's been lucky enough to live and travel all over the world.

She grew up in Northern California, where she ran around on her family's farm, raising animals, riding horses, playing flashlight tag, and turning hay bales into cool forts. She volunteers helping animals and is Eco-friendly. She feels all animals, people, and environment should be treated kindly.

## To learn more about Stacey or her books, visit her at:

**Author website & Newsletter:**
www.staceymariebrown.com

**Facebook Author page:**
www.facebook.com/SMBauthorpage

**Instagram:**
https://www.instagram.com/staceymariebrown/

**TikTok:**
https://www.tiktok.com/@staceymariebrown

**Goodreads:**
www.goodreads.com/author/show/6938728.Stacey_Marie_Brown

**Stacey's Squad:**
www.facebook.com/groups/1648368945376239/

**Bookbub:** www.bookbub.com/authors/stacey-marie-brown

Made in the USA
Monee, IL
06 September 2024

2a5162fb-dbab-439c-856b-7d7c6614d0bfR01